# AND STILL THE EARTH

# AND STILL THE EARTH
## AN ARCHIVAL NARRATION

IGNÁCIO DE LOYOLA BRANDÃO
*TRANSLATED BY ELLEN WATSON*

DALKEY ARCHIVE PRESS
CHAMPAIGN / LONDON / DUBLIN

Originally published in Portuguese as *Não Verás País Nenhum* by
Editora Codecri, Rio de Janeiro, 1981.

Library of Congress Cataloging-in-Publication Data

Brandão, Ignácio de Loyola, 1936-
[Não verás país nenhum. English]
And still the Earth : an archival narration / Ignácio de Loyola Brandão ; Translated by Ellen Watson. -- First Dalkey Archive Edition.
pages cm
"Originally published in Portuguese as Não verás país nenhum by Editora Codecri, Rio de Janeiro, 1981."
ISBN 978-1-56478-871-9 (pbk. : alk. paper)
I. Title.
PQ9698.12.R293N313 2013
869.3'42--dc23
2013002353

The publisher thanks the Consulate General of Brazil in Chicago
for its support.

Partially funded by a grant from the Illinois Arts Council,
a state agency

www.dalkeyarchive.com

Cover: design and composition by Mikhail Iliatov

For Angela Rodrigues Alves,
and for Geraldo Alves Machado
who did not live to see this dedication.

I, THE KING, make known to one and all, through this my Royal Decree which carries the weight of Law: That it has been disclosed to me by the Proprietors of Factories of Tanned Hides in the Captaincies of Rio de Janeiro and Pernambuco that inhabitants thereof, as well as those of Santos, Paraíba, Rio Grande, and Ceará, are currently felling the tree known as Mangrove for the purpose of selling the wood for lumber. Whereas the bark of the aforementioned Mangrove tree is the only example in the Viceroyalty of Brazil which may be used to produce tannin for the curing of leather; and Whereas, for that reason, the bark of the Mangrove has already reached an excessive price, with the inevitable result that in not very many years this indispensable material shall be widely unavailable; and whereas it is My desire to favor Commerce to the common benefit of all My Vassals, intending to protect particularly such Manufacture necessary to Navigation and the growth of Exports, it is My Determination that from this day forward the aforementioned Mangrove trees shall not be felled unless having previously their bark removed, the penalty for infractions being fifty mil-reis and three months in prison, except in the case of repeat offenders in which case the penalties shall be doubled.

Thus, in order to favor the enforcement of this Decree and the apprehension of Infractors, it is further made known that anonymous denunciation shall be accepted and likewise the authors of said denunciations shall receive payment in the amount of the penalty charged to the Infractors, unless the latter be without means to pay, in which case payment shall be made at the expense of the Municipal Council.

And be it further declared that the Manufacturers of Tanned Hides and their Agents, Deputies, or any or all

1

persons who sell said Mangrove bark to such Manufacturers shall be freely permitted to remove said bark without regard to location or area; in the case that the above-mentioned persons be impeded in this work, that fact shall be made known to the Board of Inspection whereupon my Determination shall be executed, to which end I concede to the Board the necessary jurisdiction.

Thus resolved, and in this regard to further insure that these measures be fully executed, this Decree shall be made known by Myself to: the Supreme Tribunal of Justice, the Chairman of the Board of Appeals, the Royal Treasury Council, the Overseas Council, the Board of Conscience and Religious Orders, the Municipal Council, the Committee on Commerce of this Domain and its territories, the Viceroy of the State of Brazil, all Governors, Captains-General, Chief Justices, Magistrates, and all People of this Kingdom, in order that they shall fulfill their charge without encumbrance whatsoever of any other law or custom, and eliminating all disposition to the contrary.

Be it therefore enacted that this Royal Decree shall carry the full weight of law fully approved by the Chancery though it shall not be so legislated; that it shall remain in force for the duration of one year; that it shall be registered and recorded in all places as such laws are customarily registered and recorded; and, further, that the original Decree shall be delivered to the Royal Archives in Lisbon. Signed in the Palace of Our Lady of Assistance, Lisbon, the ninth of July in the year of our Lord seventeen hundred and seventy.

## THE KING

**Count of Oyeras**

By virtue of this Royal Decree carrying the force of law, His Royal Majesty prohibits in the Captaincies of Rio de Janeiro, Pernambuco, Santos, Paraíba, Rio Grande, and Ceará the felling of Mangrove trees which have not previously had the bark removed, under penalties contained herein, thus decreed and declared, to be thus literally executed,

**For His Majesty to See.**

## THE SIRENS WAIL NONSTOP ALL NIGHT LONG. BUT WORSE THAN THE SIRENS WAS THE SHIP WHICH SANK AS THE CHILDREN'S HEADS EXPLODED

A pestilential stench. It comes from the cadavers, the garbage and excrement piling up in the Pauper Encampments over there Beyond the Pale. Who knows what would happen to me if they heard me calling those places by their nicknames. Isolation, I guess.

They say they've tried everything to get rid of the constant, nauseating odor of death and decomposition. No success. I wonder if they really tried. The trucks, painted a cheery green and yellow, drop off bodies day and night. We're not supposed to know this, but things like that always come out. That's the way it is.

Bodies pile up waiting to be cremated. Open-air sewers disgorge their contents into old riverbeds. The stacked garbage forms seventy-seven undulating columns—inhabited, all of them—and the sun, unbearably intense, rots the meat in a matter of hours. The fetid smell of death, combined with the ineffectual insecticides and formaldehyde, is so pungent it makes your nose bleed when there's an atmospheric inversion. It even leaks into the obligatory gas masks, drying your mouth, burning your eyes, making your skin raw. At ground level the animals are dying.

That's what makes up the noxious atmosphere that a battery of powerful fans are constantly, unsuccessfully trying to drive away. Trying to drive the stench far beyond

3

the *oikoumene,* a word the do-nothing sociologists revived from the past to designate the slender space we
live in. If you could call this living.

I turned, surprised. In thirty-two years of marriage,
Adelaide had never felt the need to yell to get my attention. Seven forty-seven. I had to be at the bus stop in
four minutes or I'd miss the S-758, my authorized transport. Funny, she knew that—so how come she decided
to make me even later?

—What is it?

—You forgot your sport coat.

—I can't stand to wear that thing and sweat all day
long.

—Souza, you know they won't let you work without
a jacket.

—So much the better . . .

There was a frightened look in her eyes. Worried, I
considered her face and asked myself a question. A question I don't dare ask. If I did, who knows what might
take shape, what might be revealed.

We had breakfast together every morning. Then she'd
walk me to the door, where I'd put on my hat (yes, hats
are back in again), gently squeeze her left shoulder (I
don't know if there's any pleasure left in this for either
of us), and look at my watch. I worry if I'm running
late.

—Look how low the haze is, it's going to be a scorcher.

The haze seems to be getting lower by the day. Six
months ago it hovered above the city like the dome of a
gigantic cathedral. The air trapped underneath, inflamed,
is unbearable. Sometimes it condenses and the smell is
sickening, it makes your head burn. If this haze keeps
lowering, will it eventually suffocate us?

—Did you sleep?

—With those sirens going all night?

—I thought it was a burglar alarm. Who can tell anymore.

—I'm sure it was a fire. Not that it makes any dif-

4

ference. I could put up with the sleeplessness, but the alarms really get on my nerves.

—As if the infernal daytime heat weren't enough . . .

—Remember when the gas tanks exploded, and the buildings burned nonstop? It was right after the Era of Extraordinary Rationing.

She handed me my gray sport coat. A waterproof synthetic fabric that was supposed to keep the heat out. Top quality. Just like cashmere. It was stifling. I noticed last year's calendars piling up on the table, she was taking them down off the walls. Huh! Today must be the fifth of January. Who cares.

The calendars are always left open to the first day of the year. The red [1], universal fraternity. Red fading to pink by the end of the year. Adelaide cleans them daily, hours and hours wiping the dust off the little pages. Living room, kitchen, bedroom. Ardently.

That eternal [1]. No reason to mark time passing, forget about it, she told me once. What good is it to know which day it is? But the hours—now they're important. Each day compartmentalized, something specific assigned to each hour. It's better to live one day eternally, everything contained inside that one day.

This attitude wasn't like her. She was a quiet woman, an ex-bookkeeper for the railroad. Never talked much. She took things as they came and showed irritation only by keeping her silence and rubbing her eyes. The hollows underneath would sort of crinkle, and her eyes became elongated like a Japanese.

At the beginning of each new year she would collect the calendars from each room and wrap them up in brown paper. As I left for work on January fifth, she would always remind me: "Don't forget the paper." Year after year for thirty-two years as we said good-bye at seven forty-seven on the fifth of January, and she never forgot. I never remembered.

The changing of the calendars on the fifth was automatic. Adelaide took them down first thing in the morning. I'd come home for lunch instead of staying downtown. After lunch I'd take a little nap, though lately, with this stifling heat, there was no way I could sleep. Even so, I stayed in the bedroom. By the time I came out, the new calendars would all be in place and the old ones would be on the table wrapped in brown paper. I would take the packet to what was supposed to be the maid's room and throw it on the pile. There they would be, piled up in chronological order: the last thirty-two years.

Eleven thousand seven hundred untouched days. Dusty, yellowing, unused, preserved. I walked into that room just once a year. We never had a maid, Adelaide always did everything herself. She said, with a touch of irony, that it was her mission. Only lately had I been able to convince her to hire someone to do the weekly cleaning. And only because maids earned so little. These days people would work for a plate of food, one glass of water a day. They didn't want money, which made it tough on some employers: "If only she'd accept cash instead of demanding food and water..."

The hoarded days. Stockpiled. Not a mark on them. Not a single mistake. The sum of all our moments. I see now that each moment was a sort of antecedent. A wait, which renewed itself infinitely. We lived in anticipation of the someday that would have to arrive.

And so our life expanded like a rubber band stretched to the breaking point, to a state of tension, nerve-racking anxiety. As each day ended, the waiting was born in us again. We hoarded the instants which would make the following day full/empty.

Instants which were lacking something, something we needed but weren't about to look for. We lived in a constant state of expectation, a real, concrete emptiness. A sort of twinge casting its shadow into every corner of the house.

We filled the apartment with objects. It resembled a bazaar, a collection of singular, unsalable articles. China closets full of glass dessert dishes, goblets, salt and pepper shakers, glasses, wine decanters. Walls covered with

6

portraits, pictures of saints, pennants, stopped clocks.

Vases, knickknacks, end tables, coffee tables, clean ashtrays, statuettes, picture frames, lace centerpieces, hooked rugs, tiny decorative boxes, empty flasks, cut-glass bowls, paperweights, lamps, votive candles, baskets of artificial flowers.

And calendars. Two or three in each room, all chosen by Adelaide. Prizes won at the Supersubsistence Distribution Centers, or purchased at church. Some had advice about obsolete customs like planting and harvesting timetables. Tide charts.

After I put away the packet of old calendars, I would look through the new ones, page by page. Pretty pictures in Technicolor: young girls harvesting coffee, orange trees single-file up a green hillside, golden wheat in the sun, men waving from hay-balers, lakeside cottages, forest fires. Scenes from long ago.

Indians, jaguars, kittens in baskets, macumba ceremonies, angels keeping watch over children wandering dangerously close to the precipice. Everything but naked women (the kind on the wall at the auto mechanic's—diaphanous blondes, thickset brunettes, smiling in tiny bikinis). I thumbed through the calendars quickly; there would be a whole year to admire them.

—Souza, I've found a white hair! And you're hardly fifty—at ninety your father's hair is still jet-black.

Her mother called her husband "Father." None of that for us. What ever happened to our child, anyway? I'm not even sure we had one. It may seem absurd, but it's true. On my honor. Everything is so mixed up in my head, what was and what should have been. What actually happened and what I would have liked to have happened.

—Souza, I had another dream.

—Again? The same one?

—Sort of, but not exactly. It wasn't the sirens that kept me awake, it was the dream. Incredibly vivid. As real as that night watching the ship leave the port.

Adelaide, no. It's bad enough as it is. We made a pact

7

to forget it, never to speak of it again. Try to concentrate on being happy. We *were* happy. Or at least we thought we were.

—It was incredible, Souza, the ship was sinking in a terrible sea. There wasn't any storm, or wind, just silence. What gave me the chills was the sound of the hot light bulbs exploding as they hit the cold water. And there was a poof of white smoke whenever the wires touched the water. The sea got darker and darker until the last light went out. I couldn't see a thing, just the sound of those little explosions echoing in my ears. Not even a moan. It's true, isn't it, Souza, they died, didn't they? You're going to have to tell me someday. What I heard was the sound of their little heads exploding, wasn't it?

—Don't be silly, Adelaide. How could their heads explode?

—Children have such fragile little heads . . .

—It was just a dream, Adelaide, try to forget it.

—I can't forget it, and you can't either, until I know.

The ship, our affliction, had been forgotten so many times. I thought we'd never come back to it. When we were younger we handled it better. I mean Adelaide, principally. She's tired now; I think she's sick. Troubled. We found out over the years that time doesn't help in forgetting; on the contrary, it feeds memory.

Seven fifty-six. If I don't run, I'll miss the bus for sure. If it weren't for my bad leg, I'd have a bicycle like everyone else. An arthrosis in my knee makes it impossible to pedal. I went through dozens of tests, hundreds of examining committees, I greased a few palms, I found out all about low-level corruption.

I pressed water coupons into the hands of functionaries. Leaving myself short. I signed away food quotas. And I waited and waited, until finally I got the almost-impossible-to-come-by authorization to take a bus. Special Circulation Authorization for S-758. And the damn bus is always on time, it's a real pain.

I open the door and the hot breeze from the hallway

hits me in the face. I'm already syrup; by the time I get to work I'll be soup. Like everybody else. A neighbor is furiously sweeping the floor in front of her door. As if you could fight the black dust, the filth. Water is not provided for cleaning the common areas of the building.

Now to face the stairs. I stopped using the elevator years ago, one ancient hotbox for thirty floors, a hundred and fifty apartments. Only invalids and the elderly wait for that jerry-rigged contraption. The lobby is full of garbage. A disgrace.

The trash piles up by the day—we're not allowed to throw it into the street and there's nowhere else to put it. The truck takes what it can, when it comes. If it comes. Rats rifle through the bags, spreading the garbage all over the hall, the odor is unbelievable. One more smell to add to the lot.

I don't know why we pay the super, he's never around, and he always forgets to hook up the Anti-Rat Sonar. A good super these days has got to be political, he's got to negotiate with the garbage men, security guards, keep up a regular relationship with the Official Water Distributor.

Ah, the barber's just unlocking his shop. In the old days there were several stores in the lobby, even a little cafe with checkered tablecloths, tea and pastries, cakes, ice cream. But they all closed long ago, sheets of plastic nailed to the window frames.

Nailed in from the outside. That's how I feel. Counting the days, minutely scrutinizing each step I take. As if I were looking at myself under a microscope magnified dozens of times. Often I don't even recognize this character sloshing through a viscous liquid. It's me and yet it can't be.

A vacant hall, with only the barbershop remaining. The old folks come down now and then for a shave or a haircut. You can hardly see into the shop through the grimy glass. I nod, and Prata motions for me to come in, he's always anxious for a little chitchat. Unavoidable, painless.

9

—You think the water will be delivered this week?

—How should I know? Ask the distributor.

—Well, I figured because of your nephew...

—Sorry, but I don't have the foggiest.

—Either they miss the delivery or they raise the prices.

—Or both.

—See what you can find out, okay?

My hand itches, a sort of burning sensation, and I notice a little hollow in my palm as if I'd been squeezing a marble, hard, for a long time. I run my finger in and out of the hollow, it tickles. An insect bite? I don't remember any. Sudden fear. You hear about the strangest things.

There's a truck delivering synthetic soft drinks to a snack bar on the sidewalk. Meanwhile, another month's gone by. How time flies.... Nonsense, what do I care about time? Nothing to do with it, anyway, so who cares how fast it goes. It's true, I really have nothing to do. Does anyone?

### SCRATCHING HIS PALM (AN ALLERGY?), SOUZA WATCHES WITH DISTASTE AS CIVIL GUARDS SUBDUE THIEVES WITH CATALEPTIC BULLETS

The bus arrived just as my palm started itching again. I wove back and forth in the aisle, no empty seats. Predictable at this hour. I nodded to the familiar passengers—the same people every day. New faces were rare. We *are* the S-758, assigned to this transport and no other. That's what our Circulation Authorizations said.

CIRCAS, as they were called, not only dictated what (if any) transportation we were authorized to take, but also which neighborhoods we could enter, and by which routes, even down to which side of the sidewalk we were to walk on. Generally people were awarded only one bus author-

10

ization, which is why we all knew each other by sight. But no one so much as smiled at each other, much less entered into conversation. We traveled in silence.

Except for me. I sing out my good mornings and watch the faces cloud over, then turn back to the landscape: sidewalks choked with people. Just another lunatic, they think. They're all positive I'll be picked up as I get off the bus. The next day they try to hide their surprise when I appear, as usual, bearing my unwelcome greetings.

A couple of stops before the end of the line (there must be about seventeen in all), my hand started itching like crazy; but we were so packed in I couldn't even examine it, much less scratch the itch. Briefcase in one hand, suspended from the rail by the other. I pushed my way toward the exit, murmuring my good-byes. Of course no one answered.

As I stepped off the bus, there was a burst of gunfire. Dry, hollow. And familiar. I flattened to the ground: reflex. We are all well conditioned—a tenth of a second was all it took. Like mice trained to eat when they hear the bell.

The number of times we had to throw ourselves to the ground in that city! If someone were to make a film of peak pedestrian traffic hours, it would resemble one of those old Harold Lloyd comedies, with the fat guy and the thin guy—what was his name?—Mack Sennet. Down up, down up. And the faces: every one of them tense, terrified.

People fought over an inch of sidewalk. Heads knocked together, people spread on the concrete face-to-face, kissing, breathing in the dust, sweating. Then we'd struggle to our feet, filthy, cursing, complaining. One day it took me two hours to walk the three blocks between the bus stop and my office. Down up, down up. Shots coming from everywhere.

Today it happens just once. The Civil Guards are famous (and feared) for their speed and deadly aim. The thief, or whatever he had intended to be, still just a boy

11

(I was never good at ages), was laid out on his back, a red capsule like a plug in the middle of his temple. Not a drop of blood.

He had been shot with a cataleptic bullet, which provoked a condition of suspended animation not unlike death which would last about two hours. By the time the victim awoke, he would already be in Isolation. After that it was good-bye Charlie. Some people say that cataleptic bullets make you feebleminded.

The Civil Guard bent down, removed the guy's wallet, and handed it to a man standing next to him. The man looked it over calmly, made a few notes, and gave it back. Security Surcharges were assessed and collected right at the scene. No more bureaucracy, paperwork, receipts, red tape, lines, long delays.

Then the Civil Guard called for a car over his walkie-talkie. He rolled the victim over to the edge of the sidewalk and announced in a booming voice: "You can get up now." But people always hesitated. You never knew when a new incident would follow on the heels of the last one, criminals liked to take advantage of the confusion.

Although they didn't have it too easy these days, either. It seemed as though for every one of them there was a Civil Guard. And the Guards walked around with their heads swiveling back and forth like robots. They were compulsive, unerring, had impeccable noses (intensive training). They didn't miss a thing.

I think someone told me they use the same methods to train Civil Guards as they do German shepherd attack dogs for the military police. But however you feel about the Guards, you've got to admit they prevent utter chaos from taking over the city. No question it would be worse without them.

Yes, we've gotten to the point of accepting the Civil Guards as a necessity. We put up with them, we even phone them in emergencies. Now and then. I'm not speaking personally here, of course. For me, calling a Guard would be worse than having to swallow cod-liver oil. Say what? Cod-liver oil! Does that still exist? The things that come into my head all of a sudden. Funny.

The Hall of Waters. I usually get here at ten-forty. I have a half hour to spend wandering through the place, drinking in the tranquility. For over two years I haven't been able to start my day without a visit to the Hall of Waters. A section a day, a leisurely stroll.

I look at my hand. A bright red mark has appeared, and I swear the hollow seems to be getting deeper. I pinch it: no pain. It still itches, but it's an agreeable sensation, oddly pleasant, a kind of shiver all over. Such foolishness at my age—standing around shivering on account of an itch.

I always leave the Hall of Waters feeling moved, moved by the irreparable. Not in relation to my own life, but to the world around me—how far things have gone. But it's not resignation that comes over me when I turn away from the last display and cross the artificially green hall. The hallway has a calming effect, provides a sort of reconciliation with reality—which I admit may not be the best thing.

I plow into the foot traffic in the concrete plaza, overshadowed by immense billboards, and wonder about the purpose of the Hall of Waters, suddenly imagining it as a warning rather than a consolation. Pure conjecture. Maybe it represents memory. Nobody goes there anymore, anyway.

Yet I realize that as I walk through that glass desert, I blossom in the emptiness of its rooms and halls, with the comfortable sensation that it's all mine. Egoism. I feel like the presence of other people would defile this almost churchlike sanctuary. A cathedral for our times.

Certainly from a practical point of view the Hall is useless, and so is what is exhibited there: a collection of items out of their place and time, irretrievable. In today's world everything functions in terms of utility, convenience. That place is maybe the last deliberate government project with no practical value for civilization.

I probably shouldn't even go there, but somehow I

feel I must. If I lose the lucidity I'm beginning to recover I'll be dead. Like the unaltered calendars sleeping their eternal sleep in the maid's room. There's got to be a way out. The thing is to find it.

People don't see clearly unless they want to. Nowadays everyone quietly accepts the inevitable. Newspapers are no help, they censored themselves little by little until they perfected the art of saying absolutely nothing. Television is monitored by official censors. Even if it weren't monitored, there's nothing on of interest. The news bulletins are completely innocuous. Soap operas, government work projects, construction plans, ministers' promises. How can anyone believe a word these officials say—most of them over a hundred. They're practically fossilized, left over from the Fabulous Era of Grand Enrichment.

People still talk about those unfathomable times, though. They live on in oral tradition, in spite of how the history books leave them out completely. If you went to a lot of trouble you could read up on the basics in the newspaper archives. Distorted reports, of course. It was a period of intolerance, gag orders, silence.

When I was a professor, students would sometimes ask about those days. Students whom the administration inevitably deemed "troublemakers," students who would end up being expelled. The authorities would listen to tapes of my classes and call me in to identify which students were responsible.

At first I simply refused. I made excuses. In a class of three hundred students, I maintained, it was impossible to know who had asked the "Unpalatable Question," as the administration referred to it. I wonder how big the classes are these days—five hundred? six hundred?

Later, things got stickier for me because it always seemed to be in my classes that "Unpalatable Questions" arose. They wanted to know why. What kinds of things must I be saying outside of class? They had me followed, they bugged my house, tapped my telephone.

Then they hit upon the idea of requiring that all students identify themselves before speaking in class. Some, as a result, stopped asking questions; others preferred to speak up and face the penalties. "This so-called Era of Enrichment never happened. It's all a lie," insisted the administration. "People shoot off their mouths a lot, but where's the documentation? It's made up, it's a myth."

"That's right, a myth. There are lots of them, you're probably acquainted with quite a few yourself. Does the Headless Horseman exist? Is Wolfman real? Pure fantasy. Fantasy that perpetuates itself with no other point than to make people afraid. Now do you understand why oral tradition is so dangerous, so unreliable?"

So why didn't the students go to the newspapers, the public libraries, the microfilm archives? Because all these records were in the hands of the government. It was (and still is) necessary to go through endless bureaucratic red tape, getting approvals, rubber stamps, official seals on all the right forms. An impossible task because of the sheer time involved.

Students wasted years shuffling from office to office with their paperwork, and when at last they got the ultimate *nihil obstat* they found the archives had been moved. Or the functionaries they dealt with before had been transferred and the new ones, tipped off to the situation, refused to recognize their authorizations. If you wanted to make yourself crazy you could begin from scratch, again and again, but the government's tactics were circular. And very obvious.

I remember walking through the streets of Circumstantial #14, blocks and blocks of towering buildings which house the National Memory. No one knows what facts are deposited there. Files that are stamped: NOT TO BE OPENED FOR TWO HUNDRED YEARS. No doubt among them are the records of the Era of Enrichment.

—Uncle Souza!
—Two hundred years, just think...
—Huh?
—Oh, nothing. I was just thinking out loud.

15

Instinctively, my nephew had raised his arm in salute. Since I didn't return the gesture he went to shake my hand, but I hugged him instead. After all, he'd always been like a son to us. He was smiling and cordial, though his body remained rigid.

—What are you doing here, Uncle Souza?

—I took a stroll through the Hall of Waters.

—A case of nostalgia?

—Could be...

—Guess what, Uncle Souza? I've been promoted. The first man in the New Army to reach the level of captain at only twenty-three.

I gave him an ironic salute. He saluted back, dead serious. Circumspect, as always, taken with notions of duty and obligation. He was like that even as a kid. Whenever he visited (which was often), Adelaide would say: "He should join the army when he grows up, don't you think so, Souza?" That's when I realized how thoroughly acclimated to the present Adelaide had become.

To a much greater extent than I had imagined. Adelaide was always full of surprises. Looking back on our relationship, I have to admit that I understood very little about my wife. When I least expected it, she would come out with some completely appropriate and realistic suggestion. In another era, the seventeenth or eighteenth century perhaps, she would have advised him to be a priest. And so, fifteen years ago, much to my chagrin, Adelaide had begun her single-minded campaign to get that boy into uniform. Not as a simple foot soldier, mind you—she wanted him to become a Mili-tech.

The best positions in the country were awarded to the Mili-techs. In banks, government ministries, multinational corporations. But what a job it was to surmount the obstacles to becoming a Mili-tech! Not only did you need to excel throughout your military career, but you had to come up with the outrageous tuition charged for training.

—How about if I drop over to celebrate, would that be all right?

16

—Of course, I insist! Let's not even tell Adelaide— it'll be a wonderful surprise.

—You've got food?

—The usual.

—I'll try to get something special from Subsistence. Do you need any extra water coupons?

—Well, sure . . . it's always good to have a couple extra, I guess. I never manage to plan ahead, they get used up so fast.

—That's what they're there for, to be used.

—I know, but it's better to ration them, make them last a little longer.

—Ah, yes. Rationing. Well, some of us are not so unfortunate.

When you get right down to it, I don't really like him. I take advantage of his position, sure. It's due to my (obligatory) contributions that the New Army exists with all its privileges. I've got to get what I can out of the situation. And besides, my nephew owes his career to me and Adelaide. All the laundry she did. All the food she cooked.

I used to get up at a quarter to six, make the coffee, and rouse that lazybones from his seemingly bottomless slumber. He spent two years living with us while he attended the Institute of Higher Integration. The worst years of his schooling, until he finally passed all the tests: Fidelity, Neutrality, Ideology, and Sensory Perception. How can I like this kid when I know who he belongs to? When I know the country will be in his hands a few years from now. If we've still got a few years.

No desire to go to work. The itch is back again, which surprises me, irks me. The hollow in the center of my palm is definitely getting deeper. I must be delirious from the heat. I grab the arm of the man next to me, he starts. (I know I'm taking a chance—when it comes to personal security any reaction would be understandable.)

—I'm sorry, I didn't mean to startle you. I just wanted you to take a look at my hand. Does it look to you like there's a hollow there in the middle?

17

He pulled his arm free and hurried off. Must have taken one look at my hand and got even more scared. Who knows if it's contagious? The only reason he didn't break into a run is that the sidewalks are so jammed with people. I'm different from Adelaide. For me, reality is this hollow in my palm, just an itch, no pain. Inexplicable.

No sense going to the doctor. The only thing to do is wait. And I won't say anything to Adelaide, either, she'd call me a hypochondriac. She doesn't believe in my headaches, my stomach problems, and she's so damn stoical. I looked up. An uneasy feeling through and through. A bald-headed man was looking at me penetratingly, menacingly.

## IN THE MIDST OF HIS RAMBLINGS SOUZA REALIZES HE'S LUCKY TO AT LEAST HAVE A MEMORY— UNLIKE THE MILI-TECHS WHO HAVE LOST THEIR MORE HUMAN FACULTIES

It was remarkable, the way he looked at me. Disdainful and penetrating at the same time. And his skin was so red, like a very pale-skinned person who had been superexposed to the sun. Not a single hair on his head, just a scalp that was as cracked and parched as the soil in the northeast.

But my initial uneasiness was overshadowed by the sensation of familiarity. I was positive I'd seen this man somewhere before. I *knew* those hands: no fingernails. Adelaide was right, I need a memory tonic.

There was a period years ago, before my forced retirement, when I became very forgetful. Willfully forgetful, about everything. I was late with the rent, forgot to pay the electric bill, put things in my pockets in the supermarket, walked out of luncheonettes without paying for my coffee. I'd forget to come home after work, just sitting on a park bench somewhere.

18

Adelaide cured me with a steady diet of fish. Fried, marinated, grilled, in soups and stews. Nothing better than fish. I never even got tired of it. How long has it been since we've had fish—real *or* synthetic? What good would it do to remember? I look the bald man straight in the eye and then head for the office, not the least bit upset that I'm late.

At the security window I reel off my name and number, registration card, Social Security number, tax identification number, office and section number. The yellow light goes on. Half an hour late, then. I don't even know what penalties they might hit me with, I've never even cracked open the Manual. Why bother, it wouldn't make any difference. Everybody knows that according to the Manual we have no rights, just duties and obligations.

—What's your excuse, Mr. Souza?

—So many security holdups it's incredible. You spend more time on the ground out there than you do on your feet.

—When will you people learn to leave earlier, you have to count on problems like that these days.

—Right.

—I think maybe you ought to make up the time on one of your days off. Come in, say, on a weekend or holiday?

—I really can't do anything about it, Dr. Alvaro...

—Right, but I can. I don't know what's happening to this country, no one's got a sense of responsibility anymore, a real understanding of duty, respect for public service...

He keeps right on talking, even after I've walked away and headed for my desk. Like a repentant student. Irritated, because in all the years I've worked here I've never missed a day, never once before been late. Forget it. What I'm really worried about is this hollow in my hand. It's turned red, and seems to be getting deeper. My God, I wonder if I have cancer?

The day's work is piled on my desk: long ribbons of yellow paper. Columns and columns of numbers from

19

the computer. My job is to check them over, one by one. In the past twelve years, no one—and I mean no one, not one of us—has found an error, an imperfection, a slipup, an omission. To the great satisfaction of Dr. Alvaro. He thinks it means we're perfect, when obviously it's really the computer. My colleagues actually review the lists of numbers conscientiously. I just sign whatever they put in front of me. Why question it?

At least I think they're conscientious. They squirm nervously in their chairs, each creating his own method for comparing the figures. They use rulers, calculators. They squint. They trace over any numbers which were printed light. Their average is only about five pages per day, so I keep to about the same pace, just sitting there staring at the numbers. I spend an enormous amount of time, then, doing nothing at all.

That's what bothers me the most—it's such an incredible waste. So much dead time. A man can't spend his life looking at pages full of ciphers. So I spend a fair amount of time watching what goes on in the neighborhood. Luckily, my desk is next to a window.

There's probably someone watching me from over there, too. Someone else who's bored, who looks at me and thinks: I've watched that guy in the window across the courtyard for so long that I'd actually miss him if one day he wasn't there anymore. I'm used to him. I know his rhythm, his habits, when he arrives and when he goes home.

Before sitting down at his desk he always removes his jacket and drapes it carefully over the back of the chair. Then he lights up a cigarette, the first of two he will smoke during his workday. He yawns, scratches his chest, and settles into his chair. But he doesn't focus on his work right away. First he turns to look out the window.

I can sense his vacant look vaguely wandering down to ground level. A shabby central courtyard, ancient-looking, full of trash. Bins of roof tiles overflowing with junk, tattered plastic bags, propane tanks, greasy windowpanes, cardboard cartons, luncheonette stovepipes belching black smoke, heaps of packing crates, broken bottles.

That man spends the majority of his day in a slow pan, pausing over each small detail of the landscape. The same view day after day, what could possibly change around here? One day he saw someone run out a door, hands at his throat in a gesture of desperation. He stepped onto a ledge overlooking a dingy flagstone patio. Frightened. He stood at the edge and seemed to be deciding whether to jump when suddenly he fell. And lay there shaking convulsively, like someone having an epileptic attack. Then he was still. No one appeared. At the end of the day the body was still there. And the following day. We watched, full of questions, from up above.

The day wore on, the body hadn't been touched. I began to worry about decomposition—it was no doubt beginning to smell. The man across the street was apparently concerned, too; he kept looking up from his desk anxiously every few minutes or so, staring out the window. Late in the afternoon he disappeared, and I imagined that he had gone down below to investigate.

I went downstairs hoping to run into him—though of course I really didn't know what he looked like. All I saw through the window was an indistinct form, no detail. Once in the street, I was suddenly confused; it was hard to know which door the man had come out of with his strange attack.

There were dentists' offices, businesses, snack bars. Could have been that lunch place, but unfortunately I didn't have an authorization: I was assigned to one farther down the street. Which meant they wouldn't let me in even if I tried the old "I have to use the bathroom, it's an emergency!" routine. Not even if I begged or broke into tears or beshat myself.

"In an emergency you're supposed to go to the appropriate First-class Urinal," they would say in a monotone. "We can't do anything for you; we're restricted

to our own patrons, a set number of people per day."
The First-class Urinals were reconditioned public toilets.
Sophisticated decor and technology.

The majority of them are concentrated in the Forgotten
Center of São Paulo. They're run sort of like private
British clubs, very exclusive. Spotless, gleaming tiles.
Soap. Forced-air machines to dry your hands. Benches
to recline on, pressing machines to crease your slacks.

The First-class Urinals provide the comfort, you provide the urine. To be eligible you need to undergo a
rigorous medical examination, including a detailed anal-
ysis of your kidneys and intestines. Once you've received
a clean bill of health, you are awarded your First-class
Urinal Privileges Authorization. What an ugly word:
FUPA.

They put the urine to commercial use. What with the
shortage of water worsening every day, they've set up a
system to collect healthy urine and pump it to a central
tank to be recycled. It goes through intensive chemical
filtering, purification, refinement, transformation. It
comes out colorless, odorless, sterilized.

They say it's good enough to drink, though you won't
get me to try it. Not even my own, much less somebody
else's. But the daily collection capacity is somewhat limited. All the more reason for the stringent selection process and the cushy atmosphere: the best for the best.

Those without FUPA's relieve themselves anywhere.
Which is one reason the streets stink so badly. An informal arrangement has caught on with those who are a
bit more shy about such things: men stand behind low
cement walls (originally constructed to keep cars from
parking on lawns), facing the street, visible only from
the waist up. Still, they look awfully embarrassed re-
lieving themselves in a row like that. The new rage is
to hold your hands over your eyes during the entire operation. That stance, combined with the controversial
system of shallow troughs dug to collect even this un-
elite urine, is responsible for the setup's nickname: the
See-No-Evil Freebie.

I swore I'd never drink that stuff, but who's to say whether I'm not already drinking it at home, on the street, in the luncheonette? If there's one thing in this country in which people put absolutely no faith, it's the word of the System.

My nephew, the Mili-tech, was the one who told me the truth. Everybody thinks the excess recycled liquid is piped to the reservoir in the Superpopulated Zone (not to be confused with the Pauper Encampments, which are farther out, Beyond the Pale, as it were)—but they're sadly mistaken. A certain quantity of recycled water is *earmarked* for the Zone, yes.

The rest is supposedly set aside. The Minister of Water has declared that in case of emergency our reserves will last for six months at least. Meanwhile, my nephew confirmed that we're actually selling water to Chile for a tenth of the price domestic consumers pay for it.

They urge us to economize "to avoid rationing." But what do our water coupons represent if not rationing? Who can make sense of it, they're so inconsistent. It's as if they tossed us out in the rain and then got boiling mad: "You're getting all wet, come in out of the rain!" So we try to come inside, but of course they've locked the door, so here we stand getting rained on. (I wish!)

The truth is that only a fraction of the excess is held in reserve. The Privileged Neighborhoods siphon off all they can. Though the information isn't from firsthand reports, the word is they even have swimming pools. In any case, if there ever is a real emergency it will be the last, because the reserve tanks must be just about bone dry.

An emergency has been anticipated for a long time now, you realize. Even before I started this job I read about the continuous red lights nature was flashing us. A full-scale alert, the scientists said—the few of them who had survived. They were doing the best they could to warn us.

Scientists. A minimal, marginalized lot these days. It's almost prehistoric the way we've become immune to the warnings science offers us. As soon as the System realized that the prognosis was bad, and would make them perhaps look bad in turn, *voila:* they started an intensive propaganda campaign in the press, fostering as much sarcasm as possible with respect to anything scientific. That was when the scornful expression "scientific paranoia" came into being.

Anything could be labeled "scientific paranoia." Being an illustrious, enlightened scientist of conscience became tantamount to being a Jew in Nazi Germany. Scientists were debunked, persecuted, and not a few of them went into hiding. Some continued their studies, issuing public announcements, denouncements. Desperately trying to engage public interest.

So, most of the scientists were hunted down and silenced. Others accepted invitations to foreign universities and institutes and left the country. Some merely retired and went on to other activities. Research institutions languished and closed, as the new order grew in numbers and power: the Mili-techs, the advanced technocrats of the new generation.

Today *Mili-tech* is a household word, a part of the language, but back then we didn't really know what it meant. We read about the Mili-techs in the press, heard them touted on government radio, but who paid any attention? There was no way we could have foreseen the danger—how were we to know that these men didn't have normal brains?

The scientists were busy proving this to be true— which was one more reason why they became outlaws. Their research indicated that the Mili-techs had undergone a metamorphosis affecting the cerebrum. They lost part of their memory. Emotions were eliminated; Mili-techs were trained to be supreme calculators.

That's where the extreme practicality of our civilization comes from. The Mili-techs spent so much time and effort on numbers, calculations, machines, systems, that they lost certain other faculties. It's the old story of body parts atrophying from lack of use.

The instinct for conservation, fraternity, the capacity to appreciate beauty, things of quality—all these died. North American social scientists specializing in the study of our country presented a report on the subject at an international convention in the United States. They had arrived at some very curious conclusions. But of course the work of these researchers is banned here. Incoming baggage, parcels—even personal mail—are subject to search and seizure.

I'm lucid enough to know that the complete, rigid control of all means of communication, insidiously intertwined with the Intense Official Propaganda, or IOP, has the effect of deadening intellect. So efficiently that this "emergency" we're living in is by now considered the norm. How soon we forget—this is the recent past we're talking about, after all!

Gone, as if it never happened. Maybe because it all happened so fast. Those who "enriched themselves" now live in luxury in isolated enclaves cordoned off and forgotten by the masses. They have been unable so far to reproduce, but that doesn't seem to bother them. They've come to be called (ironically?) The Men of Present Times.

Over the years we've adapted to (and learned to ignore) all kinds of contradictions. Didn't people in the sixties and seventies accept and adjust to (and almost enjoy) the permanent state of siege? I'm not excluding myself from all this. I too am "the people." Maybe I should bear an even greater responsibility.

I am a history professor, after all. I laughed at the scientists' objections to the way things were going. They've gone crazy, I imagined, things like that can't possibly happen *really*—it would mean the end of mankind! Now I understand. We may not be extinct yet, but surely we're pressing the outer limits.

Fear. I live in fear. That's what Adelaide is always saying. But she's from another generation, all she cares about is church. She believes in eternal life (can you imagine!), always talking about salvation. Suffering now, paradise later. What happens on earth . . . mere preparation for the encounter, face-to-face, with Our Lord Who Looks Down on Us From Heaven.

That's how she confronts her life: patient and resigned. Accepting what is given. When she wants to, of course, she knows how to see what's what—for example, encouraging our nephew to join the New Army. And what about me? I'm an old history professor with a hollow spot in my palm. I face this fact easily, naturally. It must be an effect, not a cause.

So many crazy things happening every day—like that bald guy. Who knows where he came from? And what about the people whose fingernails are falling out? Or the ones whose bones turned to mush? The people who've gone blind or lost all their teeth. . . . If scientific inquiry still existed, maybe we'd know some of the answers. As if it mattered. We're all just trying to survive.

Anyway, when I went downstairs that day, I had no luck finding either the entrance to the patio where the body lay or the man from the window across from mine. I went back up to my desk and stared out the window some more. The body still lay there untouched. And there it stayed, rotting away for days, though no odor wafted up to my level.

Then one morning I saw that the body had finally disappeared. In its place was a heap of shiny metallic bundles. They're still there today, in fact, though rusty by now—in spite of the years of consistently dry weather. I always thought rust was caused by humidity. There must be some other explanation. More useless rambling.

I look out the window; there's a man watching me. At least I think he's watching me. He looks up from his work and leans toward the window. He must be thinking: "I've watched that guy in the window across the court-yard for so long that I think I'd actually miss him if one day he wasn't there anymore." Good God, I'm delirious. So what else is new?

## A LITTLE ORIENTATION
## WITH RESPECT TO THE SYSTEM'S
## ORGANIZATION OF THE CITY
## IN ORDER TO ENSURE
## ORDER & PROGRESS
## IN THE STREETS

On General Radio (the only station there is) at lunchtime they play nothing but waltz music. For two solid hours. Old recordings of the Vienna Boys' Choir. Those boys must be long dead; or else they're senior citizens, still singing waltzes with tremulous voices. They played waltzes at my graduation dance, over a hundred couples swirling around the dance floor.

Adelaide was a fine dancer, a real champion. Even as an adolescent, at the club on Sundays, she didn't miss a number. Everyone loved to dance with her—cheerful, slender, agile, enthusiastic, and full of rhythm. How could she abandon such things and turn into a church mouse?

Sometimes she says there's no doubt in her mind that God will intervene personally and resolve the mess this world is in. In other moods she's despondent. Terrified. Waiting for the second deluge. I've come to the conclusion a deluge would be just what the doctor ordered— imagine, the world filling up with cold water! I'd dive into any old puddle and float for a whole week.

The heat is worst at the end of the day. The sun is low behind the buildings, but the paving stones and cracked concrete throw back the blasting heat. I hesitate for a moment at the edge of the sidewalk, until I find a break in the stream of people headed towards the bus stop. The line moves along slowly, overheated and apathetic.

—Get your lottery ticket here.

27

—Shark's fins, tell me now, you ever seen such nice shark's fins?

—Photos for documents!

—Pencils, three for the price of one!

—Religious medallions anyone? Better safe than sorry . . .

Once in a while the stream of traffic stops dead. People get furious. Must be some dispute up at the District Access. There's always something going on. People who've lost their circulation authorizations or let the expiration date go by unnoticed. People who are unable to prove their identity, or who get arrested for using borrowed documents.

—Wallets for all your cards and coupons, first-class synthetic leather.

—Shoeshine, need a shoeshine, mister?

—Air-ated socks, that's it, step right up!

Hands in my pockets, I shuffle along fingering my CIRCA. It's made of cheap aluminum, already worn around the edges from so much handling. Whenever I'm nervous I rub it back and forth between my thumb and forefinger like an amulet. Without the appropriate CIRCA, you can't enter the Forgotten Center of the city.

—Razor blades, mister?

—Cigarettes?

—Portable ashtrays—one hundred percent plastic!

—Cotton balls!

The street is crowded with bicycles. The rumble of car engines has been replaced by the dry sound of chains turning on toothed wheels: bicycle chains, thousands of them. Horns have given way to little bells, sharp whistles. People still curse a lot, though, just as in the good old days of automobiles.

The absence of cars doesn't prevent crowding, congestion, confusion. Cyclists cross into the bus lanes, veer up onto the sidewalk crashing into pedestrians, or try to ride along the edge of the curb elbowing the people on the outside. But the worst place to be is in the middle

28

of the crowd: you get shoved, kicked, insulted, and goosed from all sides.

It's like a horse race, the animals thundering ahead, knocking against each other without looking to the right or left. Or like Roman chariot races. Ben-Hur. From up above what you see is a continuous river of heads and bicycle tires: dirty water.

Pedal-power is big these days. The really well-appointed have chauffeurs—a couple of people pulling a small cart, extremely light, like a rickshaw, in which the Privileged One sits. But it's rare to see those contraptions in this part of the city. Too risky. The people on the sidewalks would be likely to tear them apart.

There are just too many people in this city. That's why they had to define areas of circulation. It got to the point where people couldn't get to work. The streets and sidewalks were so jam-packed that no one could move at all. The city came to a standstill. So they issued CIRCAs which authorize entrance into prescribed areas only. District Access Stations control the traffic flowing in and out of each area; without the proper CIRCA you are not admitted.

Even so, the lines of traffic on the sidewalks had to be organized to prevent tie-ups. You have to get in line and move ahead slowly, in place. At least maybe it's made people a little more patient. It simply doesn't do any good to rebel, to fight the rules. And besides, it's dangerous. If you get into a brawl over a place in line, they can confiscate your CIRCA.

The areas of circulation are reasonably spacious and each contains the necessary elements: restaurants, stores, luncheonettes, pharmacies, banks, houses of entertainment. This idea of compartmentalization was first introduced in the late fifties with the founding of Brasília. By now the concept has been substantially refined and developed.

Government teams studied the cities of antiquity and came up with the notion that man has always circulated within identifiable limits, rarely straying beyond a certain prescribed number of streets and locales. "Thus the new restrictions will not affect the sense of personal freedom which people enjoy in their day-to-day lives," the study concluded.

I arrived at the District Access, dropped my CIRCA in the slot, and walked through the metal corridor. Relief. A clicking sound would have meant an identity check to verify that the numbers on my identity card matched those on my CIRCA. District Access Stations are narrow metallic blue hallways with slots for the CIRCAs, which are checked electronically and then returned at the exit. As you enter the area you take the sidewalk to the right; those leaving, travel on the left.

Most CIRCAs have designated time restrictions as well. People who work the night shift have authorizations which allow them entry after 5:15 P.M. The Access Stations, at entry and exit, are synchronized. As each person leaves an area, one more person is allowed to enter. That way the number of people in each area at a given time is rigorously controlled. Otherwise, there would be chaos.

—Anti-Rat Sonar, top of the line!

Then it hit me, ours had been broken for two weeks. Adelaide forgot to remind me on my way out this morning, I've got to get it fixed. Or maybe I should buy a new one—the stupid things never last very long, but you've got to have one. Living without an Anti-Rat Sonar would be sheer madness.

—How much?

—Five hundred.

Expensive, but I should give it more thought. It's awfully risky to be without one this long. A little more time to procreate, and I could come home to find Adelaide overpowered (eaten) by rats. Technology has few enough worthwhile products, but the Anti-Rat Sonar is one of them. The way it works is to emit a high-frequency sound identical to a rat's squeak immediately following copulation. A squeak which means: "Leave me alone!"

The other rats understand. Fatigued and satisfied with the sexual act, the rat wants some time to recuperate, so

30

he lets out this Greta Garbo cry. The inventors of the Sonar managed to reproduce the sound with such accuracy that the gadget actually works: it prevents proliferation of the animal. A continuous high-frequency shriek effectively keeps the sexes apart.

—How can you ask double what it costs in a store?

—You don't like my prices, go buy it in a store!

These street peddlers are sharp. They know everybody hates to go shopping. Though we have to, of course, on our assigned Consumer Day. The rest of the time we're supposed to support the Austerity Regime to Avoid Recession, which means we're not allowed to buy anything without having to pay the extremely steep Excess Consumption Tax.

Before I can make up my mind whether to buy the Sonar, an Inspector arrives, and that's the end of that. Charming times we live in. Anyone could be an Inspector, they're everywhere. They get in line with the other traffic and patrol the crowded areas. Unrecognizable. They're chameleons, they look like anyone else. Once they've been identified they're transferred to another area.

No wonder we fear them. They can demand to see your CIRCA to verify that you're allowed in the area. They can look in your eyes and pronounce you ill and unfit to be on the street. If they notice a slight trembling, they may send you to Isolation. The street vendors disappear with a simple flick of the wrist, just a wave of the hand. They're magicians.

It's a complex structure we live in: there are also Inspectors for the Inspectors. Occasionally this leads to wars between groups of them, and we, the populace, utterly powerless, suffer the consequences. Don't ask me to explain how it all works, the mechanics of the system. That would be impossible; the only way to see the structure is from the inside.

## ADELAIDE REPORTS THAT
## REPULSIVE BALD PEOPLE
## ARE INVADING THE NEIGHBORHOOD.
## THEN SHE GARGLES
## WITH GOOSEBERRY JUICE
## AND GOES TO BED

Helicopters swoop down low over the larger thorough-fares to keep the crowds in line. Their blades spin with a threatening drone—metallic insects that give me par-adoxical sensations of death and freedom. They're armed with machine guns and Demoralization Spray bombs, but more often the method they use to quell disturbances is to drop nets over the throngs and balloons with colored liquid which paralyze people and give off toxic smoke. Those machines have a thousand-and-one uses, and for some reason they fascinate me. The way they hover above us, omnipotent. The discombobulated flight of some pre-historic bird. Which has the power to escape at any mo-ment, a sudden liftoff.

I lost my chance to buy the Sonar, but someone else will turn up soon, maybe even with a better price. From the corners of doorways, from the depths of the sewers, on street corners, the street vendors reappear. Until they run into an Inspector again, harassed or pursued for the umpteenth time. Sometimes it seems like it's all a big game of cat and mouse. Just to break the monotony.

It functions like an ecosystem. A perpetual-motion machine. Ah, the perpetual-motion machine my relative Sebastiao Bandeira built! Come to think of it, there are some interesting people in my family. And I take after the craziest of them, with my wild flights of fancy—at least that's what Adelaide says.

Adelaide was waiting for me at the door to the build-ing. Hidden in the hall alcove; with so many strangers around it's a good idea to play it safe. Especially someone as timid as she is. Adelaide often waits there for the mailman. She's been expecting a letter for years.

—Did it come?

—No.

—It will, one of these days.

—I'm not so sure anymore . . .

My question is automatic, like the gesture of squeezing her shoulder on my way out to work, and so are her answers. For years we've been exchanging these phrases at the doorway—a sort of proof that some things in this world are immutable. The day this impossible letter arrives, we'll no doubt feel a great emptiness.

We went upstairs. As usual, I showered and took a short rest. I tried to act normal, continue the routine. Adelaide can sense the least change in my mood. She's got a good ear, she can tell from the tone of my voice if I'm especially worried or excited or depressed. The table was set, a frying pan sat on the stove. I didn't have the slightest desire to sit down to eat.

—You've got to eat something, Souza.

—I'm not hungry.

—You never eat a proper lunch, at least have something decent for supper . . .

—It's too hot.

—If you're going to let the heat stop you from eating, you'll never eat again.

We sat down in front of the television, waiting for the evening soap opera to begin. I waited until the titles came on to show her the hole in my hand. She looked at me, puzzled, disturbed, waiting for me to explain, to say something. It's not every day your husband comes home with a hole straight through his hand and acts as if nothing has happened.

When she saw how calm I was, how indifferent, Adelaide began to cry. I know she was outraged that I was not the least bit inclined to explain. But explain what—something I didn't understand myself? Still, she's not

33

the type of person to accept anything without explanations, she likes things crystal-clear. The only exception to this rule is religion.

—Does it hurt?

—Not much.

—Did you have an accident?

—No. It just appeared.

—But, Souza, a thing like that doesn't just appear. Something must have happened—I don't understand why you won't tell me about it.

—I told you. Nothing happened. I was on the bus and my hand started itching. I scratched it and noticed a little hollow spot, it sort of intrigued me. Later, after I'd forgotten all about it, I discovered it had turned into a hole.

—I'd like to know what you're trying to hide.

—Nothing! That's the whole truth, I swear it.

—You've always been honest with me before, Souza.

—And I am now!

—But it doesn't hurt—not at all?

—Nope.

—Have you seen a doctor?

—What for?

—To let him have a look at it, of course—maybe he'd have some way of explaining it.

—I don't want any explanations.

—You've got a hole in your hand, Souza, and all you can do is just sit there?

—Why not? It's not bothering me.

—Well, what about me?

—You?

—Yes, me! You expect me to walk around town with you like that—a hole straight through? What will people say?

—Look, Adelaide, with this city in the shape it's in, who's going to pay the slightest attention? You know how many strange people there are out there.

—Speaking of strange people, I forgot to tell you. Two horrible bald men came to the door today asking for charity.

—Charity? Did you report them?

—No, it's so complicated . . .

—But it's important, Adelaide, you know that. It's for their own good. The System needs to take care of them.

—But there's so many of those people around, Souza, I shouldn't even answer the door anymore.

—You mean that wasn't the first time? Why haven't you mentioned this before? How do they get into the building?

—Oh, I guess people forget and leave the outer door open. Or they just get in, you know, the way thieves manage to get into places. All I know is they ring the doorbell all hours of the day.

—The System had better get on top of this problem, that's all I've got to say. There are all sorts of strange people, who knows where they come from. I saw one of those bald guys today—he was awful. Looked like he was from another planet or something. Those guys scare me. I don't know what's going to happen, there's no way this city can accommodate more people. It's hard enough to get around now.

—Well, there's nothing we can do about it. And besides, you changed the subject: what about that hole?

—I already told you. You know as much as I do.

She went to the bathroom to brush her teeth. Now I can hear her gargling. It's a cheerless sound, the glu-glu-glurg in her throat. Adelaide never goes to bed without gargling with gooseberry juice. Of course the stuff was made from synthetic gooseberries, but it had a sweet, fresh smell, just like I remember from when I was a child.

When she climbs into bed, that pleasant aroma fills the room. My compensation for having to listen to her gargle. I have an idea maybe that's why, in all these years, we've never gone to sleep without a good-night kiss. The taste of gooseberries is like a tonic, reassuring me, bringing back the Adelaide I knew so well.

And yet we've changed. We're getting old, maybe

too used to each other. Living such a comfortable, uneventful life together, a few emotions get lost along the way. It was almost spiteful of Adelaide to discover this gooseberry gargle. She knew very well it would remind me of the first time we met.

It was in an ice-cream parlor on a very hot afternoon. I'm always awkward in a crowd. Somehow I knocked over a pitcher that had been standing on the counter, red sticky liquid spread in a pool. The smell of gooseberry juice enveloped the room, and in the midst of all the confusion I saw her smile.

That was it, that smile of hers floated up at me through the fruity aroma. Two images intermingled in my head: the red liquid and her white teeth. It was one of those moments which becomes fixed in memory, and we relive it every night, our faces crisp against the sheets, the smell of gooseberries in the air around us.

My turn in the bathroom. I brush my teeth, put eye drops in my tired eyes. The light in the bedroom was off, there was Adelaide waiting for me at the door. For thirty-two years, every night, we'd walked into the bedroom together at bedtime, my hand on her shoulder. The gesture is good for both of us. We have our traditions.

From the doorway I looked up at the trunk on top of the wardrobe. Without knowing why. It was automatic. Just a wicker trunk sitting there in the dark. The last time it had been opened Adelaide was pregnant. Or at least we thought she was. Her belly was getting rounder and rounder, she'd missed her period, she was nauseous in the morning.

"It's psychological," said the doctor, but we didn't believe him. We were so confident. We hadn't planned the pregnancy but we wanted the child, we'd gotten used to the idea. Until one morning before sunrise I woke up to hear Adelaide playing the piano: Beethoven's *Pathétique*. I'd never heard so much despair in the piece before. Even the composer couldn't have imagined a more painful rendition. I lay there, almost in tears—I swear—just listening to the sounds she was wrenching from the piano. I suppose I knew somehow what it meant.

She was sitting at the piano, her stomach as flat as a board. There was no way for me to take it in; something snapped inside my head. Her belly had disappeared overnight. The doctor was right, then, she hadn't been pregnant after all. I've thought about that episode for years, it affected me deeply. My son was no more than a puff of air.

Adelaide was saving the baby's layette in that trunk. It had belonged to her mother's mother, passed down from daughter to daughter. Adelaide had used it for her bridal trousseau. Then, the week after we were married, she carefully laid all her things in the bureau drawers and we hoisted the empty trunk on top of the wardrobe.

Pristine, shellacked, smelling of mothballs (to keep the mice and roaches away). And she gradually filled it with little packages, all the same size, wrapped in brown paper. The same paper we use for the calendars. Every once in a while I'd try to guess what was inside. She wouldn't say.

Most of the time it was as if the trunk didn't exist. We didn't touch it, we didn't talk about it. For months at a time I'd forget it was up there full of those packages. Then, for no reason, I'd get curious, wondering what sort of stuff my wife was saving in there. Someday, I'd think, I'll have to ask her about it; I knew she'd never bring it up herself.

It's time I did ask her. What is all this foolish secrecy? What if I were the jealous type? I'd make a scene. No I wouldn't.

What could she possibly be keeping in there after all? And why shouldn't she be allowed to have a few secrets, a little world all her own?

When I reached out and put my hand on her shoulder, Adelaide trembled. And shrugged away my hand, without looking at me.

## UPSET ABOUT THE HOLE
## IN SOUZA'S HAND,
## ADELAIDE INSISTS THAT HE GO
## TO THE CLINIC & ASK
## THE EVER-COOPERATIVE (FOR A FEE)
## DOCTORS FOR A HEALTH EXCUSE

—What are you looking for?

—A water coupon. I can't find one anywhere.

—There should be one in the blue crystal, in the china closet.

—Which one?

—The one you gave me on our second anniversary.

—You mean the one with the handle, or that other one you dropped?

—It wasn't my fault, my hands were all soapy.

—So it broke, that's all . . .

—You started it.

—Just tell me which piece of blue crystal to look in, okay?

—I don't know, look around. Hey, you know who I saw today? Your nephew. He promised us some more under-the-table water coupons.

—*Our* nephew. Why do you always call him *my* nephew?

—He's your sister's son.

—Well, we're married, aren't we?

—Sorry. My mistake.

—You're always making "mistakes" when it comes to Domingo. You really don't like him, do you?

—What do you mean? Why shouldn't I like him?

—Your own foolishness. You've had it in for him ever since he lost those two books from your collection of police novels.

—Well, you're right about one thing, I *was* mad—those were rare books! Sure, it bothered me to lose two

38

volumes of *Sinete Cinzento*—I knew I'd never be able to replace them. But I'm no monster, I got over it a long time ago. And if I'm not mistaken, he also made off with a couple of my Ellery Queens. I had the complete collection of magazines, and now it's not worth a damn.

—None of it amounted to anything in the end, Souza. When you lost your job at the university you sold the whole series for a song. People don't sell love. Anyway, I never did understand how a history professor could be so crazy for police novels...

—Oh, by the way, speaking of your nephew, he's coming by to celebrate.

—To celebrate what?

—Didn't I tell you? I don't know where my head is. He got a promotion—he's a captain now.

—A captain? At his age? Oh, I knew he'd do well, he was such a good boy, studious, dedicated. Headed right for the top.

If Adelaide ever managed to find a water coupon, we'd have water for two more days. Three, if we were really careful. That's it. Which means we'll probably be without water entirely all next week. Until I get my new quota. How can they be talking about cutting back—or "redistribution" as they call it. I don't know how we'll manage.

I could hear Adelaide rummaging around in the china closet. Sometimes she looks over the glassware piece by piece, just for the sheer pleasure of it. All her trinkets. Clay figurines from the Northwest (when it was still part of Brazil), souvenirs from our tenth-anniversary trip.

The TV was still on in the living room. Survival classes. Nobody watches them. They used to be mandatory, but now everybody knows it all by heart. The most dangerous periods of the day, for example, when the sun is so bright and the streets reflect so much heat that it's inadvisable to go out at all unless you wear a hat. The segment on cooking with synthetic foods is more widely appreciated—women still avidly copy down the recipes. They're always looking for new ideas about what

39

to do with artificial black beans, but the consistency never comes out right. They're practically inedible. Either they're too soupy, with absolutely no body, or they're all stuck together, tough and rubbery.

They seem to come out with a new product every week. Some food which hasn't been available for ages, suddenly back on the shelf because some technician in the Ministry of Social Well-Being came up with a formula to produce it artificially in the lab: peanuts, olives, tomato, scallions, eggplant. Even roasted sunflower seeds. I couldn't believe what I saw in a store window the other day: synthetic squash blossoms!

Memories of squash blossom soup, with cornmeal. Chilly, rainy afternoons, the whole family snuggled up at home, that pungent aroma hung in the air over the soup tureen. Of course synthetic squash blossoms didn't smell the same as the ones you gathered yourself fresh from the garden—ah, the late afternoon, knee-deep in creeping squash vines...

It was the smell (or lack of it) that bothered me most about all this artificial food the government industries whipped up. Proof of just how fake they were. Besides, if they make water from urine, who knows what we're eating. This stuff is just too antiseptic, plus it leaves a lingering taste of plastic in your mouth.

My grandfather used to bring us a basket of fruit every Friday. Tangerines, pineapples, bananas, strawberries. Depending on the season. He knew the few remaining places which sold natural produce. The fruit was much smaller and less splendid-looking than the kind they sold in supermarkets, which always looked so colorful and attractive.

Go on, peel one, he'd say to me. Taste it. The tangerine would leave a strong smell on your hands even after scrubbing with soap and water. An oily aroma, sharp and sweet. Yikes, it's fake, I'd yell. And he'd act annoyed: it's the ones from the supermarket that are fake!

Sweet, juicy tangerines. Flavor in every drop. I'd

separate it into sections the way my grandfather showed me and eat them slowly, one by one. Each drop of juice made my mouth pucker with pleasure.

"People do everything backwards," my grandfather would say. "They eat fruit for dessert, leaving a wonderful perfume in the mouth, and then ruin everything by having a cup of coffee!" But what really got him going was a visit to the supermarket. He'd handle the gigantic fruit they had stacked in pyramids, strawberries, mangoes, pineapples, melons. Oranges with thick skin and microscopic pulp. And absolutely no flavor, it was like chewing paper. Pineapples with juice that tasted like water. Strawberries red on the outside, pasty white on the inside—if you put them in the blender with milk, you got a pale pink tasteless liquid. "Look what they're doing to the fruit," he'd say, shaking his head sadly.

My grandfather hated everything produced with chemical fertilizer: "Fruits and flowers are born of the earth and should nourish themselves on the earth." I can't say for sure that this was the root of his madness, but it seems important to me. Once my father suggested that my grandfather had probably become conscience-stricken over his years and years as a lumberman. Sounds like an exaggeration to me, but people are complicated, so who knows? It's true that he was eventually hospitalized, taken away against his will, yelling at the top of his lungs that the fruit of the world was fake, all fake. And one day, when he was eighty, he climbed over the wall and escaped (can you imagine?), leaving a note behind explaining that he was headed up north to stop the trucks.

—Adelaide, are you all right? Are you really watching that?

She nodded, silently. I know these silences of hers. There's one which is neutral, when she's quiet, running around the house involved with her chores. Then there's another which has a weight to it and almost seems to create a breeze as it moves through the house. An uneasiness. When Adelaide is moody or irritable, little wrin-

41

kles appear on her face, a kind of furrowing which makes her look much older.

—Why are you watching television? You never watch TV in the morning.

—I woke up and couldn't get back to sleep.

—Worrying about my hole?

—Yes, among other things. Didn't you hear all the noise last night on the terrace upstairs?

—I slept like a rock.

—It sounded like an awful lot of people. Like construction—lots of hammering and sawing going on. You think they're building something up there?

—The police closed off the terraces, remember? Maybe it was animals—opossums or something.

—Animals, Souza? Opossums?! Only in your head. There aren't even any animals in the zoos anymore, for heaven's sake. Just the museum specimens you love so well—and they're stuffed.

—Maybe it was a miracle.

—No, Souza, that's not how miracles work. When man puts an end to something he's got to pay for it. God isn't there to fix up our mistakes, he's there to judge us. He's just waiting for the final reckoning.

—How can you still believe all that, Adelaide?

—I don't want to argue about it, Souza. I know just what you're going to say, and I'm tired of it. I didn't sleep all night, and now this morning there's no water. You're going to have to go without your coffee, by the way. And I don't have the patience for conversation. And another thing, we're going to have to do something about that hand of yours, get some sort of treatment.

—Treatment? What for? It's already formed a scar.

—That can't be. You just hurt yourself yesterday, there hasn't even been time to go to the first-aid center.

—I don't need a doctor, Adelaide. Or a hospital, or a first-aid center. The hole just appeared, and that's it.

—It really doesn't hurt?

—Not a bit.

42

—Tell me what really happened.

—I already did. It started when I was on the bus. All of a sudden it itched like crazy. I scratched it a little, and felt a sort of burning sensation. When I looked at it later, there was a hole.

—And you didn't complain to the company?

—What's my job got to do with it?

—No, not your company, the bus company.

—They don't have anything to do with it either.

—You could get some witnesses. Bring a suit, ask for damages. Accuse the bus company of contamination. Remember Germano, from the little store on the corner? How many years' pension did he get as an invalid? At least twenty. And all because of a bee sting. They have doctors and lawyers at the Clinic who take care of things like this, everybody knows that, Souza. Why don't you just try it? That's the way the System is built—think of it as your revenge for being retired from the university. It's finally your turn, Souza. Really, you should go; I'll go with you if you want and do the talking. Yes, that's a good idea, you don't have to say a word. As if the whole experience had changed you, you were trauma-tized. What do you say?

At moments like this I get really confused. I listen to Adelaide, I agree and disagree. Her head works so fast when it comes to practical things. And for her this is a practical problem. There's even some merit to her logic. Adelaide always surprises me—the things she comes up with: think of it as my revenge.

The years the System owes me. The time I spent spinning my wheels, out of work, cursed by the stamp on my work card: COMPULSORY RETIREMENT UN-DER SECURITY LEGISLATION. Now I'm not even registered. It was my nephew that got me my job, that's why I'm in a tight spot. I owe him something more than just water coupons. I'm not supposed to argue with him, I'm supposed to be grateful. Which makes me feel just terrific, since he's not exactly my favorite person.

However. I've got to survive; I have Adelaide to support, and my parents. There are a hundred reasons to justify the status quo, my position in the world today. In a way, that's why I love this hole. It's a way of reminding me, suddenly, that the "no" exists. The possibility of change. Overnight, no less.

I love Adelaide and I hate her. Where does it get me to refuse to indulge in these little games with the System? I should go there, arrange a health excuse, that's for sure, and I could still do some odd jobs. Or I could do nothing at all, just wander around all day long. Arranging for water coupons, CIRCAs, ID cards for the best luncheonettes. Like a street hawker, a numbers runner.

Forty percent of the population live like that. It's the only way they can get by. Suddenly I hate my wife. Because she wants me to get in on the game. Not that I'm all that pure or principled. I'm no Don Quixote. I just don't want to get involved. I refuse to contribute to that way of life, from now on. Of course there's not much ahead of us anyway, the game's almost over.

Everything's all gone to hell. Until recently, bitterness was something I wouldn't allow myself. Today, meanwhile, I have to go without coffee, and if there's no water for coffee that means there's no water for cooking lunch, either. Or dinner. We're going to have to eat *cold* artificial food, shitty mayonnaise salads. I should steal a goddamned bottle of water from somewhere.

—Souza? Are you listening? What do you say? Are we going to the Clinic?

—No.

—I knew it. You're a fool, Souza. I always thought so.

—Then why did you marry me?

—I love you, in spite of it. Can you understand that?

—Sometimes.

—But I really think you should go. Promise me you'll think about it. Let it sink in, you always work things out slowly. Just promise me you'll let it simmer for a while.

Incredible how well she knows me. I do reason things out slowly. Maybe I'll even end up deciding to go. Wring some money out of the System. What I should do is take a walk through the neighborhood of Those Who Were Grandly Enriched. Take a good look at their mansions, the water they waste on their gardens and their pools. Get all worked up and feel wronged, indignant.

I probably couldn't even get in. Those neighborhoods have been off-limits ever since the Dismal Months of Raids and Robberies. You can't get past the District Access without a special CIRCA, a gold one. From what I've heard, Those Who Were Grandly Enriched never leave their houses. They keep to themselves. Besides, I don't even know how to get there, I don't even know if those neighborhoods really exist.

—The packages are on the table waiting for you, you know.

—I'll take care of it, don't worry.

—I sat and waited for you yesterday, Souza, and you forgot. The first time in thirty-two years you forgot to come home for lunch on the fifth of January.

—It was a strange day, Adelaide. I was upset. The hole in my hand—I just wasn't thinking.

—You always come home for lunch on the fifth. Come wind or high water, that's why I was surprised. Really, it was awfully inconsiderate.

—Once. One time in thirty-two years, is that so terrible? Can't you be a little more understanding?

—I understand. I understand that things aren't the same between us.

—This has got nothing at all to do with you, Adelaide. It's my own problem, it's between me and the world.

—Oh, come on, don't give me the weight-of-the-world-on-your-shoulders business. My father used to pull the same thing with my mother, and she put up with it far too long. If you think I'm going to be like she was, you've got another think coming.

—What are you talking about?

45

—I'm trying to find out what's up, what's going on with you, that's all. Something's going on here, I just want you to tell me what.

—Okay, you're right. But it won't do any good to talk about it.

—Why not?

—I've got to figure things out for myself. I've got to find a way to understand what it is that's going on around us, surrounding us...

—When it comes to changing the subject, you win hands down, Souza. You're an expert at it, you're so slippery, saying things that don't make sense. What are you talking about, what's going on all around us? Our problems are right here inside this house.

I tried to argue with her, the first few years. Then I found it was easier to agree. I should have kept on fighting, at least it stimulates you, keeps you awake. But I'd get home from the university so worn out. It was enough to have to wrangle with the administration about the students' questions I wasn't allowed to answer. Plus the fatigue from the heat.

Excuses, that's what's surrounded me all my life. But not anymore. This hole has somehow given me strength I didn't even know I had. Ever since I woke up this morning I've felt like a stranger in this house, as if I had no connection whatsoever to the place. I feel like leaving, getting away, wandering around town. Taking a look at the world.

—You should call your nephew, Adelaide. Invite him to dinner one of these nights. Oh! I just remembered something else, some bad news he told me when I ran into him.

—What?

—He's got one of those digestive bags, you know, the kind you wear inside your clothes.

—So? What's so bad about that? Lots of people have them. Why should that be so alarming?

—I didn't say it was alarming, I said it was bad news.

46

It must be awful to have a piece of your intestine in a plastic bag hanging inside your clothes.

—It's better than being dead.

—You know, sometimes I can't even talk to you. Call him, okay, and invite him for dinner.

—With no water?

—The day after tomorrow I'll get the new quota. Maybe Saturday would be good.

—Saturday I'm going to mass at Sacred Heart.

—How about Sunday, then?

—Sunday dinners around here are always so unpleasant. You have a few drinks down the street first, then you come home, eat dinner, and sleep the whole afternoon.

—Let's not start. Invite the boy for Sunday dinner. Your mother, too, if you want.

—Really? You mean it?

—Sure.

—What about the packages?

—I'll take care of them tonight.

—In the dark?

—I said I'd take care of them.

—Okay . . . but at least let me put a Band-Aid on your hand.

—Not on your life.

She gave me one of her afflicted looks. Lost. As if she were sitting on top of a cake of ice on a hot day. The ice melting, her slipping off to one side, knowing she's in trouble. She's only looked at me that way once before. The day I said: let's get married.

## SOUZA SEES THE PUNISHMENT
## OF THE BIOLOGIST
## WHO HAD BEEN TEACHING FOR 19 YEARS
## AS A WARNING FROM THE SYSTEM.
## IF EVERYONE HAD STOOD BEHIND HIM
## THAT AFTERNOON
## WOULD IT HAVE MADE A DIFFERENCE?

I opened the door and was hit in the face with a blinding brightness. I needed a pair of dark glasses, it was unbearable. Now I understand why so many people are afflicted with teary eyes. You could almost see a thin vapor rising from the pavement. Impossible, there hasn't been dew for years.

In the hall, in front of the barbershop, stood three men: bald. Like the one I'd seen yesterday. Dangerous-looking faces. What were they doing here? Did they have CIRCAs for this area? Should I go back and ask them? Or maybe phone for a Civil Guard? If they didn't have proper CIRCAs, they had no business being here.

Then I felt guilty, ashamed of myself. I blamed the sun for such thoughts. Leave the poor devils alone, they're not bothering anyone. At least it didn't look like it. If I reported them, they'd be taken away, Beyond the Pale, and left to die. They say there's no way to survive out there.

I wouldn't have the courage to turn them in to the authorities, to deliver them into the hands of the Civil Guards, probably the strangest, most mysterious citizen army every created by any government. But I hope they don't hang around the neighborhood. Everyone's on edge, suspicious, terrified at the smallest unfamiliar noise. Determined to stay alert.

I take off down the street, limping a little because of my arthrosis. A blue and white sign, with an arrow pointing left, and a visual symbol: a bus. At the corner, another sign, this one with a series of small buses, color-coded to indicate each line which passes by here and all the connections.

You don't even need to know how to read anymore. Information is portrayed visually. Instead of words, it's a specific code the government designed, with a symbol for everything: bathroom, bar, restaurant, downtown, dentist, pharmacy, overpass, bridge, tunnel, danger, ghetto, school.

Butcher, park, water fountain, industrial sector, commercial area, church, movie theater, luncheonette, hospital, crossroads, bakery, Alleviation Centers. We had to memorize fat manuals until the practical took the place of the theoretical. If they put up a sign now with letters on it, I bet no one would understand it.

At the bus stop, where there are generally about a dozen people waiting in total silence, there was a noisy crowd. The Circulation Inspector pushed his way into the middle of the group, irritated. When I got closer it looked more like fear than irritation.

—CIRCAs, please, let me see your CIRCAs. Get them out quick before the S-758 arrives.

I held out my CIRCA, apprehensive. Something was wrong. For the first time in all these years the Inspector grabbed my authorization and studied it carefully. For what seemed like a long time. Then he asked for my identification—odd, and verified the card number. He stared at me, hard. I saw that his hands were trembling slightly. He gave back my documents after checking them nervously once more.

—What is it? Is something wrong?

—Too many people, just too many people. Most of them don't have CIRCAs, it's getting impossible. Everyone wants to go downtown but no one has authorization. What am I supposed to do, they're all furious.

I had my hand out in front of me, still holding the papers. He looked right at it. I should have been careful to use the other one, keep my bad hand in my pocket. Stupid of me, these people love to ask questions. Who wants to try to explain something that's inexplicable, that just has to be accepted, at least for now.

—What's this?

—A hole.

—I can see that. What's it from? Did you have an accident, or is it a disease?

—I'm not sure.

—What do you mean, you're not sure. Explain yourself!

—Well, I had an itch, and it just appeared.

—Then it must be a disease. Of course, definitely. Speak up.

—No, not really. It's not a disease or an accident, it's just there.

—What? Hmmm... Better come with me to the checkpoint. Could be contagious.

—Look, it's really not necessary. See, it's scarred over already and everything. It's nothing.

—Come with me.

—I'll miss my bus.

—You're not getting on any bus. Give me your CIRCA.

—No way.

—Do I have to call for help?

I decided to cooperate. There was a checkpoint every five hundred meters. For verifications like this, because of all the unidentified diseases which had been appearing, mostly different forms of skin cancer. The strangest cases—suddenly, in the middle of the street, a person begins to lose all his skin, nothing left but blood.

It happens all the time, especially with the migrants from the northeast. Crowds of people have drifted south looking for shelter, trying to escape the sun and heat of the north. Many of them were expelled from their homes. When the multinationals took over their home states they became foreigners in their own land. And so the people come. To die in the south.

Facts leak out here and there from the official corridors of power. Breaches are discovered between the System's central and state authorities, who have been known to calmly declare a State of Public Calamity and then refuse any further responsibility. "It's war," our governor is supposed to have said, referring to the negligence of the System.

But the fact is that the governor doesn't have any real power, influence, or authority. There are those who insist that he's been "forgotten," left powerless in his job ever since his nomination decades ago. The few people who voice this opinion are leftovers from the Era of Casuistry, when the System changed the rules in the middle of the game without permitting a word of complaint.

It's not that the governor was literally forgotten, of course not. Posts like that are permanent, perpetual, partly because no one in his right mind would want the job. Now, you could argue: who in their right mind would join the System to begin with? And I swear I wouldn't have an answer. On my honor.

It seems like there's nothing anyone can do—the money ran out, the coffers are empty, whatever money there was was spent many times over. Any miraculous surplus devaluates before our very eyes. That's the legacy left by OOI#1 and OOI#2 (the Orderly Order of Inefficiency and the Orderly Organization of Incompetence, respectively). A common remark in those days was that we, too, were part of the OOI—we represented the Orderly Order of Impotents. All our protests, contestations, investigations, were utterly useless.

To reach OOI#1, a public servant had to pass through various stages within OOI#2. For example, if he showed maximum inefficiency in his achievements, he was headed for a lifetime career. Of course he would have to complete graduate study in cunning and manipulation, as well as demonstrate an understanding of the various genres of corruption. Eating candy without getting caught (having his palm greased without a telltale stain)—this was one of the most important lessons for the candidate to learn on his way to proving that he was worthy of the distinction of OOI#1. Which gave me a brilliant idea:

—Look, hold it a minute. Maybe we can find a way of resolving this without going to the checkpoint.

—Scared, aren't you? You must really be contagious.

—No, it's not that, it's just that all the red tape takes up so much time.

—Well, then, how do you propose to resolve the problem?

—You tell me.

—Well, I'd have to admit I'm a little hungry...

—I can give you a lunch coupon.

—For where?

—The Aurora Borealis. It's the luncheonette in my circulation area, anyone can tell you it's a real good one. But look, don't come around tomorrow, trying to pick me up again, okay?

It seemed as though it would take forever to get through the District Access, the line just wasn't moving. A dwarf who was on line in front of me said that last night they had issued more authorizations, and that he'd had a real hard time leaving his area. That's how it works, they make it tough for some and others get the go-ahead. It's all a big game.

I passed right by the Hall of Waters, not in the mood I guess. I was thirsty, and a little hungry. I spent a few coupons at the Aurora Borealis on a glass of synthetic milk, a cup of coffee, and a few cookies. If I keep using up my coupons at this rate, I'll end up having to go hungry at the end of the month.

The end of the month is the end of the month. Now's the time to worry about now, then we'll see what happens later. Things get worked out in their time. After having something to eat, I was more in the mood for the Hall of Waters. It was beastly hot inside the luncheonette. The fan turned round and round on the ceiling, but the air just didn't move.

At least it would be cool in the Hall of Waters—

maybe all those thousands of jars of water lined up on the shelves had something to do with it, who knows. Then too, the roof is designed to let in a soft diffuse light, which probably has something to do with the reason it's one of the few places left that's comfortable. The day the general public discovers the Hall of Waters is the day peace and quiet will be over.

I know the color of each room, hallway, alcove. The order of the jars of water on the shelves. They did a beautiful job designing that place, let's see—it was just before that famous short was made, "The Last Tree." One of these days I've got to visit the Simulated Virgin Forest, I'd like to see that documentary again.

As I walk along, I check the gutters and garbage cans. Who knows—maybe I'll find an old newspaper. Or even a piece of one, half shredded. It wouldn't matter. I feel like reading some news. I feel like reading, period. I'm tired of just seeing things on television or listening to National Radio. There's got to be a discarded newspaper around here somewhere.

For years, as a professor, I was authorized to get a weekly paper. There wasn't much to read in it, of course—not much of interest, at least. Bad news was prohibited. In order not to alarm us, they said. The people in power during the Grand Era of Enrichment were the ones who introduced the idea of the undesirability of bad news.

They did it gradually. Films on TV and in movie theaters, immense billboards. Exhaustive repetition, until everyone was convinced that reports of bad news impeded tranquility, as they put it. Encouraged worry and provoked stress. Increased hypertension. Caused illness, even death.

NOW IS THE TIME TO JOIN TOGETHER,
TO MAKE OUR COUNTRY STRONG!

The Grand Era of Enrichment came right after the Wide Open Eighties, which had succeeded a grotesque dictatorship. The press had gotten used to treating things

53

ironically, denouncing and making accusations by inference. This was troublesome. The Society of Inebriated Ministers found this offensive and demanded reparations.


WE HAVE EVERYTHING WE NEED
TO BE A LEADING NATION.
WHAT BETTER EVIDENCE OF THIS THAN
OUR ECONOMIC & MILITARY MIGHT.


It all started when some government minister brought suit against a newspaper which had accused him of corruption in office. The paper revealed its evidence, the System backed off, the minister fell. Of course all the remaining government officials felt threatened, so they got together and started a patriotic campaign: "What good do reports like these do for the nation? The System must govern undisturbed."


OUR DEFENSES ARE INVULNERABLE.
THE SYSTEM HAS DEVISED REMARKABLE
STRATEGIC ADVANCES.
OTHER NATIONS STAND IN FEAR OF US.


That was the general tone. A government constantly under attack has to spend time responding to the accusations and can't govern "undisturbed." The people would have to choose. If the bad news were allowed to continue on the airwaves and newspaper stands, the System would not be able to function efficiently. And would not, therefore, be to blame if the country came to a complete standstill, or perhaps even began slipping backwards.

## CONSIDER OUR SYSTEM OF DAMS, HYDROELECTRIC PROJECTS, NUCLEAR REACTORS, OUR MINING RAILROADS, OUR ENERGY POLICIES, THE DISCOVERY OF COMBUSTIBLE ALCOHOL!

The trick was to convince people to be proud of what they had. To convince them to stop reading newspapers which printed bad news. And it worked. That's how the movement to stop the devastation and partitioning of the Amazon was killed. No one wanted to hear about the destruction of the forests, felled trees, open fields taking the place of woodlands, the whole area well on the way to becoming sterile. Good news was much more pleasant, it's only human nature.

## TAKE PRIDE IN THE GOLD WHICH POURS FROM OUR MINES, IN THE SUPERIOR WOOD WE EXPORT; REJOICE IN THE BOUNTIFUL HARVEST OF OUR FERTILE FARMLANDS. LET'S CULTIVATE OPTIMISM AND CONFIDENCE! DOWN WITH NEGATIVISTS!

In the eyes of the High Hierarchy of the New Army, there were only two things worse than cancer: negativists and communists. Both were hunted down and clapped behind bars. By the time of the Great Battle Against Liberalism in the Church, communists were rare animals, practically extinct.

Partly because of the repression they faced, but perhaps to an even larger extent because of disillusionment. They simply disappeared, just as the birds and animals did. Except that the animals were given the luxury of private reservations where they were encouraged to attempt to reproduce in captivity. The communists, on the

55

other hand, already in captivity or underground, languished.

The latest news about the events up north had been released by the Minister of Real Estate Transactions, a post created because of the pressing need to control rampant speculation, not just in the large cities but along the entire seacoast as well, where the sale and division of land parcels was proceeding at a devastating speed. Rather than controlling speculation, what the new minister actually did was to take very good care of his own group which, in turn, did an excellent job of controlling and restricting upstarts and eliminating all adversaries.

I'll never forget the infamous afternoon our new Minister of Real Estate Transactions declared on national television that "we should be proud of this most recently completed conquest—a great act by a government which is always thinking of our future." History, he said, would show how the System had created for our country one of the great marvels of the modern world. Now we, too, had a Sahara to be proud of—and our brand new desert would be photographed, filmed, painted. It would become a tourist attraction, a stage for glorious adventures.

"As of today"—and he smiled rapturously—"we can boast a truly marvelous desert, hundreds of times larger than the Sahara, and even more beautiful. Utterly magnificent! We bestow on the world nothing less than the Ninth Wonder. Soon newsstands here and abroad will be flooded with images of our limitless plains, fantastically high dunes, singularly dry riverbeds."

Films produced by the Official Government News Agency did indeed depict the gradual desertification of northeastern Brazil, some of the most sophisticated photographic images people had ever seen. Public Relations firms ran campaigns inducing glossy magazines to sponsor caravans into the desert. The upper classes had a grand time dressing up as Arabs.

The First Lady received hundreds of illustrious guests under a silk tent pitched on the sand, complete with bonfires and torches for atmospheric lighting. Fans simulated breezes which stirred artificial palm trees. Decorators had screened scores of Hollywood films for inspiration for their incomparable scenario.

This all happened around the time the scientists began to be persecuted (or the first time since the Wide Open Eighties, I should say). It's my belief that this shame marked the beginning of a new era. In the last years we have moved so rapidly from one cycle to the next, hardly used to coping with one change before we have to learn to adapt to another. Incessant change.

We were so naive. Myself included. There we were, in positions from which it would have been possible, working slowly together, to introduce at least a gesture in the direction of clarity, just the tiniest bit of consciousness. Seeds of worry. Alarm. We should have been able to do that, even with all their vigilance. After all, a professor in whom his students confide is much more than a father.

There was one scientist who spoke up. Bravely, on his own. Who, today, even remembers his name? At first there was an underground black book at the university, a vivid account of the persecution suffered by professors, researchers, doctors, scientists. Until finally reports no longer meant anything. The exception proved to be the rule.

We lived with it, we got used to it. But now I find I can't get that scientist out of my mind. I was standing in the hall when he walked by on his way to his office that day. Already aware, via the afternoon news broadcasts, of what was going on. I stood and waited. The president of the university delivered the memo personally, and the scientist left without opening a drawer, without taking a single sheet of paper.

When he passed me in the hall on his way out, he looked the same as every other day. Not with his head lowered in shame, defeated. Not with his head held high as a sign of pride or indifference. Merely a normal biology professor who had just lost all his rights: the right to teach, to circulate in the city, to talk to other people. The right to live, when you came right down to it.

I was shocked. I couldn't understand what had brought this man down. A biologist with degrees taken in the U.S. and Europe. An exemplary teacher for nineteen years. With children and grandchildren. A little bit longer, and he would have gone on to a tranquil, undisturbed retirement. And yet he stuck his neck out. His indignant voice rang out loudly. Against the desert.

We hadn't counted on the intensity of our reaction, and it left us confused. What kind of intellectuals were we, if we didn't so much as have the capacity to analyze the situation clearly? People with our knowledge of the political and social reality should have been prepared. Prepared to calculate calmly and lucidly, to sift through the facts, to keep our eyes open. To see to the end of the road. All we had to do was examine the facts and draw the natural conclusion. Like taking a drink of water when you're thirsty. The fall of that biologist was a clue, a warning from the System.

Of course we didn't need that warning to be afraid. For months I had been perplexed, even ashamed. I knew I should have walked across the hall and joined his camp. If we had all done that, it might have made a difference. But we seem to lack the decisive gestures at important moments in our history.

A symbolic hand extended in solidarity. I think about that a lot. Even after so many years, I imagine the whole group of us, together, against the university. They would either have destroyed us all or they would have had to change. Instead we let things stay as they were. Which makes me furious. The guilt I carry—it eats away at me. There's nothing worse than the memory of a gesture that should have been.

From the seventies on, we were totally confused and uncertain. We lived in a world of paradoxical points of reference, rigid systems, deomocratic airs. Repression justified and justifications accepted. Democracy in a dictatorial climate. Amorphous regimes we couldn't get a handle on.

It never occurred to us that this was the form of the

System. Designed to have no identifiable shape. Our mistake was to look to our own history for models—we forgot that times had changed, that man himself had changed substantially. How could we hope to define this new order? Dissimulating Systems?

They seemed to be one thing but weren't. They were, but they didn't seem to be. A game of hide-and-seek. As if we had entered a labyrinth, a hall of mirrors, and lost track of the true image. Or perhaps all the images we saw around us were true. Should we accept them all, then, admitting multiplicity? Or keep searching for a single truth?

**IN THE DARK BEDROOM,**
**NOT EVEN A TICK-TOCK.**
**THEN THEY HEAR FOOTSTEPS**
**GOING BACK & FORTH ON THE TERRACE**
**—AND IT CAN'T BE ANIMALS,**
**SINCE ANIMALS DON'T EXIST**

A dense, brown blob emerging from green. Vague stains and blotches dance before my closed eyes. I've got to figure out what it means. I doze off on the bus, and the blob reappears, as insistently as always these last few years.

Every time it blossoms, welling up from the depths of memory, I sink into paralysis. My arms are like lead, my hands and legs fall asleep. Just for a little while. But it's a very distressing feeling. All I can think about is the stain in front of my eyes, which moves, though sluggishly. And me, numb, half dead. But conscious.

Arriving home, I find the barbershop full of activity. People sweating and making talk. Even though the temperature has, in fact, gone down a bit by now, they talk slowly, lackadaisically, as if to conserve energy. I recognize a few of them, neighbors. Others are total strangers. There are more strangers than acquaintances.

No water for a shower. My nephew never showed up with the water coupons. Adelaide complains that he didn't even phone or leave a message. "But mother will lend us two coupons," she says. I turned on the television, then turned it off. I stood there staring at the hole in my palm. I felt like leaving again already. But where would I go? If only the old public garden still existed.

Adelaide turned on the TV again—time for our soap. It was one of the last episodes, she was silent until it was over. I barely followed the story. Then she turned off the sound and looked at me with a question in her eyes. It's incredible the number of looks she's got in her repertoire, she should have been an actress. Except that she's so shy and self-contained.

—I made a promise to Our Lady Who Appeared. If she heals that hole in your palm, we'll go hear two masses. And I'll give a wax hand to her Holiness.

—I suppose the neighbors gave you that idea.

—No, I was talking to Mother, and she suggested it. No harm in trying.

—Well, I'm not keeping any such promise. Leave me alone with my hole.

Adelaide burst into tears and disappeared into the kitchen. Let her cry, it has nothing to do with me. Not anymore. I look around, astonished, at the furniture, the faded curtains, the pile of old newspapers and magazines, the china closet full of knickknacks, the pictures of saints, the dainty lace centerpiece, the porcelain ashtray.

I feel like I'm in an entirely different house. A friend's house, maybe. It's as if I've never really looked at these things. They're so ugly, so neatly arranged and useless. I never drank anything out of that glass with the blue initials. Or ate anything off those Chinese plates which are just one more thing to need dusting. And what about the flowers she buys every week?

Always the same artificial flowers. Plastic. Marvelous reproductions, really—petals and leaves which are thin and smooth to the touch. I remember staring at the petals of a white rose once—how many years ago was that?— for over an hour. I think that was the last time I saw a real flower.

It stood in a thin vase over there in the corner, on a little altar to the Sacred Heart. Every other day Adelaide would cut a fresh flower from the tiny rose garden we had out front. It turned grayish overnight, covered with a layer of grime that stuck to each velvety petal and refused to come off.

When I rubbed the petals between my fingers, they were stained black. Like shoe polish, the kind that sticks to your fingers, it made me nauseous. I remembered this as I hammered a tiny nail into the rim of a red lacquered tray, one more useless decoration we've lived with ever since we got married.

Ten days after our wedding, Adelaide had the house all set up, and it stayed that way. Stagnant. The nail was still loose. I pounded gently but ended up dropping the thing on the floor. Pieces flew everywhere. "Come eat dinner," Adelaide called from the kitchen.

Instead of sitting at the table, she stood in the corner, her plate at her chin. A cat—yes, that's it, she was like a cat. Cats were curious creatures. Dogs, I hated. I don't know why, they never did anything to me, I simply detested them. Maybe I just don't like animals who are always licking people, at your heels, servile.

For years we've gone to bed at 10:45 after listening to the news on General Radio. Adelaide is sitting there with her crocheting, not the least bit interested in the news tonight. "Time for bed?" I ask. She gives me another one of her looks, confused this time. What?—straight from the table to bed, without even listening to the radio?

We brushed our teeth, she put on her night cream. (Adelaide has beautiful skin.) Ever since we got married, the ritual has been the same: I let her go first, down the hall from the bathroom. With my hand resting on her shoulder, we walk into the bedroom together. Tonight—for the second time—she wears an expression of revulsion at my touch.

Instinctual, unconscious. As soon as she felt my hand on her shoulder (it's that automatic), she withdrew com-

61

pletely. I pulled back my hand immediately and she kept walking, without looking back, certain that I was watching her. Maybe wondering *how* I was looking at her. Surprised? Indifferent?

I felt sorry for Adelaide. Suddenly she was feeling so alone in the world. Like jumping out of a plane without a parachute. She'd entered a dangerous area and I was no longer with her. Or, rather, the man she'd lived with, the man she'd depended on, all these years, wasn't there anymore. Adelaide didn't understand the way I was feeling and I didn't know how to explain.

We left the light off in the bedroom, changed our clothes in the dark. Our nightclothes were in the same place we'd left them. Pajamas, top and bottom, and socks (no matter how hot it was, her feet were always cold). We'd be able to walk around the house blind, no problem. We knew every centimeter from memory.

Freshly ironed clothes sat on top of the dresser. Every night before going to bed, Adelaide arranged everything neatly in the drawers, and for a few minutes the room would be filled with the smell of sun, soap, and mothballs, plus a faint aroma of cedar as she opened the heavy bureau.

We pretend to sleep. I can tell she wants to talk. She's trying, but she can't get started, and she can't be still, either. Until yesterday Adelaide knew everything there was to know about me: she knew beforehand what I was about to say, she knew my gestures, my habits. Now she's ashamed to be sleeping in the same bed with me. I'm a stranger.

I feel my face redden, my heart pounds. I care about this woman, I don't want her to have to feel like this. In the past, I would have talked to her, made a joke, we might have been able to laugh about it. Meanwhile I can see she's clearly frightened, intractable, curled up on her own side of the bed, on the verge of falling out.

Lying there silent in the dark, suddenly we heard footsteps. Back and forth, back and forth, across the

62

terrace. Whoever was there made no attempt to disguise their presence. And the tread was purposeful, heavy, it belonged to no animal. Silly to even consider the idea of animals, anyway.

—Did you hear that?

—Of course, how could I miss it?

—What should we do?

—Let's go take a look...

—Take a look? Are you crazy? What if it's an armed robber?

—Turn the light on, that should scare him.

—I think we better call the Guards.

—You think so? If they don't find anything, we'll get a fine!

—What time is it?

—How can I see the clock in the dark?

—If it's after two, we're not even supposed to turn on the light.

—But this is an emergency!

—How do we prove that later?

We talked in whispers, and the noise outside was getting fainter. Without thinking about it further, I jumped out of bed. This was ridiculous—my house was being threatened and I couldn't even turn on the light or call someone to protect me? So I yelled. At the top of my lungs. Frightening Adelaide even more.

I turned on the light and looked at the clock. Stopped dead. For only the second time in how many years— twenty, maybe. The first time it happened Adelaide had just quit her job. We went out for a pizza to celebrate, and forgot all about fixing it. From then on I was apprehensive about losing track of the time and left the radio on.

Adelaide put on her dingy yellow pignoir. Jesus, in heat like this, who's going to pay any attention to her short pajamas? The neighbors go around in shorts during the day, and they're not exactly kids anymore. (The women in our building were all in their fifties and sixties.)

I put my arms around her, and she leaned up against me. The hallway was full of people with puzzled faces. Some just barely peeked out of their doors, cautiously watching the hubbub. Everyone had heard the noise, it had been that loud, and could only have been human. But doing what?

—I think they got one of them.

—Not a chance, that bald guy ran for it.

—How many were there?

—I'm not sûre, I think about ten.

—No, it had to be more. I heard it from way up on the seventh floor.

—Has anybody come up to check?

—The Security Committee.

—Did they do anything?

—Nobody knows. We'll have to wait.

—Did anyone call the checkpoint?

—They were busy with other cases, and they don't have enough vehicles.

—I don't like this a bit, there's all kinds of strange things going on in this neighborhood. What's happened to Access control?

—Some control. You think they really do anything?

—I heard the Security Committee is at Dona Alcinda's.

—Did they catch anyone?

—No, no one's even sure what happened.

Dona Alcinda's apartment was two floors down. The stairs were jammed with people, everyone buzzing in the halls, it looked like the whole building was awake. Contradictory rumors flew from mouth to mouth, you never knew if what you were hearing had any truth to it.

—Did you see what they were doing?

—What?

—Who?

—Where?

No one knew what had happened, no one could even agree on the facts, and everyone was excited. Each person tried to contribute a piece of information, but when you put it all together it didn't add up to a total picture which made any sense. So everyone just got more anxious.

—They found a hose.

—They discovered the hose.

—They lost the hose?

—Whose was it?

—Did they get to the water tank?

—They lost the hose to the water tank?

—What was the hose doing in the tank?

—In the tank? But the tank's on the terrace, and the terrace is sealed off.

—They broke in.

—Oh, that's awful! How do we explain that to the Guards?

—We'll draw up a complaint.

—Who's going to believe it wasn't us?

—The Association will have to tally up the losses. Looks like they took quite a bit of water.

—They did?

—Who did?

—There's a hose hanging out the side of the building.

—Someone's stealing our water?

—Just what we need, as if there aren't already enough problems . . .

—I'll bet it was those bald guys. There've been a lot of them hanging around lately.

—Someone saw a uniform—from the New Army.

—Noooo. I don't believe it!

—Did they get a lot of water?

—More than half a tank. We're lucky the hose broke and made a racket, that's why they ran for it.

—Sunday they robbed the building on the corner.

—There's only one solution: hire some sharpshooters. It's no crime to kill water thieves, you know. What's tough is *proving* someone's stealing your water in the first place.

—That's because a lot of the time the residents are in on it. They break into the tanks, drain their own water, and then call the Guards.

—Yeah, I heard that, too. Which is why they investigate the residents before they investigate the robbery. First you've got to establish that there was no collusion, and that takes a lot of time.

—That's right, they check to see if you've got a record, and even if you don't, it's just looking for trouble. I don't want anything to do with registering a complaint.

—Me either. Who's got the time—or the patience—to go down and make a deposition, fill out a bunch of forms. Forget it. We'll get together and figure things out ourselves.

—Right. Tomorrow the Association will calculate the water level in the tank and hand out the allotments, that is if there's anything left to allot.

## THE SYMPATHETIC NEPHEW VISITS HIS HARD-PRESSED AUNT & UNCLE, BRINGING THEM EXTRA WATER COUPONS, AND A DISCUSSION OF THE GRANDEUR OF BRAZIL ENSUES

—Uncle Souza sure has a long face. What's wrong?
—Oh, just the worries of old age.
—You getting old, Uncle Souza? You don't look it.
—His hair's getting white, that's all.
—Still clinging to your old ideas, though, I bet, hmm?
—Have you seen his latest trick? A hole in his hand!
—A hole? How did that happen?
—You think he'll talk about it? At least he hasn't told me anything.
—You'd better be careful, Uncle—are you sure it's not contagious? Have you been to the checkpoint?
—Oh, he says he went, but I don't believe him. They would have given him a prescription or something. Or sent him to Isolation.

66

—Ah, so he's afraid of Isolation . . .

—Well, he didn't exactly say that, but he is. I remember once he told me that Isolation is the end. If you get sent there, you're gone for good.

—What do you mean? What does he think happens to them?

—He swears they disappear from the face of the earth.

—Who knows, maybe there's a crematorium, is that it, Uncle Souza? A gas oven, and a pile of ashes off to one side, disappearing into the wind? Maybe that's what all this dust and grime is that's all over the place, huh? Maybe it's really ashes, is that what you think?

—Ssssh, don't say that, he's worried enough as it is. He's getting quieter by the day. He doesn't even want to go to work anymore, he says it's useless, that his job is unproductive.

—Unproductive? Why should he worry about that? Do you know how many people are waiting in line for your job, Uncle Souza, do you have any idea?

—He must. They're all over the streets, he's always complaining about the crowds. Isn't the New Army going to do anything about it? Just today ten people have been here begging for food and water.

—That's not allowed. Did they have CIRCAs for this area?

—How should I know?

—You should ask to see them.

—Oh, they're so desperate-looking, the poor things. Those bald ones make me sick to my stomach, though, what a horrible thing. Why aren't they sent to Isolation?

—It's hard to take care of everything, Aunt Adelaide, but we're trying. Now that I've been promoted, I'll be working in circulation control in the areas of Greater São Paulo. Gonna be a tough job.

—You'll get a raise, though, won't you?

—A small one. But I'm going to have to come up with a plan to keep those migrants from pouring into the city . . .

—Can't you send them back where they came from?

—They came from the foreign territories up north.

—Well, can't you negotiate an agreement, some sort of treaty or something?

—Ha. They're not the least bit interested in treaties or agreements. One of these days I'm going to bring Uncle Souza along to visit the Encampments.

—Do you think you could arrange an authorization for your uncle to visit his father?

—His father? I thought the old man was dead.

—No, they took him to Silent Protection years ago. Your uncle has never been able to visit him, not even once.

—The Protection is really far from here, you'd have to pass through at least four districts. Do you know how much would be involved in getting CIRCAs for a trip like that, with money or favors for every official along the way?

—But you're a captain in the New Army!

—Sure, but the ones with the power are the generals and above.

—This country is really something, everything's so complicated. One of these days I won't even be able to go to church.

—You never change, do you, Aunt Adelaide. Still believe God's going to solve the world's problems, eh?

—That's something I won't argue about, not with you or anyone. Leave me my faith at least.

—I remember when I was a little boy and I'd come to play in the backyard. Every day, when I was washing up for dinner, you'd say: "You should be a priest, my boy, or else you should join the New Army." After a while you left off with the priest business, but you never gave up on the New Army, you said it should be the New Army for sure. My mother wanted me to get a job with the Bank of Brazil. Or the Housing Administration.

—No, your father was the one who was always talking about the Housing Administration.

—I hardly remember him.

—He said that in the Housing Administration you

could have a career, a real future, plus a home for your family. And if you worked your way up, which was his dream, you'd become a department head. The Purchasing Department, that was his obsession, that was the department for you. I'm not sure why. "The guy who is in charge of purchasing has the whole thing in his hands." Why did he say that, I wonder?

—I'm not exactly sure, but Father must have known what he was talking about.

—But Chief of Purchasing? What nonsense.

—Ummm, and it almost happened, didn't it? I'm lucky they found out about my bad intestine and rejected me.

—And lucky the New Army was more sympathetic and accepted you!

—In a special battalion, but they accepted me.

—Not everyone has what it takes to march, to maintain order, to come out fighting. They recognized you had the head for it.

—Yes, and most of the Mili-techs have some sort of medical problem. Stomach, lungs, back, intestines. We're the generation born after the explosion in the reactor, they have to compensate us somehow. So I ended up captain.

—I always thought the young men were so handsome in their uniforms, marching through the streets or out on patrol. Your uncle was foolish. I told him, too, I said why don't you quit the university and join the New Army. But you know something? The soldiers would go by on their rounds and I could see he hated them.

—Is that so, Uncle?

—Just look at his face! He doesn't even like it when I talk about it.

—Well, then, maybe Uncle Souza doesn't like me . . .

—Don't be silly, you're like a son to him.

—There are fathers who hate their sons, you know.

—That may be, but that's not Souza. He may have his quirks, but he's a good man.

—Really? What do you think, Uncle Souza? How come you're so quiet, then, tell me that?

—He only wants the best for you.

—I'm not so sure. I've seen people like him, dangerous people. I don't think Uncle Souza is really reconciled to the way things are nowadays.

—He hasn't said a word about politics for a long time now.

—What do you say, Uncle Souza? What do you think of the System?

—Really, this is no time to discuss things like that. You came for lunch, it's Sunday. Let's relax, watch a little television, go for a walk...

—Go for a walk? In this heat? Not a chance. You must not get out of the house very often, Aunt Adelaide...

—No, I guess I don't. Well! Let me open this bottle you brought...

—Well, Uncle Souza? Not planning to answer my question?

—Oh, leave him alone. He's upset because of his hand.

—No, it's more than that, I can see it in his face.

—He's always like that. Ironic, closemouthed, you know that.

—Do you like the System or not, Uncle Souza?

—No, I don't.

—You see, Aunt Adelaide? I was right. He doesn't approve of the System.

—He's just kidding, aren't you, Souza? Tell him.

—No, I don't like the System. And I'm not kidding.

—Are you crazy, Souza? This is your nephew you're talking to!

—How could I possibly approve of the System? Everything going on out there is their fault.

—What? Everything, all the problems? Let me get this right.

—Yes, everything. The country torn to pieces, Brazilians expelled from their own territory, the trees gone, every one of them, the desert up north.

70

—It's a beautiful desert. The ninth wonder of the world.

—It's a wonder, all right. And what about the rivers? Where are all the rivers, my boy?

—Oh, so you're going to blame the System for the fact that the rivers have dried up? Be reasonable! Things change. You know that, you're the history professor. The countries who started the nuclear testing, they're the ones to blame for the changes in the atmosphere.

—Is that all you can do—repeat the official propaganda?

—It's true, it's what I learned in the Infinite Course on War. A shame it's limited to authorized personnel, it would be good for everybody to take that course.

—Tell me. Where has the country gone?

—What do you mean? It's right here.

—Here, where?

—Here, there, all around.

—But how big is it, tell me that? This big? Think a little, use your head. When I was young this country measured eight-and-a-half million square kilometers. You know how big it is now?

—Off the top of my head, no, but I could find out.

—Find out, then. And when you do, you come tell me. It's not much bigger than the palm of my hand.

—The concept of a nation has changed, Uncle Souza. It's internationalism that's important now. Multiplicity. This is just a small part of the whole. Don't forget all the other pieces, don't forget the reserves in Uruguay, Bolivia, a big chunk of Chile, Venezuela. All those prairies in Africa—you know I'd like to be transferred to Africa, you get triple pay plus a house and free food. I could save up a lot of money.

—That's perfect, we surrender our own land and go colonize someplace else.

—It's not colonization at all, it's different. We're talking about multinational reserves. You have to think about the world in global terms.

71

—Maybe I'm getting old, my head full of worn-out ideas. But I'd prefer a country in one piece, whole, instead of a world of countries inside my country, the way it is now. I told you about the time I tried to go to Manaus. Never made it. There was no way, they had me going around in circles, nothing to do but come home. It was harder to get through Rondonia, supposedly one of our own territories, than to get permission to enter Bolivia.

—You've got a very narrow vision of things, Uncle Souza. You think in terms of the individual, which limits you to a sort of defeated regionalism. Try to look at things in larger terms. Our economy, for example, has never been so strong as it is now.

—You call this strong? No one has any money! This country is in debt up to its ears. And there's no land left worth farming. Anything you want to buy costs an arm and a leg because it's all imported!

—We don't import all that much...

—Not much. Salt, sugar, iron, beans, electricity, paper, plastics. You want the whole list?

—Those aren't imports, those commodities are shipped to us under the treaties negotiated as part of the land transactions.

—How can you be so blind? We're importing from ourselves! From up north, which used to be Mato Grosso, Maranhão, Pará.

—But don't forget that those concessions aren't permanent, there's a time limit on all of them.

—I know, I know. Last year the agreement with Belgium ran out. And did they just hand over the territories they maintained in Goias? Not a chance, the System had to *buy* them back. They paid good money for land that should have reverted to us free and clear.

—The land, yes. But what about the improvements, industrial projects, buildings, crops, laboratories? Those are all worth something.

—Ruins, all ruins.

—How do you know?

72

—These things leak out, my boy, people find out about them eventually. Do you know who got rich on the Belgian concession? They say, listen to this, they say it was the Society of Inebriated Ministers. If you tell anyone I said that, I'll deny it. But it's true.

—The Society? How could anyone think they have that much power? The System has them under control. They've been under house arrest, in fact, for quite a while, they're carefully watched. And they have no power at all to speak of.

—Who can guarantee that they're in those houses which are so carefully watched? No one ever sees any of them anymore. They're working their way back into the System, you'll see.

—Be careful, Uncle Souza. What you're saying is dangerous. The current System put an end to the Era of Enrichment, and those responsible were all arrested, hunted down, exiled, eliminated, killed.

—That's what you say. I think the Society is alive and well.

—The Society is a myth.

—The System tolerates the Society. They could get reorganized and take over at any time. The System is just not on top of the situation.

—The System is in complete control. Everything is going according to plan.

—You call this a plan? Did they plan on these waves of migration? On the sorry state of the public health? I see people in the street every day who are falling to pieces, literally. There's no more water. If you didn't bring us coupons, your aunt and I would die of thirst. Do you have any idea how late they were this week handing out the water coupons? And it was on purpose, I'm sure of it, to ration the water.

—You know, I can't believe you were a university professor, with such a narrow mind. You people were always screaming for nationalization across the board. Well, here we are: nationalized. The government is taking care of everything, all sectors. So now what do you want?

—You mean to say we've reached a state of socialism in this country?

—Don't you think so?

—Is that what you call it!

—Seems like socialism to me.

—Well, I suppose if you overlook the fact that it isn't the government itself which holds the economy in its hands, but a few people who happen to be in the government's good graces. As for everybody else, the masses, they're as bad off as ever, maybe worse.

—Don't talk to me about the masses. You never cared a day in your life about the masses, the common people. You're just one of those types always claiming to defend them, it's all a pose.

—I think that nowadays, above and beyond the masses or anything else, what's important is to try to save what's left of us as a nation. To reconstruct our country, if that's still possible, and then start thinking about all of us who live in it.

—But meanwhile the System is okay when it comes to arranging extra water coupons, is that it?

—Can't you two stop arguing? Why is it you quarrel every time he visits, Souza? Why can't we be like other families? There are lots of things, pleasant things, to talk about.

—Sure, let's talk about something pleasant. I think that's a great idea, Aunt Adelaide.

—You're a smart one, I have to admit that. I just don't understand how you can be so blind to reality.

—I live in reality, Uncle Souza. This is not a dream. This has always been my reality, I never lived in any other. The Wide Open Eighties were already over by the time I was born, they didn't even figure in the history books, isn't that so? Just occasional, short references, that's all, not much commentary. So how can you say I'm blind?

—Living in reality is one thing. Accepting it, thinking that such a reality is good . . . that's another story. Hasn't it ever occurred to you that life could be different?

74

—If we don't live in an organized fashion, we'll all die. It's as simple as that. We're on the right path, rigid control is the only way.

—There might have been another way, if they hadn't done what they did.

—But they did. We can't change that now.

—Are you sure?

## ADELAIDE MAKES A DELICIOUS CAKE (WITH SYNTHETIC FLOUR) TO TAKE TO HER MOTHER, & SOUZA COURAGEOUSLY REFUSES TO ACCOMPANY HER, SENDING HER ALONE INSTEAD WITH HIS REGARDS

One Saturday morning Adelaide found a note pushed under the door: "We don't want you in this building." Sunday there were two more. They were written on yellow paper (where had the person managed to get hold of it?): "Take the hole in your hand someplace else" and "We're going to call the police if you don't move out soon."

Adelaide brought the notes to me in bed. Quarter-to-seven and I wasn't up yet, which puzzled her because it was probably the first time since she'd met me that I wasn't up by six. I had the covers pulled over my head, it was a cold morning. I heard her stop and stand there next to the bed, hesitating. Then she nudged me gently.

—Souza, wake up, this is serious.

—What is?

—The neighbors know about the hole.

She read me the notes.

—Idiots. Don't worry about it.

—I *am* worried. I didn't mention it before, but no one's talked to me for two days.

—Which is normal around here. Everyone avoids everybody else.

—Neighbors are important, Souza.

75

—You're always so worried about the neighbors. First thing you do after moving into a new place is knock on the door and say, "Hi, we're your new neighbors, just let us know if you need anything!"

—And we've always gotten along with them just fine. I don't know how to live all by myself, isolated. It's nice to be able to go next door or down the hall in the afternoon, drink a cup of coffee, bake some cookies.

—How many years has it been since you've done that?

—Do you know what I found in the hall?

—The alarm clock.

—How did you know?

—Because I put it there.

—Have you gone crazy?

Adelaide shook the clock back and forth to see if it was broken. Then she put it on the dresser, on top of the notes from the neighbors. And looked at me as if to say: there it is, we'll talk later. I know that look. There's definitely a "later" in it.

—What time should we go to mother's?

—I'm not going.

—But it's Sunday, they're expecting us.

—I'm not going.

—But how am I supposed to explain? The least you could do is put on a good face and come along, so they won't worry.

—You go alone.

—Mother will be so disappointed...

—Better her than me.

I took such a long time getting up that Adelaide had plenty of time to make the obligatory cake (synthetic, of course) to take to her mother. She made one every Sunday. The artificial flour is a yellowish powder which comes in premeasured plastic bags. They got the taste almost right, but who knows, the memory can play tricks on you. Adelaide complains that the consistency is never right, too rubbery.

She came into the bedroom again, this time to tell me coffee was ready. She left sobbing. For a moment I felt

76

like running after her, but it was so pleasant in the bedroom, so shady. She'd have to go by herself. The sun would mean instant sweat. Why should I spend the whole day away from home, out in the oppressive heat, I'd just get more depressed.

When Adelaide got home that night, she found me sitting there staring at the hole in my hand. The floor was covered with cigarette butts and leftover food I'd heated up for myself. Without saying a word, she began to clean up the mess. Nothing makes me madder than an indirect accusation, the kind that just hangs in the air unsaid.

Adelaide always cleaned house on Sunday evening, after it got cooler. Then she'd take a bath and go to bed. Of course she left the heavy cleaning for the once-a-week cleaning woman: doors, windows, tiles, bathrooms. Tonight she walks into the bedroom looking sick. Refuses to look at me. Strange—what could it mean?

—Mother sends her love. She said it was a shame you didn't come along. I told her we'd both be there next week, that you had to work today. I felt so awful, lying like that. I think my father noticed that something was wrong.

Now she's got the waxer out, waxing and polishing the wood floors. For years I've been saying: "Let's put a coat of synthetic varnish on it, save you a lot of work." But she thinks wax gives a better shine. So the smell of wax spreads through the house, reminding me of Saturday morning when I was a kid.

Soapy water running over the tiles, waxed wood floors, blankets flapping out the windows or on the line. Mattresses out to bleach in the sun. Brooms ticking the sidewalk, water splashing off hot stone, the humid smell that would rise up from the whole street, almost joyful, everyone immersed in the ritual.

Women hanging precariously out windows to wash hard-to-reach panes. Feather dusters fluttering about the furniture, big thick scrub brushes back-and-forth, back-and-forth, in the laundry room, on the veranda, in the living room. Rags tied on broomsticks to clear spider webs from corners. Linens smelling of sun and cedar and mothballs gently lifted out of their drawers.

There was only one house on the street which remained closed up and quiet, impenetrable. A block away, on the corner: a Baptist family. Imbedded like a thorn under the nail, amid so many Catholic houses. Early in the morning they closed up the house and left, maybe so they wouldn't have to witness that sacrilegious hustle and bustle.

They were as strange to us as Moses, the Jew who sold eggs. We children were bursting with curiosity, but mother wouldn't even let us talk to them. The Protestants were heretics, they refused to obey the holy Pope. The Jews had killed Jesus. I imagined Moses throwing rotten eggs at the cross.

Every two weeks or so the men from city hall would come with their sickles to cut the grass which had sprouted between paving stones. All day long you could hear the rhythmic noise of iron on stone, their tools throwing off little sparks as they worked. The aroma of cut grass would take over the whole block.

Each day was itself, with its own special flavor. Monday was white, the day of sagging clotheslines, women leaning over cement tubs doing the wash. They sang as they worked. By mid-morning there were so many melodies in the air—a weaving together of all the popular songs of the moment into a single sound.

Tuesday was the girls' day to go to the movies. Romantic movies that made them weep and blush. Wednesday, late in the afternoon, the women wound their way down the dusty streets to mass. Thursday everybody went to the movies. Friday was trash pickup, with all its particular smells. Saturday morning was for house-cleaning, afternoon for picking up clothes at the seamstress, and at night movies or dances.

Nowadays you never know if it's Tuesday or Saturday; the only day that's different is Sunday because you don't have to go to work. And they're talking about a law to

78

change that. What good does it do to remember all this? It's like a lapse into senility to even think about it. Like dreaming of the fantastic life on a lost planet.

Believe it or not, fifty is *old*. It's true. Sometimes I'm amazed that I'm alive, still on my feet, walking around. People die at thirty-five, forty years old these days. In the last decade (I heard on General Radio) the average life expectancy fell to forty-three.

"A good age," my nephew had remarked. "There are too many people as it is. Why should the System be interested in raising the life expectancy? On the contrary! After all, where would we put the extra people?" (And to think of the Wide Open Eighties when the average person lived to be seventy-four!) "We're a young country," bragged my nephew.

—You've been smoking in the bedroom.

—Just a couple.

—A couple? Look at this mess of ashes and cigarette butts. What's wrong with you, Souza? Don't you feel well? Should we go to the clinic?

—You want to take me to the clinic just because I've been smoking in the bedroom?

—You've never done this before in your life. You know how much I detest the smell of cigarettes in the bedroom.

I kept smoking the whole time she complained. It's time to realize that one day things change. How can she be so insensitive? The world out there is changing totally and she just goes on the same as ever. Of course so did I, I spent years contemplating, contemplating, without acting or reacting. Traumatized by losing my job.

I recognize now what weakness that represented. But then I'm not a very strong person. I'm just an ordinary man who tries to live his life a day at a time, who wants to be happy, to accomplish something in life. But suddenly the idea of accomplishing something doesn't make any sense anymore, because we're at a dead end. Yet I can't just sit around waiting to die.

Or waiting for them to take me to Silent Protection,

79

to an asylum. Someplace where there's no communicating with anyone. Adelaide finishes her tirade and runs off, slamming the bathroom door. I can hear her throwing up in there. When she's done, she hesitates by the bedroom door. How can I live with such a timid, fearful woman, always running around like a chicken with its head cut off?

—Souza, I've made up my mind.

I jumped. Must have been dozing off. She was standing at the foot of the bed, first-aid kit in her hand. Staring at me. A completely different look on her face now. Stern, unflinching. A look of hate, almost, and of determination. She sat down on the bed and took my hand. I pulled it away, and she grabbed it back again, forcibly. Imagine!

—Either you let me put a Band-Aid on your hand or I'm leaving. I mean it.

—You're not putting any Band-Aid on my hand. It was my understanding that the subject was closed.

## MONDAY: SOUZA & ADELAIDE'S CONSUMER DAY, THE DAY THEY MUST BUY WHAT THE FACTORIES MAKE SO THERE WON'T BE AN INSIDIOUS RECESSION

Adelaide spent the night in the armchair next to the bed. Spying on me, waiting for me to fall asleep so she could bandage my hand. She courageously put up with the cigarettes, I smoked the whole pack. Then, since I'd used up my entire quota, I lit the butts. All night I thought I heard whispering, though I couldn't tell if it came from the living room or from the hallway outside the apartment.

I dozed off, woke up; the chair was empty. Then I heard the whispering, muffled noises, I thought I heard her mother's voice. Or the neighbor whom I've never seen without a feather duster in her hand (she wages a constant battle against the dust). I dozed off, woke up. Adelaide was sitting in the chair again, maybe I had been dreaming.

Adelaide suffers so. I shouldn't feel sorry for her, but I do. I married her after I no longer loved her. I didn't know how to say no, I was stuck on all the old principles, dignity, a man's pledged word. We had been sweethearts for so many years, since adolescence, when I first imagined she would be my match, we would grow together.

The right decision. The fear of the "no." The fascination it held for me. That strange, delayed mechanism of mine, working as if I lived in a different time zone. Adelaide was a good friend to me, but I didn't have to marry her. What am I trying to prove by going over all this now?

I always accepted our marriage as an inevitable fact, I didn't fight it. Sometimes we do things we don't want to and end up getting used to them, adapting. As long as we agreed to it to begin with. That's the worst part— our passive acceptance of the idea that not everything in life is as we'd like it. But it should be.

I liked Adelaide, but really she was just an empty space, a vacuum, inside my own loneliness. She never *filled* me, she wasn't essential. I've thought about this a lot. If she disappeared, I'm not sure I would really miss her, everything would continue just the same. The discovery that my wife was not indispensable. Far from consoling me, this thought made me profoundly uneasy. For both of us.

My indifference has served to turn her, little by little, into a bitter and despairing woman—with no horizons, no promise for the future. And now, with no support from me. She had tried to build a home for us here, and instead of participating I withdrew, as if I hadn't wanted to get involved or to accept any personal responsibility for our life together.

So that I would be ready to drop everything at any moment and flee. Ever since I was a boy I've needed that feeling, that theoretical escape route. It never appealed to me to stay in the same place, making incessant renovations. What I wanted was to be disengaged, to escape from everything and live far away where no one could find me.

I don't think about it anymore. I know it's not a question of near or far away. There is nowhere, no way out, no safe haven, everything has been exposed to view. This knowledge awakens in me a strange nostalgia. Not for the days when my grandfathers were pioneers in Mato Grosso or Paraná. Before then. Way before.

I'd like to be like the explorers. Going beyond the horizon, and then beyond yet another, wandering continually until, who knows, returning to the point of departure. Which is not where I am but where I was born, where I put down the roots I'm tugging at now, bruising my hands, unable to tear them out.

What to do with this yearning? All I know is that if it weren't for the hole in my hand and everything that goes with it, I would never have run away. I'd still be there in front of the TV watching Adelaide hook rugs, dust off the furniture, wrap up the calendars, and complain about the bald men who knock at the door every day begging for food and water.

Suddenly Adelaide got up out of the chair and walked out of the room without closing the door behind her. Never, in all the years we've been married, has either of us left the bedroom door open after going in or out of it. No one but the two of us, not even a relation, had ever been inside our bedroom. It was a secret place, a refuge. Our sanctuary. Inviolate.

—Let's get going or we'll come home empty-handed, she said when she came back.

—You go. I don't feel like it.

—You go, you go. Is that all you can say?

—I never liked shopping, Adelaide, you know that. I don't want to go, not anymore.

—But you have to. A woman shouldn't have to do the shopping alone. Besides, for sixteen years we've been going out together on Monday to do the shopping.

—So what would happen if today, for once, we didn't? Is there anything we really need?

—Don't even suggest it. Things are bad enough already, I couldn't bear to get blacklisted. Remember what happened to Dona Alcinda's cousin? And she only missed her Consumer Day two weeks in a row, and it was because she was sick. No, Souza, we're going even if it's only to buy some salt. They don't want to hear anybody's excuses.

A hell of an idea—Monday shopping. The beastly haze, people moving at a snail's pace. And the sun. No shade, my head sizzling. A few of the houses we pass by have painted plastic panels in front of them—Simulated Gardens.

Anybody can buy one. You pay by the square meter. Some people hang them in their windows so they see greenery when they look out. Others, more vain, arrange the panels to face the street: status symbols. They're expensive, especially the three-dimensional ones. Or the kind that come with built-in aromas.

Adelaide walks a little ahead of me. She's embarrassed about my hand, of course. She detests me today, because I resisted so ferociously her idea of covering it with a Band-Aid. I'm not trying to be difficult, I've even got my hand in my pocket to avoid arousing people's curiosity, but that's not enough. She grudgingly accepts the situation but still avoids me.

The Shopping District makes me dizzy in this heat. Buses disgorge multitudes of people. Crowds of the Economically Exempt mill around the edges of the district, holding out fistfuls of money to anyone on the inside who's willing to make their purchases for them. Many people make a living furnishing merchandise to the Exempt, although it is illegal.

Those in the Economically Exempt category have the luxury of not being assigned an obligatory Consumer Day like the rest of us. The problem is that, under the terms of their exemption, they are restricted to shopping at smaller stores in their area. It cuts down on traffic in the Shopping District, but they are deprived of access to the wide array of goods to be bought there. Anyone whose annual income is above the minimum wage is eligible to be designated Exempt.

So, often when the Exempt have saved up some money, they position themselves at the fence and try to bargain for rare or unusual items like synthetic oriental fruit: dried figs, tamarinds, raisins. And all sorts of other things, I can't think of any more examples right now. Anyway, they stand there yelling, begging, holding out their cash or money orders while people on the inside listen and take notes. It's all based on trust. The Interceptor, as he's called, buys the item and brings it home to be picked up later by the buyer. Interceptors operate on the same code of ethics as the old numbers runners before the numbers game was legalized.

No one knows what happens to someone caught passing merchandise across the boundary because he or she is never heard from again.

Sometimes it seems as if this is all a dream, an imaginary situation I'm living through, surrealistic. A hydrogen balloon which could explode at any moment.

Today there are some of those bald men hanging around the boundaries, as well as the ones with flabby skin, and others whom I've never seen before, with their eyes almost completely sealed shut by some gummy secretion, as if their eyeballs were inflamed. It's hard to look at them. They're all jammed together in a shouting match; suddenly I feel like one of the Privileged, their problems don't affect me.

But I think of the Shopping District as torture, in any case, even though lots of other people seem to like it. Smiling and sociable, drinking and talking in loud voices, they wander in and out of the stores—which seem to be more numerous every week. I must admit the District definitely has one thing going for it: the gallerias and shopping malls are cool and comfortable. They're air-conditioned and have natural light filtering down through smoked glass roofs.

The building we're assigned to still hasn't reached its Quota Limit. The stream of people entering is continuous. In the beginning there were always people holding things up by trying to get in without authorization, cutting into the lines and causing a big ruckus. Now they stay away; there are so many Inspectors it's just not worth it. Adelaide and I have almost made it to the door. She doesn't look too forgiving but she talks to me anyway.

—I was thinking of picking up a few aromas.

—Not a bad idea.

—See? You can always find something to buy.

—How about the Aroma of Late Afternoon?

—Okay, and I'd like Water on Dry Earth. That used to be so nice—on a hot day, the rain pounding down hard, making the dust rise, and the smell too.

—Sold out, said the cashier.

—Both of them? Well, why don't you tell us what you do have.

—Dry Leaves, Rotting Leaves, Eucalyptus in Late Afternoon, Coconut Palm, various flowers and vegetables, Roasting Coffee Beans, Brand-New Paper, Cotton Balls, Brewing Tea Leaves, Cow Pies, Burned Milk, Bread in the Oven, Steel Saw after Cutting Cedar Trunk, Lavender, Jasmine, Church at Benediction, Just-Cleaned Public Bathroom, Hot Ironed Clothes, Girl Fresh from the Bath, Roasting Chicken, Toothpaste on a Child's Breath, and about two hundred more.

—Made in Brazil?

—Just the Cow Pie, Hot Ironed Clothes, Escaping Gas, and Closed-Up Room.

We bought three sprays. Milk that Boiled Over, Steel Saw after Cutting Cedar Trunk, and Coal-Burning Locomotive. My grandfather cut a lot of wood for railroad ties, I can bring back the smell of the vapor at will. I used to stand beside the tracks as they brought out the engine.

At the District Access, the Inspector stamped our cards: Consumer Obligations Fulfilled. Saved for one more week. As we waited for the bus I held my hand up in front of my face, shading my eyes. The sun shone through the hole forming a circle of light on the ground—more a blotch than a circle, the way the shadow was diluted.

I moved my hand up and down, the circle got larger and smaller. I squatted down and played with the light. I liked this image, the sun passing right through my hand, forming a symbol. A sign of some sort. Maybe it contained a hidden meaning, a message to decipher. Could be a warning.

I had spent hours in cathedrals watching the slow progress of the light at it filtered in through stained glass in the vaulted ceiling, until the moment when the sun reached the altar, perfectly illuminating that most holy of places. There had to be more than coincidence in the way it worked. Some deliberate design.

Perhaps a sort of homage: light at the feet of the divine. A confirmation that God is light. Or it might have been some message which only the initiate would understand. A message which had traveled millennia and would always be intelligible, in any age or time. Though I never liked the idea of initiates much.

There would always be men capable of decoding whatever was contained in this circle of light on the sidewalk. A sensation of comfort and peace, that's what I felt in those European cathedrals, sitting in a pew for hours on end watching the tenuous, almost imperceptible movement of light toward the altar.

Harmony in search of fulfillment. And finding it, every day, for the light, varying according to season, worked its way along the floor of the nave until reaching the altar at the determined hour. It's strange—now the whole thing seems sort of unpleasant in the way it represents the immutable.

At the same time, I felt the certainty of the immutable in the grand things of the universe. In the way they worked, in their structure. Could it be that even today light travels that same path, at the same time of day, with the same intensity? Could it be that one small example of immutability remains unaltered? I'd give anything to be inside one of those cathedrals right now.

Of course there are various notions of the immutable. The first, broad in scope, general, necessary, is the universe itself, untouchable. Then there are the other, smaller systems which we ourselves construct, and which need occasional alterations, minor adjustments from time to time, in order to adapt them to the larger, absolute order.

Or am I hopelessly confused? I'm not sure. I'm never clear on where man fits into all this. What is our role in nature, in the universe? Are we in control or controlled? And what about mankind's tremendous zeal over the centuries to dominate, to hold the reins of power?

I guess the question is this: could man, daring to alter the structure of the universe, have gone beyond the limit? Modifying things on a large scale even before understanding or controlling the smaller pieces which together make up our world? In other words: maybe we got in over our heads, and made a serious blunder. At some point.

## ON RETURNING TO WORK SOUZA GETS AN UNPLEASANT PIECE OF NEWS. THE BOSS, OF COURSE, DOESN'T OFFER ANY EXPLANATIONS: BOSSES BOSS

I made up my mind to go to work. I didn't shower or shave. Already sweating. I heated up some leftover soup. First time I've ever eaten soup for breakfast, but there's a first time for everything. Beef broth, tomato, little star-shaped macaroni. Synthetic. For years soup has been our main dish for supper.

Only the macaroni has changed. The neighborhood factory closed down a long time ago. The old man had been proud of his work and used wheat flour exclusively, but his sons were content with only a percentage of natural flour, and when the grandchildren took over they settled for chemical flour produced in government laboratories. And where did that get them—they were wiped out by the multinationals, whose macaroni came in attractive plastic packaging and supposedly had higher concentrations of vitamins, proteins, and eggs.

The truth is that during the seventies large-scale toxification was going on. People's digestive systems just didn't function properly; food turned to rock in their intestines, provoking terrible cramps. It was all the result of the excessive use of untested chemical ingredients. The technology, after all, came from abroad; the Brazilian technicians were still experimenting. It took months for them to get the process under control. Meanwhile, the press was prohibited from mentioning the subject because many ministers high up in the government had interests in the food industry.

I can still remember that mass toxification—it happened right around the time we came back from the polluted coast, a real fiasco of a vacation. At least we were smart. As soon as people started dying we headed for home. They'd go to the beach, lie in the sun for a while, and frolic in the water happy as clams. When they came out, they lay back down to work on their tans. By the end of the afternoon they were dying like cockroaches with insecticide.

Nowadays no one goes to the beach anymore. It got depressing just to drive along the coast and see the cement walls and barbed wire fences isolating the area. The stagnant, black sea. The beach—if you could call that dense, black, greasy sand a beach. The seawater wasn't even worth treating and distributing to alleviate the water shortage.

They did devise all sorts of filters in their attempts to make it potable. Completely useless. At the end of the cycle the water was gray and had the sickening smell of rotten eggs. As if it were the sea's vengeance. So they installed a gigantic system of underground pipes; now the wastes of the country flow to the ocean, day and night.

Two spoonfuls of soup, that's all. It made me nauseous. I had a sudden urge to dump it all over the rug. The rug made of scraps which Adelaide had worked on neurotically every day home alone. Ten thousand do-nothing afternoons sitting there in her chair cutting up pieces of cloth making rugs for the whole family.

Now she's asleep on the living room sofa. Or pretending to be. I made all kinds of noise but she didn't move a muscle. Nobody sleeps that soundly. I let myself out the front door and marched down flight after flight of stairs, slowly. Why should I care if I miss the bus?

In spite of it all I got to the bus stop before the S-758 did. What's the "S" stand for anyway? There are so many names, signs, numbers, little letters and symbolic designs, so many incomprehensible visuals, each one designating a division, a department, an organization. It would take someone at least a year to learn them all.

—I'm sorry, sir, but you'll have to wait for another bus.

—How come?

—Company rules.

—But that's impossible. The company doesn't know me, personally, and I've got the proper CIRCA.

—Please don't make this difficult.

—I'm not making it difficult. This is my bus; I'm simply getting on it.

I sat down. All the passengers stared at me; they didn't look pleased. I didn't recognize anyone from the usual group. There were a couple of bald guys, redder than ever. Stifling heat. Now they're giving those guys CIRCAs too? People looked nervous. They began to get off the bus. The ticket taker bolted from his post near the back and disappeared after consulting with the driver, who approached me cautiously.

—Why don't you just cooperate? It would make things a lot easier. For all of us.

89

—I paid, I have my CIRCA right here, it's my right to travel on the bus assigned to me.

Before long the ticket taker was back with a Civil Guard. As polite as usual, the Guard didn't say a word to me. (They're famous for shooting first and asking questions later.) He simply picked me up and threw me on the sidewalk as if I were a scrap of paper. Go to hell with your bulging muscles.

My briefcase flew open, papers cascaded all over the place. Still sprawled on the ground, my backside stinging from the impact, I started trying to gather them up. Suddenly I stopped. Why bother? These papers don't mean anything to me. Bills, memos, receipts, newspaper clippings, business cards, canceled checks, notices, invoices, papers with rubber stamps on them. It occurred to me these were more things my wife would care about.

Why should I waste my time gathering up this stuff? I looked down once more at all the slips of brown paper (the only kind that existed in Brazil—poor quality and rationed even so). I've lived with this pile of papers for how many years now? Why on earth carry around this archive of nothingness? It's funny, just yesterday I was lying in bed trying to remember where I worked, what I did. Why not leave my briefcase and the scattered pile of papers right here on the sidewalk? Which is exactly what I did.

The other passengers had piled back onto the bus in a hurry. I picked myself up and stood there leaning on the sign for the bus stop. Fifteen minutes later another bus came by, but only the front exit door opened, to let a few people off. It's a conspiracy. I beat on the back door, I kicked it. The ticket man stuck his head out the window, furious. I decided I was going to have to walk.

When I got to the office I walked past the boss's desk as quickly as possible, without even saying good morning. I didn't look at any of my colleagues, but then they didn't seem to be paying any attention to me, either. I've always been considered a quiet man, a fanatic for well-ordered drawers, a desktop clean enough you could eat off it, papers stacked neatly in labeled piles, a man known for his precise, eminently readable handwriting.

Someone else's jacket was draped across the back of my chair. I opened the top drawer, but things were not as I'd left them: pens arranged according to color and size, paper clips, rubber bands, stapler, stamps, each in their little compartment. Instead, everything was all mixed together. I heard an "excuse me, please" behind me and looked around. A fat man, bald, about thirty.

—Excuse me, but this is my desk.

—What?! Since when?

—Since yesterday morning.

—Well maybe we'd better go have a little talk with the boss.

—As you wish.

The imposter was sweating more than I was, but he looked awfully smug.

—What's going on here? This guy thinks he can take over my desk.

—And he has. You've been fired.

—For a couple of absences?

—Why don't you drop by the Treasurer's office on the way out.

—But you've got to explain what's going on here! What's this all about?

—When someone is fired, there's usually a reason.

—Well, I want to know what it is.

—What difference does it make? You're already fired, it wouldn't change anything. Sometimes the worst thing is knowing why.

—Look, I'll smash this place to pieces, I swear, I'll do it. I want an explanation, and right now!

—Be my guest, smash the place up. You always were a little too rebellious for your own good, Mr. Souza. And where has it gotten you, eh?

—I'm not leaving without an explanation.

91

—All right, then, stay. As long as you like. But just don't interfere with the people who work here, or I'll have to call a Guard.

I stepped out into the afternoon. The air was as thick as honey, my clothes seemed glued to my skin. Oh, for a bath. An ice-cold shower. A violent spray of water beating my body, relaxing every muscle. Ha, I live on the moon. Two in the afternoon and it's almost dark. You couldn't really call those clouds. More like metal, yes—metal plates closed up tight over the city.

The buildings hold the heat, the lines of people make their way listlessly along the sidewalk. Funny, how in the old days everybody dashed around, pushing and shoving and colliding in their haste. São Paulo was known for its speed. Meanwhile, the irritation on the faces (and inside people) is the same as ever. It used to be because they just couldn't go fast enough; now it's because of this asphyxiating, interminable heat.

Hopelessness. The lights are on already: a weak yellow. Sickly. "Under the painful light of the factory's big electric bulbs, I am feverish and I write." It was my favorite passage, I had copied it out and memorized it. Actually, I know most of Fernando Pessoa's poetry from memory. I am feverish and I think, in an infinite spiral.

The painful light of the big electric bulbs. People move in slow motion, as if they lived inside a special-effects movie. Heads lowered, breathing in gasps, following the eternal lines of bodies going in and out of buildings. Saving their energy so they can last a little bit longer and make it to the end of the day.

This is a city gone mad. I don't feel like walking in this heat, but they won't let me get on the bus. So I walk. Fewer and fewer people on the street. The downtown will be virtually empty by seven. And dangerous. But I can't stand the thought of going home to face the bags of garbage in the hall, the kitchen all tidied up, dishes in the dish drainer.

We had two trashcans in the kitchen. One for things

which rotted quickly: leftover food, coffee grounds, paper, eggshells. Things which were biodegradable. The other trashcan was for glass, tin cans, plastic. One day I observed this system very carefully. Each can, empty in the morning, would be filled gradually throughout the day. Overflowing by evening.

We left the cans out for the garbage men to pick up early in the morning. By the time we got up they were back in their places. Empty/full. The mechanism of repetition. Get up, have coffee, go to work, come home, eat, watch TV, go to bed.

Like a wheel spinning in place. Producing what? Nothing, zero, zip. A perpetual-motion machine. It went on working nonstop your whole life long. Unless someone interfered with it. Without interference, things go on and on, they become eternal. Intervention is what we need, someone interrupting things, making themselves an obstacle to repetition.

I had been walking all night. At daybreak I took off my socks, then put my shoes back on. At my assigned luncheonette I asked for bread, a hard-boiled egg (which tasted like plastic), and salt. A gray cloud still hovered low over the city, the clocks said a quarter to nine. People were already sweating. Soon there'll be mass dehydration. There's only so much water in our bodies.

Walking downtown. Strange to be free like this, admiring store windows I didn't even know were here, noticing the faces of people as they go by. I stopped paying attention to the downtown years ago. Lots of men with briefcases. My briefcase! That's what's missing, my briefcase in my hand as I walk down the street

That briefcase was part of me, like a limb, it made me feel secure. Without it my arms hang limp, close to my sides, afraid of coming unglued. I miss the office. Not the work, not the people, either—we hardly said a word to each other. It's just that I've never been free like this, at this hour of the morning, like today.

—Eighth floor, please.

93

The elevator man stared at me intently.

—We're not open until nine-fifteen.... Souza?

—Yes?

—Don't you recognize me?

—I don't think so...

—Tadeu.

—Tadeu Pereira! What are you doing here?

—I'm the elevator man, can't you see?

—Since when?

—I've worked in this building for years.

—But, so have I...

Then I realized I'd made a mistake. The lobby looked exactly the same, but this wasn't my building after all. Though of course they all look alike. Uniform. Made from the same design. The Brand X architecture of the Wide Open Eighties. Thanks to my error, I had rediscovered my old friend Tadeu Pereira. I can't believe it. He looks so worn out.

—Tadeu Pereira. Who could believe it.

—And you, Souza! What do you do now?

—Nothing. I've been fired.

—How come?

—You know about as much as I do.

—I've heard they're firing people left and right on the basis of the Secret Decrees.

—Never heard of them.

—They're secret. New from the Ministry of Planning. Mass firings, can you believe it? The System has decided to quit creating artificial jobs. There are too many already, and they think that general unemployment, even with the inevitable social problems it brings, is preferable to an unsupportable debt. They're scared to death of the foreign debt, but at the same time they use it as a justification for everything.

—Tadeu Pereira! Unbelievable!

He could never know how happy I was to see him. I never imagined I'd find myself face-to-face with this old friend again. He had disappeared so many years ago we

94

figured he was dead. It's a shame he looked so old and feeble, so stooped over, not at all like the man who had always radiated vitality, courageous in any circumstance.

### TWO PREMATURE RETIREES HAVE A CHAT. WHO WOULD HAVE GUESSED THINGS WOULD TURN OUT LIKE THIS— RIDICULOUS & OVERDEVELOPED SCIENCE FICTION?

—You mean they forced you into early retirement, too?

—Oh yes, a long time ago.

—So, what have you been doing since the university?

—Like I said, nothing.

—All these years?

—No, no, I verified lists of numbers in an office. Numbers and more numbers, all day long. Columns and columns of them.

—Who would have thought we'd end up like this, eh? Everything looked so promising in the Wide Open Eighties

—That didn't last long, did it? Though of course some people haven't even noticed.

—That's exactly what we've been discussing lately, Souza. And we've come to the conclusion that we were tricked. I suppose we should have foreseen it. It really makes me livid that so many cronies from the original dictatorship are still in power. Senile, the whole bunch of them.

—What do you mean "we've been discussing"? Who have you been talking to?

—Oh, we've got a small group, very informal—maybe you even know some of the members. We take turns meeting at each other's houses. It's a way of keeping your head in shape, you know? Of not losing touch. But

95

it's hard these days, people are scared. They'd rather stay in the dark. All that counts is the day to day. All people can think about is surviving.

—Would you believe it if I told you that I haven't had a serious conversation for about five years?

—Of course I would, that's what happened with me, too. Not for as long as that, where you begin to atrophy. My silence exploded in my face one day.

—Once in a while I talk with my nephew. He's twenty-three and already a captain in the New Army, so as you can imagine we don't really understand each other. He gets on my nerves. Makes me feel, I don't know, malicious. Corrupt—you know what I mean? Just because I accept a few extra water coupons from him.

—Souza, do you think a few water coupons could make you corrupt? Your vaunted honesty is still intact, don't worry. You always were the scrupulous one, weren't you. Too much so, with your rigid, somewhat antiquated ideas about right and wrong. Deliberate, that's what you were. You always took everything one step at a time.

—You know, I still can't believe what they've done to this country without so much as an uprising.

—I can. What impresses me is how they're not the least bit afraid of the judgment of history.

—The judgment of history? I've come to the conclusion that those guys intended to eliminate history altogether, even to blot out the future. That way they wouldn't be remembered as the new plunderers, the Attilas, of this century. They think they're powerful enough to erase our memory.

—Well, they're doing a pretty good job of it so far. Not much left besides what's in the National Memory Bank, and nobody could ever break into that fortress.

—Even if we could, who's to say there's anything in there. Maybe it's an empty building.

—Even the invaders of the Roman Empire didn't inflict that kind of damage on civilization.

—You're right! They may have been barbarians, but

96

they didn't touch the temples. Apparently afraid of the gods, afraid to violate their sanctuaries. And the libraries, the manuscripts, were all in the temples, so the training of priests went on undisturbed. Today it's different. It all started during the great dictatorship, remember? With the teaching reforms, obstacles thrown in the way of getting an education. In the Open Eighties we thought maybe we were making some headway, but there wasn't time, before we knew it it was all over. The Grand Era of Enrichment was underway.

—And the worst is that we were duped into inattention, we didn't even know what was going on.

—Yes, but don't forget it was happening in secrecy— the System made its decisions behind closed doors. Then all of a sudden they hit us with their propaganda campaign, gradually escalating until we were numb. For eight years we supplied the entire world with wood. No problem. We sold off parcels of the Amazon. Just a few sections, they told us, no great loss. Areas especially chosen by scientists so as not to alter the ecosystem. Until one day photos taken via satellite revealed the extent of the devastation. It was awful, remember? The heart of the rain forest decimated beyond recovery. What was left didn't last long, just a few short years, then the desert took over.

—The System was smart. They denied and denied everything and acted in secret. How could we believe it, how could we take in the fact that 250 million acres of forest lay on the ground? The end. Just like that.

—And we're still in debt.

—Ah, but we've got the Ninth Wonder!

—Right, and sandstorms worthy of the most developed country. No more reason to be jealous of North America's hurricanes or tornadoes, no sir. Our very own home-grown storms did quite a nice job of destroying Maranhão and Piaui. And the desert marched down to the sea, ta-tum.

—Remember those two mudstorms in Sergipe? Ara-

97

cajú was buried alive. They said the waves of mud were thirty, forty meters high.

—Monumental. As fierce as the System itself when those environmentalists came out with their international denunciations. The System unmasked.

—Do you think they're really still alive, Souza?

—Oh, a good many of them are gone, I suppose. They were all sixty-five, seventy years old. Obstinately clinging to their positions, intoxicated with power. Dazzled and kept alive by their riches.

—But you think that some of them are still hanging on?

—Uh-huh. Remember what I said before about how they thought they could save themselves? The only mistake they made was believing that if they eliminated the future no image of them would remain. They forgot about oral tradition. But they sure did one hell of a job banning books, hunting down loose-lipped scientists and professors, arresting the country's thinkers. It's almost as if it was an international plot. The division of the modern world, a treaty between the superpowers and whichever underdeveloped countries were malleable enough to go along with the plan.

—Really, it's like science fiction, when you think about it. São Paulo a walled city, divided into districts with magnetic passes to get from one area to another, superpolice like the Civil Guard, food produced in laboratories—a thoroughly systematized, regulated, rationalized life.

—You're absolutely right. We're living out a science fiction novel. All because twenty or thirty officials resolved to use their power to get rich. And the people, the happy-go-lucky people, called it the Grand Era of Enrichment. It sounds a bit too ridiculous for science fiction, maybe.

—What do you mean?

—Remember when we were all reading books by Clarke, Asimov, Bradbury, Van Vogt, Vonnegut, Wul,

Miller, Wyndham, Heinlein? All about supercivilizations, technocracies, computerized systems, societies which boasted relative (though monotonous) comfort and convenience. And what do we have here? An underdeveloped country living in a science fiction environment. Well, we always were innocent, and paradoxical, as a nation. But I never thought it would come to this. São Paulo is utterly surrounded by Pauper Encampments, diseased, starving ragamuffins who will no doubt eventually invade the city. How long can they possibly last, out there Beyond the Pale? There's nothing, but nothing, to eat!

—I know, I know. Meanwhile, here we are. You want to go for a cup of coffee? I can leave the elevator on automatic for a while.

—Love to, but I spent mine this morning...

—I should have an extra one here someplace. Just look at all these coupons, passes, ID cards, it's ridiculous. It's like birth control pills, for heaven's sake: one coffee for each day of the week. That's what it's come to. And people like us have to shoulder some of the blame.

—Wait just a minute. We couldn't be all that responsible. After all, we got kicked out of the university, didn't we?

—We weren't exactly expecting it. We thought we'd been playing by the rules for the most part. That's why it took such a long time to get used to, to feel normal again. Never mind trying to find another job. I was lucky the boys were grown up by then, at least they were working. But we sold the house, moved to a tiny apartment...

So we went for coffee: an indistinguishable dark powder, half a teaspoon of sugar, and piping hot, unavoidably suspicious, water. There seemed to be more waitresses than customers. One put the Silex on to heat, another got the cups, a third measured out the exact amount of sugar, a fourth poured the water, and the last one dispensed the instant coffee. They shoved past each other, continuously jockeying for position behind the counter. It was called specialization. The System's answer to unemployment was to expand and subdivide all jobs. Now Tadeu says that policy is being reversed. Oh, the changes. "Next month it will only be two cups of coffee per person per week," warned a blonde with no teeth.

—People got worried, but what good did it do? There were organizations sprouting up everywhere. Groups defending the rivers, associations against the proliferation of hydroelectric projects, would-be heroes fighting to stop the Angra Nuclear project . . .

—I knew they'd all fall by the wayside.

—And in the end, so did the reactor. There it sits, half buried in sand. I went to see it once, it's a tourist attraction. Looks like a gigantic ship, heeled over, half in the water, half out. What a strange thing, Souza, a monument to our times. A gigantic hunk of concrete run aground.

—A monument to immediatism. Like the Hall of Waters.

—Exactly! You know, it's funny. The Hall of Waters is the most damning evidence against the System that exists, and yet they leave it for all to see.

—Sometimes it's hard to believe there are actual people behind the System. The System, the System, that's all we hear. Old Caldeira's been an invalid for years, and still he's president. *Somebody* must be running things.

—We should get together. I want to show you something. Remember that little notebook of ours? I've saved it all this time, must be twenty-five years. It'll make you cry!

—My God, I'd forgotten all about it. Our little notebook. Yes, I'd love to see it, soon.

—All right! We'll get together again soon.

We crossed the street at a slow stroll. No one else was in a big hurry either. Everyone seemed so listless, lackadaisical. Not seemed, were. Suddenly I knew I

100

wanted to show Tadeu the hole in my hand. Maybe he could help me understand its significance. He would understand my pride, he's got a good head on his shoulders.

—Look, Tadeu—down there on the sidewalk. What do you see?

—The shadow of your hand.

—Look closer.

—There's a circle of light in the middle. Bizarre!

—What do you think?

—Oh, I see, it's a hole in your hand! The sun goes right through.

—Pretty amazing, huh?

—Have you had it long?

—About a week.

—I've seen a few other cases like yours.

—Really?

—Does it bother you at all?

—No, not a bit.

—Bizarre things like this have been happening all over the place lately. Hard to explain. You should probably see a doctor.

—What for? I doubt the doctors would know what it was. But they'd take my money anyway, and give me some useless prescription which would no doubt cost a bundle. Best thing to do is drink water.

—It's such a perfect circle. As if you'd had plastic surgery. Unfortunately, it's usually bad news when something like this happens for no apparent reason. Like all the people who've gone bald, or the ones with their skin falling off, the people who went deaf overnight. It's pretty terrifying. I've seen people who came from up north and don't have a hair left on their bodies, noses corroded by insecticides, ears leaking pus, some of them have lost all motor control. And then there are the ones walking around with artificial lungs strapped on their backs, like the gasogene cars in the First World War. But your hole is different. Even kind of pretty.

101

—I wanted you to see the shadow. Do you think that circle of light could mean something, could have some significance?

—That's going a little far, isn't it, Souza? The hole itself is enough to make me scratch my head. Don't go looking for more trouble.

—But I'm sure it must represent something. It's got to be a message of some sort.

—A message? And that makes you predestined or something, right?

—No, that *would* be going too far.

—Maybe not. I remember back in the old days you went through a period of mysticism. Who knows, maybe you were reborn...

—Gee, I'd forgotten all about that, too.

—Well, it's been great talking, but I should be getting back. I left the elevator unattended.

—We'll see each other again, then?

## THINKING ABOUT THE MAN WHO NEVER WAS, SOUZA ALMOST GOES TO A STRIP SHOW. THEN, ANOTHER SURPRISE FROM ANOTHER ELEVATOR MAN

The Forgotten Center of São Paulo, which spreads out around the bus and train stations, makes me dizzy. It's as if I'm on a hallucinatory merry-go-round, images swirling past in a flash; there's no time to fix them. They remain imprecise, speeding streaks of color, music, voices, screams, footsteps.

It's a hodgepodge of an open market, full of second-hand items: used clothing, leftover medicines, old books and newspapers (expensive!), small appliances with re-built engines, replacement parts from junked cars. And it's a free-for-all, you don't need any consumer obligation cards or authorizations.

There's a sultry, sluggish feeling to the place, though, a little like illness. The eyes I meet are dull, the mouths pursed and sour. People's movements seem retarded, almost automated. And everyone's nose quivers from the fetid smell that surrounds us, there is no way to get away from it. This city is completely out of control.

I look up: a rusty sign, peeling paint, bullet holes. How long has it been since I've seen a show like this? I didn't even know they existed anymore, and now that I do I'm sort of curious.

I walk back and forth in front of the theater three times. Peering in, interested, hesitating, continuing on, circling back. Two men face out at me from the door. I better get out of here, they might say something. Nonsense, how can I be so timid! A long time ago I saw a strange movie called *The Man Who Never Was*. An ordinary film, it came and went unnoticed.

Except by me. I was utterly fascinated by that man who had never existed. I think I'm beginning to understand why. I wind my way up the spiral staircase thinking that I shouldn't be. I've always had the feeling that I shouldn't be. Wanting to not want.

Where is this staircase leading me, anyway? Could they really have striptease acts like the sign says? It's hard to believe they still exist, museum relics, lost and forgotten in this chaotic city. I wonder what else might still be preserved in this old downtown area. I've always been intrigued by the unknown. I climb the stairs slowly, a little scared. But I climb them.

Years ago I elaborated for my students an interesting theory about the The Terrible Risk of the Eternal Known. Of course a copy of the work ended up attached to the report assigning me compulsory retirement. How could I explain? They were looking for subversion, and my brown file-folder gave them what they wanted.

There's hardly anyone here. A succession of boleros, hard rock, disco, blasts from behind a greasy curtain. Suddenly I feel free. I can stay here as long as I want, or go someplace else. Then in a split second I feel like leaving. Over the door there's a faded ad for the show: *Adam and His Seven Sexy Eves*. All of them blond and blue-eyed. Adam is holding an apple.

The hunchbacked usher looks at me with raised eyebrows: "The show hasn't even started yet, mister, and you're leaving? You can't get back your admission, you know." Adam: holding an apple, red and misshapen, obviously meant to be a phallic symbol.

The red jogs my memory: a pair of women's shoes. Shiny red sandals always turned me on. Adelaide never owned a pair, of course: "Too loud a color for a woman like me." That red apple, like a neon sign.

I've been away from home three days, maybe more. I've lost track. It doesn't matter. Walking aimlessly loses its meaning after a while. Suddenly, inexplicably, I miss my living room, my bedroom. Do I miss Adelaide? I'm tired. If I can just slip by the Inspector and onto the bus, I won't have to walk the whole way. The S-758 pulls up to the empty bus stop.

—Can I take this bus?

—Sure, why not?

—Last time they gave me a hard time.

—Do you have the right CIRCA?

—Yes, right here.

—Then get on, we don't stop people from taking their assigned bus!

As my key turned in the lock, a strange shiver came over me. Then the smell of a closed-up house. And silence. At this hour Adelaide is always watching her soap, or else the cooking show. Pitch-dark. I realize I've never smelled the smell of my own house, stale and closed like this. I walk through all the rooms. No one home.

The house was tidy, slippers lined up on the scrap rug, chamber pot tucked under the bed. Dailiness. A note on the pillow—Adelaide's handwriting. I threw the note into the chamber pot and lay down, clothes and all, leaving the light on. And lay there smoking, flicking the ashes onto the floor. The head of my cigarette fell off and I watched as it burned a neat hole in the carpet.

When I woke up, I heard noise in the street. Looked in the icebox, nothing but butter. Synthetic butter, no less, which tasted like a combination of suet and plastic. The kitchen was all in order, the floors were immaculate, the bathroom smelled of disinfectant. My whole life smelled of disinfectant. I took a pee, missing the toilet bowl on purpose. I hacked up a pearl and spat it on the tiles before going on to the kitchen.

In the kitchen I made myself some coffee (which tasted like dishwater), spilling it all over in the process, knocking cups and saucers together, and breaking two plates. I put on a sport coat that clashed with my shirt. "Honey, you can't go to the office like that—what would people say? They'd think your wife doesn't take care of you." I've let her take care of me all these years. I'm the one who made her that way, then.

A sport coat—am I crazy? In one motion, I ripped it off and stuffed it in the incinerator. The ashes were backed up, the pipe must be clogged. A cloudy day; if only it would rain. A light sprinkle slowly drenching the earth, and me, and everything else.

The definitive drought occurred immediately following the creation of the immense Amazon desert. A year without a drop of rain, and São Paulo's reservoirs were exhausted. Terrified, people made promises to saints, they filled the churches, they organized processions, said novenas, took pilgrimages. All utterly useless. Artesian wells were drilled by the hundreds; charlatan rainmakers roamed the streets making money left and right. And still the rain didn't come.

Where could Adelaide have gone? To her mother's, probably. One of these days I'll go over there. Meanwhile, a conjugal separation, a vacation from each other, is good for you now and then. What about the maid— is today the day she comes? Or was it yesterday? (Everything so neat and clean when I came home.) I shut the door behind me and head for the office. It was automatic,

I did it without thinking. Suddenly, there I was in my office building, waiting for the elevator.

The elevator man gave me an intimidating look, his face reflected in the smoked-glass mirrors of the elevator, reproduced to infinity. Indistinct, shadowy, a rough draft of a face. Thousands of them, though, and frightened, every one of them observing me carefully. It was clear he didn't know how to handle this.

—Sorry, all full.

—Full? What are you talking about, Mr. Potiguara— it's completely empty!

—Well, yes, but it's reserved.

—Since when do people reserve the elevator?

—Besides, they said you don't work here anymore. I've got orders not to let you go up.

—But you know me, Potiguara. I haven't done anything wrong.

—I don't know, you always seemed like a nice person to me, but . . . well, not anymore, not now . . .

—You mean I'm not so nice anymore?

He closed the grate decisively and stood there stiffly, alert, ready to push a button if I tried anything. I laughed and threw myself against the grate as hard as I could, watching utter fear take over his face. Just to give them something to talk about upstairs, those men-desks, men-drawers, so quiet, so obedient.

**IT WAS ALWAYS CLEAR THAT THE NEPHEW
DIDN'T PROVIDE WATER COUPONS
MERELY OUT OF THE GOODNESS
OF HIS HEART.
EVEN IF SOUZA HAD HELPED
TO RAISE HIM—
THE TIME HAS COME
TO RETURN THE FAVOR**

—On another planet, Mr. Souza?

The barber was leaning against the doorjamb. He never

106

had any customers this time of day. The little record player in the corner was playing tangos. Ever since he'd set up shop here it had been playing tangos and boleros nonstop. Piles of ancient, scratchy records, positively archaic LP's, lay in dusty heaps nearby.

I pass my hand over my face—my God, how many days since I last shaved? If Adelaide saw me like this, she'd have a fit. Where *is* she, anyway? I never did call her parents. Could she have gone on a trip? Or has she left me? It's possible. Why didn't I read the note she left? Sometimes I surprise myself, I didn't used to be like this. It's not as if it's her fault, after all.

—Do you use water here, or refined urine?

—Mr. Souza! Do you think I'd put refined urine on your face? You know me better than that!

—No, no, I'm not sure I do, anymore...

A fan, the kind in old American movies set in the Caribbean, blades spinning uselessly over my head. There's no air to circulate. This place is stifling. Out in the entryway it's a little better, but the floor is black with grime. You can't win, with this filth, it's unremitting. Today the sun came up on a cloudless sky, no haze.

—Relax, *that's* it. Here's a nice cool towel...

—Mmmm... and how much will that cost me?

—I've been thinking, Souza. Your nephew's a captain, isn't that right?

—Um-hum.

—Well, people around here, you know, just in conversation, people say he can help out in certain ways.

—What ways?

—Well, someone from the building, I'm not mentioning any names, bought some water coupons from him once.

—I don't know anything about that. And I really don't like mentioning things like that to my nephew.

—You don't have to. Just tell him the barber would like to have a little chat with him, that's all. He'll come see me.

107

—You sound awfully sure of yourself.

—Absolutely. He'll be interested in what I have to say. Just talk to him, will you?

—All right, but it's just that I never know when I'll see him. He only drops by now and then.

—He's upstairs now, I saw him come in a half hour ago.

And there he was at the door to the apartment, with his syrupy smile, crafty eyes, jet-black mustache—looking like a bolero singer. He put down his can of beer and embraced me when I walked in. There are some people you just dislike, without even knowing why. You take one look at them and you just don't like them. It's not that they ever did anything to you, it's just spontaneous antipathy, pure and simple.

—Have a seat, Uncle Souza. I came to propose a little business arrangement. I know you'll say no right off, but hear me out first, okay? It's sort of an act of charity I want you to help me with.

—You—charity? Since when?

—Oh, I'm not as bad as all that! Just because you hate the New Army, you don't have to include *me* ...

—Who says I've got anything against the New Army? It's that wonderful organization of yours, the Civil Guards, they're the ones who are hard to swallow.

—But that's not fair, we don't have anything to do with the Civil Guards.

—You expect me to believe that?

—The Civil Guards were created by a radical wing which didn't approve of the renovations brought about by the New Army. They joined up with some radical civilian police-types who didn't go along with the liberalization of the System, and formed their own organization.

—Which the System tolerates.

—Look, Uncle Souza, I didn't come here to talk politics. I'm in a hurry, and I need a favor.

—Okay. Maybe I'll help you out. What is it?

—I don't want to ask this, really I don't. But when

108

you needed coupons I always delivered, didn't I? No questions asked. And I did it with a smile.

—So that now you can ask for something in return.

—Biting the hand that feeds you, eh?

He motioned for me to follow him into the kitchen. Three people sat at a table, drinking beer. The place was littered with empty cans, packages, grocery bags. Men in their thirties. Can't say what color hair they had because they were bald. Not a hair on their heads. No eyebrows, either. Just like the ones in the street.

—These people need some place to stay, Uncle Souza, and I thought they could stay here. Do you think Aunt Adelaide will mind?

—She's not home. She'll be away for a while.

—It's only for a few days. We brought some food, there'll be more coming later. They've got water coupons and everything, it won't cost you a dime.

—We'll manage, don't worry. Oh, by the way, the barber downstairs wants to talk to you. He's got some sort of deal to propose. Says he's sure you'll be interested.

Windows all closed up tight, insects buzzing. I looked at the wainscoting: brown stains. I get a can of DDT and let them have it. No reaction. It's as if I just gave them a dose of fresh air. I blast them again. Nothing.

## SURROUNDED BY A TRAFFIC JAM OF ABANDONED CARS, TWO PROFESSORS TALK OBSESSIVELY ABOUT "THE SITUATION." WHY DO INTELLECTUALS HAVE SUCH GUILT COMPLEXES?

I crawled along on my hands and knees, cautiously throwing myself to the ground at the least suspicious noise (that part of the technique I was plenty familiar with). I had no idea how long I'd been inching forward along the hot concrete, my nose in the dust. It made me sneeze. A good sneeze is therapeutic, though; it cleans

109

you out. But my body ached from all the exercise. How much farther could it be?

—Are you trying to kill me, Tadeu? I haven't crawled around on all fours like this since I was in the military.

—We can rest a little bit farther up ahead, behind that embankment.

We crept along the center of the pavement, crouched low to the ground so we wouldn't be seen. The freeway rose fifteen meters above ground level, an empty expanse sixteen lanes wide, covered with a layer of fine gray dust. Of course I couldn't see the color in the dark, but I knew it was the same dust that came from the burned-over fields.

My shoulders burned as if they had been flayed. It was a good thing Tadeu had warned me to bring something to pad my elbows. At first it seemed impossible, but then I got into a rhythm. It's just that I'm short of breath—which is understandable, since I don't eat well or get much exercise.

—Can't we rest right here?

—No, up ahead, behind the embankment. We can't take any chances.

It hadn't been easy to get up onto the freeway in the first place. All the entrances were blocked off and guarded, plus there were high walls along the sides of the entrance ramps. Tadeu had led me through the ruins of what used to be the neighborhood called Vila Anastacio. Row after row of collapsed buildings: public housing units that had made some real estate company quite a bundle, no doubt.

We hoisted ourselves up a girder, climbing the series of metal reinforcing rods embedded in the concrete. Scared to death of falling, all I could think was that this was no activity for a man my age. I had to admire Tadeu; he climbed with the agility of a cat. In two minutes he was up on the freeway.

Once I had joined him, he showed me the best way to crawl along without bruising myself. "It'll be hard at first—painful—but you'll get used to it." We must have gone about two kilometers when a greenish light flashed in my face. There, to the right of the overpass: a veritable mountain of beer cans, and another, and another.

Immense green dunes, higher even than the freeway, stretched before us, shining in the moonlight. It was beginning to get cold. As we pressed on, I was sure I heard a strange sound, almost a lament, coming from inside the gigantic heaps of metal. Impossible! Then I heard it again.

It was a sort of low scream. Or one low scream added to another added to another until they became just one sound. Painful, but almost artificial. It must be the wind in the dunes, I thought to myself. But a wind that (literally) wails? I stopped and stared at the piles and piles of green cans, oxidized, practically soldered together.

But there is no wind. If there were, the dust on the road wouldn't be so still, smooth and flat like a newly made bed. I look behind me and see the neat furrow my body has made as I crawled along. I keep moving. Finally the sound reaches me, loud and clear. Now there's no mistaking it: human moans.

—Do people live in there?

—Thousands of them, yes. There are caves inside the mountains of cans.

—But during the day, with the sun, it must heat up in there something awful. They must roast to death.

—But they don't. It's the "Brazilian Miracle."

—I can't believe it.

—There's some sort of mechanism they haven't figured out yet. Apparently, the cans get so cold overnight that it takes a long time for them to heat up again. Just when they're beginning to, the sun's already on its way down, so it actually stays pretty cool in there. Or at least that's the hypothesis. Everything changes so fast these days you can never be sure you understand what's going on.

—How did you find out about them?

—A couple members of our group work at the first-

111

aid station nearby. I've never been there myself, I just read the reports they wrote. The majority of the people under there are crazy.

—Crazy? You mean mad, out of their minds?

—Yes, basically. They're semi-imbecilic. Incapacitated. Living in a prone position. They scream because they're in constant pain—they never sleep, they're always nervous, irritated, in a state of unbelievable tension.

—But who are they?

—No one in particular. Migrants, mostly. The majority of them from Pernambuco, slum dwellers who lived in swampy areas subsisting on crabs.

—That sounds harmless enough.

—Except that the crabs were contaminated with high doses of DDT—public health's idea of how to clean up the area. There's nothing much we can do for them now, they're condemned.

—The System should do *something* to help them.

—Are you kidding? Why should the System lift a finger? These people pose no danger, they're completely passive, they don't even get up off the ground. The dead ones are carted off by the dozens. That's the only thing the System does take care of. Think about it, why should these unfortunate people interest them? They're hardly potential consumers. At the most, they represent just another social problem.

—What's your group doing for them?

—We bring food when we can. A little water. Not much help, really, but we're experimenting, giving them vegetables, trying to detoxify them. No positive results, so far.

—You're feeding them vegetables?

—Uh-huh. Lettuce, tomatoes, squash. What's the matter, you look like you never heard of them.

—Fresh ones? Or synthetic?

—Souza! Surely you know that synthetic food is just a slower form of poison.

—Sure, but without it we'd all be dead already.

—Don't you know what they're up to with the stuff that comes out of the labs?

—Money, I suppose. Another kind of power over us.

—Sure. But in this case that's not all.

—What do you mean?

—They put chemical additives in the food, tranquilizers. Minute doses which affect the organism in subtle ways, slowly eroding individual will, making us more accommodating. Why do you think people are so passive, so calm? Because of threats, Civil Guards, this whole business of spies and inspectors? No, Souza, the system doesn't have to worry, they've found an infallible method of getting people to conform. Just introduce tranquilizers directly into the bloodstream.

We stood there, looking down from the highway. I would have liked to get down and explore on the ground, but there was no way to get there. To the right we could see the dry upper slope of the Tiete. The river was much shallower than I had imagined. It stank terribly, a thick coagulated mass of debris and slime. Just as well it was drying up, it was no more than a slow, steady stream of filth, the rotten intestine of the city.

—Is it much farther?

—Yeah, it's still quite a ways. Would you rather go back?

—No, no, as long as we've come this far, let's keep going. But slowly.

—Sure, I'm in no hurry. And I know you aren't, either, since you lost your job. Have you thought about how you're going to get along?

—Not really. I guess I'll take everything out of my savings and see how long it will last.

—And what if they haven't been depositing into your account?

—A life of crime?

Disappointment on Tadeu's face. But I mean it. I want to live. I'll try to support myself decently, but I'm determined to make it to the end, no matter what. To be the last one, if possible, when everything comes tumbling down. The last one. What pessimism. If they could hear me now. Suddenly I sense something coming from down deep, a sharp reminder of something missing, an emptiness.

Where a little bit of happiness belongs. Something to make me laugh out loud. Though I think if I did, I'd get a cramp in my side. Or strain the muscles in my mouth, because it's been so long. And it's not just my sourness, my reserve. Adelaide was always complaining: "You never loosen up, you don't know how to have fun."

It must have been hard for her, living with me all those years. The silent observer. Unable to laugh. A prisoner. But of what, of whom? And why? We used to go out for a good time on weekends—gorge ourselves on pizza and beer and go to one of those honky-tonk places to dance. Adelaide was so light on her feet, so musical.

Hours and hours without once leaving the dance floor. Sometimes it would be a tango place, other times a grand ballroom. She was so agile, and I was a heavyweight. I went through all sorts of clumsy contortions to keep up with her. A bull in a china shop. And she'd laugh at me, contented. I worked at it, because I liked her. I really did, even though now I deny it.

I'm always denying things, making up excuses. The truth is I miss Adelaide. I don't know what happened to our life together; we let ourselves drift so far apart. Somewhere along the line she stopped complaining about my silence, my private torment: "It doesn't do any good, anyway. Maybe someday you'll realize you can't live like that forever."

And she retreated into a corner. She started living for her mother and father, though she had never gotten along with them very well. And she discovered the church, who knows how. If I could find her now, I'd ask. But then if I wanted to find her, all I'd have to do is call her mother. It's just a question of wanting to. So why don't I call?

Tadeu and I were getting farther and farther away from the mountains of beer cans. The moans faded away behind us along with the tracks we left in the dust. The silence was weighty. I could hear Tadeu's breathing. He sure moves fast for a man of fifty-five.

I'd gotten into a rhythm now, my arms weren't hurting so much. I remember when I used to play soccer, I'd get to the edge of fatigue, but if I kept on playing and got past it then I could last till the end. There's a certain limit beyond which we either give up or can go on forever. It's just a matter of pushing yourself beyond the breaking point.

Somehow I guess I have. At least I'm keeping up, which makes me feel good. I was so used to the house-to-office trajectory, I was in such a rut, frightened to death of everything around me. House-bus-house-Hall-of-Waters-desk-window-bus-house. Each day a reflex, a reflection of the last.

Now I am discovering São Paulo. My São Paulo. My—ha. As if I had one before. I get caught up in the past, trying to hide the nonexistent. A free-fall into a vacuum. No wonder I'm insecure. I'm discovering a strange new city, offering new possibilities for my life. The city had gone on, while I stopped dead.

You give it out or you get it back. You've got to revise all your ideas. Set lamentation aside, adapt to this new concept, become part of it. Running into Tadeu showed me how out of touch, how dead to the world I was. He remains a mystery to me, I'm not sure what he thinks, how he sees life. But that doesn't worry me.

Suddenly we came to a spot where the freeway was jammed with cars. Not a single open space from one guardrail to the other. Greasy radiators glinting in the moonlight, rusting hoods of cars, windows broken or streaked with dust, empty light sockets. They came into view as we crawled over the crest of a hill. In their immobility they gave the impression of great speed.

Phantasmagoric, like dinosaur skeletons in a museum. A tribe of monsters, killed suddenly in the midst of an attack. Once when I was a child I went to see an old animated film called *Fantasia*. What impressed me most was the flight of the prehistoric beasts, their great desperation.

Their habitats barren of food and water, they split up into herds, strange and gigantic animals, stricken with hunger and the fierceness of the sun. One by one they fell, finally beaten, gradually becoming meatless skeletons, extinct species, fossils.

That's what came into my head looking at those old cars, maybe the last survivors from the time of the great Brazilian dream. After what was known as the Notable Congestion, the automobile factories closed down and thousands of the jobless poured into the streets—those who had worked directly in the manufacture of cars and many others who had been employed in related industries. A painful time.

—Admiring the leftovers from the Notable Congestion?

—Mmmmm . . . it's sort of a shock, since they've removed the cars from almost all the other areas.

—Here it was easier just to close the highway—the cars stretch on for a good two hundred kilometers.

—What a week that was, huh? I thought the country was going to blow sky-high. For the first time, Brazilians in open rebellion. Running out into the streets, armed, some of them, desperate to organize, to take action.

—And that's when the Civil Guards performed their first great service for the government. They were ready, you have to give them that. They were the ones who were organized, not us.

—We weren't all *that* bad . . .

—Oh, no? Just a rabble of left-wingers against a rabble of right-wingers. Remember all the leftist splinter groups? Couldn't agree with each other on anything. No mutual understanding, no way of joining forces. It was that simple.

—No, I don't think so, Tadeu. You can't just talk about the left and right as simplistically as all that. There

116

were so many factors involved, you know that. I've thought about it a lot, trying to analyze the situation. Not that I came to any conclusions—there aren't any. Total confusion.

—Of course.

—Not just the regular kind of confusion that we see in front of us every day, this is something else, do you follow me? It started in the eighties and just grew and grew. Not only in Brazil, either, but all over. Ideological confusion, conflicts. The government thought one thing, the opposition another, but in the end they were thinking the same thing, at the same time, even. The right adopted the attitudes of the left, and vice versa. No position was comfortable or secure. There was—and still is—no certainty, stability, resolution. I had a friend, a real conservative, who told me about a theory he had. I used to think his ideas were crazy, in addition to being utterly reactionary, but now I'm beginning to reconsider. Do you know what he predicted? He said that during the Wide Open Eighties the government would go so far to the right that it would end up on the left—either socialism or its reverse.

—Are you serious?

—I'm thinking. Not seriously; not joking, either. Just thinking. Look, Tadeu, they've already destroyed everything, all the structures we believed in, trusted. Maybe we're in a transitional phase, you know? There's some sort of substitution going on. Meanwhile we're navigating in a tremendous vacuum, vaguely oriented by the stars but with no true reference point. Our compasses have gone wild, spinning madly, attracted by thousands of magnetic poles. We might as well throw them out the window, they're obsolete. It's just us and the night sky, like it was for the early explorers, while we wait for new, more advanced navigational devices to be invented. My only fear is that the stars have somehow gotten out of place and will be no help as references either. But some idea will come to us as we float along; there must be a few smart sailors on the crew.

—You know what you need, Souza?

—What?

—A hat. The sun's fried your brains.

—You're right. My head's boiling over, I can't stop thinking.

He crawled on ahead, motioning for me to follow. The road was so jammed with cars we had to crawl beneath them, between blown-out tires, breathing in the acrid smell of rust. The moon beat down on peeling chrome, opaque metal: no reflection. We kept moving, breathless and sweating.

Then we stopped between a Passat and a Corcel. What year is this car? I never was good at models, never even learned to drive, in fact. Too easily distracted, too easygoing. Adelaide liked to drive, she'd borrow her father's car and we'd go out on Sundays, to the beach or for a picnic by the roadside.

Being behind the wheel gave me vertigo. The other cars all around, the way you had to pay attention to everything at once, have good reflexes swerving here and there, glancing in mirrors and out windows, it was too much. I'd much rather get in a cab, give the driver directions, and bury my nose in a newspaper. Or hop on a bus, pull the cord, hop off. To me, *not* driving was freedom.

The family—Adelaide's, mainly—thought I was an odd duck. My nephew was always harping at me: "You should buy a car, Uncle Souza, a car is what gives you freedom to do whatever you want, whenever you want to do it. What could be better?"

The people in the building were positively shocked. They didn't even try to hide their surprise, their eyes widened, their mouths fell open: "You mean you don't have a car, Mr. Souza? Ridiculous—you're joking, aren't you?" And I was, in my way. I let my space in the garage sit empty month after month instead of renting it out— even after people came to the door with some pretty attractive offers.

—Who'd have thought that one day we'd be stretched

118

out on the highway chatting peacefully among all these cars, eh?

—Here they sit, dead as dead can be. So much old metal.

—The cars were jammed up for two years in front of my house.

—That's because you live close to downtown. There weren't that many in my neighborhood.

—I almost went nuts that night, Souza. Really, I felt like killing somebody, anybody. The way they honked and raced their engines. The air was black with exhaust. Most of them kept it up until they ran out of gas, too; they just wouldn't turn off their engines. In the morning, they were all still there in the driver's seat, as if they were part of the machine! Gearshift, steering wheel, brakes, driver. They just sat there waiting for who knows what.

—On my street there were people who refused to believe the news bulletins. They took their cars out of their garages that morning the same as usual, drove off without a care in the world. Of course I had to laugh when they came back on foot.

—I remember one guy who stayed in his car a whole week, maybe it was two, he just wouldn't leave. Every once in a while he'd knock on the door and ask to go to the bathroom. No, really—and he wasn't the only one. I refused them all. What were they thinking? I just wanted them to give up and go on home. Relatives brought them food, coffee, changes of clothes. And what a show of despair when they finally realized they wouldn't be driving their cars ever again! They sat in front of the steering wheels weeping inconsolably, as if a loved one had just died. Some of the women fainted, went completely hysterical.

—I took a lot of pictures that week. Mostly of people's faces. The faces interested me more than the long lines of cars. Pathetic faces, perplexed expressions. Incomprehension, as if they'd just been thrust into the world for the first time. It wasn't rage or even irritation, it was

119

more like defeat, a kind of sad bewilderment. I photographed so many inane expressions!

—Wasn't the silence weird at first? That's when I noticed the permanent buzzing in my ears. Until then I didn't even know it was there. The doctor told me there was no cure, of course, and I've still got it today, but now I'm used to it.

—Is it much farther, Tadeu? I'm running out of steam.

—Running out of steam . . . now that's an old expression. Must have originated back when that's what engines ran on . . .

—Well, is it much farther or not?

—Up there a ways we can stand up and walk. Once we cross the Valley of Petrified Birds. It's a real deserted stretch, nothing to worry about.

—Great, but is it very far?

## ONCE PAST THE VALLEY
## OF PETRIFIED BIRDS,
## THEY REACH
## THE REGION OF PLASTIC GARBAGE.
## PARALYZED, HORRIFIED,
## THEY CAN'T BELIEVE WHAT THEY SEE

We continued to crawl through the straight and narrow corridor under the cars, at wheel level. Volkswagens, Corcels, Galaxies, Kombis, Brasílias, pickups, limousines, tractor-trailer trucks, buses, station wagons, vans. Vehicle after vehicle, some immense, others tiny, but all of them rusty and rotting away.

The insides had been completely stripped, either by the actual owners when they had abandoned them, or later by looters who took everything that could be carried away. Seats, clocks, tape decks, radios, speakers, mini-TV's, telephones, speedometers, steering wheels, air conditioners, windshield wipers, electric antennae, alarm systems.

Steering wheel lock, dashboard, mini-bar, Ray-Ban windows, heaters—all the paraphernalia which conferred status, power. The looters were highly organized and bold, and they were hunted just as the looters of the royal tombs in Egypt were hunted.

Empty carcasses, showcases of uselessness, testimony to the illusory symbols they had been. They were falling farther and farther into ruin, hollow and corroded, a demonstration of a perishable dream that had spent itself much before the moment of waking. Even now it's only a tenuous memory, dissipating more each day.

—After that pole up ahead we can go on foot.

—It's about time.

—Let's walk along the guardrail, it's easier.

—I've lost all sense of time. Do you have any idea what time it is?

—What difference does it make, Souza?

—Just habit, I guess.

—It's a mania. I can't stand it, the whole day in that elevator, people constantly asking me: What time is it? Excuse me, please, do you happen to have the time? The ones who don't ask are busy consulting their watches. And now you!

—You're awfully irritable, Tadeu.

—And you're so well behaved. What happened, Souza? You're different, full of "habits."

—I don't know what you're talking about.

There was a half-rubbed-out inscription on the post in red spray paint: *Mercury is not a vitamin!* Ten years ago the whole city was taken over by graffiti—during the last campaign in defense of the environment. The Civil Guards hunted down and exterminated the culprits. The System went on television.

"We don't need anyone to remind us of our responsibilities," declared the President. "We are well aware of the problems. Research teams and qualified government commissions are hard at work already. What we do need is peace and quiet in which to work out the answers to these questions which affect the lives of all of us. We will wage war against all agitators to the full extent of the law; order will be maintained. Relentlessly."

121

—Okay, it's straight ahead from here on out.

—Maybe now you can tell me where we're going?

—We're going to pay a visit to our little preserve.

—What kind of a preserve?

—Oh, Souza, this is really an exciting project, we've been working on it for years now. And it's going pretty well under the circumstances. We have quite a number of animals.

—Animals? *Real* animals?

—Yes. Can˙you believe it? One of the few things the System's laboratories have not succeeded in producing is synthetic animals. It just doesn't work. They've been manufacturing artificial eggs for how long now? But they just can't get them to hatch, some essential ingredient is missing.

—Tadeu! Listen to what you're saying, what you're admitting!

—I'm admitting what's true, there's no way to run away from it.

—So, tell me about these animals of yours.

—Well, the project began some thirty years ago, maybe more. I'm not good with dates. There was a preserve in Sorocaba, which in those days was a separate city from São Paulo. Scientists there succeeded in inducing animals which were about to become extinct to reproduce in captivity. It was a monumental work. They saved specimens of the black-necked swan, the tapir, the rhea, the Brazilian ostrich . . . Ah, but I won't list them all, soon you'll see for yourself. At any rate, industrial growth took over Sorocaba—as well as Votorantim, Brigadeiro Tobias, São Roque, and Cotia—and local government sent in the tractors and closed down the preserve. The birds and animals were left in their cages untended for two or three weeks. Many of them died while the scientists were negotiating the project back into existence. Studies were underway which were aimed at reducing lead contamination in the soil. Finally, the details were ironed out and the animals were brought to this preserve. It's near the site of the old Barueri barracks.

—That's in the Region of the Plastic Garbage, isn't it? Out in what do they call it—Hell's Ranch?

—That's right, and that's exactly why. Because way out here no one bothers us. You'll see for yourself.

The freeway stretched across a dull yellow plain. Sort of a mini-desert, a flat, low valley, with the sludge-filled Tietê riverbed cutting through the middle. Hundreds of strange, dark statues studded the dry expanse. They looked as though they were made of plaster, old porcelain, fired clay—who knows what all. They gave me the impression that this place had once been a great public garden, as if the vegetation had withered and only the statues remained, solitary and forlorn. Odd how you can live in a city for years and not really know it. I'd never heard of any park or garden way out here. Could it have been private property?

—What is this place, Tadeu?

—It's called the Valley of the Petrified Birds.

—I've never heard of it.

—It used to be a swamp, can you believe it? The Tietê would flood and spread out over the whole valley. There was a time when this was all a garden—part of the "greenbelt." Prehistoric, huh?

—Just look at all the statues.

—Statues. I guess that's what you'd have to call them. They used to be birds.

—Birds?

—That's right. They came from the coast. Crossed the mountains, landed here, and stayed. Never to fly again.

—Why here?

—Must have been instinct. No one is sure, but they say the swamps had all kinds of food, small animals, crabs, that sort of thing . . .

—So they came all the way from the coast, eh?

—Apparently their diet had always been fish, shellfish, et cetera, and when the ocean no longer supported enough sea life they moved on, tried to change habitats, as it were.

123

—And then they couldn't fly anymore, because of the change?

—No, their problems flying started even earlier, before they left the coast. As they dove into the increasingly polluted ocean, they came up covered with oil and sludge. It got more and more difficult for them to fly, in fact the ones that made it here were really heroic. It was their last flight. Once here, they became earthbound. The oil on their wings baked hard in the sun, closing their pores. That's what eventually killed them, actually. Now, covered with layers of dust, they perch on the barren plain, like statues, as you said . . .

—They're almost pretty.

—That's the worst part.

—You know, Tadeu, I'm not sure how much longer I can go on. It's not just fatigue, but hunger, too. It's getting to be too much.

—You can make it, it's only a little bit farther. See those mountains of plastic? It's right beyond there, we'll be off this freeway in a few minutes.

The moon seemed to be fading; it was almost sunrise. It had been so many years since I stayed up all night, I never would have believed I could still make it. A light flickered behind the huge heaps of plastic up ahead. As I stepped off the last rung of the rope ladder, my feet sank into a soft layer of dust, almost shin-deep.

Walking was difficult in the mountains of plastic. A labyrinth of toys, kitchen utensils, gallon jugs, beach balls, signs, thousands upon thousands of items made of plastic. Plastic had become the substitute for everything: aluminum, wood, cloth. So of course it piled up. Grimy and misshapen, perhaps, but colorful and indestructible.

—Get ready, Souza. This place is almost sacred, if you'll forgive the expression.

Silence. I imagined he was moved by the thought of entering the preserve. I felt a coldness in the pit of my stomach. Tadeu turned and walked a little faster, we were almost there. I thought I could even smell manure, whew, it was making me light-headed. Another chill. But not

124

as intense as the one I felt when Tadeu let out an excruciating wail.

I stopped dead in my tracks. The sound went on and on. I don't know if it was an echo or if Tadeu had lungs that strong. I couldn't see him anymore—the trail was narrow and winding here—but his scream paralyzed me. When I caught up with him he was shaking terribly, and I wondered if he'd had a heart attack. Then he turned, bewildered, and I saw the tears in his eyes.

—Look. Just looooook...

He bit his lips till the blood ran.

## WHEN THEY GET TO A CERTAIN AGE, PEOPLE TEND TO REMINISCE ABOUT THEIR LIVES: SOUZA REMEMBERS HIS GRANDFATHER WHO, AS IT HAPPENS, WAS A LUMBERMAN, A PLUNDERER OF THE FORESTS

The preserve, or what was left of it, spread open before me. The tottering mountains of plastic were like backdrops to the swath of land which extended into the distance. I could see that it had been a beautiful place, in spite of the present devastation. Tadeu bent down and cradled a skeleton in his arms.

It must have been some small creature like a dog, cat, rabbit, fox cub, coati. Shreds of singed meat still clung to the bones. Not long dead, then. Flames crackled in the nearby buildings: twisted roofs, doors, windows. Everything made of plastic. Horrified, but anxious to investigate, I pulled Tadeu along with me. He followed like an automaton.

All the buildings were empty. Furniture in pieces. No sign of human casualties, at least that was relief. Tadeu poked here and there searching for more animal remains. There were bones everywhere—on the paths between buildings, the yards, porches, ruined gardens. Gardens? What kind of plant could possibly have grown in earth like this—hard as rock? As usual, I'm full of questions.

125

It's the sun again, making my head soft. I swear I saw bruised, trampled plant life, with real leaves, not plastic or nylon. I touched them and my fingers came away green. The experiments on this preserve must have been highly sophisticated. Evidently they had come up with synthetics that were realer than real.

—Tadeu, this is amazing, could these have been real plants?

—Bah, what do I care about plants? Let's keep looking for animals.

—Okay, okay, but it won't do any good. It's pretty clear they've killed them all.

—Something must have survived. Animals flee when the forest catches fire.

—I know, I know . . .

We searched for a full hour. Shacks, cages, holes in the ground, charred shrubbery. Whoever had invaded this place had destroyed everything, had most likely eaten or carted away anything that could possibly be considered edible. And I saw in Tadeu an even greater ruin. He was disconsolate, maimed even.

—Do you think it was the Civil Guards?

—Why would they do such a thing?

—Who can begin to explain anything they do?

—Yeah. All I know is there's nothing left. Nothing. Thirty years of research, and not a straw, not a toothpick. They even finished off the plants.

—Then they were real plants!

—Of course, can't you see? Are you turning stupid in addition to getting old?

—Tadeu, Tadeu, what good will it do to get mad at me? I had nothing to do with what happened.

—I know, I know. But you don't need to make it worse.

—Let's walk some more. Take a look at the whole place, as long as we're here. Come on . . .

—I don't know. Every little thing I see—Look at that tiny bird, half eaten . . . I don't know, it's too much . . .

We pushed on, rummaging through charcoal (charcoal—that means there was wood here?!), poking around in the houses. It looked like the wreckage of a war in the Middle Ages, an alien invasion, nothing but ashes, the population exterminated. I worried more and more about Tadeu. His slumping shoulders expressed such utter defeat. And I think the worst was not even knowing what had happened.

—What was that? Souza, I heard a noise!

—Probably just my stomach growling with hunger.

—No, it was a kind of whining sound, I swear, *I heard it!*

—You don't have to yell.

—Come on, we've got to look for it. Something whimpered, I tell you.

—The wind, maybe?

—What wind? Have you gone crazy?

—I'm getting there. Just like you.

—Best thing for you. Let your head explode.

—I already did. Now it's a question of picking up the pieces. If there are any left.

We found a man lying facedown, pinned beneath a large cage. He was indeed moaning, but very weakly now. Some of the iron bars of the cage were embedded in his upper back. A skinny mulatto, his lips were cracked from the sun. Dried blood stained the ground all around him. His eyes were dull and lifeless. As gently as we could, we dragged him into the shade. It was beastly hot.

—We've got to find him some water.

—I thought I saw a tank back behind the mountains of plastic. Why don't you go have a look? Right down that path, to the left.

Vague directions, but I went looking. Just to look. All that wreckage made me uneasy. Something pressed up from my stomach, weighing heavily on my chest. The blob. It was back, brown on green, and I was paralyzed. Wanting to walk, but unable to move. Brown/green. Something familiar.

Then it was over, and I just felt sort of dizzy, like when you're lying down and you get up suddenly, you see stars. I held my head in my hands. The hole in my palm!

I'd forgotten all about it. I'd learned to live with it. It did me no harm, I was even intrigued. Where did it come from, though, and why? Save it for later, Souza.

I came around the corner of a wall of plastic and began looking for the water tank. It was well camouflaged, but I found it. A few inches of dirty water in the bottom. I scooped up what I could with a plastic pail. It wasn't much. The view on the way back gave me a better idea of the extent of the destruction. It seemed to go on forever.

Bones, smoking tree trunks, debris. It's true, there had been trees here. I saw two or three timbers at least a meter in diameter. Unbelievable. The kind you'd see in the old days at the lumberyard, piled up, aromatic, waiting to be made into planks.

Museum artifacts. I scratched at one with my fingernail, scraping off some of the rotten stuff which covered the bark. Crumbly. I smelled it: sort of moist. Odd. I scratched some more to see what color it was. What kind of tree could it be? Unidentifiable. Funny, I knew so much about trees when I was a boy.

Then, right there in front of me, with the giant timbers and charred earth as backdrop, was my grandfather. Yes, it's him, here he comes with his short, rapid footsteps, coffee steaming in the cup he made himself out of a Toddy can. He's coming to see me, in bed, the sun's not up yet. He shakes me insistently by the shoulders.

A sixty-year-old man, thin but muscular. A rascal, Grandmother always said. I jumped out of bed, splashed a little water in my face, no time to dry. Besides, the morning air on my wet face helped wake me up once and for all. I gulped down some thin, reheated coffee my grandmother had made the night before.

It didn't matter to us, me and my grandfather. We'd drink it cold, even, we liked it any old way. (Even today, I don't mind the synthetic stuff, I drink it like crazy, always running out of coupons. If I had to go very long without coffee, I'd be capable of stealing some, I mean it.) After morning coffee, we'd be on our way.

Grandfather heaved his saw over his shoulder; it was

bigger than I was. The blade made a wonderfully musical sound when it was drawn across the whetstone. But it had to be angled just right, or else the sound would be weak and dull, no echo. I swear I actually *saw* the sound waves shimmering in the air.

How could I ever forget that saw. Years later my admiration gave way to a lingering sense of a guilt. The intellectual in me, as Tadeu said. The image of my grandfather had dimmed and disappeared; only the saw remained. A symbol. I felt, well, I guess you could say I felt like an accomplice.

I condemned my grandfather unconsciously, and myself as well, for having gone with him so many times. I felt guilty for having admired his handiwork, standing for hours at the corner of his workbench watching toys, furniture, doors, windows take shape in his skillful, raw-boned hands.

I've lived with these conflicting feelings for a long time. When the Great Desert, the Ninth Wonder, claimed Amazonia, when the Great Chasm divided the country, when the punishing rains began beating down the northeastern scrub, which hadn't seen a drop of water for years, my confusion brought me to the edge of madness.

I became unhinged. Of course I got better eventually, realizing it was a case of mental apotheosis. Delusions of grandeur, to imagine taking on something so big single-handedly. Sure, I had my cross to bear, but so did everybody else. We all let things happen the way they happen. Without lifting a finger.

And I can't discount the official propaganda, the ever-convincing IOP. It's a killer, it's in the air we breathe. It's the only truth we have nowadays: an impenetrable curtain. Like a fun-house mirror, transposing things, fat/skinny, ugly/beautiful.

So I carried all these worries around with me, gradually letting myself be eaten away by them, almost as a kind of atonement. What foolishness. It may have taken me awhile, but at least now I see how useless my hostility was. Thick-skulled. My grandfather was not just a simple exterminator of trees, I'm sure of that now.

My head was full of all sorts of confused notions, born of things remembered and imagined, things my father had told me. My father was an unpretentious railroad worker; whenever his days off coincided with one of the big land-clearing projects, he'd come along too.

The executives arrived the same time every year to recruit people. Then truck after truck would set out for the forest in early morning. It was always a long drive, first a day, later two. Each year the logging site was farther off, the railroads having advanced farther, farms growing up behind them.

I'm not exactly sure how old I was. It doesn't matter. I know it was very hot and dry; we slept in open lean-to's. Rice and beans and meat every day. Animals were killed, cleaned, and preserved in salt and spices. Animals that had lived in the forest the men were felling.

I remember being in the forest watching the axes fly, red-white shavings spraying in all directions. An enormous V widened at the foot of the tree until it teetered and fell to the ground. My father lifted me up onto a piece of freshly cut trunk and my grandfather counted the rings one by one and said: "Three hundred years old, eighty meters tall. This was a hard one to bring down."

He was proud, almost defiant. It must have been a fantastic tree. And he had cut it down, bested it, with his calloused hands, his solid arms. Sitting in the middle of those magical rings, I looked up at the old man. Happy. Fairly bursting to be the grandson of a man who could be intimidated by no tree, however daunting, however majestic.

The first time I saw a tree felled, my father was standing next to me. The noise was so horrifying that not even his presence could reassure me. I cried. Now I wonder: was it pity I felt that day? No, that would be rationalizing the feelings of a frightened child. But to this day I remember the horror of that tree thundering down.

A defenseless giant cut off at the feet, suddenly swaying free and hurtling down with incredible speed. And the noise. A cry, a lament, rage, S.O.S., despair, a giving

130

in. I had the feeling as it fell that it was trying to appeal to the trees around it, hoping to break its fall on the fragile shrubbery that surrounded it, silent, impotent.

Too weak to be of help. But with a spirit of solidarity. They would all go down together, beaten, dragged off. At the same time, that immense tree seemed to be trying to find something to lean on, it seemed ashamed of its weakness. Ashamed to be cut down without a fight. And so it roared its hate. Could it have resisted? I don't see how.

Then suddenly, irrevocably, it fell. Pulling smaller trees down along with it, with a burst of noise that sounded to me like a waterfall, or a dam bursting open. In Vera Cruz once I saw a dike break, first just a crack, then the water rushing to open a small cavity, finally the walls exploding.

Those men did what they did to earn their living. What they did couldn't really be considered extermination. The battle between my grandfather and the tree was hotly disputed hand-to-hand combat. Man vs. tree was different from machine vs. tree, after all. A machine represented unbridled power, uncontrolled slaughter. Ruthless destruction.

My grandfather's pride came from the fact that he believed his profession was noble, worthy of being passed on to the next generation. Surely he never imagined there would come a time when there were no more forests providing the link between heaven and earth, height/depth, darkness/light. Man against tree was a slow process, allowing the forest time to reestablish itself.

Under the earth is the deepest darkness. Like before creation, my father would say. Above the earth is the light. Trees unite these two worlds, bringing light to the terrible emptiness. Trees bring air from the depths of the earth, air which they need to recreate, to nourish, life.

Along with water, my father would go on, the tree is symbolic of creation. No other form represents life so clearly. The roots breathe the humus, the trunk is the

131

axis, the branches represent expansion, they dominate the terrestrial sphere. Leaves and flowers with light filtering through them are imponderable forces.

I listened as he expounded. He brought along a fat notebook, he wrote things down in it all the time. My father's gnarled handwriting, slanting backwards, impossible for me to read. Even when I got hold of his notebooks years later, I discovered I couldn't decipher them. I would need his help. I knew there was something very important written there, something about my grandfather.

But by then my father had been put in Isolation. And he'd gone deaf. We never managed to communicate through letters, I just couldn't understand his handwriting, no matter how many times I tried. And it got more and more difficult to visit him, Isolation was overloaded, visiting passes were impossible to obtain. Or did I avoid going to visit him?

I managed to understand a letter here, two syllables there, three or four words at a time, a symbol, a scribble. But it never made sense. His writings seemed to be notes, almost in code, for future development. I spent long nights recopying sections, comparing passages, looking for some key to understanding. I tried getting outside help. And I ended up understanding very little.

One page had a Leonardo Da Vinci sketch: a ship setting sail with a bear on it and a tree in the center. My father had written:

*The tree is the sail* → *life* → *the motive power which gives the impulse* → *the vertebral column.* The arrows were in red.

*The fruit of human knowledge is the tree of life.* This notation was in green. Then came the Latin phrase *Produxit Dominus Deus lignum etiam vitae in medio paradisi.* Disconnected quotations: *disappeared Cedars of Lebanon and Assyrian Cylinders* → *3 thousand years before Christ* → *Arar,* to plow.

*The garden of Olive trees.* This notation in red. I don't know what the colors signified. In black: ÁRVORE, *arbor,* tree.

132

AEO.

A → liquid → life

AA (German) → *aqua,* water

R (rushing noise) → AR → running water, rampant, torrent.

*Mount Ararat.* In red. *Noah's Ark,* in green.

ÁRVORE  RE/RA  the sun, Egypt.

ÁRVORE—ARTERIES (the tree retains water)

A = *agua,* groundwater

R = absorbed by the roots

V = harvested via the trunk

O =

R =

distributed through the branches. Restitution of air through absorption of carbon contained in the atmosphere.                 fire

I hadn't the slightest idea where he was headed with all this. I just couldn't follow the shape of his logic, it seemed to be nothing *but* keys. For whom? Sometimes whole paragraphs were indecipherable. If only I'd had access to his library, maybe then I would have been able to get somewhere.

ARAR, capitalized, in red. *To turn back the ara = altar,* to till the earth = *mother.* Preparing it for the *árvore. Duplication of AR = life. The chain of life. To turn back, return.* Then some more "logic." *Reverse AR → RA = the sun.* Therefore, Arar → *Expose to the sun.*

Here, things were a trifle clearer. To take something from the subterranean earth and expose it to the light = creation. Arar = to create life. Then came a very long list of words in green. I memorized them all. I read them over and over in my eagerness, like a litany. Sonorous words, resonant and round.

Maybe I was too young to understand what was on an adult's mind. Besides, I didn't think about it all that long, I'd just remember pieces once in a while, especially the imponderable. Melodious, provoking, and completely impenetrable.

I liked shuffling through the soft ash, still warm to the touch and soft as cotton. We'd kick through the stuff to the center of the clearing, where one large clump of trees still stood. An island of trees. Presided over by silence.

I never saw the final ritual with my own eyes, not even my father had, but Grandfather told us about it. As they cut more and more of the forest, the animals would flee from the men and the noise and gather in the one stand the men had left uncut at the forest's center. They stayed there, as if waiting. In solidarity. As if they knew.

The loggers left that stand of trees for last. There was a little of everything hiding there. Opossum, monkeys, apes, armadillos, mice, tapir, paca, jaguar, snakes, otters, deer, rabbits, bats, hedgehogs, capybara, wild dogs, ferrets, ground squirrels, peccaries, wolves, even sloths.

All packed in together in close proximity, no fighting, no rivalry. Crowded. Watchful. When the last day came, the camp was always bursting with excitement. The men shined and oiled their rifles and spread out around the remaining clump of trees. A great silence fell all around. Then someone set fire to the first bush, and smoke rose in the sky.

The animals, forced to flee their burning shelter for the cleared land, were cut down one by one. With ease. Much of the meat was consumed right then and there. Some was salted and left to dry in the sun. A few of the men only had eyes for tapir skins, jaguar pelts. Once the men had gone, what was left went to the vultures.

Much later, plows ground up the bones, mixing them into the earth like fertilizer. And that's what I see before me here, all over again. The scorched earth, strewn with bones, covered with a blanket of ashes. Repetition. Nothing new under the sun. I bring the pittance of dirty water to the injured man, wondering if it will do any good. What he needs is a doctor.

The skinny mulatto drinks greedily. It doesn't matter to him how filthy the water is, it's liquid. Tadeu still has the look of a dead fish about him, he's in no shape to take charge of things. I'll have to manage somehow, to bring these two back with me. But how? Can I crawl all that way on the freeway dragging a man behind me? Or should we leave this guy here?

—How do you feel?

—Mmmm, mmmmm.

—Better?

He moans, opens his eyes—white, glassy. Tadeu leaps up and grabs him by the shirt collar, shaking him roughly. I can see the blood start to flow again from the wounds on his back. It doesn't take much to separate the two. Tadeu looks like he's hallucinating, and strangely, the attack seems to have revived the injured man.

—Have you gone completely off your rocker, Tadeu?

—He's got to tell me what happened.

—Let's bring him back to São Paulo with us.

—First, I have to know.

The man was still bleeding, but slowly. His eyes were beginning to come back to normal. Sort of yellowish, though. It almost seems as if he recognizes Tadeu. At least our presence and concern is making him more energetic, excited even. I prop his head on my knee and give him the rest of the water. He spits it out. Maybe he's noticed how dirty it is.

—Can you talk?

—Mmmmm, mmmm.

—You don't have to say much. We'll ask questions, you just nod your head yes or no. Understand?

—Mmmm.

—Who came here? The Civil Guards?

—No.

—The New Army?

—No.

—People from the System?

—No.

—Then who?

—Lots of men ... the encampments ...

—People form the Pauper Encampments?

—Oh my God, they've started.

135

—Started what, Tadeu?

—Getting out of control, it was bound to happen sometime.

—So they came, killed indiscriminately, and filled their bellies, eh?

—Of course. With good reason. And we can't tell anyone.

—What do you mean?

—Do you have any idea what those encampments are like?

—No, but nothing justifies what they did here.

—Not even people starving to death? Suddenly the preserve seems like such an elitist idea...

—What are you saying? What about the scientific research? The preservation of the species?

—Does it really make any sense, Souza? Now? That's what I'm asking myself, I'm so confused. Can it make sense, in a world like this?

—Of course it makes sense. You *have* gone crazy.

—Which is more important—the preservation of animals or of human beings, human beings who are literally starving?

—No one can answer that, the way you've posed the question. But this is an entirely abnormal situation.

—Sure it *should* be abnormal, but it's not, don't you see? This is our day-to-day, Souza, our reality. People dying of hunger right alongside us, and we can't do a thing about it.

—Are you sure?

**SOUZA RETURNS HOME
TO FIND HIS APARTMENT
IN A STATE OF TOTAL CONFUSION.
WHY ARE THEY STOCKPILING FOOD THERE?
WHAT KIND OF STRANGE BUSINESS
IS THIS NEPHEW OF HIS INVOLVED IN?**

The neighbors will think I'm drunk. Reeling. My stomach is growling, I'm nauseous, my head's splitting.

136

Hunger, fatigue. Better get out of this sun, it's getting hot much too early. I smell bad, my clothes are filthy. I need a shower, and bed, yes, I need to sleep a whole day.

No one around, thank goodness. The buildings are all closed up, shades drawn against the heat. The entryway hall is dark and almost totally obstructed by trash. Flies. Red insects. The blades of the fan in the barbershop turn uselessly. I walked in, looked at myself in the mirror. What a sight. I look like a hobo.

If Adelaide saw me looking like this, she'd run for her life. I slumped into the chair and the barber bustled over with a hot towel. In this heat. It smells awful, too, I refuse it. This place is getting nastier-looking by the day. How can he let it deteriorate like this? The mirrors are peeling, the chairs are getting ratty.

—You'd be better off with the towel, Mr. Souza, that's one tough beard you've got. Where have you been?

—Around.

He looked at me, his eyes full of questions. No way to interpret my dirty clothes, I've always looked so proper with freshly ironed shirts, the knot of my tie just so, shoes shined, hair in place. After all, he's had this shop thirty years; he's known me since we moved here.

—Your skin's all dry and blistered. Been out walking in the sun?

—A little bit.

—You should be more careful, Mr. Souza. Look at this blotch, a discoloration. Better put something on it when you go home.

—I'll do that.

—Oh, by the way, your nephew and I came to an understanding, everything's just fine. Thanks to you.

—He came by, then?

—Yes, sure, he's been coming by every day. He brings people, takes people with him. Lots of traffic around here lately.

—Is that so?

—In fact, the neighbors are starting to complain. You

know how it is, this is such a sleepy building. Any hoopla scares the pants off them.

—Well, I'm back now, I'll put a stop to all that.

—Oh, have you heard about the new rules? Every night at seven-fifty they lock the front doors. Orders from the superintendent.

—What?

—With the new energy conservation law, they're only allowing one street light per block, so for security reasons they decided to lock the place up tight after dark. Really something, huh? But, it's true, there's all sorts of people hanging around asking for food, water, charity, a place to sleep. Yesterday I heard there was a shooting, they killed some old couple right in their own apartment. Tough world, I'm telling you. I wish I knew how they got into the neighborhood in the first place . . .

—Ask my nephew. The New Army's responsible for controlling the Access Stations.

Now for the stairs. (The ancient elevator was out of order. Definitive, or only temporary? Hard to tell.) I climbed slowly, one step at a time, the stairwell was like a furnace. My key wouldn't turn in the lock, but when I gave the door a push it opened. I'll have to have a talk with that nephew of mine. Only that lughead would leave the door unlocked in these times.

All the ashtrays in the dining room were full and a red sport coat was slung on the back of a chair. I don't own a red sport coat. Voices whispering in the kitchen. Like people murmuring at a funeral parlor, telling stories. I walked in and the three men just stared at me. Me at them. Like imbeciles.

We all hesitated for a moment, looking each other over. Surprised but not startled. As if I had expected to find them here; as if they had known I might walk in at any moment. Though they were all bald, and one had scaly skin, they were not the same men my nephew had with him when he asked me for the use of my apartment.

—Is this your place, my friend?

The question was superfluous and its formality hov-

138

ered, ice-cold, in the atmosphere around us. We were strangers to each other, but accomplices somehow. Oddly familiar. No way to explain things like that. No way to explain the shame I felt admitting that yes, I owned the place. It's a crazy world.

—Make yourselves at home.

—We've already been using the stove, and the refrigerator, of course. But don't worry about water—your nephew left extra coupons.

The man at the head of the table—I'm not sure if he was the leader or not, but it seemed like it—introduced me to the others. We shook hands. They spoke with accents, but perfect grammar. The third man, who was eating candy, noticed my hand. He asked to look at it.

—It's nothing much, just a little hole.

—Does it hurt?

—No. Never did, in fact. I'm used to it by now.

—Have you seen others like it?

—No, I guess I'm the only one.

—I don't think so. I met some migrants from the Northeast, around twenty kilometers from the Great Chasm, and they had holes like these, every one of them. That's why I noticed.

—What do you think it means?

—I have no idea.

—Maybe some sort of sign?

—More likely a disease.

I feel like talking, describing how the hole appeared, how I lost my job. It would be a relief. But they seem to know all this already. I don't see how, but that's the impression I get. They looked at the hole in my hand casually, as if everyone had one. Who are these men, anyway? The man-who-was-eating-candy comes over to me, solicitous.

—Would you like something to eat? We can heat it up for you.

My hunger, the shower, I'd forgotten everything, even how tired I am. But at the mention of food my stomach started complaining violently. I said sure, I'd like a piece

139

of meat, it looked pretty appetizing surrounded by onions and green beans. I know it's all synthetic; the taste is the same whether it's egg, meat, or vegetables. It's the mere suggestion of food that interests me.

The bathroom was not exactly clean. Not like when Adelaide was around. You could tell only men lived in this apartment now. Urine-splattered tiles, ashes, wads of toilet paper in the corner on the floor. I took a long, hot shower, who cares if I use up the water coupons— easy come, easy go. Hot water is so relaxing; it regulates your body temperature.

—Now you look a little happier.

No hostility in the air, they were smiling. It hadn't been fair of me to consider them invaders. How can I complain, I lent out the house. These men had nothing to do with the agreement. If it bothers me, it bothers me. I keep thinking I'm in a boarding house, a hotel or something, which is disconcerting. I wish I felt more relaxed, since it *is* my house. Neurotic.

They cleared off a corner of the table. I ate in silence, the three of them watching. I didn't strike up a conversation and neither did they, simple as that. A mountain of plates, glasses, pots and pans, silverware, plastic bags, coffee cups peeked out at me from the sink. All around the trash bin lay orange peels, beer tops, coffee grounds, cigarette butts.

—I'm going to bed, I was up all night.

—Ummm, your room...

—What's wrong with my room?

—Don't get upset...

—Is there someone in there sleeping?

—No, no... We just put a few things in there, for safekeeping, that's all.

A few things! Hundreds of canned goods and he calls them a few things! The bed had been moved up against the wall to make room. I wondered if I'd be able to sleep in the midst of all this. Every type of canned food imaginable—shredded beef, sausages, hams, pâté, peas, sauces, soups, jam, powdered milk, instant coffee.

Heaped all over the room in no apparent order. Since the cans themselves are made by government industries, they're all the same except for color-coded labels and a picture illustrating the contents. The right side of the room was entirely taken up by this unexpected and diverse cache of food. My bedroom as pantry.

I couldn't sleep. Not just because the bed was out of position, but also because the room was stifling. My headache came back, though not so bad as before. I chalked it up to fatigue and tried to relax, but I couldn't stop thinking about those three men and this immense stockpile of food. I should have asked them about it.

Why is it here? And how did they get hold of it, anyway? Was it bought, stolen, appropriated? My nephew's got to have something to do with this. Is he that powerful, or are there others involved in this little game? What *is* the game? What's the point of hiding these people in my house? Finally I fell asleep, questions floating around in my head.

When I woke up, the bell was ringing insistently in the hallway. I was about to jump out of bed, but heard voices and realized the men had answered it. The voices stopped, I decided to get up. Now they were in the living room watching TV. It's as if they move all of one body; where one goes they all go.

—That woman's been here at least three times already.

—Really? What does she look like? The people in this building usually keep to themselves pretty much.

—Blonde, wears a lot of makeup. A cleanliness fanatic. She dusts and sweeps the hall at least fifty times a day.

So it was the neighbor-with-the-bleached-hair, bright red lipstick, and lots of wrinkles. Her lipstick drove Adelaide wild, it was engraved on her face, lit up like a neon sign announcing first-run movies. But then you saw the rest of the face: eroded by time, water, wind. A complete wreck.

I imagine she's paid for her sins, Adelaide would say, in a certain ruthless tone of voice. My wife had a certain

141

streak of incomprehensibly rigid intolerance that must have originated with her extreme Catholicism—an intolerance she exercised continually, at home as well as in the world. That's one reason we grew apart from each other. I think.

Every time we met the bleached blonde strolling in the hall with her son or playing in the empty playground, Adelaide would give me a look. Something between criticism and condemnation. As if her imperfect child were proof of the hypothetical sins and aberrations committed by his mother.

Of course the beginning of this story dates back before the Great Cycle of Sterility, which was followed by the Era of Exterminated Children (which is still going on today). My thoughts jockey for position in my head. I can never be sure of the chronology.

Sometimes I'm not even sure how old I am. Then, too, I could be any age. These days time is relative, measured by the stages we reach rather than days, weeks, months, or years. The significance and duration of each stage are relative to the individual.

Things which happened a long time ago often seem, to me, recent occurrences. Today's events are so unreal it's almost as if they haven't happened yet. People materialize or disappear into a cloud of smoke, the touch of a magic wand, stars which spring from my fingertips. Each of us is master of his own time; we do with it what we like.

Even so, I do have a notion of when my problems with Adelaide began. The worst phase of our marriage occurred after her conversion. She turned from spiritualism to Catholicism on the wave of a feverish missionary campaign undertaken by the church (which had been spurred to action by a papal bull written especially with Brazil in mind).

Let's see, that must have been between the Era of Grand Enrichment and the extremely short period referred to as the Phase of Hushed-Up Financial Scandals. Faced with potential "chaos in the largest Catholic nation

142

in Latin America," the Vatican issued its "warning bull." It was considered hopelessly ecological-minded by the conservatives and was declared "treacherous surrender" by the liberals. Clearly there was more than a simple question of ecology at stake.

As the years went by, Adelaide lost some of her reformist fury. Her tendency toward criticism diminished. But there was by then a large barrier between us. I can't say it was all her fault. Everyone had a terrible anarchy inside them. And I kept my silence when I should have been trying to open her eyes.

In any case, the distance between us seemed unbridgeable. I thought about separation, but in addition to being old-fashioned about such things, I really liked her a lot. I had no idea what to do. I've never been good at relationships. There's a certain deficiency in me when it comes to understanding people, getting through interpersonal crises, analyzing social situations.

I'm slow to get to know people. Scatterbrained, even, the way I don't pay the slightest attention to gestures, turns of phrase, the little things which are sometimes highly revealing. Maybe I'm too (innocently) confident. The worst is my laziness when it comes to thinking things through, lining up the facts, finding connections, remaining observant. Or is it just that I'm too wrapped up in myself?

For instance, lately Adelaide could hardly stand to cross paths with the bleached blonde, and I never managed to figure out the reason for her extreme antipathy. The woman had never done anyone any harm as far as I knew. Like everyone else, she limited herself to the usual inconsequential conversations, the blah-blah-blahs at the door, the inoffensive "he said this, I heard that."

There had always been very few children in our building. The couples who moved in these days were generally middle-aged, with grown kids living on their own. Most of the youngsters who had grown up here were away at college and now only appeared for quick visits at holidays and school vacations.

The nursery school next to the playground had closed for lack of students. Each building had been required to provide one so the children would be safe, so they wouldn't have to go out and mix with unknown kids in the streets. That was before they organized and controlled circulation. Before sterilization.

Anyway, the dark hallways, the filth, the closed life inside a shuttered apartment, the fear of the street, the asphyxiating heat, the neighbor who had a son while Adelaide didn't—all this had its impact on my wife. It changed her disposition, fostered attitudes that weren't really hers to begin with. Rudeness, severity, these were qualities she acquired after we moved.

And all of these feelings somehow converged in a dry and piercing hate for the-neighbor-with-the-bleached-blonde-hair. Which was not lost on the woman herself, of course. She and Adelaide would never come up in the same elevator; they avoided walking into the supermarket or the hairdresser at the same time. The neighbor started the rumor that Adelaide had something against her son because he was handicapped, and that she was trying to have him expelled from the building.

So of course everyone turned against Adelaide. They called her the monster without pity. I took advantage of every trip to the barbershop to deny this gossip, but unfortunately women don't go to the barber's. It was a hopeless situation. All because of a poor retarded kid, and the mysterious aversion Adelaide had toward him.

For some reason the boy disturbed her. Profoundly, uncontrollably. Her skin crawled whenever she saw that dwarfish creature with skin the color of Coca-Cola, a sticky secretion constantly dripping from his eyes, black-spotted gums protruding as he drooled and babbled. He used to go from door to door looking for other children to play with.

It was then Adelaide's dream about the brightly lit ship sinking in a calm sea first started. Every afternoon when I came home I'd find her waiting at the door for the mailman. Sometimes he would arrive before I did, but still she'd be standing at the door, motionless, and she'd hand me the mail with a nasty look.

Junk mail, direct mailings, bank statements, all sorts of notices, advertisements, religious chain letters, an occasional card or letter from a student. "I don't know why people waste so much paper, never mind time and postage, on this worthless stuff. I don't want it filling up my drawers and piling up on the furniture—anything you have no use for you should throw away right now."

The people in the building kept more and more to themselves. The retarded boy made everyone uncomfortable, he was an embarrassment. Plus he rang doorbells, threw things down the stairs, rode the elevator up and down, broke windows, peed in the hall, left little turds in the doorways, smashed light bulbs, pawed through the trash.

He howled like a wolf the whole night long, and the sound echoed to the top floor through the central stairwell. He opened transom windows and threw garbage and feces inside. Finally the tenants signed a petition to have him locked up. Eventually it was discovered that there were other children like him in the neighborhood, lots of them.

The retarded children's parents called a meeting—which was unusual, because people didn't often communicate like that, they hardly went out of their houses. Each building had a life of its own, like an overcrowded transatlantic liner. Isolated, afloat on a tempestuous sea, unable to help each other. So this was a valiant endeavor.

At the meeting it became clear that dozens of children born during the same period had all kinds of problems. Abnormally large heads, missing limbs, born blind or deaf, strange marks on their skin, pigmentation irregularities, liver problems, intestinal or kidney malfunctions, atrophied genitals, leprous lips, arthrosis.

An association of parents was formed to analyze the situation, and as research proceeded, thousands of cases came to light: abnormalities linked to the Ingestion of Food Contaminated by Mercury. They ran to the doctors with their statistics, and some of the doctors, in turn, tried to start a movement, make plans, raise the public's consciousness.

It's my conviction that these rumblings of discontent are what eventually led to the Cycle of Sterility. No one talks about this, of course. No one's crazy enough to go looking for trouble. Bringing up the Era of Exterminated Children is the same as talking about the Pauper Encampments. Pure subversion.

Sterility, Extermination, the retarded boy, the brightly lit ship, the letter Adelaide was waiting for (I wonder if she's still waiting for it, wherever she is)—there must be a connection between all these things. Or else I wouldn't think about them so obsessively. I'm sure there's a link; I feel as if I've almost discovered it.

But everybody keeps their mouths shut, a rule of silence like in the Mafia. The more the parents pressed for investigations, the greater the silence. Doctors were transferred. No explanations. Some of the most determined parents were scared off. They saw what happened to the ones who insisted: a truck would appear and they were moved away. No one heard from them again.

—Hey, are you listening?

—Sure, sure I'm listening.

—You could have fooled me. That's some glazed look in your eyes. I was talking about that neighbor woman. You know the one I mean?

—Yeah. What did she want?

—She said she'd be back later. She seemed awfully suspicious, really looked us up and down, tried to peek into the apartment.

I go looking for the clippers, my nails are incredibly long with lots of dirt underneath. Can't stand it when they get that way, never could. But the nail clippers are nowhere to be found. It used to be all I had to do was ask, and Adelaide brought them to me. She's the one who knew where everything was. The house was her domain. I can't even find my own shirts and socks.

I'm getting to know my own house in a different way,

146

discovering things. The bureau drawers, perfumed, made of cedar. Papers accumulated in the desk, in spite of her recommendation that I throw them out. How many years has it been since I took a single item out of these drawers? I just keep putting things in, more and more useless stuff. The story of my life.

What life? Some story, a memory which is never consulted and which will be thrown in the trash as soon as I die. I'm not much for order. Papers, photos, bills, notes. What do they matter? Documents of what? An ordinary man. Bah, has history ever been interested in the common man? Why should it be?

Mementos. They don't even jog my memory or tell me anything about myself. What significance can a receipt for a pacifier have? It proves a child existed, yes. But the question is this: did we have a child, here in this house, or did we buy one as a gift? A pacifier as a gift— ridiculous.

So there was a child. The records in my head have been erased. I'd prefer not to think. That's why I avoid desk and dresser drawers. This house. The office. They have made up my world for a very long time. Nothing existed beyond these walls. And me with my eyes closed, then inexplicably opening them with the appearance of the hole in my hand.

I didn't even dream of a resurrection anymore, the third day, the raising of the dead. I was so accustomed to my comfortable sarcophagus. There was a time when I imagined rays of sunlight and clouds across which I dashed on horseback toward an intense point of light. The intensity disappeared and all that was left was a small, painful electric bulb. Yellow.

But that intense and blinding light would one day shine through me, striking the ground, opening like a fan, joining me to the rest of the world. I kept waiting for the light to come, but it went out, I can't even tell where it's gone. When I found Tadeu I realized that things could make sense again.

The doorbell ringing. With a vengeance. What does

147

that woman want, and why is she so insistent? I open the door. Two men push past without so much as looking at me. They're repulsive, hideous. No hair, a hole in place of a nose, yellow drool running down their mouths.

### PERVERSITY OR PRACTICALITY? SOUZA IS CONFUSED WHEN HE'S NOT ALLOWED TO GIVE WATER TO TWO MEN WHO ARE DYING OF THIRST

They burst into the living room and were confronted by my three lodgers, who stood there as if expecting them. Ready to react electronically at the first sign of danger. Faces tense. The one-who-was-always-eating-candy held a gun.

—Where do you think you're going?

—Food. We want food.

—We don't have any.

—Food and water. Give us something to eat.

The intruders moved forward; the man-who-was-always-eating-candy calmly cocked his gun. The click echoed like a thunderclap in the silent afternoon. We were all sweating, panting from the heat. My head was pounding. Intimidated, the intruders gave ground, trembling, drooling, heads hung low. They were in no shape for a fight.

—We just want some food.

—We told you, there isn't any.

—The woman next door said you had lots of food over here.

—It's not true.

—She told us people bring in more every day.

—She's lying. It's over at her house there's lots of food, go talk to her.

—No, it's here. A guy in the hall said so too.

—Bah, get out of here!

This could go on all afternoon. The man-who-sat-at-the-head-of-the-table left the room, I followed him. I figured he was going to come up with something. He glared at me: "I don't know how they got in, but we can't give them anything. I know it's hard, but if we did, this place would be invaded tomorrow, and I mean invaded."

So he was determined not to give in. The man-who-ate-candy was holding his gun steady. The intruders were still trembling and drooling, indecisive. All I could think was: Who am I not to at least give a glass of water to these pitiful creatures? I went to the kitchen. Who cares about tomorrow's invasion. Who knows if there'll even be a tomorrow. What a pretty thought.

The man-who-sat-at-the-head-of-the-table trailed me into the kitchen. "I know how you feel, but forget it. One glass of water won't solve anything, they need a lot more than that. Water, food, a good hospital. Besides, it's not our job to solve Brazil's problems."

—Just a glass of water, that's all.

—They need a tankful of water. They're dying. I know the symptoms, the trembling, the drool. You'd be wasting it.

—So what's one glass of wasted water?

—You've got to accept the way things are, my friend. That glass of water should go to someone who can survive a little longer.

Ugly and hairless as this man was, his eyes were calm, not the least bit violent. He didn't look irrational, hot-headed, worried about his own survival. Something about him made me trust him. Judiciousness. A certain air of determination I had also seen in Tadeu Pereira. Maybe you could call it sincerity.

But sincere or not, I keep thinking over and over: how can I refuse these men a lousy glass of water? What difference does it make that they're dying? All the more reason to be charitable—at least they'll die with a belly full of water. Meanwhile, the third man was waiting in the hall to intercept me.

—Don't do it, pal. Foolhardy. Make it all the worse for us.

149

—This is my house. Have you forgotten?

—Our house. There's no such thing as "my" anymore.

—What are you talking about? I could throw you out of here in a minute if I wanted to.

—Think again. What are you going to do—file a complaint?

—You leave that to me.

—Your concern for those two living dead shows you have a heart. That's good, man. Why not show some concern for us, then? Do you think it's fair for you to live all alone in this big place, with so many people dying out there from disease and heatstroke?

—Okay, let's make a deal. I'll just give them some water and tell them to leave. If they make any trouble, we'll throw them out.

—Throw them out and they'll tell the world we've got food and water. No, no water for them, and what's more—they're not leaving.

—What?

—We're going to lock them up in the room in the back, the one that used to be the maid's room. I checked it out, it's just full of packages. We'll take all that stuff out and put the two of them in there.

—And keep them prisoners until they die?

—They'll be leaving tomorrow. The truck will take them.

—What truck?

—The supply truck.

—You've got more stuff being delivered?

—Lots. This place is going to be a central warehouse. From here we'll send supplies to the other distribution centers.

—Distribution centers?

—Don't you ever stop asking questions?

—Look, just let me give them this one glass of water, okay?

After all, who does this guy think he is giving me orders in my own house? The blood rose in my head. Which almost never happens, or never happens when it

150

should, rather—which is why my life is the way it is. This was a moment of decision. Determined now, I switched the glass to my left hand and, with my right, pushed the man out of my way.

He fell back, surprised by my sudden bravery, and I darted into the living room. There wasn't even time to offer them the water, they dove for it with such frenzy that they knocked the glass out of my hand. The man-who-sat-at-the-head-of-the-table burst out laughing.

—Are you happy now?

—They're animals.

—Animals, no. They're desperate.

They were licking the floor like dogs, disputing each little puddle that had formed between floorboards, frantic to stop the water from disappearing into the cracks. They pushed each other feebly, falling to the floor. Clearly exhausted from the effort.

—Take the two of them out back, said the guy I imagined was the leader.

—We still haven't finished getting all the stuff out.

They were clearing the little cubicle completely, piling packages of calendars in the kitchen. So many years wrapped up and buried on the fifth of January. They meant nothing anymore. Old paper to be sold by the pound. Or just the thing for the Museum of the Representation of Time, a deserted monument, dead archive.

The doorbell rang again. I opened the door: no one there. I closed the door. Someone better go downstairs and find out what's going on. They rang the bell again, I let it ring. I disconnected the buzzer, slammed the door. Loud knocking. The men came from out back where they had secured the two intruders. We looked at each other and the door.

They made a sign: leave it to us. The man-who-always-ate-candy fired right through the door. Two shots. A scurrying, and silence. Then a moan. I got a chair and leaned it up against the door. Looked up at the pane of blue glass in the transom above the paneled door. It had never been opened. This building is ancient.

151

—Jesus, that was a stupid thing to do, I said.

—Now that it's started, no one's safe anymore.

—Someone had to let those two guys in in the first place. There's an electronic grate, an automatic lock, a television screen, for heaven's sake.

—But who?

The transom gave way with a swift kick. There on the floor was a man, bleeding. His shirt was soaked. I peeked down the hall: no one. But of course they could be hiding, waiting for us to open the door. Or ready to call the Guards.

We dragged the man inside and dumped him in the maid's room, too. I felt like vomiting. This is total madness. I had something to eat and went to bed on a full stomach, which gave me terrible nightmares. I've got to wake up, I've got to shake myself free from this obsession. None of this is really happening. All I have to do is deny it with all my strength. I swear it's not happening.

There's nobody here but me, those bald guys don't exist, I haven't got a hole in my hand, it's not hot, I don't have a headache, I didn't lose my job, Adelaide didn't leave, there is no Beyond the Pale, the city isn't overcrowded, it's definitely not hot, my house is empty, tranquil. Rest in peace.

It's all a dream. We're not shooting people, the neighbors aren't ganging up on us, there are no beggars and mutants coming to the door. In a little while I'll go back to my daily routine, imperturbable. I'll wake up, take a shower, have coffee, Adelaide will walk me to the door, and I'll go to the bus stop and get on the S-758.

I'm ashamed to think what Tadeu Pereira would say if he saw me in a situation like this. But what would he do? What could anybody do? He'd berate me: "You accepted what happened at the university, impassive, you turned yourself in without a fuss, you let your life trickle away. How can you complain now?"

The judgment wasn't Tadeu's, but my own. Complying is the same as becoming one of them. It's me that I need to face up to. Wrapped in my own thoughts, I hadn't even noticed the images flickering across the television screen. Familiar images, a familiar place. It can't be! One more thing that's just not happening!

## A DAY OF SHOCKING REVELATIONS REGARDING: THE HALL OF WATERS, THE INSTALLATION OF SOLAR GENERATORS, AND THE ACTIVITIES OF THE MULTINATIONALS

Broken shelving, pieces of glass scattered all over the floor. Men gathering up metal tags. Civil Guards overseeing the operation, prisoners being shoved into police vans. The Hall of Waters in ruins. Rooms that I know like the palm of my hand, glass by glass, object by object. Rooms that were my refuge.

The prisoners: toothless, aggressive-looking mulattos, wizened northeasterners, short orientals, people without noses, ears, hair, eyeballs dangling from a thread of scabby skin, stubs for arms, a guy with a hole in his hand. He's out of sight before I get a really good look— but I'm sure it was just like mine.

The announcer does a voice-over in a serious, ceremonious voice, like whoever reads the official news on General Radio. A Civil Guard holds up a glass of water, the only one left intact. Water from the Tucuma. Where the devil was the Tucuma? There's the governor, and the director of the museum. And the monotonous voice drones on.

*At two o'clock this afternoon an unusually large influx of visitors converged on the Museum of Brazilian Rivers, known popularly as the Hall of Waters, located in what used to be the Largo do Arouche in metropolitan São Paulo. Suddenly, to the total surprise and amazement of the guards, hundreds of people began streaming in and scattering throughout the building, apparently interested merely in looking at the thousands of liters of water which*

153

*include samples from rivers, streams, brooks, springs,
lakes, tributaries, headwaters, wellsprings, marshes,
ponds and inland seas from all over Brazil. The Hall
of Waters was the most extensive hydrographic museum
in the world, universally admired and appreciated by
experts who came from all parts of the globe to further
pursue their hydric-research. Though work on the project
was originally inaugurated in the eighties by scientists
from the Federal Universities of São Paulo, Rio Grande
do Sul, Espirito Santo, and Paraíba, with the collabo-
ration of researchers from the entire country, enjoying
great popular cooperation and enthusiasm, the museum
took twelve years to reach completion. It was laid out
geographically, with each room representing a particular
region of the country and containing hundreds of liters
of water of varying colors, in addition to engravings,
photographs, graphs, maps, and inscriptions. A main
library, a film library, and a record library—containing
relics like the sound of waterfalls, in particular the Igaçu,
the roar of the extinct tidal wave, and the murmur of
tiny streamlets—completed the complex.*

*As soon as the guards had grown accustomed to the
size of the crowd and relaxed their patrols, everything
began to happen at once. In a matter of minutes, without
a chance of stopping the catastrophic events. All over
the museum people began opening the glasses, drinking
the water, or splashing it around, soaking themselves,
laughing with glee. By the time the Civil Guards arrived,
minutes afterward, only one glass was still intact. Most
of the marauders had escaped, breaking out through
doors and windows. A few were taken prisoner. Authorities suspect that this action was incited by some as yet
unidentified subversive organization. Witnesses do report that earlier this afternoon a rumor circulated that
the Hall of Waters was poorly guarded—and that it was
therefore a potential source of a great deal of free water.*

*One of the prisoners, under examination, commented:
"Who wants to go look at water from some river? We
were thirsty, that's what, so we came to drink the water*

*which was ours by right. Like me, for example—I looked
for the water from a little stream which used to go through
my hometown. A river I went swimming in every day
when I was a kid. So that's what I drank, that's the water
right here in my belly. Let them take it out if they want
to."*

*Others who were interviewed said that people just
couldn't endure today's temperatures, which were recorded in the official registers as the highest so far this
year. The sun must have in some way altered people's
behavior, a few meteorologists ventured, stressing that
the temperature is in fact on the rise, even more than
would be expected during these months which correspond
to what, in other times, was called summer. The System
is prepared to take two actions in this regard. One is to
impede further migration to metropolitan areas, since
the resulting supercrowding causes so many problems.
The second is to adopt measures such as the construction
of a giant Marquee to protect the people from the intense
heat wave which is presently beating down upon the
nation.* A commercial for the System. Images of artesian
wells superimposed on shots of dry riverbeds. The rivers
disappear, limpid water gushes from the wells. Thousands of plastic cups parade down a conveyor belt, machinery filling and sealing them. Children laugh happily,
optimistic classical music in the background.

The official voice announces: *In two minutes and thirty-
two seconds, we'll be back with the latest word on the
break-in at the Museum of Brazilian Rivers. New information directly from the bastions of government. And
something else of interest: a rare rerun of an old documentary, today a classic in the genre of historical short
subjects. Please stay tuned for "The Last Tree in Brazil."*

Another commercial, this one showing the installation
of solar generators. Citizens shaking hands with the
technocrats from the System. They don't really show
people, just welcome banners, signs with slogans painted
on them. A sound track with applause, shouts of hooray,
well done, long live the System. Bells and gongs.

—Leftovers. It's all a bunch of leftovers. Do you think that equipment was really imported from Germany? Not a chance. It's all from the Multinational Territory of Germany which used to be Pernambuco and Rio Grande do Norte. That machinery is at least ten years old; the multis must have decided to put in something more modern, some model that can stand up to the heat these days. So they sell their scrap metal to Brazil.

—How do you know so much? Whatever happens, one of you has got an explanation for it, a story to tell.

—I know because I saw it.

—What? I find that hard to believe. I find *you* hard to believe, and him-over-there-at-the-head-of-the-table, watching everything so intently. What is it with you, anyway? Why do you always sit at the head of the table?

—Are you serious? With all the things you have to worry about, you're asking me why I sit at the head of the table? I suppose you've fretted over stupid things like that all your life. Who sits at the head of the table, who smokes his cigarettes down to the filter, who used a green handkerchief to blow his nose. Why don't you just live and let live, huh? You'd be a lot better off.

—Okay, you want me to live and let live? Fine, that's just fine, except you three have got to live someplace else. Not here. I mean it. Why don't you just get out of here, this is my house.

—Our house. And we're all going to live here together for a while. Whether you like it or not.

—Well, I don't like it. And you can just go start packing your bags.

—Right. And you're going to throw us out, is that it?

—That's right, I am. Don't laugh. There are still laws in this country. What you're doing is not right!

—Maybe not. But by whose standards? Are there universally recognized standards here? Maybe each person, each group establishes its own set of standards, beliefs, whatever they need to survive. Fine by me, fine by the System. After all, the government is one thing,

156

the country's another, and the people a third. The System is just security. Or an attempt at security, I should say. They try to tie our hands so we won't kill each other. As long as the System manages to keep people's stomachs from grumbling too much, the structure is maintained. Just how long do you think they can keep up the juggling act?

—I don't know . . .

He made a sign to wait. Familiar music on the TV. I close my eyes. I know these images by heart. Violins, a little brass, an epic sweep. The music picks up tempo with a certain calm confidence. Then another crescendo, a crash of cymbals. Mussorgsky's *Night on Bald Mountain*. A forest fills the screen, nothing but trees as far as the eye can see. The music fades out and the announcer intones:

*The vandals who raided the Hall of Water this afternoon did not spare the irreplaceable archives in their burst of destructiveness. Photographs, films, tapes, recordings, documents were torn up, smashed, trampled, and otherwise destroyed—which is hard to understand since the marauders themselves declared they only wanted to drink the water, nothing else. Whatever might have led them to devastate everything else in sight is a mystery which the troubled Civil Guards are anxious to unravel. Looters who were arrested at the scene will be subjected to the usual persuasive treatment, scientific and painless, designed to make them of their own free will reveal exactly how the events took place. The objective of this questioning is to determine if, as the authorities suspect, a provocateur was involved.*

*As we all know, the System is very concerned about maintaining records of the past, keeping our history documented and intact. Unfortunately, very little archival material remains after the shameful events of this afternoon. One short film of note, however, did survive. "The Last Tree in Brazil," a film characterized by straightforward reporting style with no artistic pretensions, is somewhat of an oddity. Though shot in Super-8 by an*

157

*amateur, the historical importance of the piece is clear. When it was shown in Brazil for the first time, this short film provoked considerable controversy, including televised debates, protests and demonstrations in the streets, discord in the military sector, and international denunciations. Such intense agitation was not something the government was prepared to deal with. It led to anarchy, corruption, absolute chaos. While "The Last Tree" may have been merely an unpretentious, amateurish short film, it helped precipitate the fall of the elite group in power during the Era of Grand Enrichment, thus paving the way for the installation of the present System which, as we all know, was able to resolve our country's grave internal and external problems. And so we invite you to watch with us now the ceremony of the felling of the last tree in Brazil in the little village of Santa Ursula.*

The music swelled, images danced across the screen. Distant shots of forests, swamps, lakes, rivers, waterfalls, creeks, colossal tree trunks, the solemn announcer enumerating each species. If the footage of these trees, so long extinct, hadn't been so visually breathtaking, it would have been a completely uninteresting film; it certainly didn't reveal the slightest bit of imagination on the filmmaker's part. And how many times had I already seen it?

—Ah, yes, Santa Ursula, the city that never existed. A complete fabrication, said the man-who-eats-candy.

—So now you're a know-it-all, too? Got some story for me, I suppose. Well, I'll tell you, I've had it with stories. And besides, everyone knows that Santa Ursula was flooded when they constructed the hydroelectric plant at Manguinhos.

—That's what they told us, sure. Who's got proof? Manguinhos itself disappeared in the earthquake.

—How do you know?

—I worked in Paraíba, at the geographical and statistical institute. When so much was made of this little film, I decided it was a good idea to do some investi-

158

gating. I found no record of this charming village of Santa Ursula.

—You must have got it wrong, then. The film shows the town, the ceremony, and everything. It was in the São Francisco valley.

—That's right, there was a Santa Ursula in the São Francisco valley, I wrote to them down there, compared photographs. Something didn't jibe. The town in the film doesn't look the least bit like the photos they sent me. Totally different.

—So?

—So, the film is a fake. The town, the ceremony, everything: fake.

—But why would anyone go to the trouble?

—I think that's pretty obvious, but then again maybe it's not...

—You guys are too mysterious for me.

Suddenly I didn't feel like watching that famous documentary yet one more time. Not because of what this guy said, I didn't believe a word he, or any of them, told me. We were stuck here together, they made things up just to pass the time. They had something to say about everything. A bunch of bull. I turned off the TV. We'd been in the middle of a conversation sort of like this one earlier. I turned to the man-who-sat-at-the-head-of-the-table.

—You were saying, before...

—Before the TV? Hmmmm, I was talking about... trust, yes—belief, something like that.

—Right, you said we all need to believe in something. But what?

—I'm not sure. People, maybe. Each person's ethics, his behavior. I get second thoughts using the word *ethics,* though. It doesn't make sense in a situation like ours. But I still believe in the importance of the individual man. The problem is that everyone is preoccupied with survival. To the point that they're even willing to kill.

—Even if there is something to your theory, that doesn't

159

give you the right to take over my house. I'm the one who paid for it, and lived here practically my whole life, I struggled for it. I *am* this house.

—As a phrase, very pretty. But think about it. If your life is nothing but this house, what kind of life is that? No, don't say a word. What you don't seem to understand is that we had houses once, too. We fought for them, sweated for them, paid for them . . . and lost them. There's a Belgian living in mine, if it's still standing. A South African's living in his, and a Chinese in his. And it's not just a matter of houses. We had to leave our land, our hometowns. Expelled without recourse. Expatriated. Can you understand what that means? To be expatriated in your own country? They banished us from our own states. Just put us on a bus one day and sent us away. Then— surprise!—they let us out about two hundred kilometers from Maceió.

—When did all this happen?

—About two years ago. People from all over. Entire families pushed out by the multinationals. To make room for their families, the foreigners. When they kept any Brazilians around at all it was for manual labor, or as servants. Which is exactly what we did to the blacks and the Indians five hundred years ago.

—And the government didn't do anything about it?

—Those reserves were handed over unconditionally. They became foreign territory, with their own laws, their own structures imported from the homeland. Nonintervention was part of the deal.

—I can't believe it.

—Even when you look around you? Where do you think all the people are coming from? Or why?

—I've got a friend, an ex-professor like me, who was talking about these migrations, something like what you're saying. I keep asking myself where will it end?

—You were a professor? What did you teach?

—History.

—Why aren't you still teaching? You're awfully young to be retired.

160

—Compulsory retirement can strike at any age.

—Ah.

—Ah? Just "Ah"? Aren't you going to even ask why?

—Do you think I need to? Do you know what I am? An agronomist. At least ten of my friends are in your position. I think it must have been an epidemic in this country for a while. Every family had somebody affected. Their private shame, the hidden sinner.

—I'm not ashamed. I consider it my badge of honor.

—But you don't act that way. You're a strange person, Mr. . . .

—Souza.

—Very strange. Apathetic, while the whole world falls down around you. You don't react, you're indifferent to everything. I've been watching you. Today I even provoked you on purpose. Remember when I said there was no way we were leaving? I was testing you. And after a slight objection you gave up. All you could muster up was a rough draft of anger, when anybody else would have thrown us out, physically if need be. But not you. It's hard to believe you're a history professor. Or were. You're stuck in time, impassive; I can't imagine you doing anything to upset the System, anything that would lead to compulsory retirement. What happened? What made you change?

Maybe I could answer that question. There are so many variables, it's just a matter of putting them all together. Not so difficult. Not at all. This guy will laugh if I tell him my head opened up because of this hole in my hand. Sometimes I look at it and think it doesn't really exist. It's just a figment of my imagination. Too much sun on my head.

I imagined things. It was my way of regaining consciousness. For many years I felt like my brain was closed down. No matter how lucid a man is, there's a point of no return. After that, his conscious mind becomes cataleptic. And all the while, the unconscious goes on working, defending itself. Reacting.

When I came to, I found a world I didn't recognize.

161

I entered it a little at a time. I'm finding out that what I need, first, is to recognize myself again, to establish my identity. I must confess it's discouraging. From one minute to the next I wonder if it's worth the trouble to survive, much less to be reborn. It's a hard question.

—There's a woman's picture on the dresser in your room. Are you a widower? Divorced?

—No. I'm still married.

—Then where's your wife?

## NEIGHBORS ARE FINE (HELPFUL, NECESSARY EVEN), BUT WHEN THEY THREATEN TO INTERFERE IN YOUR LIFE, THEY ARE, AT THE VERY LEAST, IRRITATING

—She's away.

—When do you expect her back?

—Do you really think that's any of your business?

This time he had gone too far. He's got some nerve, sticking his nose into my personal life. Though of course to him it's no big deal. He looks at things differently. I realize I hate this man not for his insolent attitudes, but for what he makes me see in myself.

Inside my head: a small, almost imperceptible movement—the brown blob. The brown is separate, disconnected, it has nothing to do with the green part. It's as though it's resisting connection, though some relation must exist, since one seems to emerge from the other. My uneasiness is becoming oppressive, it's knocked the wind out of me.

Piano music, out of tune, in the middle of the afternoon. I regain control, almost shaking free of the paralysis—I can do this at will now, instead of depending as I used to on some remote and unknown mechanism in my brain. The *Sonata Pathétique*. When I first met Adelaide she was learning to play the piano; she practiced for hours on end.

She dreamed of becoming a concert pianist, she would specialize in Beethoven. So many facets of Adelaide disappeared with time. And I didn't see it happening, I stood by as parts of her evaporated. I remember her hands on the piano—so white, such slender fingers, her nails chipped and splitting. It was inevitable.

She spent all day in the kitchen, hands submerged in detergent, in and out of the washing machine. We like our house clean, quiet, everything in its place. Adelaide had created the perfect nest for us, and as she arranged all the pieces that made it what it was, she would tell me her dream.

Once in a while when I'd come home sick in the middle of the afternoon (I've always had stomach problems, it's this synthetic food) or when I'd get off early because of a *coup d'état* (they were frequent), I would surprise her at practice. I could hear the piano from out in the hallway.

The *Pathétique*, over and over. It was an obsession. In the beginning I confess I felt sorry for her—it was obviously a piece that Adelaide would never be able to play. Not well. Not master. Not like the great pianists; probably not even as well as the mediocre ones. Her performance would remain, what shall we say: reasonable.

I've always wondered: do most people have a sense of their own limitations? A limit which perhaps functions as a protection, a shield against the perception that they will never go beyond a certain point? If not, surely there would be general despair. I found this an interesting idea—and maybe the answer was right there in front of me.

But of course I never discussed it with Adelaide. Sharing such thoughts with her would have been a condemnation, a judgment, would have reduced her to merely a shrewd housewife, capable of creating in the midst of this chaotic city a refuge stopped in time, outside of everything, like a bird lost in space.

So whenever I came home I was cautious, watchful.

She invariably heard me coming, she could detect the slightest noise in time to close the piano, put something on the record player, and pretend to be dusting the record collection. Hundreds of LP's, all classical. Adelaide never admitted that she had been playing the piano.

Sometimes, after dinner, I'd open the piano, gently finger the keys, and ask her to play a little something for me. She always reacted first with surprise; then I saw the hidden pleasure in her eyes. I sincerely wanted her to play for me! Though it's true that moments like these were few.

—I don't feel like it, I'm tired.

—Just pick something out and play, anything. You know how I like *Night on Bald Mountain*.

—No, Souza, look at my fingers, how stiff they are. I'll never be able to play.

—Just give it a try, come on, do it for me. It's been such a long day, so many people coming by to talk politics and all, my head is exploding.

—No Souza, forget it, my fingers just won't cooperate.

I'd leave the piano open; the next morning it would be closed. I knew she got up in the night, she sat for hours on the piano bench, her hands sweeping the keyboard without touching it. Silent study, practice without sound, maybe so she wouldn't wake me, who knows. I feel guilty just thinking about it! And I should, shouldn't I?

To a certain extent it was me who stifled her, remaining so distant, instead of trying to help her overcome the obstacles. Why couldn't a housewife be a pianist? I didn't realize it meant so much to her; to me it was nothing more than an occasional distraction. She'd learned to play like any number of girls of her generation.

And she abandoned it gradually as the years passed and she matured. Until the night she sat down and played for real. I woke up sweating, the sheets and pillow were drenched. I got up and went to the living room where

164

Adelaide was pounding the keys furiously. She saw me come into the room. She kept on playing.

The music was terrifying, incredibly intense. Sounds which literally hurt. Adelaide was sweating too, maybe more than I was. Maybe those days and years of misunderstanding, nerves, emptiness just exploded inside her.

That's the last image I have of Adelaide, like an old movie, in sepia, with odd movements, a bit off rhythm. The next morning I found her asleep on the sofa. I made all sorts of noise but she didn't stir. Maybe she was faking. When I came home three days later, she was gone.

The piano I hear now is not a memory. The sound comes from two flights up, it's an old man who lives alone. He plays poorly—even I, with my tin ear, can hear how he's messing up the melody. Such an obsolete instrument, an anachronism. Appropriate only for someone from another epoch, someone who believes in the resurrection.

The old man never leaves his apartment. They've tried to get him out several times, to take him to Isolation and give the apartment to someone else, but it didn't work. He must have some protection, family or close friends in the System. No one ever comes to see him, though. He just plays the piano, any hour of the day or night. Sometimes when it's very late you can hear the neighbors' windows open and close in irritation.

At least he's got something to believe in, and he certainly throws himself into it. I only wish I could settle into something like that, instead of always finding myself in quicksand—scared to death that I've jumped in, yet terrified that someone will throw me a rope and pull me back out. Where do I look for values, for something to situate me? Values. That's a joke.

I'm afraid of struggling naively with good and evil, right and wrong, without being able to comprehend that the concepts themselves have changed. How can you know where you stand with people so distant from one another, in the absence of newspapers, with libraries inaccessible? I responded to the feeling of being lost by marginalizing myself without even noticing it.

There must have been a revolution in human thought during the years I've been isolating myself. Or being isolated. I = everyone. That's an important thing to remember, to know, if you're interested in thinking about the universe, in rethinking it, I should say, in figuring out how these modifications relate to man. Identifying man's new image, that should be my objective.

Maybe that would help me find my place, anyway. I = everyone. A concrete idea would give me something to lean on instead of all this shifting around. Right now I'm adrift in a sea of perplexity, wanting to believe that certain concepts, old as they are, are still valid. Because they affirm mankind, or at least mark our existence.

The incoherent digressions of a man asphyxiated by the heat. And the lack of air, too. It's been like this for days now. Just a little while ago I looked out the window, it's so bright and hazy everything's out of focus. A very strange brilliance, unnatural. As if everything were on fire, rocks, windowpanes, roof tiles.

The aging professor hallucinates, under threat of losing his house. Not that old, I guess. Age generally brings inflexibility, and here am I: accepting everything, intransigently. Meanwhile getting myself ready, open, receptive. Not that I know why. Extreme heat fries your brains, I've said it before. Or was it Tadeu? No matter.

More knocking on the door, the bell ringing insistently. "Here they are again," yells the man-who-eats-candy, bringing me back to reality—my living room, the pathetic piano. The man-who-sits-at-the-head-of-the-table says: "Go get the gun." Not me—I don't even know where the trigger is!

—You answer it, you're the man of the house.

—And what if it's more people asking for food?

166

—Get out of the way and let us handle it.

—I don't want you killing anyone else!

—What are you talking about? We didn't kill anyone.

—Just about.

—Look, sometimes there's no other way. It's us or them.

—I know, I know, but why...

—Hurry up and answer the door, or they'll break it down.

It was the neighbor-with-the-bleached-blonde hair, heading up a group of other residents, four or five of them. Middle-aged people with pallid faces, sunken eyes, breathing heavily. I recognized one of them, he was always walking around with a mask on and occasionally collapsed in the halls. Suffered from a lack of oxygen or something.

The woman craned her neck to see inside, not even bothering to hide her curiosity. I flung the door all the way open and stepped out of the way so she could get a good look. My attitude intrigued her, I could tell, and she didn't hesitate to take advantage of the chance. She stared at the three men standing in a line in the living room, defiant, guarded, ready for action.

—If your wife could see this. . . . What a disgrace.

—What disgrace?

—It's obvious the place is a complete mess, plus these bums traipsing in and out all day. Look at them, they look like bandits, all we need now is for a bunch of blacks to move into the building.

—Don't you worry about my apartment, everything's in order here.

—Some order. It's a shambles, I can see from here. Would you like me to do a little straightening up for you? After all, your wife always kept things so spic-and-span.

—Why is it you've decided to meddle in my affairs?

—Your wife was a good friend of mine.

—That's a joke—she detested you!

167

—How can you say that?

—It's true, she hated your guts, she couldn't even stand the sight of you.

—Don't be ridiculous, you don't know anything. Your wife and I were like this! (The cliché gesture)

—Look, why don't you just go back upstairs to your own apartment, okay?

—Are you throwing me out, Mr. Souza? *You,* one of the most prominent residents in the building? Everyone respects you, the famous professor. That's why we can't understand what's going on here. If all of us were to open our doors to these people, it wouldn't be long before the mobs outside the city found out about it, they'd be all over us.

—They need somewhere to live, too.

—You say some dangerous things, Mr. Souza. Can you imagine the chaos if those people from the encampments invaded the city? What would happen? And what about food?

—Even if they don't invade the city, what's going to happen, tell me that!

—We get along as best we can. The government's keeping the situation under control. The System must remain intact.

—Fine. And now why don't you go home? I'd like to close the door and be left in peace.

—Not so fast. We're from the Security Committee, and it's our job to monitor the well-being of the entire community of residents. These men are just going to have to leave your apartment, that's all there is to it.

—This is my home. I'm the one who gives the orders around here.

—To an extent you're right, Mr. Souza, but each building's resident committee has the ultimate responsibility in that regard, for things like security, you know. I'm speaking for all of us.

—That's right. We've heard you're being coerced into letting these guys stay here, we can help you get rid of them.

168

—Coerced, my foot. These men are here because I'm letting them stay with me, they're my friends. And they're not going anywhere.

—I can't believe you've got friends like this, Mr. Souza.

This last was from the guy with the oxygen mask who was always stumbling and falling in the hall. A ridiculous figure. I had had it. "Would you excuse me for just a moment," I said calmly, and headed for the kitchen. While they waited, perplexed, I put on a pan of water to boil, and a few minutes later I was back with the pan in my hand. The commission had edged closer and closer and was now practically inside the living room.

—It's time for you to leave.

—We need to talk.

—I'm afraid there's really nothing for us to talk about. So please leave.

As the bleached blonde moved toward me, I heaved the steaming water straight at her. She let out a scream that must have been heard around the corner. Especially with such pervasive silence as a backdrop. The man who had been standing behind her glared at me, so shocked he was sputtering. My friend-with-the-mask said:

—You'll pay for this dearly, Mr. Souza. We're going to have to call the Civil Guards.

—You're going to have some lawsuit on your hands, added another.

—Send me the bill from the clinic. I'm pressing a suit of my own—invasion of privacy. This is private property, in case you'd forgotten.

—In our capacity as members of the building commission we have the right to enter apartments when we deem it necessary. You know we do. And in this case we deem it necessary, no doubt about it.

—Sure, come on in, I'll just go heat up a little more water . . .

They left. The woman was crying, clasping her hands to her chest. I hope I burned that white cockroach's skin to a crisp. Can you believe it, a friend of my wife's!

169

"We were like this." Then I thought: what if they *were* friends? I'm at work all day, Adelaide could have told me one thing and done another. It was her right, after all, to do as she liked.

It's come to this. Thirty-some years together, it's hard to believe I'm thinking this way all of a sudden. I used to complain that we had no secrets, no surprises, and now I'm completely thrown off guard, in doubt about everything. Whatever happened to the solidarity we felt toward each other?

The idea of a lawsuit scares me. If the bleached blonde decides to press charges, I'm in trouble. Not right away, of course. Things like that take time, lawyers are expensive. There are inevitable delays. The de-bureau-cratization which began in the late seventies came to a screeching halt just a few years later.

Lost in the very whirlwind of decrees that were aimed at cutting down on excessive paperwork. So at least I know I won't have to worry about it right away, unless her husband is waiting for me out in the hall someday. It's happened before—people taking the law, or lack of it, into their own hands. The System refers to it as Personal Problems Resolved Between Parties.

A convenient name for it. A convenient out, too, for the organs of security. We are our own police. But we must take care of our business cautiously, because excessive violence can lead to Large-Scale Intervention. And that means curtains for everyone involved.

We waited. Silence in the corridor, silence in the city. A strange silence, because we knew there were noises out there being stifled. Every once in a while the elevator creaked, carrying a load of chattering old people. After a certain time of night, no more sounds at all. As if there were a curfew.

—They're up to no good, you can see it in their faces, said the man-who-sat-at-the-head-of-the-table.

—They're busybodies. I never trusted them, they're always dying of curiosity.

170

—No, it's more than that. They want to throw you out so they can take over the apartment.

—That's ridiculous, what are you talking about? This apartment is mine, I've been here twenty years.

—Holy innocence, as my mother would say. Sometimes I get the impression you don't even exist, you're so innocent. I'm surprised you've survived this long. You must be hibernating, on ice all this time. Those people have their eyes on your apartment, can't you see? How can you think it's just a question of gossip, nosiness? They're looking for a way to get their hands on this big, comfortable place.

—I've got legal claim to this apartment, guarantees.

—Legal claims, guarantees, what nonsense. No one is guaranteed anything. Not even life. Who's getting bent out of shape about all the people out there dying, disappearing, who's worrying about why or where?

—Have you forgotten about my nephew?

—I know about your nephew . . . they don't. The best thing would be to get him on this right away before they get someone higher up involved, because then you can forget it.

—You're too suspicious.

—And you're not suspicious enough. I've seen too much, that's all. Do you have any idea how much an apartment like this is worth nowadays? There are people out there who'd be willing to pay any amount of money, food, coupons, *anything,* just to sublet your back room. You could make thirty, forty coupons a month, at least.

—And you three are installed here gratis, how about that? You just took over. You're not the least bit worried about me, my property, you're just afraid of being pushed out yourselves.

—You bet. We did take over. And we're ready to stand our ground, to defend ourselves, if necessary.

—You admit it . . .

—Sure. So what? Do you think I'd rather be a guest in the Pauper Encampments?

171

—But just invading my home like this, it's not right.

—That subject's getting a little tired, you know? Would you like to discuss the theory of personal property one more time, is that it? Ownership, these days, is a gas, a liquid, something which dissolves, slips through your fingers. So keep your eyes open, those people are going to be all over us. They're going to lay siege to the apartment, I've seen it happen before, upstairs. We'd better be prepared. Is the barber a friend of yours?

—I think so. You never know.

—See if he can find out what they're up to. Offer him some water coupons in exchange, some canned goods.

—He wants some favor from my nephew, I know that much.

—Okay, use that to our advantage, get him to find out what he can.

—All this seems so neurotic . . .

—It is. What can you do? Everybody has to take care of himself. Tomorrow we're going out to get more supplies.

—There's hardly room for anything else.

—We'll make room.

—How?

—We could get rid of some of this furniture. Who needs it, anyway?

—I do. It's mine. What do you think?!

—I think it's in the way.

—I've spent my whole life with these things, I need them.

—That life you're talking about was something else entirely. It doesn't exist anymore, it's over. And we're going to have to get rid of the furniture.

—If it goes, you go.

—Stop the tough-man act. We can't fight over every little thing. It's obvious that to get along with each other we all have to make concessions.

—Up until now the only one making concessions has been me. I've given up my house, my food, my privacy, and now you want my furniture.

—Don't make such a big deal about it, we'll leave the beds and a couple of chairs. Who needs the rest? Why does it mean so much to you?

—These things are my memories. The knowledge that I lived.

—You're alive, isn't that enough? Memories, bah!

—Life isn't just from this day forward, you know. What about everything that went before?

—Memories. You're the last person in this whole country to still be talking about memories. What good are they?

—They give you a vision of yourself. Of what you were and what you're becoming.

—Only if the world were still following a normal cycle. You're a history professor, or were, you should know that. For centuries and centuries, historical and social coordinates functioned as expected. But for the last thirty years everything has been out of synch. The acceleration of history changed everything, the dynamics are totally different now, the dynamics are everything, total conception—or else transforming constantly, minute by minute.

—This new order has a name. It's called chaos.

—No, that's too strong a word. Chaos implies complete disorganization, anarchy. This is confusion, but not total chaos. Maybe *disorder* would be the right word. A change of givens. A disordering of facts. Like someone taking apart a motor and spreading the parts on the ground in apparent disorder.

—Except with the motor the pieces can be put back in their precise places.

—Unless the mechanic invents a new motor. Which is completely possible. Something that works in an entirely different way. And the thing is that the world, unlike a motor, isn't static.

—This is all just talk. You're not laying a finger on my furniture.

It's suffocating in here. I'm tense. I look at the thick layer of dust on top of the piano, the photograph of

Adelaide. And I feel like crying. I'm a monster. What have I done to find my wife? Nothing. Not a damn thing. And yet, day by day, I feel like I'm finding her inside myself. I don't want her to turn into a memory.

## TENDERNESS REAPPEARS IN A HAND-TINTED PHOTOGRAPH, AND ROOSTERS, THOUGH THEY DON'T EXIST ANYMORE ARE STILL CROWING

Looking at Adelaide's picture makes me feel lonely. I bet my friends here would die laughing if I told them that. And the one who seems to be in charge would find all sorts of arguments to prove to me that solitude is not an appropriate complaint these days. He'd say we're all alone, and no one else is complaining. Just me.

So maybe he's right, but I'm not like everybody else. My solitude weighs on me. Think about something else, look at the world around you, get it through your head that it's impossible nowadays to have subjective feelings. That's what he would tell me. He seems like a practical man, concrete in his proposals. Pure speculation, of course.

But I understand why he wants to eliminate memories. There must be something in his past, something irretrievable he left behind, whose loss causes him pain. To do away with suffering he did away with memory. An apparently simple surgical operation, the only remedy. Except that I can't pull it off, everything's too alive inside me. Too agitated.

Adelaide is there somewhere, hidden in her own fear. As time went by she got more and more frightened. One day she asked me not to go to work, not to leave her alone. She couldn't explain why, as soon as I closed the door, she always went into a panic.

Why was it so impossibly difficult for her to get control of herself? She'd close all the doors and windows, and not just to keep out the heat, but because the people around her were total strangers, complete unknowns. "I never see a single familiar face in the supermarket any- more—where are our neighbors, our friends, our rela- tives?"

Adelaide, too, had noticed that the crowds in the city were growing daily. We discussed this observation calmly, not really realizing what was going on. Proof that the days were slipping away from us. I wasn't worried about where all the people were coming from, or why. Or who they were.

But the streets were getting remarkably crowded, more impassable by the day. The first real circulation problems were developing. And Adelaide was right—all of a sud- den the faces I was used to seeing every day at almost the exact same time began disappearing. As if into thin air.

Staring into this closed, compact mass of people was like staring into fog, half-light. We walked shoulder-to- shoulder, face-to-face, but without looking at each other. Instead we looked from side to side, unfocused, or at the ground. And then the deformed and bald people began appearing. People missing limbs, people with their eye- balls hanging out.

Only a few at first. The police arrested them, took them away. But the number steadily increased; they seemed to be multiplying. I remember a comic strip I read when I was a kid about certain creatures called schmoos which adored human beings, practically lived to be petted, and reproduced like jackrabbits.

For some reason that long-lost story from childhood comes to mind when I think about the days when the blind or bald or deformed people began appearing. The Civil Guards did what they could to keep them out, even going so far as to install the electronic barriers which to this day separate the city and the Pauper Encampments. I couldn't tell Adelaide about all this. It would only have added to her fear—which was instinctual, because she really didn't see much of what was going on. She rarely went out, and our neighborhood was still one of the safer ones.

Now I understand our long, silent nights for what they were: stupefaction. We lay in bed holding hands, staring at the ceiling, and listened to the noise from down below in the street. People dragged themselves along on all fours, moaning, screaming, raging, begging. The Guards would come beat them, click on the handcuffs, and cart them off.

We didn't look out the window. Not out of pity, but pure fear. We were terrified, just like all the other residents of the building, of all the buildings on the block. The next day there would be bloodstains and pus on the sidewalk. Or stuff that looked like dried flour and water which we supposed was the scaly skin of some poor unfortunate.

Adelaide just couldn't look at it, it was nauseating— lots of people threw up right there on the sidewalk. But no one mentioned it. Not a word. Just a conspiratorial silence filling us with guilt. After all, we were protected behind closed doors. We thought we were secure.

Having no one with whom to share my anxiety is what really makes me feel lonely. A self-centered attitude, I know, but I can't do anything about it; that's how I feel. Years ago, I don't even know how many, sharing was a real possibility. Pain and happiness were not solely individual. You could dare to use the word *community*.

We were all in it together, we said, we could count on each other, and that made everything easier, more bearable. All you had to do was ring someone's doorbell, run out to the front gate, pick up the telephone—people shared the good and the bad. Adelaide noticed the loss of all this long before I did.

In the past we hadn't felt so solitary, buried behind four walls, all the locked doors, empty hallways. Noises from outside were normal. People could look each other in the eye without flinching, without their tongues getting dry, hearts beating wildly.

Mortality statistics came across my desk as a matter

of course. I always examined the causes with the pleasure of a necrophiliac. Of course these statistics only represented the deaths that had been recorded, those which took place in patrolled areas. What happened Beyond the Pale was unknown, purposefully ignored.

Many people died from heart problems—heart attacks, hardening of the arteries, all sorts of cardiological complications were listed as "cause of death." Or was it a pack of lies? Camouflage. And why was it that people only twenty years old, sometimes younger, were having heart attacks? It was all pretty hard to believe. On the other hand, what good did it do not to believe?

One afternoon, before we were married (though we had already bought a house), Adelaide and I went out window-shopping. It was Saturday afternoon, the stores were closed, no one on the streets. Strolling happily along, we met a photographer who had installed himself on some street corner and was sitting there with such a long face that we decided to let him take our picture. One with our arms around each other, one kissing, and one close-up of Adelaide. Suddenly full of ambition, the photographer adjusted the angle of Adelaide's chin, tilting it this way and that like dramatic poses advertising a professional's studio.

Though the pictures were ready on the spot, the man asked for extra time so he could hand-tint the portrait of Adelaide. Her mouth came out too red, in my opinion, but he managed to get her brown hair and eyes just right. It turned out to be our favorite photograph of her, maybe because we were so happy together that afternoon. Under a favorable aspect, astrologically speaking.

For years whenever we passed that spot we saw the same photographer, always looking dejected. That was his way, either to lure prospective clients out of pity, or because it was his general attitude. We never had another photo taken, I guess because we liked that first one so well, it was exact. Just as we wanted to be, always.

Looking at the photograph now, I realize how steady the man's hand was, and how acute his powers of observation. No one ever again succeeded in capturing that serene look of Adelaide's on film. But that's the way she was, delicate, sensitive, without being passive. At least not in the first years.

Could it be that I've changed that much too? Or was it the situation which changed? Adelaide saw the world differently than I did; she appreciated tranquility, stability, she worried a lot about security. The world had solid values—it would have been difficult to change them, but you could accept them, secure that they would last at least a lifetime.

And by the time things changed, we had been prepared, people were conditioned; it wasn't as if everything exploded suddenly scaring us out of our wits. Things changed the way fashions, fads do, they just appear quietly out of nowhere and become part of the present. Like when it became *de rigueur* to wear something leather to local holiday festivals, then something blue. Or like when people took to burning blessed straw to make the rain stop.

Simple customs, ceremonies, rituals, habits. Things that lasted centuries, passing from grandfather to father to son to grandson and on. Spontaneous gestures, popular sayings, foods. They endured. They gave us a feeling of solidarity. Made serenity possible, because they themselves provided a certain continuity.

That same afternoon we bought a picture frame, very simple, made of plain, unvarnished wood. The space was larger than the photo, so Adelaide inserted a white background which by now has yellowed. The colors in the photograph haven't faded, though, they're the same clear pastels. Serene.

I miss her hand on my shoulder. I miss the slightly scandalized reprimand at dinner when I make too much noise with my soup. Instead of *Pathétique* and classical recordings, there's this invader's transistor radio playing music from the outback, cowboy music. Those three are planning to clear this place out completely, I've got to save the portrait of Adelaide.

I'm surprised at myself, suddenly caring so much for that photograph, rebelling against the idea they might take it away from me. Adelaide has disappeared, and I sit back and indulge in philosophical meanderings, angry at the idea of losing my home, my furniture, yet insensible until now to my largest loss. Why did it take me this long?

Maybe it hasn't been all that long, after all. I have no notion of hours, days, weeks. How much time elapsed, for example, between discovering the hole in my hand and Adelaide leaving me? I don't know. It probably doesn't matter. Tadeu Pereira (I must look him up again) is right: it's not the days and months that count anymore, but the situations and events.

The sun's coming up. I spent the whole night on the sofa, I don't even know if I slept or if I've been ruminating all night long. I slip the portrait of Adelaide in the dresser drawer between ironed shirts, socks, and underwear. The city is still quiet. Nothing from out in the hall, either. Have they given up?

—A truck will be coming by tonight. You've got all day to sort through your things, said the man who seemed to be in charge.

—Just like that, so soon? I thought I had a few days.

—There's a war on, my friend, we can't waste time.

The kitchen was total chaos, Adelaide would die if she saw it this way. It bothers me, this business of sorting out furniture, choosing what to keep. I want to keep all of it—I'm a prisoner of tables, chairs, piano, knickknacks, pictures, bureaus, end tables, bookshelves, plant stands.

Somehow connected to every useless item that does its part to fill each room. The empty flowerpots on top of the plant stands. Adelaide never allowed plastic plants, she hated them, no matter how perfect they looked. The ones with "natural" scents were even worse.

Only the very rich have real plants. They're sold in art galleries, for incredibly high prices. Plants are worth more now than paintings were years ago. At the big auctions they trade Picassos for ferns, Porinaris for potted palms. Duke Lee for geraniums. Oiticica for dumb canes.

There are plant collectors, plant dealers. Air-conditioned greenhouses where the plants are cultivated. The entrepreneurs supply the water. The privileged few. Because anyone caught wasting water is a goner. Isolation for sure, and that's fatal. There are some people, evidently, who are above the law.

Even though it was synthetic, the coffee smelled good. Nothing in this country is more highly developed than the industry which creates artificial aromas. It's a shame they don't use the technology to get rid of the terrible smell which dominates this city most of the time. (Maybe they tried and it didn't work?) Meanwhile, the coffee has practically no taste, it's all in the aroma.

The doorbell rings, and the man-who-sits-at-the-head-of-the-table goes to answer it. He's gone for some time. Muffled voices. Then he's back with an ironic smile and a piece of paper. He doesn't have to say a thing, obviously it was the neighbors again. What are they up to now? He hands me the paper.

—A subpoena.

—For what?

—To appear at the District.

—To do what?

—To file a deposition. It says we're supposed to bring our Employment Identification Cards, to prove we've got jobs.

—And if we don't?

—How should I know? All I know is we're not going. We leave here, and those neighbors will break down the door and make themselves at home.

—What about the subpoena?

—They must issue thousands of those things. People denouncing each other left and right. They send the forms out, sure, but they can't possibly keep track of all of them. Now it's a matter of luck. The advantage of chaos is that it means the absence of control in all areas, which in this case works to our advantage. The guy who sends

180

out the subpoenas is paid to sit at his typewriter and churn them out, that's all.

—That may be, but don't you think our friendly neighbors will be all over him? They'll do it for free, the government doesn't even need inspectors.

—It's not the same. If you're not an inspector you're not authorized to inspect, supervise. Each department operates within its specific jurisdiction.

—But you can buy the inspectors, can't you?

—Of course, that's practically the only way they function. You buy them, someone else offers a little more. The more you got, the less you cry, as the saying goes.

—This whole thing scares the pants off me. You just never know with official things like this.

—Everything scares you. Relax, old man, easy does it.

—I don't know, things were okay for a while, almost normal. But suddenly I don't know where I am. I'm nervous, that's all.

—Sure, I understand. You're terrified. You and all your kind. When the big calamities were going on, nobody got upset, nobody lifted a finger. It's now you're worried.

—You're always preaching at me. As if you were so perfect. Save it, okay?

What a bore. The keeper of "truth," always spitting out rules to live by. That's why I can't stand this guy, not because he took over my house. He's got a theory to fit every situation, a hypothesis, a formula. He knows the answer, he makes his pronouncement. And I'm stupid enough to admit I'm confused—I listen to what he says and doubt myself.

This house is so full of stuff—where do I start? I wander around looking everything over, the stacked-up furniture, the mountains of canned goods. Bags, boxes, cartons. I was intimate with everything in this house: pins, towels, soap, toothpicks, socks, sheets. Piece for piece. The wicker trunk.

The trunk! I'd forgotten all about it. So many years

181

of our lives hidden away in that trunk, preserved. I have
a passion for saving things. So does Adelaide—we got
along well in that regard. The trunk must be in the maid's
room, buried under the piles of calendars. But what about
the men they locked up in there?

I stand with my ear to the door. Not a sound, not even
breathing. Could they have died? One was badly wounded
to begin with, and it's so crowded in there, maid's rooms
are about the size of solitary jail cells. Stifling, pitch-
dark. And as far as I knew, no one had brought them
any food.

They must be sleeping, it's still early. Or passed out.
The key's half fallen out of the lock, maybe they dis-
lodged it trying to escape. I hesitate, unsure of myself.
Then I fit the key back into the hole, carefully, sound-
lessly. So far so good. Fingers crossed, I turn it gently
in the lock. Just a dry click which makes my backbone
tingle. I stand there, my hand glued to the knob, paralyzed.

Just as I decide I've waited long enough, a rooster
crows. Distraction. I come to my senses. Wait, that can't
be a rooster—impossible. (How long *has* it been since
I heard a rooster crow?) Must have been a record, they
sell all kinds of sound effects, voices, animal noises. Just
some nostalgia nut who likes to turn on his stereo at
dawn. Artificial or not, I let the lulling, harmonic sound
of the rooster wash over me. If I give my imagination
free rein, the memories will explode. All sorts of conflicting images will tumble around me.

I open the door as if it were the most decisive act of
my life. More decisive than when I faced the examining
committee with my doctoral thesis. Or when they called
me to Administration to notify me of my compulsory
retirement. Or when I went to the Political Police to sign
my Rebellion Card. Or when we saw the ship off.

Even more decisive than when I discovered Adelaide
was gone. In none of these situations had I felt the kind
of fear I'm feeling now. It's as if my life depended on

this small action—yes, a matter of life and death. What am I talking about—me and my well-nourished imagination.

There, it's open. Nothing happens. The men are slumped on the floor. The wall is covered with blood. Ay—but there's an extra one! An older man with white hair, lying facedown. Nauseated, I turn the body over. The barber. Stabbed to death.

## IN THE KITCHEN SOUZA BECOMES HYPNOTIZED BY THE FASCINATING MYSTERY OF A POT OF BOILING WATER WITH AN EGG IN IT

I just couldn't take it in. I was paralyzed, between the brown blob dancing in front of my eyes and the stab wound that cut across the body. I simply could not believe what I was seeing. Why had they killed the barber? And when? How had they sneaked the body in here?

The barber was a harmless sort, he kept to his barbershop and didn't meddle in other people's lives. Whatever he knew about the goings-on in the building he heard from the older residents who would go down to the barbershop just to have a chat, as old people do. It couldn't have been one of them, they wouldn't have the strength to do this.

I'm no expert, but it looked to me as though the barber had put up a fight. His shirt was completely torn open to reveal several puncture wounds that were smeared with dried blood. If he'd been shot, the holes would probably be rounder, smaller, I reasoned. It had to be someone quite strong, decisive, and cold-blooded. A professional.

Not the work of some golden-ager—old people are emotional, a scene like this would be too much for them. Says who? The things that come into my head! It's strange, though; that the barber's body is in my back room bothers me a lot more than that he was killed like this. But it's also sort of intriguing to have him hidden here.

Stupid! Of course it was one of my three friends. But when did they drag him in here? While I was dozing? I'm such a light sleeper, though, the slightest noise wakes me up. And I was on the sofa, which would be right in their path. Maybe they drugged me?

Well, it won't do any good to stand here thinking about it, I'd better come right out and ask them. And we've got to get this body out of here, it's stiff already, won't be long before it starts to smell. Contaminate the whole house. No, I'm not crazy about the idea of living with a dead body. This is getting to be too much.

I no longer feel paralyzed, but the brown blob lasts a final few seconds. It's not stationary, I'm quite sure now, there's something moving inside it. I can see more of a shape every day. If I'm patient long enough, maybe I'll eventually see it clearly enough to make out what it is, and why.

So many things to figure out these days, trying to understand all the confusion around me and, at the same time, struggle with my own inner problems. If I had the courage, I'd see a doctor. Courage and money. Who can afford what they charge these days? And besides, they take so many tests, far too many tests as far as I'm concerned.

Once you put yourself in their hands, there's no escaping. And of course no doctor would ever get to the bottom of what's wrong with me. I'd be passed from specialist to specialist, leaving all my blood, feces, and urine behind in their laboratories. I'd be sucked dry in more ways than one. And then comes the fabulous round of pharmacies.

That's why people avoid going to the doctor. Plus, if the doctor can't find a definitive problem, he sends you to the shrink. And that's curtains: the primary function of psychiatrists is to convince you that you are incapable of taking care of yourself, i.e., that you're crazy. Without so much as a second thought, you're pronounced insane.

Crazy people are sent to Mental Isolation where, as soon as a patient is checked in, his material goods are automatically transferred to the Isolation Treasury ostensibly to pay for his treatment. So you can see why there's what amounts to a head-hunt in this city. The shrinks are brilliant, they even manage to get the rest of us into the act.

If you put the finger on someone who is mentally deficient, you are rewarded with extra water coupons or some other type of privilege. So you understand why people go through the streets as if they're walking on eggshells, afraid to talk to anyone, and why they avoid so much as making sudden gestures or raising their voices.

Any suspicious behavior or deviation from the norm could be seen as a symptom of a disorder, and here come the psychiatrists, drooling like mad dogs. People would rather not even go out. You never know. All of a sudden you sneeze funny and it's bye-bye.

Meanwhile, right now what I feel most like doing is running out into the street, screaming and jumping up and down. The shock of this man stabbed to death, abandoned in my back room. Oh, Adelaide, it's a good thing you're gone, you wouldn't be able to take all this. Not that I can, not that anyone could, but we have to face whatever's in front of us, our daily life, our rice and beans.

How many years have I been saying to myself: this is my lot, my particular quota, I've got to learn to live with as best I can. Everyone thinks that way, so things just go on as they go on. Years ago I thought that if one could manage to institute reforms at the grass-roots level, a general revolution would be possible.

Each person operating within his own particular group, and all the small daily reforms would add up to change. Of course there would need to be a general direction to follow, something that would give unity to the movement. I thought and thought about it, but I didn't do a damn thing. Too worried about surviving, supporting the family, the house.

I worked hard for a house, I accepted the trade-down to an apartment, I fought to get a job, I accepted what they gave me, scared to death of having no future. And look where I ended up: in the non-present. Looking back, I see that I lived in a non-past. With terrifying results.

The man who lived a non-past and then fell into a non-present, that man doesn't exist. What an odd and crazy idea. I don't exist. Here I am, I can touch myself, grab myself by the hand. I think, I consider, I conclude. I look at my whole self, but there's no reflection, no image.

It's bizarre: because I managed to think, I don't exist. There is no me. I was not and I will not be. And meanwhile, here I am. I'd like to see that wise guy's face, the one who always sits at the head of the table, when I hit him with this new train of logic. What will he have to say to that?

In the kitchen, I find the three of them having coffee and crackers. Their teeth gnash the dry crackers with a uniform, monotonous noise. It's the only thing to be heard besides water boiling on the stove. Then I see the egg in the pan, and I'm thunderstruck. An egg. A much more fascinating discovery than any cadaver.

An egg floating in a pan of boiling water. These men must be very powerful. My nephew must be a good deal more influential than I had imagined, and I haven't been taking advantage of it. A magnificent white egg, twirling around in the bubbling water. I can't contain myself, this spectacle is hypnotizing.

There's nothing simpler than an egg. And nothing more impossible. And yet there it is, I could reach out and touch it, feel the heat. What a comfort, what a sense of security. This egg instills in me the certainty that something lasts. The egg is a truth. I feel like I've got myself back again. And at the same time the egg is a total mystery, a mystery which gives me pleasure.

186

—There's a dead body in the back room, I said to the man-who-always-sits-at-the-head-of-the-table.

—Oh, did one of those poor devils kick off?

—No, one of you killed the barber from downstairs.

—Mr. Souza, how could you even suggest such a thing?

—It had to be one of you. Who else would leave a dead body in there?

—Beats me.

—Stop being so flip for a minute, will you?

—I'm not. It's just that I really don't know what you're talking about, it's news to me. Let's go take a look...

—I already did, and I didn't like what I saw.

—Murder is serious business, my friend. Why is it you're so sure one of us killed him? Maybe he just fell down dead outside the door and we did the only decent thing and brought him inside. Which, incidentally, is exactly what happened. He knocked on the door real early this morning moaning for help, bleeding something awful. We carried him into the kitchen, but he died before he was able to tell us what happened.

—Oh, that's nice, yes, good to see you've got quite an imagination. So why didn't you wake me up?

—What for? Could you have saved him? Since when are you a doctor?

—This is my house, how many times do I have to tell you? What if I hadn't looked in the maid's room? The body would start to rot in a few days and stink up the whole place.

—Take it easy, a smell can't kill you. If smells could kill, there'd be no one left alive in this town, right?

—This conversation is madness. There's a dead man in the back room, that's what we've got to deal with here.

—We'll take care of it, don't worry, it's all planned. Just don't rush things.

—What's all planned? You mean there's some oper-ation going on here which I know nothing about, and it includes murder? Great, just great. It's too much, really, I have no control over the insanity going on in my own house.

—Slow down, man, keep cool. We were going to tell you all about it, we were just waiting for the right time. And by tonight it will be all taken care of.

—What do you mean, taken care of?

—Leave that to us.

—Every time I do, something else goes wrong.

The egg was bubbling loudly, the man-who-ate-candy looked at his watch. Must be his egg, then, or at least he's the one in charge of cooking it. He glances at me, sees my look of amazement, but betrays not the least hint of reaction. Not a smile, not an offer, no impulse whatsoever to share.

Oh well, it's his egg, he can do whatever he wants with it. I've seen so many things I can't have, I'm getting used to it. I'm not about to get bitter now, over just one more, and such a small one at that. But I just can't get the image of the barber's lifeless body out of my head. An obsession which I begin to understand: death is very close by, all we can do is try to escape it.

So I'm mad at the barber as well as at these three. They all make me think about something I've been trying to push away, fight off, forget. In battle, people must struggle to abstract the idea of death, even with bodies falling all around them. The only way to survive.

The sight of that cadaver forces me to admit: I'm on the list too. I could be next. So I want to get him out of here fast, eliminate the thing that's forcing me to be conscious, go back to my cozy isolation. The problem is I can't really be alone, I'll never get rid of these guys. My new family, ha. Whether I like it or not.

The terror I feel with a dead man hidden away in the back room, the other two, wounded, unconscious (I imagine), everything is spinning around in my head. I feel like screaming, heaving myself against the wall, to hell with it. Let these creeps take care of it, let them take over the house. Stupid house just makes me crazy. Why bother to defend it?

I'm always a prisoner to something—people, objects, thoughts. I end up where I end up, like everybody else. The thing to do is to follow Tadeu's example, he's got a good head, and he mentioned a group, people you can talk to. I've got to get out of here, away from these men. I don't even know who they are, they never told me. But then of course I never asked.

—How's the roof on this building? Is it in pretty good shape? asked the man-who-sat-at-the-head-of-the-table.

—Yeah.

—Want to come up and have a look?

Instead of waiting for the elevator, we went up on foot. He took two stairs at a time, I had to ask him to wait for me—what good would it do at this point to have a heart attack? The stairway is filthy, each step covered with layers of black grime, miraculously sticky and slippery at the same time.

My companion doesn't seem to notice, or to mind, the filth, the stink. We feel our way up the stairs in the dark, they never replace burned-out light bulbs any more. The walls are like coals, I expect to see them glowing. It must be brutal out there today. Worse than yesterday, worse than the day before yesterday. And much better than tomorrow.

Sweating, we stop on the twenty-ninth floor and listen to the sounds of plates and pans, a hiss of escaping gas. At least gas is one thing that doesn't have to be rationed, since it's recycled from garbage. God knows we produce enough raw material for that process. Faraway noises, like cannon blasts, or dynamite exploding.

One more flight and we're finally at the top. The door to the roof is locked tight, a rusty padlock and chain. No one's been allowed up here for years. When we first moved in, Adelaide would come up once in a while and find young girls sunbathing. The girls grew up or moved away.

189

The man-who-sat-at-the-head-of-the-table took out a gun. For some reason I never imagined he carried a weapon; I thought he left that to the others. Two shots and the lock flew open. Strange how you get used to all sorts of noise, gunfire sounded almost natural. The door was still jammed. He gave it a swift kick and it opened like in a movie.

The roof was immense, and looked like a desert with all the dust and sand which I suppose was blown here slowly, gradually, over the months and years when there was wind. Broken chairs, a tabletop, heaps of bottles. All sorts of things made of plastic. Indeterminate mounds covered with dust.

We sink in: dust up to our ankles, as we walk we leave deep footprints in the stuff. For a few seconds (one of those rare moments), there's complete silence over the city. Just for an instant, though it seems like an eternity, we're so used to deafening noise.

I consider these patches of silence a real mystery. It's as if they were planned, rehearsed at great length according to a precise program, timed to the millisecond. Everything just stops. Voices, footsteps, screams of orgasm, fistfights, explosions, coughs, throats being cleared, music, scratching noises, crashes, whistles, whispers, laughter.

As if human life itself had ceased to exist. We float free, like the astronauts, those men who suited up to explore space fruitlessly in the sixties. Walking on the moon, kicking through dust deposited there millennia ago.

Here on the roof I feel like the moon, floating in space, isolated from the earth, from the world, ready to begin again. The desert extends in front of me, and in a little while larvae will surely emerge from this dry and trampled dust covering the building, cocoons, amoebas, new species adapting to the sun, the heat, the dryness.

I'm delirious, of course. My sight blurs, the sun beats down on my head, my shirt is soaked. I head for some shade, there's a little shed for the extra roof tiles, though it's locked. The man who seems to be the leader is exploring the roof, stamping his feet, examining the edges. What's he up to now?

—Hey, can we go back down now? I shout. It's too hot.

—Okay, okay, just a minute. I've seen what I wanted to see, I think it's going to be fine, just fine.

—What?

—It can take the weight—it'll be a quick operation.

—Why did you bring me up here?

—To keep me company.

—That's all?

—Why not? You were getting hysterical inside. You need to get out, get a little air. Why don't you go downtown anymore? You've still got a CIRCA, and special permission for the bus.

—I feel shakier in the city than I do at home.

—But your apartment's not a home anymore, you act like it's a prison.

—I like my apartment, I feel good there.

—Look, someone left their clothes on the line.

Undershorts, shirts, a nightgown, a pair of pajamas, hanging on a nylon clothesline. They were completely ragged, and stiff, hanging like stalactites. Whoever put them out to dry must have left in a hurry. Had the person been arrested? Or perhaps just run away. Who can explain mysteries like this. Could even have been simple forgetfulness.

I touched the nightgown, couldn't tell if it was silk, nylon, or cotton. Fossilized clothing, I thought to myself. How many years had it hung here exposed to the weather? The cloth had become fragile, as if dissolving into dust. It left a fine, pale stain on my fingers. The legacy of fossilized fish, birds, animals.

Petrified trees, too. You could study the past, reconstruct eras, just looking at them. Our legacy to future generations: fossilized consumer goods. Clothes, cars, electronic devices, and thousands of other products, useful and useless, the marks of our civilization.

191

Our history summed up right here on this clothesline. All the insanity of the era could be reconstructed from what we leave on our terraces, vacant lots, subway stations, cellars, abandoned apartments, supermarkets in ruins, empty churches. Ah, if the washerwomen of yesteryear could see me raving like this. They'd have left the clothesline full of laundry to rot and fade, they'd giggle to each other: let's help the poor boys out, they'll need a few clues or that'll be the end of history. What would history be without the washerwomen of the past? And I do mean past—handwashing went out with my grandmother.

My friend here and I gaze out over this private desert, then down at the lower buildings. We discover other suspended deserts just like this one. There was a time when the Civil Guards sealed off the roofs all over the city on account of snipers.

In fact, rooftops are still classified Security Areas. We shouldn't be seen up here. But I'm transfixed: wherever I look I see flat, empty surfaces covered with dust. If it ever rained the dust would turn to mud, I wonder if the roofs would be able to support it. Can you imagine— swamps on the tops of buildings?

—It's exactly the same. Makes my head spin, said my tour guide.

—The same as what?

—Where I came from, the places I passed along the way . . .

—It looked like this?

—Well, worse. Much worse. I try to forget about it, just avoid the topic completely, but it's there in my head, it's not something you forget. You know hardly anything about me, about where I come from, now do you see why? I've tried to wipe out memory, imbecile that I am. Instead of wiping things out we should be doing the opposite, remembering everything, keeping the horror alive, so we can keep on fighting.

Here comes the speech-maker, theorizing again. I know all about theorizing. I don't need to take classes from

192

him. Is that why I have such an aversion to this man, I'd like to understand it. What is there about him that I'm allergic to, that makes me itch? The other two practically don't exist, they walk around as if they're invisible.

But not this one. Maybe it's how confident he is about everything. Or maybe it's just that I see him as the organizer, the instigator, of the invasion of my home. The man who's occupying my private space and trying to prove to me that there's some new concept of privacy. Some concept—it's rationalization, that's all. And he's a real bullshit artist.

—It's worse up there, huh?

## RECESSION IN THE NORTHEAST, THE MORTAL DANGER OF HAVING A JOB, & THE GROWING HEAT POCKETS— THE ONLY PROTECTION FROM WHICH IS A BLACK SILK UMBRELLA

As the man-who-sat-at-the-head-of-the-table rambled on and on, I listened and recalled (like a good history professor) the first Crusade to Jerusalem in 1099, as related by d'Aguilers in *Historia Francorum Qui Ceperunt Hierusalem:*

Some of the Moors were decapitated, which was a sweeter fate than that of those others who, pierced with arrows, saw themselves obliged to jump from high towers; others, after long suffering, were given to the flames and consumed. In the streets all over the city one could see piles of heads, hands, and feet. Knights and soldiers opened a path right over the cadavers. But all this was nothing compared to what took place in the Temple of Solomon, where the pagans celebrated the rites of their cult. What went on there is beyond the limits of what can be believed.

This, then, is the tale my companion told me:

193

"I worked in a textile factory until it closed down. By then, when I finally left the Northeast, everything was pretty much over, it was near the end of the Great Epoch of the SI's. The Sighs, as the people up north called them, were the Steadfastly Incompetents. They ran the show, remember, for six years. Three different administrations, each lasting two years. One coup d'etat after another, like clockwork. Every seven-hundred-and-thirty days a new Sigh was substituted for the old one, and each one went on to demonstrate even more incompetence than his predecessor. The Sighs proved they were not so incompetent, however, when it came to lining their own pockets. If they had wanted to, they could have tried their hand at governing the country. Meanwhile the System was manipulated so that top positions remained "in the family," completely inaccessible to any ordinary citizen. But I guess it's sort of silly, telling this to a history professor—you probably know more about it than I do. After all, I'm just an enlightened worker. At least that's what I consider myself: a product of those wonderful, lucid men who were exterminated during the Period of Chronic Liars. My father disappeared during that time, swallowed up. Of course the Enlightened Workers tried to form a movement, to organize, to raise the consciousness of the rank and file, but the Chronic Liars emasculated the leadership, suppressed all rebellion, appeased the skeptical, bought off the weak, and fooled just about everyone. Though I'm sure that's not news to you either. In any case, I call myself an enlightened worker because I didn't start out an ordinary worker *per se*. First I went to the university and got a degree in sociology, and *then* I fell into the void—the seemingly endless search for work. An odd job here and there, and finally I wound up in the personnel office of a medium-sized textile factory in the upper São Francisco valley. By that time, after years of devastation, the river was in its death throes. All protective vegetation gone. Serious erosion was taking place, with superficial runoff increasing dramatically; silt was beginning to clog rivers, dams,

194

everything. By the time the São Francisco had dwindled to a fine thread trying to survive in the hot sand, nobody noticed. And no wonder: dry sluices, empty reservoirs, cattle lying dead in the scrub, the sun getting hotter and hotter, children dying like flies. The Great Epoch of the SI's coincided with the end of the children of the Northeast, exterminated even before the System initiated the general sterilization of the masses after the nuclear accident. Anyway, there were days when the factory itself was an oven, people fainting, suffocating, sweating buckets, dehydrating. I remember wondering where all this would end. There seemed to be no way to stop the process, it had begun years before and now it was snowballing. How could we change the climate? By pushing the sun farther up into the sky? That's what we felt like doing—anything to put a stop to that unbearable heat searing our skin, burning our heads, singeing our feet. The earth was no longer earth; it was sand or rocks. I felt desperate being unable to do anything. Put the mountains back in their places, replant the forests, pump water up from underground and create a river where there was none. You think I'm joking? No, of course you don't. You know it's the only way these days. What do you do when you feel like denouncing the errors of their ways, confronting a government as untouchable as ours? And besides, what good were denunciations? Hadn't they ushered in the Lamentable Period of Giant Shell Games? The System's clever web of lies and tricks: do something, undo it, and then deny it? For years the *powers that be* had been isolated, inaccessible, uncommunicative, immune to contact of any kind with the population. And what could the people do—desperately worried about keeping their jobs, scrounging up food, getting from day to day. They said to me: 'What do you want us to do—stop working? Complain to the boss and get fired? Organize and sign a petition?' And they were right. Dozens of movements had fizzled from lack of interest. And what about the thousands upon thousands of petitions which were duly signed and then merely filed away—if in fact they even made it to the tomb of national memory? The thing that mattered most was making sure you didn't lose your job because that meant death, literally, for the whole family. At least a job in the factory meant a minimum water quota, a pitiful salary, and the guarantee of a hut in which to live. But of course, no security: the unemployed would do anything to take your job. Anything. The number of dead bodies found in vacant lots, back streets, unbelievable. Patrols were formed to pick them up each morning. Imagine—people who had been murdered with sticks, stones, knives, guns, fists, feet. Trenches were dug surrounding the factories, or any place people were working, veritable moats like they had around castles during the Middle Ages. Even the guards were not immune to attack; vigilance and security were professions themselves, after all. Once I was walking through the scrub in early morning, nauseated, my head splitting. Do your remember that old American movie, it's famous, they show it on TV all the time, *Gone With the Wind?* Well, there's a scene in a railroad station where the camera does a slow pan of the floor which stretches into the distance, covered with bodies. It's fantastic, a classic. That's the kind of scene I saw walking through the scrub. I'd never seen so many dead people, never mind all in one place. But now I know that was no movie, what I saw, it was real."

I listen to him with the same horror I felt when I read the story of the first Crusade. Every one of d'Aguilers' words fixed in my mind. Suddenly here it is acted out again, not in 1099 but at the beginning of the twenty-first century, *in the Temple of Solomon crusaders rode knee-deep in blood, nay, up to their horses' bridles.*

He went on: "The violence was always worse after a holiday, I'm not sure whether it was the drink or the carelessness. No one could stay in the house all the time, living like a prisoner, surrounded by four walls, being transported to work in an armored truck, then buried in the factory for twelve hours, trembling just to think of the daily slaughter. We had to live with the constant threat

196

of death, we adjusted, sort of, we made a deal with tragedy, accepting it as a daily presence. Our capacity to make mental accommodation continually surprises me. The way we learn to adapt to horror. We must possess some sort of perversity which allows us to accept terror as normal, or even to go so far as to desire it, as long as it doesn't touch us directly. A perversity nourished by that abstract entity, the System, which proved capable of maintaining itself in the midst of anarchy, chaos pretending to be order, anomaly disguised as progress. No, don't interrupt, let me talk, I need to spit it out, yes, I need to vomit up all I saw and swallowed and accepted. I guess I felt like the Jews walking their long walk peaceably to the crematoriums. Knowing and impotent, hopeful until the last minute that the fire would go out, the gas would somehow miraculously lose its deadly effect, the Allies would arrive in the nick of time. What I want to know is, Can we fight, alone, for our salvation, as isolated individuals, or do we have to depend on outside assistance? They did everything to lump us together at the same time that they isolated each person within himself, making us ferociously individual, closed to everyone else, neither offering nor accepting support, fearful of our own personalities. You think I'm crazy, I can see it in your face. Maybe. It's better that way. I wish this was all a lie, a hallucination. Traveling through the streets in the night's heat melted my brain, I left it in puddles by the roadside. All that's left inside is a light cloud, the shadow of what had been a mind, a mind which could reason, which could make me act. Maybe I'm looking for excuses, so I don't have to shoulder such a weight. I would look around at the Northeast, devastated like a battlefield, more and more horrible each day as the sun came up on the freshly dried blood of those who had been killed during the night. Killed merely because they had a job. Merely! Every death represented a vacancy which was violently disputed at the gates of the factory. It was a silent, undisguised war, consented to—even encouraged—by the company, ignored by the System. The words of Isaiah echoed in my head: *'Make the heart of this people fat, and make their ears heavy, and shut their eyes; lest they see with their eyes, and hear with their ears, and understand with their hearts, and convert, and be healed.' Then said I, 'Lord, how long?' And he answered: 'Until the cities be wasted without inhabitant, and the houses without man, and the land be utterly desolate. And the Lord have removed men far away, and there be a great forsaking in the midst of the land.'* It was all foreseen! *'O my people, your leaders mislead you, and confuse the course of your paths.'* It's all there, written down and repeated for two thousand years; now, finally, realized. Take out the references to God and it's a science fiction made real. What's odd is that we fled there and came here, but it adds up to the same thing. The employed versus the unemployed, in the fiercest battle since the war with Paraguay. And over and above it all, the sun. It seems to set millimeter by millimeter. I don't know if that's even possible, I don't know much about science. But possible or not, when we looked up our eyes teared, our heads exploded. It became impossible to go out at all. Hats came back into use, but they didn't do any good. Then came the umbrellas. Someone apparently discovered that the sun couldn't penetrate umbrellas made of black silk. No other fabric worked—after two or three days the cloth would disintegrate. Except for silk. For some reason it lasted, it protected you from the sun, providing a pleasant spot of shade. Don't ask me why. Don't ask me anything. No one explained any of this to me, no one explains anything in this country. There were other strange phenomena, like the heat pockets: areas of intense heat, impossible to stand in or even pass through. You'd be walking along and suddenly you were enveloped by incredible heat, you'd start to run, to try to escape, some of the heat pockets were small enough to come out the other side. In the beginning it was a sort of game. Dramatic, amusing—how all of a sudden someone in front of you would begin leaping about in confusion and run, screaming, back in your direction. Then everyone would hang back, aware that this behavior meant danger ahead. Later, when we went on our long trek, we saw that there were heat pockets everywhere. In certain regions they were immense, extending for kilometers. And then came the Period of Intolerable Weather. You just couldn't be exposed to the sun at all anymore. You'd go out in the street, and in a matter of seconds your face was hairless, burnt, and peeling, twisted out of shape. The light cut like a laser. In time the danger of the heat pockets increased. Once inside, there was no way out. Sun like a drill, it would kill you instantly, for sure. At least that was the image we had of what happened, because the person would let out an enormous wail, hold his head between his hands, eyes popping out of his head, mouth open gasping for air. In seconds he would fall to the ground, stiff, not a twitch of life left. You could see from a few steps away how the body shriveled, dehydrating completely, skin flaking off like dry leaves; and in a little while the bones themselves would vanish. You don't believe me, do you? Of course, you've never heard of such a thing. No one said a word, the press never reported it. Even the scientists who studied the phenomenon were perplexed. All they managed to determine was that the heat pockets were definitely growing a certain percentage larger by the week. Maps were distributed so that the population could avoid them; they changed the traffic flow; people were dislocated; they moved the roads. Children played games, pushing dogs or cats into heat pockets. (Until later when all animals, even pets, were seen as food and the adults wouldn't let them be wasted like that.) Naturally, the heat pockets were perfect for the designs of the Civil Guards. Difficult prisoners, the disaffected, potential subversives—they'd push them into the pockets and watch while the bodies disappeared. Where there's no evidence there's no crime, says the law. They'd wring confessions from people by dangling them at the edge of a heat pocket: 'Now talk or in you go!' The people talked. The pockets disappeared at night, of course—it must have been a phenomenon related to the dramatic

199

change from hot to cold in the desert after sundown. At night families wandered the streets and neighborhoods of the city looking for the ashes of relatives they imagined had been consumed, though obviously there was no way to recognize them. It was a search guided by the most fragile and relative information: the boy who had been sent to the corner grocery, reminded by his mother to be careful of the heat pocket near the plaza. The father who'd gone to an auction in the suburbs to buy some smoked meat. The daughter who had simply gone shopping, never to be seen again. The aunt who was on her way to visit grandmother. The girl sneaking off to meet her boyfriend. And the search was always useless, everyone knew it. No one could ever be sure they were bringing home the right ashes. They could just as well be the ashes of a dead calf who strayed in the wrong direction, though that in itself would be a rare event, the few animals left were guarded more closely than newborn babies. The truth was that people just couldn't stand to stay in their houses. They went out at night to see each other, friends coming along for the search. No one went out alone, of course, for fear of being attacked by the Stalkers of the Gainfully Employed. These were fearful strolls, people were terrified; whenever they saw a group coming their way they changed direction immediately. What you'd see, if you could watch from overhead, was practically a ballet: figures coming and going, swerving, wandering off, meeting another group, withdrawing, circling back, walking backward, twirling around. What madness. Who could take such tension? Finally people stopped going out altogether, night or day. Even the ones who had black silk umbrellas. They just couldn't believe in their purported invulnerability. And besides, what good did it do to go out—everything was closed. The baker no longer made bread: no flour to be had, not even the artificial kind. The bars were cleaned out, and so were the drugstores, not a single pill left in stock. Deliveries just never arrived, perhaps swallowed up by some heat pocket along the way. The lakes dried up. People with jobs could get

200

along eating at the factory canteen, but even supplies there were dwindling. Life was so desperate that people entertained themselves occasionally by throwing leftover food (if there was any) out the windows, or garbage, scraps of paper, whatever. Sometimes it caught fire in midair, even before hitting the ground. The nights were pitch-dark, there was no electricity, no energy left at all but in the factories. It's true that some solar generators were shipped to the Northeast, but you can guess where they ended up, can't you? Providing energy for what was left of the colonels, the important families, the people connected to the multinationals. What can people do when they're really flat-out, bellies empty, no way to live anymore at all? The only thing to do was to leave. I know this must sound like there was nothing left of any value, no good whatsoever, but there was: the people's will to live, their refusal to give up, which is why they began to come out of their houses once again. It was an automatic decision, unconscious, the kind that just arrives whole. Groups began leaving at night—get this—with the *protection* of the Stalkers. From their point of view, the more people who left, the better. And so they began actively aiding and abetting the exodus."

—What? *Abetted* the exodus?

—Yeah, what's so strange about that?

—It's been at least sixty years since anyone used that word, abetted. . . . Sounds funny to me, that's all.

—I can see how seriously you're taking all this.

—Maybe too seriously. That word just hit me. . . . Go on . . .

And of course he did:

"The Stalkers of the Gainfully Employed began practically forcing people to migrate. Of course people only left at night when the heat died down. By the wee hours of the morning it got really cool, and everything actually froze up. A short period of three, maybe four hours. People grabbed their suitcases, bundles, satchels, bird cages, and went. Some had giant packing crates that required two or three people just to lift them. Others

201

dragged carts full of clothing, paintings, statuettes, knickknacks. It was incredible how people simply refused to part with their possessions, they were attached to these objects, it was clear, depended on them, even, to feel secure. The very first group flight was a tragedy. In the morning when the sun came up there they were, still parading down the road a few kilometers outside town, in the center of what turned out to be a heat pocket. They looked around for help, realizing they had made a sadly mistaken calculation. The road cut through the scrub, cracked and creviced earth stretching as far as you could see. The asphalt was molten, sticky lumps scattered over what had been a road. Some ran for it immediately, and the one or two who made it back deserved Olympic gold medals for their speed. They reported what had happened. A few others spied an abandoned house, any sort of primitive shelter, and made a mad dash—the sprinters of the group, as opposed to the long-distance runners. They pushed each other aside, disputing desperately for each scrap of shade. So many people crammed inside one mud-and-stick hut that it completely collapsed. Those who didn't manage to find a place out of the sun piled whatever they had on top of their heads: clothes, hats, planks of wood, paintings, umbrellas. The sun was boiling, the ground burned the soles of their feet. People jumped up and down in a macabre dance, toes hardly touching the ground, then flying up in the air again as if they were on springs. They shrieked with pain. As the morning went on, this dance of death reached greater and greater intensity. A collective hysteria, as if some spirit had simultaneously possessed each one of them. Then it diminished as the sun consumed their clothes, paintings, umbrellas—at least those not made of black silk. It devoured hair, skin, flesh, and bones. By nine A.M. there were heaps of ashes all over the area, mixed with molten asphalt. The few people who had survived, huddling under whatever shelter they could find, waited for nightfall to set out again. They had watched the others eaten before their eyes, and they were determined to be more careful the next time. Without much to go on, they headed south. The maps of the pockets were no help since they never seemed to be where they should be— were they movable after all? In any case, the migrants knew that the road would be full of detours, they'd have to bypass the multinational territories, areas which were closed to Brazilians, but you know all about that. What they hoped was that in the central or eastern or southern parts of the country there were places the sun had not yet reached."

—Wait a minute—I'm curious: weren't there any heat pockets in the multinational territories? Those corporations couldn't be all that powerful, to be able to construct a barrier against climate, could they?

—I don't have the slightest idea. I've never been there. The Brazilians who lived in the territories were forced to leave before it was a question. No one knows what goes on inside, it's a mystery to all of us.

—Someone must know!

—You tell me who. Can I go on?

A rhetorical question.

"So, little by little the crowds moving south swelled with people from cities along the way. They converged at crossroads, in town squares, across the parched fields. As they passed through a village the population would join the march. The sick ones stayed behind, waving from behind doors and windows. I saw lots of families leading old people—at their own request—out into the middle of the street to wait for daybreak. They couldn't walk well enough to travel, yet they didn't want to be left behind to die slowly all by themselves. So they decided on the middle of the street. Standing in groups, calm, making talk, women with rosary beads in their fingers, waiting for the sun to rise. Though of course there were some who screamed and leapt about, trying to join the people streaming southward. A few managed to trail along until the end and make it here. Virtually

203

everyone jumped on the bandwagon if they could: 'Let's go, we're headed south to the big city, there's work there, and food.'"

—Yes, I remember, months later, when they finally allowed reports of the migration to be shown on television. They showed some footage filmed from a helicopter, it was amazing the number of people, it looked like the Pope was visiting or something. Do you remember those pictures from the eighties, when the Pope really did come to Brazil? That multitude without end, hushed and waiting. My God, how we longed for leaders in those days. It was a sort of transitional period, I guess, people didn't understand that the era of leaders was over, that there were no more, plain and simple: no heroes. The masses weren't ready for that, they felt orphaned, abandoned, helpless.

—You're changing the subject.

—Well, it's just that it made me think of the Pope's visit, you know? It looked a lot like all those crowds of people moving south, the same kind of hope in people's eyes. The Cyclopean March, they called it. Only the sociologists, nothing better to do, of course, could invent such a silly expression. A mania for naming, labeling, it's been that way for years, every fact, every event needs to be baptized, catalogued. Instead of remembering dates, we have catchy nomenclature. Everything with its clever designation.

—Designation or no designation, the march south, the exodus, was madness. Only the very strongest survived.

—I'm awfully tired. Dizzy from this heat. How about going back down now?

—Don't you want to hear the rest?

—Not really. I don't believe half of what you're saying.

—Do I look like a liar?

—What does a liar look like?

—You think you're better off not knowing about things like this, is that it?

—What good does it do? I'm sweating, I want to go back downstairs, my knees are like rubber.

—I just don't understand you, I mean it. There's so much more to tell. I haven't even mentioned the people with their eyeballs hanging out.

—Oh, let me guess. You mean like the famous hanging gardens of Babylon? Or maybe the famous hanging deserts of São Paulo?

—Okay, okay, let's go downstairs. There's a lot to do before tonight. Do you think you can manage to get your things organized?

On the way back across the roof to the stairs, we passed the solar generators. Every building has them— they run the elevators, hallway lights, etc. Any surplus solar power, along with the gas produced from the garbage, is used for the needs of individual apartments. Television antennas and solar panels: the symbols of our civilization.

—The haze doesn't look like it's going anywhere. That means a hot one for sure.

—Why don't they just erect a series of geodesic domes and cover the whole city? Put a little inventiveness into improving people's living conditions.

—How should I know? Sounds like you've got better connections than I do.

—And you know what else—this haze is getting to be permanent. It was with us the whole trek, a little higher one day, a little lower the next. We got so we could foretell the next day's temperature, depending on the height of the haze. I've never been able to understand that. Scientifically, I mean. The relation between the two. One of these days I'll figure it out...

—Would you mind telling me what we came up here for, anyway? Just a chat and a stroll on the roof?

—I needed to inspect the area, there's a chance this roof is going to come in handy.

—Oh, you're planning a little St. John's Feast Day celebration up here, with a bonfire and everything?

205

—Have you forgotten, Mr. Souza, about the dead man in your apartment? We'll need to get rid of the body somehow. And carefully.

—Who killed him? I want to know.

—Not us, believe me. I swear it. And I'm not one to hide things, really I'm not. As if it would make any difference at a time like this.

—So?

—So now that I've got all this off my chest, I feel better. You can't keep things locked up inside forever, they poison you. Those memories give me heartburn, I try not to think about them. I needed to get it out, deal out the pain—isn't that a line from an old song? I was a singer once, can you believe it?

—No kidding? Professional?

—Well, Saturday nights, on the hometown radio station. That's why the girls were always after me. I even won a couple of contests, and sang on TV, you probably even saw me and don't remember. I sang at the last Miss Bahia pageant.

—No, I never watched that kind of show, musical specials, things like that. For me it was just soccer, the news. Of course my wife wouldn't miss an episode of her nightly soaps. Debates, too, I liked debates.

—Oh, no, how could you?

—I enjoyed them, really. Speaking of naming things, I remember one period I called the Sterile Epoch of Useless Debates. They talked and talked and talked and absolutely nothing ever came of it. The System tolerated it, of course, because it was a complete farce. People screaming and yelling, accusations flying left and right, and what changes were made? None. Everything stayed exactly the same. There's a French author I read a lot of when I was young, Cassou, who said that all battles are lost causes; but that what survives each battle is the battle within oneself, and that remains the property of the individual combatant. Understand?

—Not really. While you were thinking about things

206

like that, the country was going backwards, side to side, tipping over, anything but forward.

This guy just doesn't like me. He always finds a way to get me up against the wall, to show I'm wrong. Meanwhile he's a perfect saint. We climbed down the germ-infested stairs. Sweat trickled down inside my clothes. There's such a surplus of water coupons around lately, I think I'll just jump in the shower.

Hunger in my belly and a sharp pain in my neck. I think about the day in front of me. Absolutely nothing to do. The furniture—how could I forget, I've got to decide what to keep and what to let them get rid of. My indifference amazes me. Those are my possessions, a part of my life which is slated to come to an end tonight!

It's useless. I just can't get excited about it. Let them take it all, it doesn't affect me. I want to be touched by something, I want to get emotional. I'm better off not picking anything, let them decide. Except maybe I'll pull out a few things that remind me of Adelaide. Wonder where she is . . .

I don't even have the slightest idea where to start looking. Could I be procrastinating on purpose? No, I'm not like that, just the idea makes me feel bad. Is it possible I'm simply afraid of facing the truth? Which is simple: I didn't lift a finger to look for my wife. I just let her go, and waited for her to come back.

For Adelaide that would be a serious offense. She left. She's not coming back. She hasn't tried to get in touch with me. And of course I want to know where she is. Well. I suppose wanting is one thing, doing another. Thank God we're almost at the bottom of these stairs, in heat like this descending is just as hard as going up. We're both panting like crazy.

—So what are you planning to do with the body?

—We're going to wait until tonight when everything quiets down, then we'll start the operation.

—On the roof?

—You don't need to know the details. If it looks like

it's going to be hard to pull off, we'll get help. Your nephew knows all about what's going on.

—You mean he already knows about the barber?

—He knows a lot more than you think.

—What's that supposed to mean?

**ADELAIDE'S SECRET
LIES BURIED
IN THE PACKAGES
IN THE TRUNK
FORGOTTEN
ON TOP OF THE WARDROBE**

I simply can't tolerate the mess. I've always been extremely orderly by nature, that's why Adelaide and I got on so well: everything in its place, nothing untidy. When my nephew was a child and came to visit for a weekend, I'd go crazy picking up after him.

He tore up paper, I picked up the pieces. He dropped his chewing gum on the carpet, took his toys apart, messed up the neatly made beds, left his pen open on the floor. I just couldn't stand the confusion. Adelaide, calm as usual, would tell me: let the boy play, when he leaves we'll clean it all up.

Now I realize that I almost never played with him, really. I was too busy worrying about messing up the house. And now these men have installed total chaos, setting up their headquarters here, indifferent to whether I like it or not. They don't bother to take into consideration what I think, I'm just here.

I'm hungry, but this kitchen makes me nauseous, the table is covered with empty cans, leftover food. If only they weren't such pigs—they live here too, after all, wouldn't they just as soon the place was clean? Maybe not. And I doubt they even hear a word I say. One's got his ear glued to a transistor radio, the other's eating candy, and the third one, the most enigmatic of them all, is forever making pronouncements.

I've lost all sense of time, which is something else

that makes me uneasy. Wish I still had my watch, who knows why. Maybe so I could verify that it's time to eat. Hard to break bad habits. If I don't eat at the right time I get a headache. And if I'm not careful, it turns into a migraine, and then I have to spend the day in the dark.

Each day used to be parceled out, compartmentalized, just so—easy to live in. Coffee, bus, work, lunch, work, the commute, home, Adelaide, TV, news, bed. Precisely on schedule. Well, we tried to be reasonably flexible. But now everything has fallen apart, I feel lost, no wonder I feel like taking refuge in clock time.

—Is there anything in this mess to eat?

—Huh?

—Is there any food?

—Speak up, I can barely hear you.

—I'M HUNGRY! ANY FOOD?!

—Food? There's some fried eggs in the frying pan. If you don't mind eating them cold.

—I do mind. I mind fried eggs, hot *or* cold.

—What?

—I said I don't like fried eggs, in fact I detest those synthetic eggs.

—Yeah, me too, eggs are good. Even these...

—They taste like plastic, and their texture is really weird.

—What?

—Look, I'm not going to stand here in my own kitchen shouting like an imbecile. This guy must be deaf—no, he's a cretin, that's all. And here I am arguing with him about synthetic eggs. This must make me one too. I can't take much more of this. And the worst of it is I'll end up eating fried eggs, *fake* fried eggs.

—You say you don't like them?

—THAT'S RIGHT!

—Why?

—Because I don't, okay?

—You've got the luxury. I mean if you hadn't seen an egg for years and years, like me, and I mean years, you wouldn't look like you had a bad taste in your mouth

209

before you even take a bite. I walked in here and saw the refrigerator full of eggs, I swear I almost went off the deep end, my head was pounding, I got the shakes. It's an impossible thing to describe—how good an egg is. The last time I saw one was in the icebox at the canteen, at the company where I worked. Nobody but nobody was allowed in the kitchen, but the boss sent me to get a knife. I walked in, the cook wasn't there, so I thought I'd at least have a look around. When I opened the refrigerator I almost went crazy. Know what I saw, can you guess?

—An egg?

—Huh?

—An egg!

—That's right, you got it, how about that. Yup, there it was, amazing, huh? An enormous egg, shiny even. That's when the cook came back. I was pretty out of it. I asked him:

—*Whose egg is that?*

—*The superintendent's.*

—*But where did it come from, if there aren't any more chickens?*

—*Ask the Superintendent. He just walked in one day with a carton.*

—*A whole carton? You mean there were that many? And he didn't share them with everybody?*

—*What are you, nuts? The peons get the regular food, no big shot's good fortune's going to change that. There was some uproar over this egg, though, I'll tell you that. They already wasted one guy caught trying to steal it. So I'd suggest you close the door after you and forget you ever saw it. And don't look so crushed, you know the bosses of this molehill are real tightwads. But I heard it's going to be a different story on the next site—a goddamned mountain—all you can eat.*

—So, anyway, I thought it was wrong to flaunt an egg like that in the refrigerator, when the workers only ate soy meat, soy chicken, soy milk, and laboratory soy, no less. I don't know who the jerk was who invented that so-called food.

—If some jerk hadn't invented something, you'd have died a long time ago.

—Yeah, but couldn't they make it taste like something? That stuff smells okay, like food even, the food I remember from when I was a kid. If they can do so good with the smell, why not the taste?

—What did you do for a living?

—Ten years I've been wandering around, no job, nothing. Last time I worked was when I saw that egg. That was some job, though. A big excavating company, I mean it was gigantic, you hardly didn't even mind working. Those machines were real beauts, the way they ate the dirt, swallowed whole hills, nothing was too big. I didn't mind a bit, no sir, operating a rig like that. Everything was hydraulic, it was a piece of cake, you just flipped the lever and it scooped up everything in sight, level the place and fill all the dump trucks in no time. I worked about twelve years with that machinery. The yellow beast, that's what I called it. The size of that shovel on the front! No one argued with that machine, I ran it all by myself. A rig like that makes you a big man, nobody could mess with me, nobody. You know, it was even a little scary climbing into that baby, but I got used to it, me and the beast, bosom buddies. I'd get in and yell *Let's eat dirt!* Knocking down hills all day long, I don't even know how many we ate, I think once I leveled a whole state up there near Maranhão, have you ever been to Maranhão? Now that was some excavation job, took a whole year, with three hundred machines pushing the dirt around, mountains of rock, looked like a hellhole by the time we were done with it. Rock, dirt, trees, all yanked up and torn down, we leveled it flat, just red dirt, like an endless red beach. No dunes though, of course. I don't know what they were planning there, some said build all new cities. Another guy told me it was for farming, but you tell me, you ever heard of leveling acres and acres for farming? Didn't make a whole lot of sense, but my boss—he was crazy about his work, really bonkers. I mean we'd get there at the crack of dawn and he'd already be at it, and he stayed after we left, too, he was made of iron, that guy. Anyway, my boss's dream was to level all Brazil, no kidding. He said then Brazil would be the flattest country in the world, it would be worth the investment on account of the savings when it came to building railroads, highways, whatever they wanted. I don't know. But that company sure leveled a lot of dirt, probably would have changed the whole country if someone asked them to. But tell me, really, it's not such a bad idea, is it? Save a lot of asphalt and cement, without all this going up and down, you wouldn't need embankments, bridges, viaducts, nothing like that, right? And people wouldn't get so tired, all the cities would be completely flat, no slopes at all, and energy savings too, that's what my boss used to say, and I agree with him, he was a smart guy. For instance, we put a couple of rivers into underground pipes, it's sort of the same idea. And one of them was a real gusher, but we got it under control, put a nice cement covering over it. Course the sound was wild, you could hear the battle going on down there, came up through the drains. It sounded like the river was going loco from being confined like that, but it behaved real pretty. And think of all the space we gained, all the land over the river. That's what my boss told me, you know that guy shouldn't have been just a foreman, he had it in him to be top dog, owner of the whole company. He had the head for it, kept everybody in line, no slipups—he loved those machines, and anybody who didn't take good care of his rig would get fined, then suspension, then fired—sometimes even beaten up, there were some gringos who took care of that department.

Christ, I thought to myself, this guy has suddenly gone bananas. All because of an egg he saw in a refrigerator ten years ago. How do I turn him off? I'm hungry, I'm going to rustle something up here, maybe some of those famous canned goods that have taken over my bedroom. I'm in the mood for a nice hearts-of-palm salad. Lettuce, tomato, a little grilled meat on the side . . .

Maybe I should take another look in the back room, what if the barber's already starting to smell? Decomposing in this heat. Why not just hand him over to the overnight Cadaver Collectors? Forget it, how do we explain the knife wounds? They'd call in the Guards to do the Necessary Investigation. And then what.

But that body is bothering me, I've got to figure out a way to get it out of here, and fast, no one likes a cadaver in the vicinity. Or even not in the vicinity. Much less someone you knew, someone you saw every day, and suddenly you find him murdered. Though I must admit the barber was a pretty nasty and unlikable guy.

What really makes my hair stand on end isn't the presence of the body in the back room, but thinking that one of my housemates is the killer. There's no other explanation. But why kill the barber? An awfully boring target, all he did was bother people with his petty requests, always trying to get ahead, sucking up to everyone.

But that's what everybody does, it's the only way to survive. We're acting out a charade—whoever gets the right answer wins. How to crack the System. Find the microscopic fissure. Nothing is allowed, everything is tolerated. That's the formula—so the whole country won't blow sky-high.

How many emergency solutions. We've lived in a State of Emergency for, maybe, ten years. I did the same thing as Adelaide: isolated myself from the passage of time. Everything disappeared in the deranged sum of days and weeks, hours and months.

Perhaps it was all a trap. Premeditated or accidental? Hard to say. The power they have over us, the means at their disposal—it's possible that they're behind this fission of the conventional frontiers of time. A perfect way to take our attention away from the concrete, physical barriers they've erected around us. Like turning São Paulo into a walled city, the barbed-wire fence marking the no-man's-land between the Urban Zone and the Pauper Encampments, the system of CIRCAs that restricts travel in general and, specifically, makes it impossible to get anywhere near the "bell jar" neighborhoods.

All necessary, of course. Organization is necessary to allow us a semblance of normal life, so chaos won't take over completely. But what do they think chaos is? That's what I'd like to know. Got to give it some thought, get my head working again. Maybe have another talk with Tadeu Pereira...

Their objective is clear: to blur the line of time and simultaneously impose strict boundaries on our physical space. Which would explain the partition we feel in our heads, that vague incoherence.

—Hey, you're not even listening.

—I'm hungry.

—I haven't even gotten to the best part yet...

—Save it for later.

—What if I don't feel like it later?

—What if I don't feel like it now?

—You're a rude old fart, you know that?

—So what.

—But I bet you'd be interested in the dams I worked on. A real pretty piece of work, we closed off almost all the rivers in this country, we made lakes that looked just like the ocean...

I turn my back and he rattles on and on. I walk out of the kitchen carrying a sausage wrapped in strange, brown-colored bread, suspiciously soft. Whenever I eat sandwiches my bridgework gets all screwed up. Luckily, it doesn't taste half bad, the bread at least smells fresh. Artificial, but relatively tasty.

I go into the bedroom. I've been thinking about getting rid of the bed, it takes up a lot of room. I can sleep on the sofa, I'll find a sleeping bag or something. I look up at the trunk on top of the wardrobe. I'm not even sure why, it was automatic. The wicker trunk. So it was in here, not the maid's room!

That old inviolate trunk. Just like me: filled up. What's the usefulness of everything stashed away inside me all these years? In order to find out, I'd have to drag it all out. Look it over, send the superfluous stuff to the trash heap. The useless leftovers of the years. How could they be worth anything now?

I hesitate. People throw things like this in the fire, things that just take up space. I could open the trunk and see what's inside. See what Adelaide guarded so mysteriously. Not that it was a rule *per se*. One time she just said to me, "These are just some of my things, I'd rather you didn't bother with them." So I didn't. Why should I?

As I climbed onto the chair to get the trunk, it hit me. Coldly, calmly. I would clear out the whole house, tear everything off the walls, empty out the bureaus, eliminate both our presences. At the same moment I realized that it would be dishonest, unfair to Adelaide, to open her secret trunk.

Besides, what could I possibly discover in those packets of brown paper? Love letters? A diary? Old photographs? What good would it do to invade Adelaide's past like that, since she herself is the past? No, better to leave it behind. Of course it would be a completely different story if I were to find her again.

If that was even remotely possible. An actual meeting. I think about how I spent years, prisoner of the aroma of gooseberries, while real life went on spinning around us. A whole world of things going on, changing, and I was just waiting for night to fall, for the smell of gooseberries.

I thought that was what life was about—the little things, the details. A patchwork quilt, a jigsaw puzzle, lots of tiny tiles which placed side by side make a whole floor. I never was one to understand the world as a whole, the world in the largest sense. I was a collector of pieces, moments, particles, instants.

Whenever I tried to concentrate on everything at once, what did it all add up to? If I tried to codify my life, essential elements were always missing. I gave up on the essential, tricked again. Given a choice between the aroma of gooseberries on the perfumed lips of my wife each night and her white hands poised over the keyboard of the piano in the living room, I preferred the gooseberries. Dead wrong.

If only I'd stayed awake maybe I would have perceived, right afterwards, the smell of her breath itself. The human smell, actual, not something produced by a synthetic substance purchased at the drugstore. I lived with distortion and accepted it as reality. Well, it seems by now we've all lost the sense of what's real.

Not that I'm trying to get myself off the hook. But I do have the right to plead confusion: no coordinates to depend on. Delirious. Nonstop thoughts. Labored breathing, swollen feet. I never had swollen feet before, but now, overnight, my shoes don't fit anymore, they pinch my feet.

I can't stop wondering whether I have the right to open that trunk. It's not just a simple question of opening it up and taking out the packages. And it's not really a question of whether she's coming back, either. We had an agreement. Why should it end here? I dredge up a modicum of loyalty. I should destroy the trunk without ever looking inside.

How many times have I climbed onto this chair to put the packages inside as she passed them up to me? Her instructions were always precise: "This side up, the tape on the left." I wonder why? The trunk smelled of mothballs, we added some more every month to ward off mice and cockroaches.

She would hand up the packet and look at me as she did. If there was anything truly pretty about her, it was her way of looking at me. A reward. Her eyes half lowered, yet observing everything. She looked timid, downright shy. I liked the way she had of looking at people, I noticed it that first day when I knocked over the sweet-smelling red liquid which would become so important to me.

216

I've always been terrified of anyone who looked me straight in the eye. People who stare force you to look at them too. I always hated staring contests even when I was a kid. I always lost. So when I first saw her, watching me with her eyes half closed, so that I was barely able to notice, I fell in love with her.

Maybe I *am* out of my mind, but it's the only mind I've got. I'd just as soon my head stayed where it is, firmly attached to my neck, doing its business of thinking. Funny, how my life with Adelaide was a series of rituals. We maintained them through it all; they maintained us. So, I feel kind of lonely looking at this trunk. I've never before touched it without Adelaide standing there below me, handing up her bundles. Then I'd climb down and put my hand on her shoulder and we'd go into the kitchen. As if to a party, a celebration.

It was a celebration, in a way—in our way. We were very dependent on each other. We got along so well, even in the midst of the enormous silence that surrounded us sometimes. We'd go into the kitchen and brew up some herb tea (she hated regular tea), and Adelaide would open a tin of goodies.

There were rows and rows of them filling one whole kitchen cabinet. She made something new every day, a cake, cookies, biscuits. Circular, square, star-shaped, triangular, holes in the middle, sugar sprinkled on top, jam in the middle, cheese-filled, guava paste. Each tin carefully sealed to keep them dry and crispy. She opened a new tin on a fixed, rotating schedule. On the rare occasions when we had company, the table would be covered with all different kinds of treats, whimsically arranged on dessert plates.

Coffee, milk, and herb tea. A little while after we got engaged, Adelaide asked me if we could have a wood cookstove. A dream she'd had since she was a child, she said, because of her grandmother's stove, which she recalled as being continuously burning, hot-to-the-touch, the smell of woodsmoke filling the house.

What would it cost to satisfy this nostalgia? If she

wanted a wood cookstove, she would have one. After we were married, we moved into a small house in a friendly neighborhood. A house which was always pleasantly warm. In the wintertime all you had to do was close the place up tight and let that dry heat spread through the rooms. Imagine the craziness of a stove like that nowadays, living in this furnace of a world.

Food was so different back then—oven roasts, steaks, rice, black beans cooked in clay. Just thinking about it makes my mouth water! It's not good to remember things like that, but what was good was good. Of course there were inconveniences. It got harder and harder to find wood for the stove.

Impossible, in fact. All of a sudden there was none. When I was a kid in the interior, I remember the woodcutter coming down the street with his cart, making his daily deliveries. His stockpile was around the corner, we used to play there, climbing around on the heaps of wood, making huts and clubhouses.

We stole some of his wood every year for the St. John's Day bonfires. It was a complicated operation, that woodcutter had his ears to the ground. One group would create a diversion while another made off with the goods, sneaking out under the fence.

I remember my parents complaining when the woodcutter started spacing out his deliveries. The stockpile was dwindling. People began buying electric stoves. Then one day the first gas tanks appeared in town. Soon after that, the woodcutter sold his burro and went away, and his lot turned into a storage depot for construction materials.

My father, who knew all about this business of forests and lumber, saw the handwriting on the wall: "Canefields and pastures surrounding this town now, that's all. No more trees anywhere around, not even those scrubby things. Wood's got to come from farther and farther away, bound to be more and more expensive." It seemed to make him sad, but he went out and bought a gas range.

Adelaide was disconsolate when after a year and a half, we had to leave our cozy little house. A big real estate company was putting up high-rise buildings, buying up the land all around. They pressed us to sell. We resisted. Tractors came and dug up everything around us; our house was left standing alone amid the mess.

Trucks and earth movers tore the street apart. Street-cleaning crews came and sprayed water everywhere, it turned into a mud pit. They put up signs: *Sorry for the inconvenience—we're working for the future of the city.* Stone-crushers arrived at night to break up what the men had dug up during the day, as if they just happened to be in the neighborhood at 12:30 A.M.

Pile drivers worked around the clock. It was useless to phone the local authorities; you got a recorded answer, a message machine. Antiaircraft spotlights flooded the area with light, we lived with the shades drawn. To save Adelaide from the Funny Farm, I sold everything.

It wasn't even a sale, really. We traded for this apartment. What she missed most was that wood stove. "Maybe we can set one up in the maid's room," she suggested. As if condominiums didn't have rules and restrictions. Oh, my innocent Adelaide.

Well, she learned to bake her treats in the gas stove. Even when flour and other ingredients became of necessity artificial. We cut back, true, on other small pleasures, because of the gas. Not that it was rationed—but the price! Who could afford it?

The situation finally improved when Adelaide got brave enough to do a simple thing: to ask her nephew for extra gas and water coupons. And since he was well acquainted with his aunt's home-cooked goodies, he brought them gladly. He's no dummy—it's not for nothing he's managed to become a Mili-tech, fancy house and all. Fancy house? What am I talking about?

219

## THINGS GET COMPLICATED: SOUZA IS AT A LOSS TO UNDERSTAND WHAT HIS SCHEMING NEPHEW IS UP TO— AND HE SEEMS TO BE UP TO A LOT

I don't know what I'm saying—my nephew's fancy house! Am I as out of it as all that? Adelaide was right, it must be the sun. Your brain gets soft and you can't remember anything. It hardly matters in this steam bath. The only thing on your mind is finding a little shade.

A little fresh air, some ice water. My lips are split and peeling, like everybody else's. I hate to admit it, but I don't have the slightest idea where my nephew lives. He's never invited me to visit. He told us once that he was set up nicely; Adelaide suspected that meant he lived in the Acrylic Palaces.

How do you like that? I don't even know his address or phone number; if I needed him in an emergency there'd be no way to reach him. No, he couldn't live in the Acrylic Palaces with all the superfunctionaries. He's capable, sure, on his way up, but he can't have reached the upper echelon of the invisible high rollers, at least not yet!

Totally sluggish, I lie back in bed, how about a nap. The fan stirs the hot air, and off I go

I open my eyes, not a sound, and think I smell something rotten all quiet

—Hey, what's happening? You going to sleep for a week?

—I must have dozed off . . .

—Dozed off! We thought you were dead, you slept a day and a half. You'll do just fine in hell if you can sleep like that in this heat.

—A day and a half, you're crazy! I've never needed that much sleep.

—Your nephew's here, he came to organize the removal.

Years ago it would have bothered me to have slept so long, such a waste of time. Now, if I could, I'd dive into sleep and wake up next month, next year. Hibernate like a bear. Hibernate, no. Summerate. Waiting for cooler, more comfortable weather. What an idea. Must not be awake yet.

—What's going on here, Uncle Souza? You haven't sorted out your things.

—No, and I'm not going to. Let them take what they want.

—You want us to choose?

—First tell me this: is there any possibility I can have my house back, all to myself, again?

—I'm afraid not, Uncle Souza. In fact, that's what I wanted to talk to you about. More people are on the way.

—More?!

—Just four more. Just for a few days.

—What kind of weird business is going on here? Are you going to explain what you're up to?

—Charity, that's all. I find shelter for people who would die without a roof over their heads.

—Sure. And what about all the people in the Encampments? How come you're not finding shelter for them?

—What are you talking about? Those people are condemned, they don't count for anything. These men are important technicians.

—Right. That guy in there, the one with the radio glued to his ear all the time—that guy is no more important than he is a technician. He's a total idiot.

—Maybe he's pretending, did you ever think of that? Watching everything very carefully, taking it all in.

I never thought of that. Maybe he is. There are types like that around. A well-known phenomenon. They spy on everybody, go around collecting information like nobody's business. I don't know what kind, or why, or what they do with it. But then this business of "information" has become a neurosis.

If he wants to inform, let him. How much do you want to bet that radio of his is a transmitter, sure, and he's getting his orders, passwords, all in secret code. Plus of course he passes on the information, like what's going on in this house. An infiltrator in every house, what a boon to the System, total security. Nah, that's going a bit far, it's just my own foolishness again, delirium.

None of it makes any sense at this point. If he were an informant, they'd know about the dead barber and the Cadaver Collectors would be knocking at the door. With their threats and subtle insinuations, money-grubbers that they are. Relax, Souza, the man with the radio really is a cretin, he went bonkers from moving so much dirt around.

—So you're really not going to choose anything to save?

—Not a thing. Take it away.

I help the men pile everything in the living room. Tables, chairs, china closet, the bar made of cedar. I couldn't care less. Each crystal glass, purchased by Adelaide a few at a time. We never had enough money to buy a whole set all at once. One day I remember she burst into tears, she wanted a tea set so badly.

A pair of pink glasses with gold lettering: HIS / HERS. A wedding gift from her mother. Adelaide used to empty out the china closet once a week and wash everything in it, dust all the panes of glass. When everything was back in place, she'd hide the key, no one could open it but her.

I gave the china closet a swift kick. Cups, glasses, wine goblets, liqueur glasses, crystal dessert dishes, all sent flying. I threw them out the window one at a time, waiting to hear the pieces explode on the sidewalk below before lobbing the next item. My friends liked this little game. They joined right in.

"That one's mine!" I yelled as the man-who-eats-candy reached for the rose-colored glass. My fury startled him so that he dropped it. I ran to pick up the pieces, dropped them again, stomped all over them. Then I grabbed the mate and tossed it out the window. Soon there should be a committee of neighbors at the door to complain.

—Have you gone completely mad, Uncle Souza?

—I'm just having a little fun, nothing wrong with that.

—But Aunt Adelaide loved all that glassware.

—I know. And where is she now?

—Where?

—She's at your house, isn't she? I'm sure of it.

—Why do you think she's at my house?

—You reacted to her disappearance so naturally. Never once so much as asked me where she'd gone. And the two of you always adored each other. Like mother and son, you two. When I realized where she was, I stopped worrying. Safe with her darling nephew. Isn't she?

He didn't answer, just walked off to give more orders. If he had any to give. Those Mili-techs love leadership, authority, they imagine themselves terrific logicians, strategists. Even in the middle of an apartment, cleanup duty, moving day. They can command a trip to the bathroom, let you know when to flush the toilet.

I just kept throwing things out the window. Someone knocked on the door. It had to be the neighbor-with-the-lipstick. But it wasn't. (I never was real good at premonitions.) It was the old man from upstairs who plays the *Pathétique* all day long. He wanted to know if I was moving or what. He walked through the living room, thin as a rail.

A fragile type, white-skinned, hard to guess his age. Somewhere between twenty and a hundred. Sunken cheeks and long white hair down to his shoulders. But meanwhile, his hands were perfectly smooth, as if he really were only twenty. He had one good eye, which was blue, and another made of glass, immobile.

—I don't want to interrupt anything. It's just that I heard all the noise and, well, I thought you might be having a fight with your wife. I'm a friend of hers, I thought maybe I could help.

—If it really had been a fight, what makes you think you could have helped?

—Well, I just thought . . .

—So you two were friends?

—Yes, Adelaide and I were good friends. She used to come upstairs in the afternoon and we'd play the *Pathétique* together. And discuss our different interpretations. She could have been a great pianist, you know. Why did she give it up?

—You'd have to ask her that, she never told me. I've been thinking about it lately, though, and I feel bad. I keep wondering if I was at fault somehow.

—Your wife was having a lot of problems, Mr. Souza. She was very self-enclosed, she kept everything inside, would never just let herself go, not even in her music. She always stuck rigidly to the way the thing was written. Stubborn. It took a long time for me to convince her that the score was a broad outline to follow, that sticking to it rigidly was correct but cold—the music had no feeling, no texture. Much later, after watching what I did with the composition, she began to take a few chances, to put a little of herself into it. But she discovered this freedom very slowly, incredibly fearful. Someone who's spent years tied up in knots, whose limbs have atrophied, needs a lot of space and exercise and direction to learn to use them again. The idea that she could do anything she wanted completely turned her head around, I thought that was probably why I hadn't seen her lately. She stopped coming upstairs even though I kept playing the *Pathétique* over and over, afternoon and evening, never giving up. I hoped any moment she'd knock on my door.

—When did all this happen? (And I thought to myself: he played it and played it, all right, and almost drove me nuts.)

224

—Maybe two months ago, let's see, yes, the turning point must have been a little over two months ago, that afternoon she made a banana cake and I had stomach problems. These artificial bananas are good for nothing, I can't tell you how bad I felt. It ruined the whole afternoon, I couldn't sit still long enough to listen to her play, I had to keep running to the bathroom. The cramps were unbearable, I almost cracked my dentures from gritting my teeth so tight. That was an important afternoon for her, and it was for me too, once I finally managed to forget about my stomachache and immerse myself in the painful *Pathétique* she was playing for me.

Adelaide. So it was then that she withdrew from me, she was only waiting for the right moment. Something to justify the break. The idea whose time had come, she was praying for an opening, a way to tell me without hurting me. At least we had that much between us all these years.

We didn't hurt each other. We handled each other with kid gloves, no all-out attacks, no sudden moves. Just friendly discussions. One of us would always give in when a real argument threatened. A peaceful life. At least we called it living. Ah, woman, you noticed before I did. If only we'd been in the habit of telling each other what was going on inside us.

—Is she asleep?
—Who, Adelaide?
—Do you have some other wife?
—She left.
—Where did she go?
—Just disappeared.
—She didn't leave a note or anything?
—It was because of this.
—The hole in your hand?
—It doesn't shock you?
—Sure. Like a mouse.
—Well, it shocked Adelaide.
—That can't be. She was so serene. And she'd seen

people before with holes in their hands—two of my students have them. She was upstairs when they were at the piano, many times. At first she thought it was strange, but then she got used to it. Nothing abnormal in this city.

Adelaide, you traitor! This man knows more about you than I do after all these years. It's not fair. If I had had any idea, I would have learned to play the piano, we could have sat side by side, playing, talking. All right, yes. Now I'm beginning to understand, now I see what happened.

Who knows, maybe I would have gone with you when you left. In freeing yourself, you got free of me. And your abandoning me has made me discover you. The hole in my hand was just a pretext, a convenient out, an excuse. A way to show you were upset, a way to disappear. Will I ever get the chance to tell you all this?

—I better be going, I don't want to miss "The Superheroes." I love TV cartoons. They've got a new Superman series based on Sartre's *Being and Nonbeing*, have you heard of it?

—Superman or Sartre?

—Whichever.

Don't give me that ironic look. I've got the definite feeling this old man is going to disappear, evaporate into thin air. He doesn't really even exist; he's a genie from the Lost Forest, completely misplaced in a modern city that doesn't have trees, much less myths. That one blue eye staring at me: just a fantasy.

—Do you have visitors? There seems to be a lot of noise in the kitchen.

—So, you're the curious type, eh?

—I like people, that's all. They're good for me. I hardly ever go out. Once in a while I visit my relatives, but they're always eating. I'm surprised it hasn't killed them, all they do is gorge themselves.

—Then you wouldn't like my visitors. They're always in the kitchen feeding their faces, too.

—Relatives?

—Friends of my nephew. That one over there is my nephew.

—He's a captain?

—Yeah. You memorized all the insignias? What for?

—I don't know, I just know them. Awfully young to be a captain. Congratulations.

—Do you live in the building, professor? (My nephew just has to get involved in everything.)

—Yes, two flights up. For the last twenty-eight years.

—You like it here, then.

—I can't stand it. I'd rather live in a barrel like Diogenes. I just can't take all these golden-agers. Some bright idea of the government to put all the old people in one place, middle-aged in another, young people someplace else.

—Our Planners for the Social Well-Being know what they're doing. The proof is that society has got on well with it, just as expected.

—You talk like an official document.

—Do you live alone, professor?

—Uh-huh.

—How would you like a few people to keep you company?

—Tenants?

—Let's call them companions. Friends. Just for a while.

—Listen to the P.R. He'll set you up all right, they'll come and take over your whole house, like they have mine. (I tried to warn him.)

—No, no, nothing like that. My uncle is just upset about his wife's disappearance. It would be good for you, professor.

—Only if no one would tamper with my piano.

—I'll take care of that personally, no one will so much as touch your piano.

—There's one more problem. I don't know, I don't know...

—Speak up, professor, for us problems don't exist.

—Well, for me they do. It's my pajamas.

227

—Pajamas?

—Yes. It's always been a problem for me, my whole life.

—You need pajamas? We'll get you as many as you need.

—You think you can solve everything with money, don't you, Captain?

—You bet.

—Then it won't do any good.

—Well, tell me the problem and we'll see. I don't have a lot of patience for guessing games.

—I don't know, it all depends on my piano and the pajamas. No one can mess with my piano.

—Don't worry, none of us even knows how to play.

—That's just it, it's people who don't know how to play who like to fool around at the keyboard...

—Anyone who goes near the piano will be thrown out immediately. I promise.

—Easy enough to say, but how do I know you'll carry through?

—I give you my word.

—The word of someone who works for the government? You know how much that's worth...

—Okay, okay. What about the pajamas?

—They have to be folded. Neatly.

—What do you mean?

—Folded up neatly and placed under my pillow. There's nothing I dislike more than folding pajamas. But I can't stand to have them lying around on the bed or on the floor. The place for pajamas is under the pillow.

—You're absolutely right, gramps. We'll fold your pajamas, no problem. Completely organized, in shifts. One of us each day. And anyone who doesn't cooperate, I already told you, out they go.

—That's a promise?

—You bet. A promise. Just tell me one thing, though. In heat like this, how can you sleep in pajamas?

—Well, there could be a gust of wind in the wee hours, you never know.

—Wind? There's no wind at all, much less a gust of it.

—Will they really fold my pajamas for me?

—Don't give it another thought, it's done.

—Then come on up, Captain. We can listen to some nice music, one of the pieces your aunt and I used to play. And Mr. Souza, if you hear anything from your dear wife, please let me know. I'm worried about her too, you know.

—I'll be back down in a minute, Uncle Souza. You can keep on piling the stuff in the living room.

—What about the body?

—Body? What body? asked the old man.

—It's just slang, a private joke...

—Pretty strange slang, if you ask me.

They headed for the stairs. No sooner had they left than the lights hit the windows. Violent floodlights. The same antiaircraft searchlights they used to drive us out of the house we didn't want to sell. Plus a terrifying noise. I was stupefied. Ran to the window. All the neighbors were peering out timidly from behind the curtains.

My nephew was back in a flash. "They got one," he yelled to the men as he rushed past on his way to the kitchen. Lots of loud talking. I stood there looking at my things all piled in a heap. I should be saying goodbye to them. They've been with me my whole life, after all—friends, as it were. As if objects could be humanized.

The men came dashing out of the kitchen and ran past me into the hall. "Everything ready, Uncle Souza?" It was and it wasn't. As far as I was concerned they could take whatever they wanted. My nephew ran out the door shouting, "Here they are with the helicopter." So I thought I understood what was going on.

Seemed like a lot of people were involved, but involved in what? It's hard to believe that my nephew, at his age, could have such influence. Which just adds to the chain of questions: influence over whom? In what areas? To what purpose?

229

If only I had some idea of how the government is organized, but these days no one can begin to identify the various hierarchical differentiations, the groups which dominate. The mechanisms of power used to be more comprehensible; in what now seems like the remote past we followed the ascendancy of the various political parties closely, and we knew what each coalition and alliance stood for. Factions splintered off on the basis of common ideas and, though of course it was all a game of approximate, opportunistic combinations, the power was divided up somehow, parceled out. Each group continued to jockey for position, but they actually took turns holding the reins of government.

But that was well before the seventies and eighties, when the wind changed dramatically and the technocrats gained the upper hand. Their troops took control without so much as giving us time to adapt to the change. They made a definitive, if not clean, break with the old system and installed themselves, confident that the future was theirs.

This arrogance lasted for some time. Ensconced in the administration, noses in the air, they had neither the time nor the inclination to recognize the new rising class— the Mili-techs, who would eventually go them one better (?!), adding military organization to their doctrine of rationalism. The trademarks of the Mili-techs: hierarchy, rigidity, discipline, and some very curious ideas about the nature of power.

The first Mili-techs came from very prominent families and took divine right for their own. They were implacable, hunkered down in their fortresses. Power was divided among them according to pacts, conspiracies, tenuous alliances; they revived the lost art of the political deal, placing shrewd and practiced negotiators in all the major government posts.

Often the university students studying political science asked me to explain the structure of power. They didn't dare ask other professors for fear of being accused of formulating Unpalatable Questions. But I couldn't help them—we lacked the basic information on which to build any theory.

I can think of only one analogy: Etruscan civilization. Historians, for all their painstaking research, learned very little about how that society was organized. All they had to go on was fragments of information from surviving shards—ceramics, painted artifacts, and the like, which furnished only incomplete, isolated glimpses of the Etruscans. There wasn't much chance to get a sense of the whole, to put together a wider vision of social or political organization. And our recent past is similarly unfathomable to us today.

Because suddenly everything went completely dark. If my memory still serves (as it should, considering that I was a history professor), the turning point occurred just after the Shameful Lines for Black Beans. It was a difficult time—hunger, starvation, massacres. I remember it well because I had my own difficulties to overcome, obstacles to the future.

Adelaide and I hadn't even set a wedding date yet, but my prospective father-in-law-'s teasing sounded more and more serious: "You're not getting married until you have a sack of black beans, you know. I'm not about to turn my daughter over to a failure. Sure you've got a house, furniture, nice clothes, a car, a NOW account, savings certificates—but you've never faced that line for beans, am I right? You're not quite a man yet, my boy."

It was a challenge: come up with some black beans, or else. Not that it's unusual for there to be tension between the father of the bride and the groom-to-be. It's typical for the father-in-law to act like he's joking and meanwhile keep needling the younger man, trying to find out exactly what he's made of, this fellow his daughter has chosen for herself. Behind the irony I felt his true disappointment. My big test: to ferret my way to the head of the line.

Which meant bribing officials, paying off guards, greasing palms left and right. But how, when I knew there would always be somebody else offering a bigger

231

payoff than I could? And besides, even unlimited funds were no guarantee you'd get anywhere. Some of the authorities were particularly honest, I'd heard. It was a supreme distinction, then, to get to the head of the line without making payoffs.

But ferrets, as they were called, were a feared breed. They were considered contemptible, something along the lines of those who collaborated with the Nazis during the occupation of France. Their heads would be shaved, they'd be stoned in the streets, lynched. And each time a ferret got lynched, the police were inspired to go after them even harder.

I just wasn't the adventurer type! Adelaide and I decided the only way was to take turns in the line. At first I thought maybe I'd get lucky and find a weak link, just casually slip into line near the front, but of course it didn't work out that way. I don't know if I've ever experienced worse torture than standing in those Shameful Lines. They extended for miles and miles, full of twists and turns like the old-time railroads when the engineers were paid by the mile. And I'm sure they chose the locale, up in the hills of Cantareira, on purpose. A little game to make things more difficult, compliments of the Ministry of Provisions.

Of course the climate hadn't yet reached today's unbearable level of sultriness, but it was extremely hot just the same, which made it almost impossible to clamber through dust and stones up the steep inclines, gouged by erosion, and still manage to protect your place in line. I hope I never have to go through anything like it again. I'd die.

In Ibirapuera—once Saõ Paulo's largest park, now reduced to an immense, obsolete parking lot—there's a monument to the people who did die. Not ten meters from the Obelisk in Memory of the Fallen of 1932. It's an enormous pyramid of smooth black stones—surrounded by barbed wire, naturally, so people can't get close enough to light candles and carry on. Each stone respresents a victim of the Shameful Lines for Black

Beans, and was donated by the victims' families who, in fact, financed the entire monument. For a long time it was a Rhetorical Rallying Spot, but when rhetoric lost its meaning the pyramid was forgotten.

Anyway, Adelaide and I took turns in line. I missed three days of work and she missed seven. We came back triumphant, with eight glorious kilos of beans, and my prospective father-in-law was completely won over. He looked at me differently, I was no longer a good-for-nothing. He introduced me to his friends, bragging about my great achievement. His eyes sparkled, full of pride. Whenever he asked me how I did it, I'd play along with him for a while, cunning and mischievous, then change the subject. He'd wink at me like a co-conspirator, fully believing he was talking to a ferret, someone who knew how to maneuver easily through the proper channels.

He talked about those beans until the day he died. And he died in terrible torment, his armpits eaten away by cancerous spray. I visited just about every day, it was on my way to work. Doped up on morphine, he was rarely conscious, but whenever he was he'd look at me and croak "beans."

Thousands of people died, disfigured, by those aerosols. Still, the government didn't ban deodorants. It was the people who finally took the initiative and stopped using them. The pharmaceutical industry reacted by tightening the screws: you could only buy toothpaste or aspirin if you also bought a can of deodorant. Unused aerosol cans multiplied in the trash heaps, or were fished out and brought home by the extremely poor to be used as perfume for Saturday night. How could they know they were playing with fire? The media said nothing, the community health centers issued no warning.

All you had to do was walk through a slum area, any conglomeration of ramshackle hovels, and there are thousands all over the city, and you'd see hideous examples of faces without skin, necks with chunks missing, mutilated shoulders. Eaten by deodorant.

When I first discovered the hole in my hand, it oc-

233

curred to me that it could be from the soap I'd been using. Or the lavender cologne I'm always splashing all over myself to disguise other smells. The idea really scared me—there's no cure for these infections caused by chemicals.

But that's another story. What I was trying to say was that nothing impressed my father-in-law, not a diploma, not an A-plus thesis on the actual number of casualties in the Battle of Tuiuti, not an all-expense-paid trip to the United States to evaluate the historical methods of the top Brazilianists. But those eight kilos of beans had him bursting with pride. He took to clapping me on the back (an uncharacteristic gesture), murmuring: "Ah, if only we had courage like that in the old days . . . these young people will go far, they're fearless."

My nephew burst back into the apartment, his acolytes following close behind. The man-who-was-alway-listening-to-the-radio kicked the china closet, glass shattered and flew everywhere. The one who seemed to be the leader of the three ran to the telephone and tried to get a dial tone. Each time the call failed to go through, he slammed down the receiver with a bang. Even my nephew was frowning for a change.

—Well, that pretty well screws up our plans. Those guys are really on my tail, and I even know who's behind it. But the worst thing is I was really counting on that helicopter . . .

—Forget it, Captain. We can carry everything downstairs and pile it into the pickup.

—I'm not so sure. That's what this is all about, they want us to have to transport the bodies in the pickup. They'll have the Cadaver Collectors on top of us in a minute, and how are we going to talk ourselves out of that one?

—Since when do you have to answer to them, Captain?

—It's not that, really, it's just that I know this business is a trap, I don't like the smell of it.

234

—I think you're being overly suspicious. You're always on your guard.

—Who isn't? It's a safe bet they're setting me up for something. Nabbing a captain red-handed, with a cadaver no less, that would be some coup. Worth quite a bit of visibility, I'd say, plus a promotion and all kinds of special privileges.

—Sure, but they don't know about the bodies, do they? Nobody does.

—My uncle here does.

—He's never even left the apartment, how could he have talked to anyone?

—What about the crazy piano teacher? How can we be sure my uncle didn't slip him a note?

—You're forgetting he's your *uncle,* pal. You're a guest in his house, we all are.

—That's exactly the point. Didn't you tell me he hasn't been acting too happy about our taking the place over? It would be a perfect chance for him to get rid of us.

—Well, he's your relative, you know him better than I do. It's all up to you—both of you. But I can't see what good it does to stand around talking about it. Let's get moving.

—What about the helicopter?

—Forget about it!

It took hours to bring the furniture down in the elevator. I had no idea I owned so many things. Chairs and smaller items were carried down the stairs. The man-who-was-always-listening-to-the-radio and the man-who-ate-candy were sweating, on the verge of collapse. But if we'd done it all by elevator, it would have taken months.

I plucked up my courage and snuck off to the maid's room. Empty. The bodies must have gone down already. Strange, the way I'm referring to them: the bodies. Were they all dead, then? And why is it that I feel nothing, absolutely nothing? I should be horrified, sickened— violence has always terrified and shocked me.

I walked from room to room like a cat checking out

235

his territory. The empty house, dispossesed of my belongings, had lost its personality. Just a house. Could have been a complete stranger's. We left our marks on the objects alone.

The idea startles me. We humanized objects, we made them our representatives. They expressed who we were, they defined us. They *were* us. In effect we were joining, promoting, a cult which is nothing more than a misshapen substitution of things for people.

Maybe it's just as well. This isn't really hard for me. It doesn't pain me to look around the empty house. Even straining my brain, I don't come up with memories, reminiscences. Good. Maybe that means we're abandoning our need to cultivate the tragic, to deify the dramatic.

—You call this a pickup truck?

—Ha, no, I made a swap when I saw how much there was, I knew we'd never fit it in the pickup.

—How did you manage a "swap" just like that?

—I manage what I manage. And you always manage to ask too many questions.

The man-who-ate-candy did the driving. He seemed to know the city well. The headlights beamed into dark corners, church portals, under viaducts, lighting up columns supporting obsolete freeways. The sudden flashes of light revealed people darting here and there, startled faces, desperate for some place to hide. Eyes wide with fear. The man-who-ate-candy blew the horn. People scattered. Some tried to climb the grillwork on buildings; they screamed, bodies shuddering, and fell to the ground. They had forgotten that the grillwork was electrified.

Groups were gathered around bonfires, eating from cans, dressed in rags. So amazed at our interruption they didn't even move, just huddled there, paralyzed, wondering why we didn't stop. Unable to imagine who we could be if not a dawn patrol out to round them up or at least harass them.

We turned a corner, and the man-who-ate-candy had to slam on the brakes. Great oil drums, cement pilings,

236

blocked the road. It was common for people to close the roads past their houses. A spotlight lit up the truck. "Identify yourself," a voice shouted through a megaphone.

The driver put it in reverse, shots ricocheted off the hood, the fenders. We ducked, the shots kept coming. A group of bald guys chasing after the truck. Before we got up to speed, I peeked out and saw them running alongside with their red skin, not a hair on them.

—It's cool tonight, but if the blue haze keeps lowering we better be ready for a scorcher tomorrow. Worse than the Northeast.

—Worse?

—This city is nothing but cement, asphalt, rocks. Things that get superheated. Up north at least there's dirt and sand, they absorb the heat a little, instead of throwing it right back at you the way concrete does.

—We ought to get hold of a black silk umbrella for our friend here.

Suddenly another bald man appeared in front of the windshield, lunging onto the hood of the truck. And another. The man-who-ate-candy braked and swerved, the two of them lost their balance and fell off. He hit the accelerator. Before long another one jumped on the hood.

The man-who-sat-at-the-head-of-the-table took out his gun. Now him? I'd taken him for a peaceful sort, not the least bit violent. Without hesitating, he stuck his arm out the window and began shooting. Resolute. One of the bald guys fell. The others jumped off. Yapping like monkeys.

Above the rumble of the engine and the sucking noise the tires made on the soft asphalt, we could hear a loud whooshing sound which echoed throughout the area. Like a steam locomotive, parked in the train yard, raring to go. No light in the windows. A watchtower now and then, with a yellow gaslamp silently turning, slow motion.

And meanwhile the sensation of being watched was

pervasive. For a minute I thought I heard the blades of a helicopter throbbing overhead, but there was nothing to be seen in the dark sky. Unless they made blind flights. But my neck is burning, someone must be watching us. But who?

The truck continued advancing and retreating, zig-zagging in and out of blocked-off streets, turning back, inching forward. I hadn't the slightest idea where we were, these were streets I never dreamed existed. The man-who-ate-candy was a skillful driver, and he seemed quite familiar with the vehicle.

We brazenly moved in and out of lanes reserved exclusively for official use: ambulances, tanks, police cars, army transport buses carrying prisoners, vehicles coming from Isolation. During the day that would mean immediate arrest, no questions asked. How could they abandon the city like this at night, anything goes?

The neighborhoods changed for the worse the farther we went, more and more ugly and dilapidated apartment buildings. We crossed a wide street and entered an area in total ruins. A little farther on we passed the dim hulks of rubbled apartment buildings.

—Are we still in São Paulo?

—What a question!

—I must have fallen asleep, we've been driving so long.

—We're near Quarta Parada.

—Quarta Parada! That's really a ways out. What are we doing here?

—We're going to dump the trash.

—Why not just dump the furniture in the street? The city's totally deserted.

—And the bodies?

—Ah, so they all died, all the men in the back room.

—Yeah, they were pretty bad off.

—Or did you kill them?

—I swear to God we did no such thing. The only one killed was the barber. The others just didn't make it, the chances for those two bald guys was pretty slim to begin

238

with, they were contaminated. Condemned. People like that are dying like flies.

—And the barber? Who killed him?

—Look, this is no time for another one of your dissertations.

—What's the big deal? Just tell me.

—The important thing now is to unload the bodies without being seen.

—I still don't understand why you didn't just leave them on some street corner. It's pitch-dark.

—What about the Block-Watchers? Or the Vigilant Trustees of Night? You think they're not watching from behind their windows, hiding in doorways, watchtowers, spying with infrared cameras? Every last one of them watched our progress as we drove past.

—So why didn't they turn us in?

—Because we were just a truck. And what if they were to turn in Someone Who Counts? They'd be in some trouble. Now if they saw us unloading dead bodies, that would be something else.

—It's hard to believe that dead people make any difference at all in this city, there must be so many of them.

—It's not the dead people that matter, it's the political game you can play with them. It's a system of trade-offs, bargains, lucky hits.

The sector we were passing through now had quite a bit of activity. Which increased gradually until we were slowed to a crawl. People stared at us—that same look of fear and surprise. Everyone was carrying something. A bag, a box, a chair, plastic canes, an odd-shaped bundle.

Each block, more and more people. They carried lanterns made of tin cans and wire with a candle inside. Feeble lights which hardly lit their way. Memories from childhood of processions during Holy Week, the litter of the Lord on Good Friday, all the faithful following behind with their candles, the funeral dirge.

There was no song this time, just a dense murmur. Almost rhythmic. And above all the smell. Horrific. Pes-

239

tilential. There was a really pedantic geography teacher in my high school who used that word all the time, for anything and anybody. He considered it the highest insult.

For me it became a symbol of mystery, a kind of code. Synonymous with terrible things, unthinkable. It's not even in many dictionaries, at least not the abridged ones, and that makes it even more special. Pestilential. What I smell is the smell of death and decomposition. Garbage and excrement, sewage and sweat.

A bitter, penetrating smell. Sharp-edged. How can these people stand it? The crowd gets denser until finally we reach a wide-open space—if I saw it in a movie I'd criticize the scene for looking unreal—full of mountain upon mountain of garbage, all of which were crawling with people trying to carve out a comfortable niche for themselves.

Gigantic piles of plastic junk, towering columns of tin cans. Heaps of scrap metal, worthless knickknacks, broken-down furniture, every sort of rubbish, refuse, debris. I don't know if it looked more like a gigantic all-purpose junk shop or an open-air flea market swarming with incomprehensibly enthusiastic shoppers.

A miserable rabble, shabby, fleabitten, wandered the alley-upon-alley of trash with the same excitement Adelaide and I felt at the Super-Subsistence Centers on our obligatory shopping days. As if these heaps of useless items were breathtaking displays of rare, imported goods.

Many people stood around large bonfires. They were burning plastic bags, more smoke than fire. Bands of ragged-looking kids climbed the mountains of trash, searching for treasures. They stopped and watched our truck make its way slowly across the valley of ashen filth and grime.

—Aren't there any Civil Guards on duty around here?

—Beats me, said my nephew.

—Don't these people have fights and things? This place looks chaotic.

240

—Who knows. But it would be just as well if they did, the idea is to let as many of them die as possible.

—On purpose? That's crazy—I can't believe it.

—Are you kidding? These people live like millionaires compared to conditions in the Pauper Encampments where everyone's piled on top of everyone else without even the strength to breathe, much less get up. And people like you wonder why they don't rebel! The only thing they *can* do is open and close their mouths, begging for food and water. Just like so many baby birds—exactly the same, except they don't utter a peep.

—But that's horrible!

—Horrible? What are you talking about? Horrible. You talk just for the sake of talking. Meanwhile, you've got a cozy life, you've managed to stay inside the city limits, with a house, enough food to eat, an influential nephew . . .

—Not all that influential, apparently. Whatever happened with that helicopter, it showed a breach in your influence.

—A street scrap, jealousy, that's all. No problem.

—If you're so influential, how come you never helped me find Adelaide?

—She's fine. Leave it at that.

—What do you mean she's fine? You've heard from her?!

—No . . . well, I mean, not exactly . . .

—Tell me, tell me everything.

—Take your hands off me, Uncle Souza. The other day I heard she was at a friend's house, that's all.

—How did you hear? What friend? Did you talk to her?

—No . . . someone called me . . . with a message . . .

—I knew it, she's at your house, isn't she? Admit it.

—Don't be ridiculous.

—I always thought you were much too calm about the whole thing, you never even mentioned her after she disappeared. And the two of you were so close. You may

241

be independent, ruthless, even, but you always depended on her. I'll tell you something, if there's anyone you ever cared about, I mean really fell for, it was your aunt. Ever since you were little.

—You don't know what you're talking about.

—When you were ten years old you'd hide under the bed, just to get a good look at her legs, remember?

—All children do things like that.

—Maybe. But you kept it up even when you were eighteen...

—Me? At eighteen?

—How many times did I find you peeking through the keyhole into the bathroom, huh?

—You're sick, Uncle Souza, really sick.

—How come you never got married, then, tell me that? How come the only girl friend you ever had looked just like Adelaide? It was a family joke—that she was our daughter and you were engaged to marry your own cousin!

—Sick.

—And when she had that accident and had to have plastic surgery, what happened? Her nose and chin came out a little different, not bad, mind you, but different, so what did you do? You broke up with her. No explanations.

—I didn't like her anymore, that's all.

—Of course you didn't like her anymore, she didn't look like Adelaide anymore, that's why.

—Shut up, Uncle Souza, I've heard enough of your foolishness. I mean it. Or I'll have you sent to Isolation.

—Even if it would hurt your Aunt Adelaide?

—She never cared for you anyway.

—You sound awfully sure of yourself all of a sudden.

—I am.

—How would you know something like that?

—She told me. We spent a lot of time together, the two of us, remember? She'd play the piano all day long. She was different during the day, happy, she'd sing, she'd get all gussied up.

—All gussied up . . . You talk like an old man.

—What did you ever do for her? Before you came home the piano would be closed up tight, the nice clothes went back into the closet. Her best clothes spent most of the time in the closet. Why was that, Uncle Souza? Why was it you never let her wear flashy things? Low necklines? Once she told me that you were the jealous type, she said the two of you had a big fight before you got married over a miniskirt.

—It never mattered to me what she wore. Just once, she bought a dress a size too small, it was really tight, she was hanging out completely. It wasn't even a fight, really, I just calmly told her she shouldn't go out like that.

—And what about her mind, Uncle Souza? What about her thoughts?

—What do you mean, her thoughts?

—What did she think about life, what did she want out of life?

—What is this, an interrogation?

—You started it.

—Is she at your house, I want to know. She is, isn't she? Are you holding Adelaide prisoner?

—Ha, you watch too much television. I saw a late movie the other night, come to think of it, a real old one, I had insomnia. This guy is in love with a girl, so he kidnaps her and keeps her prisoner in his house. What was the name of it?

—How should I know?

—You're big on movies, you must remember it.

—Sounds sort of like *The Collector*.

—Right! So, anyway, you think I kidnapped Aunt Adelaide, huh? You'd better go over my house and check.

—Loan me your CIRCA and I will.

—You think you can get in that easily?

—Is this okay, boss?

The man-who-ate-candy brought the truck to a stop in the middle of a small open space. People stared at us

243

from the surrounding mountains of trash, uneasy, suspicious. The blue haze was extremely low to the ground. The tallest peaks disappeared into the haze. A picture postcard from the Alps.

The sun was just beginning to rise, and the mess all around looked even worse in that indecisive light, plus the smell was unbearable. How could things like this go on without our knowing? Not even hidden. Right here, in the open.

Odd. We hadn't gone through one District Access station, though we had passed through several neighborhoods. I don't remember seeing a single checkpoint in operation. And as far as I know they're not supposed to close at night; on the contrary, they redouble their vigilance, because of the ferrets trying to sneak into districts they don't belong in. Maybe the truck's painted the official colors or something like that.

As we got out of the truck both the man-who-ate-candy and the one with the radio always glued to his ear looked wary, guns in hand. My nephew, on the other hand, seemed almost distracted, as if he were used to such situations. They began unloading the furniture. People cautiously gathered around.

They watched in silence, stunned I suppose to see so much furniture being discarded. And how long would it have been since they'd seen anything made of wood? A bald man climbed down and approached with a disinterested air. He reached out casually and touched a chair, then suddenly grabbed it and bolted. We watched as he hurriedly broke it down into pieces and threw them onto his fire.

Soon others plucked up their courage and pressed closer. Afraid to make a wrong move with the revolvers in full view, they stepped forward one or two at a time, surprisingly orderly, and picked an item out of the pile. Then they each retreated to their group and began breaking the furniture into pieces, feeding it to the fire, looking pleased with themselves.

My nephew walked over to a group of blind people

who probably couldn't understand what the hubbub was about. He held up a bottle of water and shook it back and forth. I can't say their eyes lit up, but their toothless mouths curled into sick-looking smiles. A few of them made strange, guttural sounds, and they all held their hands out blindly in front of them.

—You want some water?

—Mmmmm, mmmmmmmmmm.

—Then you've got to help dig, okay?

—Mmmmmmmmmm. Mmmmmmm.

—You'll have to dig really deep, understand?

—Glerg, glerg, mmmmmmmmmm.

The man-who-ate-candy opened the truck's side compartment and took out picks and shovels, then handed them to the blind people. My nephew kept shouting to dig really deep, that he'd tell them when to stop. He had to get them organized and involved in the work before they had time to start fighting among themselves with the tools he'd distributed.

I stared at the fire. Tables, chairs, bureaus, chests, bedside lamps. My wedding bonfire. We had picked it all out together, bought on credit, paid with difficulty. Up in flames in a second. Nothing. Wood. Man-made objects. All gone now.

In a flash. I could tell these men the story of each piece of furniture. What had been in each drawer. Every piece of paper that had crossed the desk, every piece of clothing, paper clip, straight pin. What did it matter to save things, to keep everything neatly arranged? Suddenly I feel foolish standing here, transfixed.

A man with his eyeballs hanging down in front of his face starts to drag off the trunk. Another comes over to help him. And a third. All of them with their eyes out of the sockets. There's a scuffle, the lid tilts open, and I see packets of brown paper go flying, small thuds as they land in the dust and filth on the ground. What would Adelaide say? What wouldn't she say? What the hell.

More men with their eyeballs hanging out trudge down from the heaps of trash. It seems as though people had split into groups according to their particular afflictions. Maimed, deformed, bald, flabby skin, cancerous armpits. Should I be looking for people with holes in their hands? So I can join my class?

There's something familiar about these men, but what? It's just a feeling I have, the brown and green blob comes back and the whole left side of my body is momentarily paralyzed. This time along with the blob comes a stabbing pain, an awful throbbing in my neck and forehead.

I close my eyes, but the blob of color is still there. The motionless green mass and the brown moving inside it. An image begins to form, a clear one. And then unforms in an instant. I feel better, I can move again. And looking at those men with eyeballs popped from their sockets bring me back to my childhood.

In the blob, the green is fixed and the brown moves inside it. An image just beginning to form, yes, it will be crystal-clear. If I could just get it to last longer, I could find out what it is. But I'm no longer paralyzed, the image dissolves. Becomes liquid, brown and green running together.

And what comes back to me, violently, is my childhood. Gangs. Street battles. Nothing criminal, just boyhood bravura based on a pretense of loyalty to the neighborhood. Fraternizing with kids from outside was out of the question, the thing was to stick together and keep all the invaders at bay.

The minute a stranger appeared, we'd run to check out who it was: new resident or enemy spy? If he couldn't explain what he was doing on our turf to our satisfaction, he got a beating to remember and had to slink home with his tail between his legs. Then we knew we were in for retaliation.

Always ready for a good fight. There were strategic positions behind trees, niches in garden walls, on rooftops. Luckily, not many cars passed through the neighborhood because when we got going, rocks, sticks, broomhandles flew through the air. One of our specialties was marbles propelled by slingshot. The battles never lasted very long.

What was important was the sense of adventure, the magical transformation of movie duels, cowboys and Indians, cops and robbers, into real life. As soon as the first injury occurred—goose-egg, skinned knee, cut foot—the bands dispersed. We unconsciously avoided aiming for the face.

There was a certain undeclared code of ethics, an unsigned pact. It was a good, clean fight—cheerful in a way. A way of blowing off steam. The next day we'd all see each other in school. No grudges. A few ugly looks, sure, the most macho of the bunch asserting themselves with a snarl, but nothing more than that. Sometimes groups from a couple of neighborhoods would team up together if the outside threat was particularly intimidating. That battle over, the alliance was dissolved, and it was back to being enemies.

Until one day, for the first time, the police arrived in the middle of a battle. Summoned by some intolerant neighbor, no doubt. Unaware of the implicit codes underlying the fight, the cops overreacted. Or maybe it was out of malice, their natural sadistic instinct was well known.

In any case, down came the clubs on our heads, but surprise: the boys fought back. Twenty-odd crazy kids up against a half-dozen policemen with real weapons. Of course there was no way to win, they were experts, and efficient, but it seemed all part of the game.

Until one of the cops pulled out his gun and shot into the middle of the crowd. Total confusion. Everyone dove for cover, climbing trees, leaping fences, jumping in windows, down manholes. Only one boy, stunned and disoriented, remained in the street.

The police got in their cars and were gone in a flash. The boy simply stood in the middle of the street for a few dazed moments. It seemed to take him awhile to begin screaming. The rest of us slowly emerged from our hiding places.

I was in a room in some house, I didn't even know
whose, and I remember jumping back out the open window, terrified. I think I was the first one to reach him,
and what I saw made me throw up and begin shaking
uncontrollably. The bullet had taken out a piece of bone
next to his eye, I don't know how, but the eyeball was
hanging out next to his nose, blood spurting from the
socket.

Blood and yellow mucus. I passed out and came to
back at home. My father gave me a good scolding: "It
could just as well have been you, do you see what comes
of your foolish games?" I didn't sleep well for months.
Years later, even, I'd wake up with the vision of that
eyeball sprung out of place, sickeningly bloody.

It was my first contact with actual violence. We'd
played at violence without really having any idea what
it was. And that shot marked the end of our fantasy. The
last gang war. Reality struck home.

It was the talk of the town—mostly because the policeman responsible continued on the force, unsus-
pended. He got off scot-free. "All in the line of duty,"
said the chief, and that was that. The injured boy's father
was too unsophisticated and unassuming to press a lawsuit. He didn't even have the courage to register an informal complaint.

For a while the whole bunch of us roamed the streets,
singly and in pairs, slingshots in our pockets. If we had
run into that cop there would have been a massacre, who
knows what would have happened. We were ready for
anything, we wanted revenge. But our parents inter-
vened.

They made us give up our hope for vengeance. I don't
think I was ever able to reconcile having followed my
father's advice: "It will only make things worse, better
to stay out of it. It's settled, over, forget it." The same
with the other boys. Our hate turned inward toward ourselves.

—Fire above their heads, why don't you? Disperse
this rabble.

248

—What for?

—Look what they're doing to my things.

—You're a strange guy, Souza. I just can't understand you. We brought that stuff here to get rid of it, didn't we? Let them do what they want with it.

—But they were my things!

The men with their eyeballs hanging out were shouting and struggling with each other, rolling around in the mess, falling into the fire. Furniture to feed bonfires. They grabbed at the bundles of brown paper, tearing things out of each other's hands. Everything got mixed up in an infernal confusion of clutching and shrieking.

I don't know how the thin shreds of tissue which connected their eyeballs to their heads weren't torn off in the confusion. They seemed to look out for each other in the midst of their ferocity. The brown paper wrappings were begining to be torn open. I stood and watched, utterly fascinated.

So it was true. I was looking at the confirmation. Confirmation of the irreparable distance between me and my wife. Thirty years together without knowing. And in less than half an hour the revelation came to me whole. As the brown paper fell away to reveal—finally—what had been inside.

### THE ADELAIDE WHO EMERGES FROM THE BROWN PAPER BUNDLES LEAVES SOUZA PERPLEXED— WHICH IS HIS WIFE'S TRUE IDENTITY? AND WHAT NOW?

So it was true. It made me furious to see that my nephew was right. Him of all people. I felt miserable, as bad or worse than I did after I agreed with my father not to try to get revenge for the boy who lost his eye. The brown paper bundles contained clothing of Adelaide's that I had never seen before.

Silk and satin. Bright patterns, flashy colors, gigantic

249

flowers, crazy designs, low necklines, miniskirts. The women with eyeballs hanging out of their sockets shrieked as they wrangled over each piece of clothing. They were ferocious, but not stupid—they'd do anything to get hold of one except tear it. I've never seen a fight so full of *politesse*.

Right in front of me, those horrible women shed their rags and put on Adelaide's showy dresses. Then they really looked like aberrations: princesses turned to frogs, it was a Black Sabbath, witches dancing in the moonlight on the patio of miracles.

I tried to imagine Adelaide in those clothes, but I couldn't. I was so used to her delicate figure in tailored suits or discreet, dark-colored dresses. In my mind, at least, flashy clothes just didn't suit her. But what if that were her true image—extroverted?

Suddenly my world was completely off balance. The rhythm fractured. And the pieces, like a jigsaw puzzle with ragged edges, no longer fit together. Everything had to be rethought, done over, conversations had to be renewed which had never been started, tendernesses reclaimed which had never been initiated. The woman I loved never existed. I felt hollow.

For I had loved Adelaide. In my way. Maybe it wasn't the right way, but it was my way. What good does it do to theorize now on the ways of loving? There's just one question aching inside me: is there still time, or has it all slipped away? How many chances does a man get in his life?

What to say, then, about our fleeting insomniac nights? Would it have been any different if I had know about this other Adelaide? I was hit with a sensation of loss. Boundless. There's a word my grandfather used often when he talked about the forests: incalculable. It's not fair to have to lose something in order to understand that it was yours.

Of course there's no way to recover those lost nights. Those gestures, caresses, murmurs, moans, sweat, smells, laughter gone forever. It's like being cut in half, BAM, under the wheels of a train. The upper limit of pain that the consciousness can endure without anaesthesia.

What wildness we could have experienced in that bedroom. Exploring each other to the limit. Limits. They were always there, barriers, at least in our heads. We could have gone all the way. Or beyond, if we'd known what "all the way" was. Meanwhile, in silence, we settled for lukewarm.

A love that was well-behaved, unchanging. Full of respect, or at least so we thought. No, not we—Adelaide had nothing to do with it. It was I who thought in terms of respect, she would never have used the word. And at this point I realize I can't answer for her anymore, we're no longer the inseparable couple I thought we were.

A life totally dependent on the "if." If I'd done, if I'd looked for, if I'd tried. An existence based on a hypothesis whose time had gone. I read a phrase in a newspaper once which made no sense to me at all: salvation with no tomorrow. Now I think I understand what that means.

I climbed one of the piles of debris. It was hard work, and what a stink. They say this is where the cemetery of Quarta Parada used to be. Acres and acres of graves, tombs, monuments. And the real estate companies made the most of it, once there was no more cemetery space left in the downtown area.

After the last house was razed and the last building erected, all there was left were suburbs stretching off into the distance. And the cemeteries: traditional, first-class deluxe, potter's fields. Cemeteries for Catholics, Jews, Protestants, Evangelicals, Mormons, Leftists. And no more room to bury anybody, regardless of affiliation. So they got the brilliant idea to build straight up.

There was an intense publicity campaign, ads everywhere. They gradually prepared people to accept the idea of seeing their sacred loved ones moved. The new monuments were breathtaking—tall spires, white needles piercing the clouds. Distraught families competed for the upper levels, those closer to the Lord, according to the advertisements. The real estate companies multiplied a hundredfold the return they could get from a given plot of land. And their towering mastabas were built on a foundation of ash and bone.

There's no way I can be sure this used to be Quarta Parada. Circulation limitations were established years ago, and since then I haven't been able to walk around the city much. All I can see from the top of these pyramids of trash is the same nondescript building repeated again and again to the horizon. Identical. A monotonous panorama.

Building after building, smooth concrete walls, windows with grates over them, bare facades. Of course they look alike—they were built with standardized plans. The designs, floor plans, materials, all uniform, to lower the costs. The only differences were in the pompous names: Edifice Rimbaud, Marie Antoinette Manor, The Versailles, Noble Hall, Babylonian Gardens, Villa Royale, Lustre of Florence.

Tadeu Pereira and I used to walk a lot. We covered the whole of downtown on foot, and sometimes we went as far out as the older neighborhoods of Elysian Fields, Higienopolis, Bras. We searched out the vestiges of Finland and Lithuania in the back alleys of Vila Zelina, forgotten pieces of Japan along the lanes of Liberdade.

Sunday morning was always a good time for long walks, while Adelaide was at mass and then visiting her parents. She grumbled that weekends had all but disappeared, she missed our weekly barbecue. Meat was already getting scarce in those days.

Neither Tadeu nor I was good with a camera—even the most automatic models gave us trouble. So we noted our finds on the clipboards and pads we carried along. It was slow going, absorbed our full attention. Like combing the city with a fine-toothed comb. But we were in no hurry. Time was ours.

Once in a while Tadeu would attempt a drawing—nostalgia from art courses in college. (He had wanted to be an architect, not a calculus professor, but he failed the college entrance exam for architecture on account of a few multiple-choice questions.) The two of us walked along noting each old house, mansion, odd building. Architect friends of ours helped us pinpoint styles and eras. We discovered hidden, protected villages in the sprawling downtown area. Parks which were well-kept secrets, streets left intact since the twenties, pockets of buildings that had somehow resisted the advance of the real estate mongers.

An ancient fig tree on Piratininga Street. A collection of art-deco stained-glass windows on Bresser Street. Statues of Calixto deteriorating in a forgotten chapel in Santana. The leftovers of the Warchavchik project, completely deformed by the addition of a plastic paneled garage and cheap mosaics applied to the facade.

A Brecheret sculpture lost among ceramic dwarves. A colonial convent transformed into a body shop. Treasure in the Armenian Basilica: bas-relief from the Church of Althamar. A bronze door in a synagogue in Bom Retiro.

We had no scientific method, really. We did it for fun, and a little bit out of nostalgia. I guess we felt like finding ourselves again on the geographic blueprint of the city we wandered at random. We wanted to feel that there were still points of reference. Maybe we were looking for a kind of security in that.

Flowerpots in the window on a gloomy block of Rua Aurora. A rickety wrought-iron staircase leading to an abandoned veranda. Rusty garden gates. Facades with inlaid marble or porcelain. Vaulted passageways. Cupolas, pavilions, greenhouses, terraces, belvederes, pillars, entablatures, ornamented archways, fine stucco, cornices, rosettas, domes, columns, art-nouveau doors, baroque, gothic. All of it duly recorded and added to our register.

Until one day Tadeu and I looked at each other and shook our heads, unable to look each other in the eye. It hit us like a bolt of lightning. Suddenly we felt so self-conscious, so distressed, that we split up. Without saying a word. Each knowing, implicitly, why. The more we wandered, the closer we had gotten to the periphery of the city. Our self-conceived work weighed on us, it had somehow become useless, inconsequential.

What we'd been doing was not radical, nor could you call it revelry. Good grief, that word hasn't been used for centuries. And I forgot all about that little notebook of mine—to imagine Tadeu still has it! My curiosity is piqued once again.

Today I see (although still nebulously) a certain sense to our fixation. But wait—here come the bodies, one wrapped in Adelaide's precious embroidered sheets, no less. But I don't get it—there are five bodies, instead of four. My God, what's happening to this world? They've killed them all, I know they have the three who came begging for water, and then the poor barber. If you ask me, it was the guy-who's-always-listening-to-the-radio. He's obviously a paranoid. Still, there should only be four.

That fifth bundle is bothering me, I've got to climb down off this pile of trash and talk to my nephew, find out what they're up to now. What an incomprehensible muddle. All I know is that behind his mask of impunity is fear. But of what? Of whom?

—You don't look too chipper, Uncle Souza. It must be the smell.

—It has nothing to do with the smell. I want to know who's in the other bundle.

—One of the guys from the back room.

—There were only three of them.

—Four.

—I may be old, but I'm not senile. There were only three.

—Yeah, but another guy, just as bad off, came another time. We didn't bother you about it, you were asleep.

—I want to see for myself.

—No way, Uncle Souza. They're all wrapped up already.

—Wrapped up or not, I want to see.

254

—What good would it do? You don't know him. He's just a deaf guy who came around looking for food.

—Let me see, it will make me feel better.

—Forget about it, we don't have time. It's almost dawn. If the sun comes up all of a sudden, we'll be dead.

—For the love of your aunt, I beg you . . .

—Don't start that again, *please*.

—Tell me who it is.

—A deaf guy, I already told you.

—So what does that mean, there are thousands of deaf guys in this city.

—What is that—you want to know why he went deaf? I think it was a buzz saw.

—Very funny.

—It happens, you know.

—Cut the jokes.

—You're awfully jumpy today, you know that?

—Who is it? I have a bad premonition about this . . .

—Keep concentrating, I think you've got it . . .

—Just tell me. Is it the piano teacher?

—You got it!

—Why? Good God, why?

—He had a heart attack, we had nothing to do with it. He never even made it up the stairs after hearing that Aunt Adelaide had disappeared. He collapsed.

—Bastard, shameless bastard—

I threw myself on top of him as the others watched, impassive. With just his left arm he tossed me into the garbage. Child's play for someone who had been scrupulously trained according to the rigid notions of physical education of the Mili-techs. I hate to be hit. Pinching is even worse, drives me crazy.

I advanced toward him again, blindly. There's a difference between fighting believing you can win and fighting when you know from the start it's a lost cause. For me it was just pure rage. It wasn't even a question of honor anymore, none of this "I'm invulnerable" business. Again he was able to restrain me with just his left hand.

255

—Enough, Uncle Souza. Think about your heart.

—You worthless piece of . . .

—That's right, Uncle Souza, curse me, curse me good, make you feel better.

—You'll pay for this.

—On the installment plan?

—I can't believe you, I listen to you and I just can't believe you.

—This conversation is over, Uncle Souza. You're really not getting to me, you know. And it's a very old conversation at that, I don't even know how you survived this long the way you think.

—I feel nothing but contempt for you.

—And I couldn't care less. Do you think it matters what you think of me?

—Tell me it wasn't the piano teacher.

—But it was.

—An abomination. I'll turn you in to the Guards.

—And I'll kill you first.

—Would you dare?

—Do I have to?

Would Adelaide recognize this nephew as the boy to whom she dedicated herself all those years? Our substitute son. We taught him all we could. Nothing took. I'm sure of it now, absolutely nothing. The only thing he hasn't done—so far—is to kill me, I suppose due to some last-ditch residue of decency.

The helicopter loomed above us all at once from behind a mountain of garbage. We heard the noise, and by the time we looked up it was already overhead. The sun hadn't quite come up yet, just an undefined flush. And then two spotlights from the belly of the machine exposed us.

A rotating machine gun started its whirl, sparks flying everywhere. Intensely brilliant, intermittent ribbons of light shot through that dim brightness. Gunfire struck the ground in soft thuds, setting off small explosions. There were shouts everywhere.

256

## FOLLOW THE SIGNS TO
## THE ALLEVIATION CENTER

Based on the Japanese model, the Ministry of Social Well-Being has constructed, adjacent to all Privileged neighborhoods, Alleviation Centers, which function like private clubs, with monthly fees, and also offer hourly rates. They are tiled gymnasiums, stark and spacious, with dolls made of plastic, foam, or synthetic rubber suspended from the rafters. Patrons, called therapeutic patients, may punch, beat, insult, scream at, spit on, or even urinate on the doll of his or her choice. If a patient would prefer to shoot at a doll he or she must sign up for a private room. If stabbing is the primary desire, there are special dolls which bleed. A visit to the Alleviation Center near you will relieve suppressed tension, reduce stress, nervousness, fatigue, chronic headaches; patients relax and make themselves comfortable. Regular attendance can help avoid the domestic or professional dissensions which result in divorce and unemployment. On the social level, the Alleviation Centers eliminate the possiblity of Isolation.

Bald people, cripples, old people, the lame, the ones with their eyeballs hanging out, everyone went running. My nephew rolled to the ground with admirable agility, bullets flying after him. Combat. I didn't have the slightest idea what to do, I was terrified.

## FINALLY, AS A RESULT OF SOUZA'S PRODDING, THE NEPHEW REVEALS THE TRUTH ABOUT THE BARBER— AND IT'S PRETTY HARD TO BELIEVE

Gusts of wind from the helicopter blades hurled ground-up trash in all directions. Something rotten hit me in the face, splashing into my mouth, stinging my nostrils. A piece of it stuck to my forehead. Unidentifiable, bitter-tasting, the consistency of snot. It dripped down my neck.

I felt so disgustingly filthy that I'd completely forgotten the bullets spraying around me. My capacity for abstraction is a constant amazement to me, how, for instance, at a moment like this, I can be distracted from the sudden reality of death—the biggest abstraction of all.

But they're clearly not trying to kill anyone. Nothing would have been easier than to hit any one of us with those machine guns swiveling around like a carousel gone mad. Even so, we ran. After rolling to the ground, my nephew got up and dashed off zigzagging like a real expert.

There was a time when I associated the sight of helicopters hovering over the city on patrol, the noise of the blades whipping the air, with freedom for some reason. I don't know where that idea came from, it has nothing to do with anything. Now the sound produces panic. I'm paralyzed. In my immobility the green and brown blob comes back.

This time it's the inverse reaction: the paralysis came

first, then the colors in my head. The brown part moves from the inside out, like a lizard slithering through jelly. The green is stationary—no, wait, it's not, either, there's a slight oscillating movement. If it lasts a little longer, I'll find out what it is.

Why worry, let the blob take over. I used to be scared that it would grow and grow and overwhelm me. I'd dive behind it as if I'd fallen into a black hole. Now it doesn't matter to me where it takes me, all I want is to understand it.

It's so close, and yet I can't quite reach it—like having a word on the tip of your tongue and still not being able to get it out. It's agonizing. The green part's movements are getting broader, like wind sweeping through brush. The splotch takes over, I'm beginning to see into it, and the wind from the blades of the helicopter scatters branches everywhere.

Vegetation. Tree trunks, twigs, leaves. I don't understand how the wind from the helicopter got inside my head like this, furiously shaking this forest which is, after all, part of a memory. The idea of death comes looking for me again, and arrives in one luminous burst like one of the bullets spraying around me.

Which fly from the potbellied helicopter in intermittent flashes, allowing me to see the green part defining itself as the forest. My eyes undergo a succession of transformations, very gradual: magnifying glass, binoculars, microscope, long-range telescope.

I'm right up close to the trunk, I make a cut in the flesh of the tree, the leaves, I see nervous offshoots, cells, I have the sensation of becoming part of this vegetation. And it's all happening so fast, there's no time to figure out where I am, I keep getting lost in the blob.

I still can't identify the brown part, it can't be the earth because it's moving, it comes out of the green, becomes separate, has a life of its own. As if it fled, after having been broken open. Another feeling of separation. It makes me shudder. If only this infernal noise would stop.

If only that helicopter would let me think. Sure. And I'll keep standing here like an imbecile, completely exposed. I run behind one of the oil drums, crawl into a pile of trash, I can hear the bullet eating away at the mountains of what must be flammable stuff.

The narrowest of margins. By the narrowest of margins, I don't get hit, but neither do I discover what that blob is. I see the man-who's-always-listening-to-the-radio stand up, he's got something in his hand he's about to throw, but the helicopter swoops down over him. Closer and closer, without firing a shot.

Then it's practically on top of him, he's knocked down and the object in his hand rolls next to his head. The helicopter neatly lifts back up into the air, what a magnificent animal! Then a blinding flash, as the man-who-listens-to-the-radio's face explodes.

It was hard to take, let me tell you. The man was a stranger, he'd invaded my house, but still we had become connected somehow in the few days we'd spent together. Maybe it wasn't exactly a connection, more like habit. Someone to talk to, if I felt like talking. Or listening to, when he wanted to talk. And he sure was a talker.

Then to see him explode like a balloon at a child's birthday party, right there in front of me. Some things are just impossible to accept. This is one of them. I refuse to take it in, file it away as a part of life. I know that if I keep saying to myself over and over: "Okay, accept it, that's the way it goes," it would finally become reality instead of such a blinding shock.

But have you ever seen a human head disintegrate before your very eyes? It was a first for me. Engraved on my consciousness in slow motion. A sudden, violent clarity. Odd, I don't remember hearing a sound. Maybe I was so terrified that I retained only the image, repeating over and over like an instant replay.

The flash of light from the object—bomb, hand grenade, who knows what it was, I don't know anything about such things—lit up his face and then ate his skin, eyes, nose. Teeth flew into the air, shattered. His bones were ground to a pulp, pulverized, turned to dust.

And then bones, teeth, flesh, skin, pulp seemed to join together again, all turned to dust. Taken by the wind, which was nothing more than the air dislocated by the blast of light. I don't know if you can understand this, but it's what I saw in that short space when time stopped.

I'd like to talk to Adelaide about it and ask her if the children's heads exploded that way as they hit the freezing water. But that's crazy, that was just a dream, a specter that persecuted her for years, a vision she nourished while she waited for the letter, which never came.

—Hit the dirt, Uncle Souza, are you shell-shocked or what? Lie down, or hide behind the garbage or something!

Sure, if I could find room in this heap of people. I watch my nephew leap up and kick his way through all the figures crouched on the ground: a real trailblazer. Nimbly making a human trench out of those bodies. If I told a story like this to Adelaide, she'd never believe it.

The helicopter had moved a little ways off, but still hovered overhead, its blades purring softly. Of course it was watching us, bristling, ready to swoop down on us again at any moment. Cat and mouse. Obviously my nephew is involved in something big, something serious, this is no child's play.

Would this brute of a helicopter waste ammunition just to hunt down some poor unfortunate, some petty water thief? All they'd need to subdue this pack of ragamuffins living off garbage is an unarmed Civil Guard. Just seeing a uniform scares them, a light tap would knock them over, a raised voice makes them run for their lives. I'm not surprised at how they cower in fear.

An awful lot of prayers for so few sins. And what about me? I'm with Pilate, I wash my hands. I could have been at home, I've got nothing to do with all this. They must have brought me along for some reason. They

261

must have wanted me out of the apartment. But why? The pieces just don't fit together, no matter how much I rack my brain.

Could I have been in the way somehow by staying behind? Was there something they didn't want me to see? If I made a list of all the questions I've asked myself in the last few years, I'd have enough to fill an encyclopedia.

The helicopter was circling, as if searching for something. A man leaned out the window, peering through binoculars. My nephew and his two remaining acolytes kept their heads buried in the trash, just a few meters from where I was huddling. A sign they, too, were scared.

Probably more likely they'll die from contamination than from their enemies' bullets. I still can't tell if the people up there are trying to intimidate them or if they really want to wipe out the whole band. All you can hear are those engines, the crackling of bonfires, and the wheezing of the people with their heads in the trash.

Scattered weeping. Everyone waiting. I discover that I'm completely exposed again, I don't know how to protect myself, which place is the best place, the position where the machine-gun fire can't get me. After all, I've never been to war, I don't even understand strategy in movies.

Time passes, we stay motionless, like fools, like sitting ducks, spied on by a metal vulture that seems unable to decide what to do. Nowadays you have to spend a lot of time telling yourself to be patient, the hell with that. All of a sudden I feel utterly ridiculous lying here in the filth for no apparent reason.

I was about to say: I'm talking to my buttons. Have you ever heard anything sillier? Even if you're a tailor! But I've told myself over and over again it's no use looking for explanations. You just have to accept things, live from moment to moment, survive.

Summing up the fragments to see if in the end they add up to a life. When I was a child my mother drummed the dogmas and biases of the church into my head. There

262

were forbidden words: Why? How? Jesus is in the host. How can that be? He just is. The Pope is infallible. How? He just is.

Adam was made by God. And God? Yes, well, He is, and was, and always shall be. He had no beginning—my father always said that God was like a perpetual-motion machine, sufficient unto Himself. Years later I spent hours in the backyard of a relative everyone in the family considered crazy, Sebastião Bandeira.

Sebastião was trying to build a perpetual-motion machine. He was an uncultivated man, with no book-learning whatsoever. He didn't understand a single principle of physics. But he built a contraption out of sticks and wire that would spin for days and days. Still, Sebastião wasn't satisfied because he had had to start it moving.

The helicopter came back shooting. Low to the ground: arms, legs, pieces of heads in the line of fire. Smoke, screaming, garbage scattering like swallows in the summertime. Some people didn't react, they stayed in the garbage, seemingly indifferent.

Others ran for it. If you could call it that: an awkward dragging movement. Like a sack race hopping along off balance, crazy to get somewhere, anywhere.

The helicopter made four or five passes, still firing. Some of the bullets started new fires. Smoke from burning plastic and rotting stuff filled the air, but the worst was the burning rubber. My eyes stung terribly, my tongue was scorched, my throat was raw.

Coughing came from everywhere, along with the moans and cries of the wounded. Where are the Civil Guards? Why haven't they appeared to prevent a total massacre? Ha, Souza, we're all birds of a feather here. From their point of view, the more who die the better, fewer problems for the System.

It was impossible to see through all the smoke, but the noise of the engine seemed to be farther off. My nephew raised his head out of the trash, there was that insolent grin again. The man-who-always-ate-candy looked dazed, probably didn't have the slightest idea

263

what had happened. The man-who-sat-at-the-head-of-the-table stood up. He looked worried.

—Did you get hit, Uncle Souza?

—No.

—Scared?

—You could say so.

—That was nothing. They just wanted to give us something to think about.

—And look at all the casualties...

—All the better. These people are already condemned. Sooner or later the Civil Guards would have rounded up the majority of them, anyway. After all, they're escapees from the Encampments. Who knows how they even managed to get into the city.

—So what now?

—Let's go home.

—What about the people you killed? All forgotten?

—I didn't kill anybody, Uncle Souza.

—Oh, it was me, then?

—You certainly have a one-track mind—and what's that worth these days?

—It's worth something to me.

—What's worse, you're a real bore, an old moralist at heart. Forget about your head, all it does is rattle around. Your ideas about death are ultra-old-fashioned, you know that? But I'll let you in on a little secret—my rank in the New Army gives me permission to kill.

—Permission?

—Surprised?

—Well, maybe permission to kill thugs, okay. In the line of duty, et cetera. But not the barber, not the piano teacher, not those poor sick fellows who came to the door asking for charity.

—Those poor sick fellows invaded your house, have you forgotten?

—And you and your friends didn't?

—That old story again? This is getting repetitive...

—It must be hardening of the arteries, said the man-who-sat-at-the-head-of-the-table.

—And the barber, Uncle Souza, the barber was no prince.

—He was a good man, I've known him thirty years.

—Oh yeah? Maybe you'd like to know something about him, then. He was the leader of a neighborhood gang, bet you didn't know that, huh? A gang which specialized in robbing water. And in driving people out of their apartments. Remember when he wanted you to put him in touch with me? When he found out I was a captain he got scared, that's all. He wanted to join up with us in the worst way. To infiltrate, so he'd be protected, so he'd get special information.

—I don't believe a word of what you're saying.

—Well, you should.

—Have you got any proof?

—Uncle Souza, do you think the Information Service of the New Army furnishes notarized, signed testimony, in triplicate, to the press?

—How else can I believe you?

—It's okay with me if you don't. No one worries about such things anymore, just you. What's important is living the best you can until someone gets you.

—The guys in that helicopter almost got us this time, said the man-who-ate-candy.

—I guess it wasn't our time to go, eh?

—Tomorrow we'll take care of them.

—And what about the music teacher? Who killed him? And why?

—Ha! How will we ever be able to satisfy this Sherlock Holmes over here? Or is it Poirot? James Bond, perhaps? Which one did you read when you were a kid, give me a hint. That's what it is, isn't it, Uncle Souza? I remember a whole bookshelf of yours full of police novels. Not even counting the magazines.

—Who killed the piano teacher?

—You figure it out. You want to play a little game? We'll supply the clues, you conduct the investigation. Clue number one: it wasn't the captain.

265

## THE USEFULNESS OF DISCOVERING
## WHO WAS RESPONSIBLE
## AND A CURIOUS
## DIALOG
## WITH THE GIRL WHO
## SPINS IN CIRCLES

—Clue number two, said the man-who-sat-at-the-head-of-the-table: he has diabetes, but don't worry, it's not fatal.

—Clue number three: he's always eating candy.

—Clue number four: he's standing right next to you.

—Clue number five: he's dying of laughter.

—Clue number six: he's half-cracked, but strong as a bull.

—Clue number seven: it was me, old buddy.

—Have you got it yet, or do you need more clues?

The day was perfectly clear. We were sweating. The blue haze hovered above the mountains of garbage. The fires only added to the oppressive heat, making it almost impossible to breathe. I couldn't stop coughing. I had to get out of there as soon as possible. So I gave up the idea of arguing with them. Who are they, anyway?

Clothes dripping with sweat, practically glued to my body. I was stinking, filthy. Life seemed to have returned to normal around us. The beggars, blind people, cripples—all of them moved like androids, rummaging for something usable in the rotting heaps of debris.

—Take me home.

The three of them looked at each other. Without pretense. Enough for me to understand: they don't want me to come back with them. Where in heaven are they going to leave me? My nephew steps back, the man-who-sat-at-the-head-of-the-table grabs me by the arm. When I resist, he tightens his grip and gives a decisive push, meaning: this is no game.

—Let me go.

—You're coming with me.

—Where?

—Home.

—What about my nephew?

—He went to get the truck. That's the only way we can get through the Access Stations.

—That's not how it seemed like last night.

—Everything changes with the sunrise.

—How poetic.

—Let's get moving . . .

—You're not taking me home, so just tell me, where *are* you taking me?

—Home, home . . .

—Christ, it's hot.

—If we don't hurry we'll end up in a heat pocket.

—Have they spread this far south already?

—Sure, there are lots of them around here. Relatively weak ones, though. Not like the ones in the Northeast. Here the sun blisters your skin but it doesn't kill you. Yet.

We snaked along through the alleys of smoking garbage that were still crawling with "the damned," people moving like automatons, almost in slow motion. Much more sluggish and awkward than the people downtown. Of course the people downtown eat, drink, and have somewhere to live. My God, I think we're all damned.

—If the pockets get worse, there'll be fires everywhere.

—You said they are getting worse. At least in the Northeast. So what will happen when there's nowhere else to go?

—The System, the Mili-techs, will find a solution.

—People will have to stay inside their houses.

—Sure, the ones who have houses to begin with. What about everybody else? There are five or six times as many with nowhere to go.

—And the System couldn't care less about them, they're all from the Encampments, right?

—I'm afraid not. There are plenty of middle-class people wandering around homeless, too. One of these days they'll discover the black silk umbrellas.

—What?

—I told you, remember, in the Northeast the only thing that could save you from the sun was a black silk umbrella.

—But there's no silk anymore, everything's nylon, synthetic.

—Yes, but there's synthetic silk. It works, but it's expensive.

—Where can you buy it?

—That's what we're trying to find out. And we were getting awfully close, too, before they threw us off the track. There's a whole lot of people out there looking for the same thing. A discovery like that doesn't stay a secret for long. We were right on the verge of a breakthrough; that's why we were using your apartment for headquarters. Something in the air, in the neighborhood.

—Did the barber have anything to do with it?

—We thought so, but it didn't turn out that way. His scam was stealing water and taking over apartments. He was into bad stuff, real gangsterism. We're not like that, we don't like to hurt anyone.

—Oh, that's cute! You don't like to hurt anyone! That really gets to me.

—Here's the truck.

It was moving slowly toward us, weaving around the crowds of people, horn honking persistently. The miserable wretches dragging themselves along looked up startled and ran off. People who were slow to react were pushed aside. The man-who-sat-at-the-head-of-the-table suddenly punched me, hard. I fell.

Stunned, the wind knocked out of me—it was as if someone were trying to strangle me. I clawed at my throat, trying to clear the air passage. There was no obstruction, it was just the effect of the blow, he got me in the Adam's apple, then glanced off my chin. Almost a knockout. Finally I was able to breathe.

With difficulty at first. Fuzzy vision, my head spinning. Once I realized what had happened, there I was on my knees, people standing around laughing. The laughing faces of ragamuffins. I don't know what was so hilarious. The truck had disappeared without a trace.

I could barely struggle to my feet. That Northeasterner is some bull. Probably wasn't even from the Northeast, I don't believe a word he said. He made up all those stories, I'm sure. Just my nephew's hired thug, that's all, probably a recruit for the New Army.

Whoever he was, he knocked me for a loop—I didn't even have time to defend myself. But I guess that would have been worse, then I would have really gotten pounded. Who would have imagined I was so weak...

Shit, now what do I do? How do I get out of here? For once in my life I'm up against something concrete. Limited. If I hang around here waiting, I'll turn into one of these worthless excuses for human beings.

Waiting for what, anyway? I've got to get out of here or I'll explode. If there's one thing I never could take, it's unpleasant odors. I decide everything on the basis of smell. That's how I fell in love with Adelaide, she was always so fresh, so perfumed. Delicious.

Get your head in gear, Souza, you'll never get out of here without a circulation pass. Unless there's a shortcut, some alley between blocks, I could try to walk parallel to the bus route. Ridiculous. I don't have the slightest idea where I am. And who could tell me?

Wait a minute. I've got to find what's left of the guy who always listened to the radio—I could go through his pockets, might get lucky. Not a bad idea. Just got to get my bearings. What a maze. All the piles of trash look the same. But that boy over there with no nose looks familiar—ah, there's my friend. The one with no head.

Sick at what I'm doing, I go through the dead man's pockets. Amputated legs, pants and all. I struggle not to vomit. A little money, a couple of unfamiliar ID cards in his wallet, tokens for the telephone, but no CIRCA. Damn.

Maybe he hid it in his shoes. Dark brown boots like the ones from the army, laced up tight, twisted out of shape. He must have been a recruit, I'm sure of it, not some nameless migrant from the Northeast. Cut from the same cloth as the rest of them. I wonder if he was in on killing the piano teacher, too.

I can't remember which direction I came from, but then what difference does that make, since I didn't know where I was. I was just following that guy who was planning all along to ditch me as soon as the truck appeared. Imbecile, I knew something was up. Why didn't I keep on my toes?

A group was gathering around a radio, how appropriate, if only my dead friend had ears left to hear. Badly dressed couples dancing slowly, out of synch with the agitated, hot music. No one is crazy enough to shake it up in this heat. Who's got the energy. A bolero slowed to a crawl.

Two steps forward, one step back, just for the pleasure of dancing, reclaiming old customs. The sun is somewhat filtered by blue haze, unmoving. The humidity. The people around me are weak, even feeble, but they seem oddly carefree, ready to party.

As if it were a national holiday—indefinitely. Man having attained the highest degree of freedom, work banished from daily life except for the bare minimum necessary to survival. Evolution. Humanity rediscovering its prehistoric predilection for the carefree.

General Radio plays World Music, a formula developed to make us more international. The musical composition is structured in such a way that a Frenchman could confidently assert he's listening to French music and a Brazilian has no doubt he's hearing a good *chorinho*. Brilliant, don't you agree?

They programmed computers with the characteristics that typify music from country to country throughout the world. They made scrupulous listings of chords, tones, melodies common to all. Of course it was a project that took years to complete, requiring the dedicated labor of the best technicians.

They gathered experts, critics, professors, specialists in music notation, arrangement, harmony, alteration, transcription, transposition. Commissions studied the possibilities of all combinations. They worked out a code to be used by composers, extremely complex, requiring intensive coursework, naturally sponsored by the recording companies.

In the case of spontaneous creation, which the Militechs pejoratively refer to as "nightclub music," there's a special process—if the composition passes muster. The composer brings his tape to a recycling center where the piece is adapted to World Music Standards. In general, "nightclub" composers don't have access to the special classes. It's more or less like someone from the Encampments trying to penetrate the Inner Sanctum.

Suddenly the announcer interrupts the music to report the current temperature, forecasting that the blue haze will lift and give way to full sun this afternoon. He warns everyone to take adequate protective measures. Trying to sound animated, the monotonous voice asks for our undivided attention, he's about to read an important communication:

*The authorities of the System have become concerned of late with the nation's worsening climatic conditions. A few days from now, in his end-of-the-year speech, our Chief of State will address this important question. Painstaking research shows that the Pessimism Index is becoming problematic. That is, for the first time in many years, our country's consistently high rating in the Optimism Index, attained by the System during the Wide Open Eighties, and considered by one international commission to be the best on the planet, has registered a slight decline. As there are no apparent explanations for this phenomenon, arrangements are being made for extensive research into the problem.*

*The System requests all citizens' general cooperation*

*and understanding. This will be absolutely necessary especially if the need arises for a campaign to raise the people's spirits. Everyone knows how important it is for all of us to have high levels of optimism, without which the nation would not be able to proceed with its Rising Scale Development. For practical purposes, this understanding will translate into a short-term tax, divided into six monthly payments, in order to finance the proposed promotional campaign to rebuild positive thinking, which tax, after all, should be considered an investment in the best interests of the people, since pessimism, left to spread, engenders discontent, confusion, depression, maniacal compulsions, suicide, and defeatism. Don't let yourself feel like a failure—collaborate with the collective optimism.*

Of course! Why didn't I think of it before? As soon as I find a telephone, I'll call Tadeu Pereira. Definitely. I'm not exactly sure what he could do, provide a little orientation, guidance, maybe. I can't ask information at the official checkpoints, or from the Guards—I'd have to explain why I don't have a CIRCA for this area.

No one on the street. I leave the trash heaps behind and walk for blocks, it seems like an eternity. My leg is bothering me again, my joints ache. The windows are all closed, undoubtedly to keep out the heat, it's like an abandoned city. If there were such a thing as wind, I'd expect to see dead branches blowing along the side-walks—a vision from ghost towns in old grade "C" westerns.

The air is so still and so hot you almost try to avoid breathing, afraid of catching fire inside. I imagine my lungs thin lampshades, bursting into flames, crumbling to ashes any moment. Mirages appear in front of my eyes: luminous fountains surrounded by hot asphalt, an open hydrant on the corner gushing cool water.

A park made entirely of concrete. Deserted, swings hanging motionless, a rusty iron railing. I wish someone would explain to me how things can rust in such an arid climate, I thought rust had to do with humidity. Unless at night there's just the smallest amount of dew?

The gates of the reservoir open, water floods the park with the force of an earthquake. But it doesn't frighten me a bit, I want to be engulfed in its refreshing fury. And suddenly the water is gone, completely evaporated. All I see is a shabbily dressed girl spinning in circles.

She spins from left to right, then back the other way. I count them: twelve turns one way, twelve in reverse. Then eleven each way. Then ten, nine, eight. Until she gets to one and starts all over. Only this time she starts at thirteen, repeats the sequence, and begins again at fourteen.

I walk up close to her. She sees me but doesn't stop her routine, or ritual, or whatever it is she's doing. Young, dark-haired, sunburned. There's something pretty about her. How can she keep spinning like that without getting dizzy? She has the startled and undernourished look of any normal person these days.

—Can I ask what you're doing?

—Spinning around, can't you see?

—Yes, but I thought maybe there was something else to it.

—Don't be silly. All you need to do is look to see I'm simply spinning.

—But why?

—Because if I stop, I won't be moving anymore.

—Sorry, I phrased it wrong. What for?

—Do I need a reason? Is there some law against it? You're not a Guard, are you?

—No, no, don't worry. You can keep right on spinning.

—This city is full of lunatics. Now they want to know why I'm spinning!

—I said I was sorry. I just wanted to know if it felt good, or what.

—As good as standing still. You like to stand still, I like to spin.

273

—Right. Thanks. I'll be on my way . . .

—Where to? Why not take advantage of the deserted park? Nobody watching.

—I'm looking for a telephone.

—You need to call someone?

—No, I'm looking for a phone so I can give it a kiss!

—A kiss! What for?

—Just kidding. You take everything so seriously.

—*You* I take seriously. I was spinning around, minding my own business, and you started asking questions. If at least you'd spin too, then I could trust you.

—I don't feel like spinning.

—Not even in a deserted park like this?

—Deserted or crawling with people, it just doesn't appeal to me.

—Who are you going to call?

—Tadeu Pereira.

—Mmmmm.

—You know him?

She didn't answer, just kept on spinning. Without even looking at me. She had an interesting face. Slightly dirty. Her hair fell in a disheveled braid to the right side of her face. A long braid, it had obviously been some time since she'd last cut her hair.

Another mirage, like the bursting reservoir. My head's on fire again. I invented this girl, made her up out of thin air. There's something interesting about her, sensual, which appeals to me, excites me even. I hope she smells good. Of course if she exists, it's clear she's completely nuts. How to talk to her.

All she does is spin round and round, her hips gyrating like there's no tomorrow. Who knows if there is? She's got a nice derriere, though. Round. Pretty curvy for such a castoff. And all alone. Odd. Why isn't she in the Garbage Heap like everyone else?

But then, I'm alone—and I don't consider myself all that strange. Ha, maybe she does, though! So what? Derriere. Why didn't I just say ass? I'm so tied up in

274

knots when it comes to worldly things. People *or* situations. Stifled, under wraps, inhibited. Who was it that said I go through life with the brakes on?

It must have been Adelaide. No, couldn't be, she always had the brakes on, too. We wore down the brake pads for years on end. If Adelaide were here, I'd lie down with her on the hot cement. It would fry her ass, or mine, but we'd make love in the sun, spied on from behind closed blinds.

The sun's definitely frying my brains. I can't say I'd really like to participate in that scenario, never mind Adelaide. Fantasies provoked by the dark-haired girl spinning around. Nutty. She's probably thinking: this guy is nutty. It's a stalemate. Two people who've lost their minds. The truth is no longer so singular; everybody's got their version. I am, you are, he/she is.

I'm wandering again. I love it, though, don't I? Maybe they've got a phone in that bar on the far side of the park. Above the door, a sign: the System's logo. Characteristic of the Intense Official Propaganda, uniform size and design. They must think we're all blind, the billboards are so big.

AT LAST—A SOLUTION:
"THE ENDLESS MARQUEE"
COMING SOON!

There's been talk about that marquee for a long time. As subtle as usual. Suddenly another campaign is upon us: signs everywhere announcing (or should I say unveiling—it wouldn't be too dramatic) the new visual symbol to be used on street markers, maps, pamphlets. Rumor has it that the marquee is finally ready.

# SENSELESS RUMINATIONS
## IN A BAR,
## THE USELESSNESS OF LOGIC
## IN CERTAIN SITUATIONS,
## AND A PHONE CALL
## WITH A TERRIBLE OUTCOME

An ordinary neighborhood bar. Dingy Formica, hammered tin and peeling chrome desperately in need of polishing, half-empty shelves, disassembled coffee machine, lots of dust. Wall tiles with panoramic landscapes. Reminiscent of the Interesting Epoch of Portuguese Dominance in Cafés and Pastry Shops.

This is the kind of bar that flourished before they instituted the World Luncheonettes, built for and patronized by the Multinationals: fast-food places. Efficiency, cleanliness, fast service. When I was a teenager we had a nickname for them: Foot-in-the-Ass. You go in, eat, and get out, fast. Or else.

The World Luncheonettes took over completely in upper- and middle-class neighborhoods, and in commercial areas where people had money to spend. They didn't bother infiltrating the run-down residential neighborhoods where the old-fashioned Formica-chrome-tile landscape bars and snack shops still operated, though tenuously.

God only knows how they survived at all, competing with the "big time." Especially considering the home delivery businesses that proliferated after the onset of the Great Fear of Going Out Into the Street. That was a period which was stressful to us all. It was like being in jail.

Who would dare stick his head out the window, much less his foot out the door? Iron grates, closed-circuit TV, newfangled locks, security guards, alarm systems. Relative security at home. But outside, forget it. People stopped going to work. Production levels began to fall. That's when the System sat up and took notice. This was serious.

A general security system had to be devised, and fast. Things were even more precarious than during the crisis in the late Open Eighties when people stopped being good little consumers. As a result, businesses began failing, industry entered a recession, there was a wave of layoffs. Luckily, the new Sophist Economics worked miracles.

The famous Consumer Quotas were established. Everyone had to maintain a monthly consumption level that varied depending on an individual's classification based on his Federal Income Tax bracket. Which sounds fairly egalitarian, but income or no, there was a set minimum consumption requirement.

Whether you had money or not, you had to fill your quota: your Consumer Classification Card had to be stamped monthly, otherwise life wasn't worth living. You would not be allowed to travel, work, have a bank account, a water quota, or send your children to school.

You wouldn't be allowed to lock your bicycle or retain your alcohol coupon booklet. That's how the Consumer Quotas saved business and rehabilitated industry. And that's when I gave up trying to understand economics.

Why didn't the country explode? Don't ask me. For one thing, credit limits were raised, payment plans extended, all kinds of commercial credit consortiums flourished. The use of credit cards, or plastic, as the people called them, reached incredible proportions. Everyone, I mean everyone, went into debt. To banks, finance companies, loan sharks. The premise was this: if Brazil, with its overwhelming foreign debt, remains afloat in 1980, all the rest of us will too.

Of course some people did lose their shirts. House, furniture, land. Repossessed. People with no cash reserves who didn't understand how to maneuver within the System. The car was always the last thing people gave up—they'd fight to keep it till the end. A noble struggle.

For better or worse, then, the economic crisis was turned around. But the problem of security was different; things are always different when it's a question of life or death. Fear kept people locked up tight in their houses. Only total security would get them back out on the street. Security at any cost. A challenge to the System.

So out of the desk drawers of various government departments came, in stages, organizations of the you-don't-know-me-but-I'm-a-cop-and-I've - got-my-eye-on-you type. Plus the there's-a-guy-on-my-right-who-might-also - be-a-cop-spying-on-me -soon-we'll-all-be-in -Isolation variety. They came up with the Agents Who Are Suspicious By Nature (ASBN), the Inspectors, the idea of giving Guards and certain members of the New Army "permission to kill," the confinements, etc. The Intense Official Propaganda agency also contributed to this grow-ing climate of insecurity for marginals with their famous ads and mottos, like: *Criminals Beware, You May Dis-appear at Any Moment!* Until finally people felt safe enough to go out again. Of course, the tranquilizing additives in our food probably helped, too. In any case, things calmed down considerably.

Life today seems positively pleasant compared to what we've already been through. How we managed to sur-vive, to get past all these hard times, is a question I don't really want to ask myself. We just did. Sometimes it's easier than you think, and easier than *to* think—fear is, after all, a product of the imagination.

The bar's windows are empty, dusty. Unlit fluorescent tubing. A couple of sleepy customers, heads bobbing on their chests, nose to nose with their shot glasses. Not sugar-cane brandy, as in the old days, but synthetic brandy, straight. Same taste, same rasp in the throat, but no telltale breath smell.

Three waiters, obviously unnecessary for a joint like this. But if the owner wants to keep his license to operate, he has to guarantee work for a fixed number of employ-ees, regardless of business. I'm sure they make next to nothing. Probably live on tips, eat at the bar, and bring home the scraps.

Dirty, sticky, sweaty, smelly (I make myself sick), I lean at the bar. A waiter comes up to me, dragging his feet. He can't stop sneezing, his nose is red, his eyes are watery. A deplorable figure, but he must think I'm a bum, the way I look. The two of us put together add up to zero.

I ask to see a phone book. There are two Tadeu Pereiras listed. I check the addresses. The first is in the northern sector, a working-class neighborhood, the second in the Privileged Functionaries Zone near the dry lake beds, in what used to be the Botanical Garden. Must be the first one. It better be.

—Hello, is this the Tadeu Pereira residence?

—Yes. (A woman's voice.)

—Tadeu Pereira, the elevator man?

—Yes. (A hesitant voice.)

—Is he at home?

—No. (A pained voice.)

—Oh, he's gone out?

—Yes.

—Then, I can call later. He'll be back?

—No.

—I don't understand. Has he moved?

—No. He died.

—Died? How? When?

—Tadeu committed suicide yesterday.

—Then it can't be the Tadeu Pereira I know, I must have the wrong one. Don't I?

—How would I know. Our Tadeu is being cremated this afternoon.

—Where?

—Who can tell? Once you turn the body over to them, do you think they tell you what they're planning to do with it?

279

## AND NOW, A LITTLE ACTION:
## A FISTFIGHT, A VISIT TO JAIL,
## AND EVEN AN UNEXPECTED
## SEX SCENE,
## COMPLETE WITH STRANGE SMELLS,
## IN AN UNUSUAL LOCALE

—Hello? Are you still there?

—Yes.

—Well?

—Could you tell me, was this Tadeu Pereira who died . . . did he used to be a university professor?

—Uh-huh. Many years ago. During the Decade of Incoherent Presidential Proclamations in Direct Conflict with the Paradoxical Assertions of His Cabinet, I think it was.

—Everything was so confused in those days. So Tadeu was retired, then?

—That's right, or they retired him, I should say. They didn't like the lectures he was giving.

—My God, it is him. I wanted so badly for it not to be him. Oh, Tadeu. Did he leave a note or anything, any kind of explanation?

—Nothing.

—Are you his wife?

—His sister-in-law.

—My name is Souza, I'm an old friend of Tadeu's. Weren't you worried that I might be an Agent Suspicious By Nature?

—Not really. What else could happen? Oh! Hold on just a minute, Mr. Souza, I'll be right back . . .

—

—Hello? My brother says there's an envelope here with your name on it.

—Really? An envelope?

—Tadeu left it for you, a thick envelope, sealed shut.

Feels as if it has a notebook or datebook or something inside.

We were cut off, I'd forgotten about the three minutes. I dug out a second token and dialed again, but the line was busy, and the telephone ate my token. Bad luck comes in streaks. Paralysis. The blob is back. Aside from overwhelming surprise, I feel nothing. No pain, no emotion. Maybe I'm too confused to feel.

—Ay! She's back!

Dark hair, light eyes, the typically Bahian type, like that famous Miss Brazil, I can't remember her name. It was the girl from the park. The usually apathetic employees clearly were not happy to see her. Her dress hung open to show two small breasts. Pink nipples.

Long, greasy hair. Who doesn't have greasy hair these days? A gold sandal on one foot, the other bare. Or at least the sandal had apparently been gold at one time. A chip of blue glass hung around her neck by adhesive tape. She recognizes me, and installs herself next to me at the bar. I like this woman.

I'm attracted to her. A cold sweat, on top of my normal perspiration. My right foot taps nervously on the foot rail. I couldn't control it if I wanted to. A violent struggle going on inside me. As if I'd walked into a room and my very look had thrown everything into chaos—furniture flying around, papers stuck to the ceiling, typewriters typing all by themselves, wastebaskets dumping the trash out the window. I'm dizzy, I'm being taken over by her smell. Sweat and skin, little droplets trickling down her forehead, her arms, falling from her unshaved armpits.

A close-mouthed smile, her lips just slightly parted. I can't see her teeth, but I think about biting her, biting her teeth, what foolishness. I'm embarrassed. What if the waiters should notice. Never mind, they're leering brazenly at her open dress, staring at her firm little breasts.

—Her again? Throw the tramp out of here!

It's the owner of the bar, or a man I imagine is the owner, yelling at the top of his lungs. Foaming at the

281

mouth. What could she have possibly done for him to be in such a fury? Screaming, pounding on the bar, his dentures dancing in his mouth.

It's pretty funny, really. The top dentures clack against the bottom ones, and with each word they threaten to fall out, but he pushes them back in in the nick of time. Closes his mouth, shoves them around with his tongue until they're firmly in place, then lets out another yell and the dentures shake loose, he has to stop and slip them back into the groove in his gums.

There's even a certain rhythm to it. I let out a giggle. A chortle. How long has it been since I laughed like this? The dark-haired girl has been enjoying this pantomine, too, she grabs my hand and we stand there together doubled over with laughter, leaning on each other so we won't fall down. In an instant I recover the great peace that used to be inside me. As if with a wave of a magic wand.

Serenity washes over me, as if injected into a vein. A sense of satisfaction with the world, because the world is what's out there, there's nothing we can do about it. All of my usual apprehension, anxiety, goes out the window, the same way garlic drives away the smell of sweat.

The somnambulant waiters pushed the girl out of the bar. She came back. They kicked her out again, literally, leaving her flat on her back in the gutter. A minute later she was perched at the bar asking for a sandwich. The man with the loose dentures grabbed a 2 × 4 from behind the bar: "I'll show you we mean business here!"

I got between him and the girl. He hesitated. But not for long. "Get out of here NOW, or I'll give it to both of you!" I wanted to follow his suggestion, get the hell out of there, and take the girl with me, but she began to knock the dusty bottles off the bar, glass crashing everywhere. I tried to stop her but it was useless, she was possessed.

The man with the dentures swung and missed. "Call the Guards! Call the Guards!" he shrieked. The waiters

282

were holding the girl, I saw the club come crashing down. They laughed as she flailed her arms and legs, breaking anything within reach.

She fell, and they began kicking her in the face, in the chest, in the stomach. She struggled to roll over, the adhesive tape came loose, her chunk of blue glass rolled out onto the sidewalk. Her face was bleeding. I looked at the bar. The glass sterilizer was boiling away. Inspiration. I pulled as hard as I could.

I never thought I had that much strength. The sterilizer went flying, wires and all. Sparks flew, I got a jolt. I heaved the whole thing at the owner of the bar. This time when his dentures came loose it would require a miracle to keep them in his mouth, he opened so wide with the scream. The boiling water hit him in the face, in the chest, in the stomach.

I peeked at him through the hole in my hand. Kicked him in the stomach, as he'd done to the girl. The waiters shrank back in fear, their boss was on the floor gasping for breath. Any kind of exercise kills you in this heat. We were all red in the face and wheezing. The waiters moved toward me, they had to do something.

I ran out into the street, calling after the girl. She staggered to her feet. Maybe she was used to situations like this, had built up some some sort of resistance, immunity. She looked at me uncomprehendingly. Maybe no one had ever defended her before. Little did she know that I was as surprised at myself as she was.

Then we were surrounded by Civil Guards. That's the way it is, all you have to do is think about them and they materialize, they have paranormal powers. In seconds they had us handcuffed. Luckily, they didn't use their cataleptic bullets—I've heard the headache they give you is unbearable, after you come to.

Thrown in the paddy wagon, we became canned meat. A dark, fetid cubicle, no air. We tried to catch our breath. When our eyes adjusted to the dark, we could see tiny air vents, minuscule spots of sunlight. It was hot, an oven turned up to broil. If they left us in here very long, we'd be D.O.A.

All of a sudden the girl fell against me, dead weight. Asleep or passed out. She was having a lot of difficulty breathing, a sort of rasping noise in her throat. It made me feel like stroking her arms, squeezing her nipple. Kissing her on the mouth. My breath must smell awful, I haven't eaten in hours. Completely forgot.

It was strange, this violent attraction I felt for her. Suddenly her nipple is hard—could she be awake? Or was it just a natural reaction? Her skin is sticky but smooth, soft, my fingers slide inside her dress, I can hardly make out her shape in this half-light, but her body smells good, excites me.

It's not a clean smell, but nonetheless seems natural, appropriate. I think if she had been fresh as a daisy it would have bothered me. Who can understand, much less control, how the human mind works? What happened to my phobia for smells? Null and void. Which makes me happy, I'm regressing.

The police van was moving now. A slight breeze came in through the air vents. Not much, but enough. I nudged the girl from my shoulder, she woke up. I stood up, bent over, and pressed my nose against the air vents, our only contact with the outside world. Ah, how pleasant! Once in a while the roof seemed to catch fire, I could smell a sort of scorching smell.

Were we traveling through heat pockets then? The van would suddenly accelerate and careen around corners— they must have been trying to hightail it out of there. Having no notion of time, I thought about counting; at least I could approximate the distance. But what for? Just let time, and the van, roll on at their own pace. All I want to do is get there. I struggled to see her face in the dark.

—Wonder where they're taking us.

—Who knows.

—You think maybe Isolation?

284

—Maybe. Maybe not.

—Have you ever been arrested before?

—A couple of times.

—How did you get out?

—They got tired of screwing me and let me go.

—That's why they let you go?! Because you . . . acquiesced . . .

—I don't know. That's a funny way to put it—acquiesced. I never heard that word before. You a lawyer?

—No, a professor. I mean, I was.

—Professor, eh? What's your name?

—Souza. What's yours?

—Elisa.

—Pretty name.

—What? It's not pretty, not ugly. A name like any other name.

—No, it's pretty! It's from the Greek. It means "free." Do you think your parents knew that when they named you?

—Maybe. My father was no dummy.

—Where is he now?

—Ha, he's a naturalized Russian. Imagine. A guy from Vitória turned into a Russian, working on their multinational reserve up north. That threw me for a loop, I'll tell you. And I thought I was used to his dramatic moves.

—What about your mother?

—She's around. She refused to become a Russian, so she divorced him and went to live with some doctor who worked in the Department of Family Sterilization. We lost touch.

—Do you have a place to live?

—My father left each of us a small apartment, I have three brothers, much older than me. But I lost mine.

—How?

—A gang of thugs kicked me out into the street, just like that. Nothing to do, nowhere to go. And the worst was that no one believed me.

—I do. The same thing happened to me.

—No kidding!

—Let me ask you something. When I met you in the park, spinning around like crazy, I asked you if you knew my friend Tadeu, the one I was going to call. You said you knew him, remember? Do you, really? Or were you just making talk?

—Give it a little thought, okay?

—What do you mean, give it a little thought? Why won't you answer me?

—It's a lot more fun to watch you, with that ridiculous, quizzical look on your face, thinking: does she know him? or not?

We went through several heat pockets, some worse than others. At times we heard voices, people screaming, and realized we were passing large groups of people in worse trouble than we were. Other times a terrible smell would come in through the air vents, worse even than the stench in the Garbage Heaps. The van stopped in what seemed to be a shady spot.

The Guards got out. We waited for them to come around back. Nothing. Silence. Their footsteps faded away, boots echoing as they hit the ground, which meant we were in some enclosed place. Some sort of garage? We were baking in that furnace, it was unbearable.

—Where are we?

—Does it matter?

—I've got to get out of here, I don't feel very well now that we've stopped. My stomach is in my throat, there's a weight on my chest. And I need to urinate.

—Urinate? Didn't I say you use strange words? Why don't you just take a piss, if it hurts so bad?

—Here?

—No, over yonder in a marble bathroom with your name on the door, hot showers and everything. Shit, are you a cretin or what?

I turned my back on her, feeling foolish, and urinated. It won't be long, in this heat, before this place smells awful. Better the smell than my bladder exploding, I guess. It was sort of exciting, actually, urinating in front of her. Only you can't really see anything in here, anyway. It's like we've been buried alive.

—What did your father do before he became a Russian?

—All sorts of things. For a long time he was a dislodger. That was our best phase, money all over the place. My father was something.

—A dislodger?

—It's slang in the construction business. Say a construction company wants to buy a certain lot, but the owner isn't selling. It may sound hard to believe, but there were people who were attached to their houses, even though they represented financial insecurity. That's what my father said, anyway. After all attempts to negotiate a sale had failed, that's when they called him in. A dislodger has to be a diplomat, a negotiator, he's got to be inventive. My father would rent an apartment in the building next door, preferably on the side closest to the house in question. Then he'd make friends with the super and some of the other residents, he was a charmer, it didn't take him long. Then the campaign started in earnest. All hell would break loose. Things fell on the roof, cluttered the yard. Rocks, hunks of metal, heavy flowerpots, garbage, turds, plastic bags full of piss, you name it.

—The people in the house never complained, or went to the police?

—Oh, my little innocent, have you forgotten the Cycle of Judicial Inversions? Anybody who tried to bring a suit against someone with money or influence got it thrown back in his face, a magnificent legal maneuver. There were Inversion Specialists. The police would go to the apartment building, get their payoff, and bye-bye. The campaign continued. Pets would be poisoned, clothes on the clothesline smeared with mud. My father's apartment was an arsenal of the most incredible objects. Once a

287

burro even landed on somebody's roof, the family was away on a trip and came back to find a dead carcass stinking up the living room.

—You're telling me your father was a criminal!

—He never killed anybody, never robbed anybody, he just put the squeeze on people. There are a lot worse.

—That's a cozy way to see it.

—Look, old man—what did you say your name was?

—Souza.

—Well, Souza. Whose idea was it to talk about my family in the first place? Not mine.

—Just passing the time.

—There are better ways to pass the time.

—Like what?

—You *are* an odd one. Is there something wrong with you? Don't I turn you on?

—Of course. I mean, yes...

—Then why haven't you made a move?

—It doesn't work like that, it's not that simple: get a little turned on and just make a move.

—Of course it is, there's no other way.

—I was... I was waiting for an opportunity.

—An opportunity? That's a strange word for it! I think I'm going to put together a dictionary here, the Souza Dictionary of word usage...

—I don't see any reason to kid me about the words I use.

—What do you mean, opportunity? The Great Ball, New Year's Eve, some scene with candles and champagne? The opportunity is now.

—Now?

—Of course.

—Just like that?

—Don't you want me? If not, you're the first. Most guys are panting before they even approach me.

—You think you're pretty sexy, huh?

—Sure.

—And what if I'm not interested?

288

—Now you're the one who's kidding around.

—I'm nervous, that's all. I tense up just thinking about it. It's just that it's been a long time, I'm a little scared.

—Scared?

She screamed a lot. So much I was afraid the Guards would come. What if they did? We're already prisoners, nothing to lose. And it would be pointless for me to let my fear keep me from losing this chance, this moment, the same way it made me throw away so many moments my whole life long. As soon as this thought came to me I started screaming too.

Elisa's flesh. Firm, palpable, slippery. Her legs were damp, juice flowed from between them like a waterfall. I've never seen anything like it. But then I haven't seen all that much, have I? Just a couple of women. None after Adelaide. We satisfied each other, I didn't need anyone else.

—Was it good?

—Was it good? Of course it was good! You need to ask?

—Don't you ever ask?

—What for?

—To know if it was good for the woman.

—Not really. My wife would never talk about it.

—Did she like it?

—I think so.

—You think so?!

—She was always happy afterwards, I could see it in her face.

—And you never felt like asking? What about when you just weren't meshing, didn't that ever happen?

—If it did, we figured it was an off-day, that's all, it would be better the next time. And it was.

—The perfect couple.

—I wish. So what about you, was it good for you?

—Ah, you asked! What do *you* think?

—I don't know, you seem to have a lot of experience.
. . . You were so relaxed, and I was scared.

—Of what?

—Nervous, I mean. Tense. Scared of not being able to perform. You intimidate me.

—You're silly. It was good. The first time you were stiff, you wouldn't let yourself go. The second time was delicious. Deep down, you're calm.

—I'm dead tired.

—And I'm dying of hunger.

—You had to mention it! I'd forgotten...

We lay together, entwined on the floor of the van. It feels a little cooler. I'm exhausted, it's a miracle I did what I did. I wonder if it's true that hunger makes you excited, sharpens sensation. How long will we be locked up in here? Have they forgotten about us? Or is this a trap?

A way to weaken us, wear us down. Nonsense. We're just two street rowdies. Nothing political about our being here. The thing to worry about is how soon they'll come back. I've got to eat something, I'm getting a headache. It won't be long before I'm dizzy, that'll be even worse.

I know myself. Elisa still has an alternative. She could do like the people of Bologna centuries ago. The city under siege, food run out, so the women took daily doses of the men's sperm. I wonder how much I could produce in a state of inactivity. And of course it remains to be seen if it would be sufficient quality, with enough vitamins, to keep her alive.

—What are you thinking?

—If you only knew. More silliness.

—Tell me.

I'm too inhibited. I wouldn't mind a bit, though, if she took advantage of the idea. I'd even try to show my appreciation, pay back in kind. That was a common practice in my childhood! My God, where have I been all these years? In Rip Van Winkle's cave? In a space capsule, like the men in *Planet of the Apes?*

Suddenly waking to a world that's completely beyond me. I've got to try and catch up. I've been swallowed, it seems as though I've lived my life in a place like this, a dark cell, unimaginably deep. Funny, what I'd like to do most of all right now is to wash my hands. Typical.

—Isn't anyone coming to get us out of here?

—What do you think they'll do to us when they do?

—We're okay now. Let's leave it at that.

—Aren't you worried, just a little? Wouldn't you like to know what's going to happen next?

—I'd rather be surprised.

—Don't you think about it at least?

—No. I wipe the slate clean, I think white. Infinite white space.

—And you can turn everything white, presto-chango?

—I turn it into nonthought.

—Feel like talking?

—Isn't that what we're doing?

—Well, I thought maybe you'd rather be quiet for a while or something.

—Do you need an authorization for everything?

—I don't like to bother people. Is there anything wrong with that?

—So why do you let everybody else bother you?

—That's the way I am, so where's the harm in it? I'm happy.

—Are you? Really?

—Don't pressure me, okay? I don't like it, it's irritating.

—Aha! A reaction!

—I don't feel like arguing. I'm tired.

—Me too. A good fight will wake me up. I'll feel better.

—We're different then.

—A brilliant conclusion, my friend, worthy of a philosophy professor.

—History.

—History, philosophy, both useless.

—You sound bitter.

—But I'm a brilliant conversationalist.

—Tell me about yourself. When I saw you in the park I thought you were completely off your rocker. Now I don't think so, but you *are* strange. I can't figure you out.

—What's there to figure out? You're like all the old people I know. Always asking questions. Why, what, when, how.

—You ask a lot of questions yourself.

—What I'm asking you is whether we really need to understand everything around us, you know? All the time we spend trying to understand things we're not really living.

—That's not true.

—And it's not a lie. So then what is it?

—Just a phrase.

—What I do know is that we live in a dirty world. What is there for me to look forward to? At least you've lived your life; but think of it, what about me? Do you know how old I am?

—Twenty-six?

—Nineteen. See what I mean? And they want me to work, to produce. They're always saying: Let's face facts. Or: Brazil is your problem too. Always trying to shift the blame. I'm supposed to solve problems I had nothing to do with creating, things that were here when I was born. Let's face facts. If I face facts it's obvious the best idea would be to kill myself.

—Then you have no hope at all?

—Do you?

—I guess you'd have to say I lost my way. I don't have the slightest idea where I'm going, I just go.

—You and everybody else. What do you think my friends do?

—Where *are* your friends?

—Around. Hunting up food. Stealing water. A little breaking and entering, maybe. The problem is, you have to wait till people go out. And, meanwhile, it's not good to be out wandering the streets with the sun getting hotter by the day.

—It's better in here, then?

—At least there's some shade, plus we can make love.

—If we last long enough. I'm going crazy from hunger.

—You can take it, believe me. Have you ever been hungry before?

—That weak sort of feeling you get waiting for dinner when it's late?

—No, I mean real hunger. Days and days without eating.

—No, thank God.

—I have. The first time was in college, we had a hunger strike.

—Over what?

—The basics. We wanted good teachers, money for research, reasonably priced books.

—Did it succeed?

—We were arrested, they closed the campus. None of us was able to finish our degrees anywhere else. Blacklisted. But in the end what difference would it have made if we did?

—How long ago did this happen?

—Two years ago. I got an ulcer from the hunger strike. The doctor said I should never again let my stomach get that empty, I have to eat a little something every few hours. That's a joke, huh! Once in a while I throw up blood. And the pain is fucking awful, it ties me in knots.

—I feel pretty awful right now.

—Tomorrow will be worse.

—Isn't anyone going to come get us out of here? Do you think they really forgot all about us?

—We're not important to them. Calm down. Sometimes it's better if they forget.

—I'm cold. It must be getting late.

—We'll have to sleep wrapped in each other's arms.

—Don't sound so enthusiastic about it.

—I was just kidding, don't worry.

—But really. Do you like me?

—You're pretty old-fashioned, and conservative, but yes, I like you.

—Conservative?

—I'm not sure how to explain it, it's something I feel. You want to be so correct, so right, that's what irritates me. It makes me feel confused, insecure. For instance, I know you're still worried about having made love to me. As if it implied some sort of responsibility.

—You're right. That's the way I am.

—Turn it off, can't you? I made love with you because I wanted to. I felt like it, it was good. I needed to. If it hadn't been you it would have been someone else.

—That's a real nice thing to say.

—The world isn't nice and neither am I, I'm not the least bit interested in nice. I am the answer to everything, I'm the creation, not the creator. Understand? Why should people feel guilty, that's what I'd like to know. Why do people your age carry around so much goddamned guilt?

—It must be our Christian upbringing.

—Christian? I'm the Christian. The last Christian in a fucked-up world.

—That's sweet. One lone Christian in the ruins of the world.

—That's not funny. I didn't say anything about ruins, did I? Maybe the world looks like ruins to you because you're a relic from the past, you see things in comparison with the way they were. For me, this *is* the world. When I get old like you and start to founder, then maybe I'll see things that way, but meanwhile it's a new world, a wonderful, old world. It's all I've got, the only thing to do is live in it.

—And you call this living?

—What am I supposed to call it? I'm nineteen years old, for Christ's sake. Do I have anything to compare it to? When I'm your age, maybe then I'll say I've learned something.

—Life doesn't teach you anything.

—Fine. I never said I wanted it to. When I was in college I wanted to learn, and I got beat on. So now who gives a whit.

294

—A whit?! That's something my mother used to say. And you talk about me. You use some pretty antiquated expressions yourself. Founder. Whit. It's been at least a decade since I heard that word.

—It's just a kick I'm on. A salvaging campaign.

A car with a loud engine parks nearby. It coughs and sputters as if it's about to die any moment. One thing they never solved with the synthetic fuel, or with solar energy either, for that matter, is the frequent need for tune-ups. The way they make motors ping and smoke, it's unbelievable.

I was so anxious for someone to come for us. Now, hearing actual noises, I'm not so sure. Doors opening, steps receding. Then another motor, doors, steps. In a little while a third, and a fourth. This must be a garage. The Guards coming back from their rounds.

If we pounded on the walls of this thing, they'd hear us and come investigate. Would that make things worse or better? Let's wait awhile and get used to the idea. The moment will come when we're ready to face them. Ready or not, we know it won't be easy, they're not exactly kind to anybody, they've been well conditioned.

Elisa fondles me, I'm getting excited again. Surprised at myself. What a day for discoveries, it's terrific! My mother always used to say "Don't ever give up hope!" Even on the road to hell there's a chance for salvation, a shortcut to heaven. She was right.

I put Elisa's hands between mine. It's always seemed important to me to feel the hands of a person I like, to stroke their fingers, explore their palm, it's my way of getting to know people. I depend on it as a way of sensing receptiveness or rejection. Warmth, sweat, a sense of surrender, it's all in the tactile.

Her fingers are long and thin ("Hansel, stretch out your finger so I may feel if you are getting fat."), nervous. They send out sparks, energy. Sharp-pointed sticks. They turn to hooks and catch hold of my fingers, I can see she, too, is uneasy.

There's such a feeling of helplessness being locked up like this, the two of us are very alone. And there is nothing we can do—that's part of the condition. The human body, divided into head, torso, limbs, and loneliness. It's physical, an integral part of us.

Rhythmic footsteps cross behind the van and move off. Whispering, a burst of gunfire. The footsteps disappear. It's quite cold now, we cuddle up together. My head's exploding, it's like I'm hearing from behind a cloud. The walls of my stomach scrape and grind.

—I feel terrible.

—Today and tomorrow will be the worst, you'll feel like dying.

—I already do.

—Don't think about it. Try to distract yourself.

—How?

—Get it through your head that you can't die. Life is here in front of you, it's important, you only get one shot at it.

—Look who's talking! Just a little while ago you were saying it was a dirty life.

—A dirty world, not a dirty life. My life is mine, I have a right to it. I want to see it through to the end, they can't take that away from me. Fucked or not, I want all life has to offer, good and bad. I'm not ready to turn myself in—for free, no less—the way you are.

—I'm not, either!

—Well, you're not putting a helluva lot of effort into it.

—I'm a lot more tired than you are, remember.

—When it comes to survival, there's no such thing as being too tired.

—Lights. They're coming to get us. They put the lights on.

—Lights in your head. It's just as dark as before.

—No, Elisa, it's light, it's clear as day. I can see the shadows on the ground, there's a lot of people sitting there. They're eating mussels the waves washed up onto

296

the beach. But wait, the waves aren't made of water, they're shells. Listen to the noise they make. Where are you? Give me your hand, or we'll lose each other in the crowd! I can't hear you, Elisa. They've got my head, what are they going to do, they're letting me have some of the mussels . . .

—I'm the one holding your head, Souza. Calm down, now, don't yell like that, or they'll come for us.

—Run for it, Adelaide, run for it! And don't eat the mussels, I'm telling you, don't eat them, they're poison. Look at the people having convulsions, the mussels are bad, Adelaide, look how they're vomiting up light bulbs full of water. Light bulbs which came from the bottom of the sea.

—Souza, stop shouting, ssssh, my love, ssssshhh.

—Adelaide, look at the heads of the little children rolling down the beach, they're being eaten by mussels. You were right, Adelaide, I never denied it, you were right, the children all died at sea.

—Stop it, Souza! I mean it. Stop, or they'll hear you.

—It's lucky I found you, Adelaide. What were you doing down here on the beach? You hate the sea, I know, it's because of the ship. Ah, now I understand, you came to wait for the mailman, didn't you? Here he comes on horseback with his trumpet blaring, how can an old nag like that gallop so beautifully? Look, Adelaide, isn't it wonderful? The mailman is Tadeu Pereira! No, Tadeu, don't give me the letter, get back in your elevator, get out of here with that lazy nag, you'll both be pulled under. What did I tell you, Adelaide, the waves are too high, Tadeu won't come out of that dive in one piece—see, the waves took everything, he's gone, but here's his bag, I saved that at least, let's look for the letter. Nothing in his bag but polluted mussels, nothing but poisoned mussels, isn't that sad . . .

—Souza, Souza . . .

—Somebody hit me!

—It was me.

—You hit me, you rotten lunatic!

—I had to. You were hysterical, like you were having some kind of attack.

—You're the one who's hysterical. What are you doing here? Who are you?

—Elisa, your friend Elisa, remember?

—I don't have any friend named Elisa. I know what you are, you're a Civil Guard in disguise. You are, admit it, YOU ARE!

—Stop, Souza!

—You hit me again! I'll kill you, woman, if I can only . . .

—Please stop.

—What's going on here, Elisa? Where's the beach? What did you do with Adelaide?

—Wake up, Souza, there is no beach. And who is this Adelaide you're screaming for?

—My wife.

—I didn't even know you were married.

—I was. She disappeared. I just found her again, on the beach.

—It was a hallucination, Souza.

—A hallucination?

—From hunger.

—But I'm not hungry.

—That's natural, that's how it works.

—I'm not so cold anymore, either. Where are we?

—Locked in a paddy wagon.

—Let me just rest my head on your shoulder . . .

The brown blob with the gelatinous green inside, back again. I can see a truck carrying immense logs out of the forest, then another, there they go, all in a line. That's what the brown is, the log trucks, it's perfectly clear to me now, I've got to stop the trucks but I'm paralyzed.

My grandfather is standing there behind the trucks looking a way I've never seen him look before. Pain and hate on his face. He was such a relaxed, happy-go-lucky guy, never a flicker of anger or violence in his gestures, on his face. It can't be my grandfather.

Another slap in the face. What the devil does this woman want, hitting me like that? What are we doing here in the dark? And what if Adelaide walked in and surprised me on this nice-smelling shoulder? I can hardly believe this myself—this woman is naked, her pubes are tickling me.

—How about if I tell you a story, Souza? Yes, you like stories, I know you do. I'll tell you about the terrific job I once had, me and my boyfriend. We painted murals on the sides of buildings. People hired us to paint woods and meadows on walls all over town. We loved it, day and night, creating trees, orchards, branches, foliage, vines. My boyfriend was incredible, you'd look at a fern he painted and swear it was real, all those tiny little leaves, just perfect. He painted maidenhairs, orchids, all kinds of delicate plants, he had a knack for it, they came out three-dimensional, you felt like reaching out and touching them. He was the one who taught me to paint, though I never got to be as good as he was. Can you believe it—me, who never even saw a real tree in my life! Year after year, stuck in São Paulo, somehow I never managed to travel, I always meant to. Until just a short time ago there were still forest and game preserves, weren't there? My boyfriend planned an excursion, we were going to take a trip to see real trees and plants so then I'd be able to paint things I'd actually seen instead of just from pictures, he had lots of slides in his studio. But we never went.

—What happened to this boyfriend? Did you have a fight?

—I don't know, we lost track of each other somehow. He was working on some senator's villa, I didn't have a CIRCA you needed for the district, top-security clearance, so all we could do was talk to each other on the phone once in a while. Then he stopped calling me. I called and called, but no one answered, I think it was disconnected.

—People don't just disappear.

—Oh no? What about your wife?

—Well, she left of her own free will. She went into hiding. But I have a suspicion where she is. My problem's the same as yours: no CIRCA.

—Then the Ministry of the Environment cut off funding and the studio closed down. Although of course it wouldn't have been much without him, anyway. I got a job at an artificial-rain movie house.

—Oh, boy, remember those, they were great. That's one job I wouldn't mind having, instead of comparing lists of useless numbers like I used to.

—They did a good business there, that's for sure. It's a shame it was a fad and only lasted a short time, like bowling, roller skates, discotheques. There were so many fads. Remember the fights-of-flying-wings? Or the monocle-of-patience?

Wouldn't it be good to have one of those showers right now? I'd go inside in the middle of the afternoon and stand fifteen or twenty minutes surrounded by the wraparound screen, water gushing from all directions. I felt so fresh and cool when I left that place.

More footsteps. This time it's for real, someone's fiddling with the lock. I feel like messing in my pants. They shine bright lights in our faces, and my hunger comes back, violent, like a knife being twisted in my gut.

—Naked, you sex fiends! Just what have you been up to, eh?

—Nothing.

—It was the heat.

—The heat! Well, how about a shower, then?

—That sounds like a great idea!

—No, no, not that, please, for the love of God.

—Oh, did you hear that? The little whore doesn't want a shower.

—What a shame! Sorry, sweetheart, it's not time to put your clothes on yet.

They led us through a corridor of cells crowded with prisoners. They had to push me along, I was still half blind. An unidentifiable smell in the air, worse than a day when there's an inversion and the odor of shit and rotting bodies dominates the atmosphere.

If there were any food in my stomach, I'd definitely throw up. The prisoners are crammed in, standing shoulder to shoulder, pressing up against each other, there's so little room. Every ten meters, a sign on the wall, white, with fat, block-print letters: BE PRODUCTIVE: WORK IS FREEDOM!

Howls from the cells as we pass by, the men leering at Elisa. They yell obscenities, invitations, they whistle, stick their hands out between the bars. But even their excitement seems to be in slow motion, vague, muffled.

Elisa walks by, naked, indifferent. She's been through this before, she doesn't let it bother her. I'm impressed by her calmness, it's encouraging. Why be frightened of men behind bars? For a few moments I let myself be fooled into thinking they were the danger, not our escorts.

They left me in an empty cell. Which was fine with me. They must have realized I wasn't a common criminal like the rest. Although with the Civil Guards, you never know, criminal or not they bring you in and beat you up. They don't even want to know. They took Elisa with them.

We didn't even have time to say good-bye, the guy pushed me in here and slammed the door. A little while later, a short guy with rotten teeth appeared, a monkey wearing blue plastic. He opened a cupboard in the wall and rolled out a hose. Told me to stand a meter away from the back wall.

The first violent blast of water threw me against the wall with such force I was sure my ribs were broken. I'm glued to the wall as the water pounds my belly like a battering ram. I feel my intestines roll over, everything that was inside runs down my legs, oh my God, what shame.

—Enjoying your shower, old man? That's why you had your clothes off, all ready to go, right?

301

The water is poorly recycled urine, it smells like ammonia, it's in my mouth, my nose, seeping in my pores...

...can't breathe, lungs full of piss...

...a blast from the hose dislocates my liver, my bladder, everything inside me...

...icy water revives me, I float around the cell...

...Tadeu comes down the elevator shaft to save me. He throws me the sack of letters for Adelaide and gallops off furiously down the beach, his horse runs on solar energy...

...he attacks the guy with the rotten teeth, he's out of control, he misses and his lance plunges into my chest, yellow liquid runs down and drips into a plastic pail...

...Adelaide tears up the letters and throws the pieces into the big cell where the men are singing in harmony that old refrain: WORK IS FREEDOM, and they jump all over each other to grab at the letters, fighting for shreds of paper...

...you shouldn't do that, Adelaide, those letters are for the other mothers, they're waiting as anxiously as you were, desperate for news from the ship, I wish you wouldn't do that, Adelaide...

...the man with the rotten teeth sloshes pails of yellow water around the cell, thousands of prisoners are drinking and howling...

...the hose again, no, I'm already hamburger, this will finish me off for sure, where's Elisa, I want Elisa, what have you done with her? Adelaide walks down a beach littered with—no, *made of* broken light bulbs, she's reading a letter, ah, that means it finally arrived...

...the truck moves forward, loaded with logs, why are you standing in front of it, quick, get out of the way, you can't stop the truck, they'll run you down...they hit the brakes and skid on the leaves covering the ground, logs tumble everywhere and the truck rolls over on top of my grandfather (what was he trying to do?), no one can stop it, look at all of them, lines of trucks leaving

302

the forest, listen to the chain saws, grandfather, there's nothing you can do to stop them, listen to crash after crash, trees falling on top of each other, a house of cards collapsing one card at a time, throw away your machete, grandfather, lean it against the wall in a corner of the shed out back, you can chop firewood for grandma's stove, if there's firewood left...

... why did you stand paralyzed in front of the truck, it was brown, as it rushed out of the greenness? What good did it do, grandfather?

... I'm floating in space, Adelaide is floating too, hovering above the letter, a sad smile on her face, she looks like a sepia photograph on a gravestone...

... foulness running from my mouth, no more water, the hose shrivels in his hands...

... they carry me away, I'm weak, so weak, they've amputated my legs, they're going to shoot me now...

... my body is so dry, so parched, how long have I been here?...

... I pull off patches of skin, not sure if it's stuck-on piss or some strange disease...

... I know I'm strong, I can take it as long as I have to, staring at the portrait of Elisa on the wall, lit by a torch which appeared out of nowhere...

... there's just one thing you said that's wrong, Elisa, because the reason we carry all that guilt around with us, the reason is because we're guilty, yes, adapted to the world, it's easier not to change anything, it's easier, we're guilty...

—How about some food, old man?

A plastic plate with something gummy, jelly-like. Nauseating. I know I should eat slowly, and very little, that's what Elisa told me. If I bolt this down it might kill me. Funny, my head seems to be working again. The man with the rotten teeth waits, watching me eat, he must be my valet.

—You're being transferred.

—Those aren't my clothes.

303

—Everything belongs to everybody here, do you think we've got a coat check, with numbers on the hangers? Just get dressed and let's get going.

—How long have I been in here?

—How should I know? With who knows how many thousand prisoners, a couple hundred showers a day, you think I take notes on the comings and goings? A week, maybe a month, or two months, for all I know.

—Without food?

—You ate a few scraps. Looked like you were asleep even when you were awake. A real survivor, huh?

—Where are they taking me?

—I already told you, professor, I don't know.

—But you know I'm a professor. How?

—The commandant recognized you. He was a student of yours.

—Really?

—Said you were a real dangerous character, subversive. Wanted to know if you were still teaching.

—Why didn't he ask me?

—No time.

Instead of the paddy wagon, I was thrown in the backseat of a regular cruiser. The clothes they gave me are too big and filthy dirty, the idea of wearing someone else's clothes makes me nauseous. My skin still looks crusty—dirt or disease? What about Elisa? A stab of longing. The urge to see her, embrace her. No use asking, there's a glass shield between me and the driver.

I don't recognize any of the streets. Anonymous, deserted sidewalks, sun beating down. It's hot in the car, too, sweat begins to loosen the dried skin. Leprosy must smell like this. The blue haze is lower than usual, I've never seen it this low, utterly stifling.

All the windows are closed. Every once in a while I see a gigantic billboard: *Citizens! The Problem of Shelter Has Been Solved. The System's Extensive Marquee is Ready!* And underneath: *Work is Freedom.* My skin crawls, I wish there were at least one person on the street, it looks like they've killed everyone.

304

The cruiser seems to turn a corner every few blocks, I wish I could open the window, get a little air at least. Wait a minute—maybe it's me they're going to kill. I can't figure it out. Why this privileged status: still a prisoner, but out of jail? At the door to a Baptist church the driver lets me out. At the curb there's a lean-to made of sheet metal.

The sun beats down with such intensity you can almost hear it hit the metal roof. Everything above the third story is enveloped in blue haze, it's as if I'm in a gas chamber. I wait for the cruiser to leave. I'm dripping with sweat, unbearably thirsty. It has never been this hot.

I have to get home somehow. Find out where I am, and find a way to get through the Access Stations. If they pick me up here without a CIRCA, I'll be tossed out Beyond the Pale and finally get to see what the Pauper Encampments look like. I'd rather not. If only I could find a telephone. But who would I call?

Bulletproof glass, watchtowers, electronic systems of surveillance and identification. It would take a super-brain to get around all these obstacles. Ha, and I've read so many mystery books, people slipping out of locked rooms, detectives full of clever tricks and ruses.

The odd thing is that I'm not hungry, it doesn't even occur to me. Indifference. Maybe my stomach shrank so much I don't need food anymore. I've changed into a human perpetual-motion machine. If only Sebastião Bandeira could study me now, he'd be able to perfect his failed invention.

This city is more of a mystery to me every day. We live inside our daily trajectory, we reduce our surroundings to that limit, and we shrink along with them. I've got a thousand theories in my head. Ah, remember the Terrible Risks of the Eternal Known. I've lived surrounded by risks without managing to ever take any. Dreaming about navigators, explorers, who searched for the horizon beyond the horizon. Or astronauts in search of the moon.

Okay, professor, use your head. Rational thought used

to be your forte. Find a way to trick a security guard. Concentrate on the problem at hand: have to make a phone call, eat something, any old thing, have to ask someone for help. Have to get home, and find Adelaide. Yikes, so many things to do. And you know something? I don't feel like doing any of them.

## LISTEN UP, SEBASTIÃO BANDEIRA, EVEN IF IT'S TOO LATE: IT WAS THE REST OF US WHO WERE CRAZY

Wide, clean streets, handsome buildings with granite facades. The absence of foul odors is what really surprises me, I didn't know places like this existed. Why did they leave me here? Panels with beautiful artificial gardens painted on them, propped up in front of each apartment building. Some of the doors have one-way glass, I see my image reflected as I walk by. And what an image.

A frightened, unshaven man, bony face, wide-eyed expression, trembling hands (did I pick up some kind of virus in jail?), wrinkled, ill-fitting clothes, no socks, scruffy boots. At first I couldn't even look at myself, I'm embarrassed and ashamed. But there's no denying it's me.

I have to take responsibility for myself: the man reflected in the door is a possibility that's present in all of us. It's just that it really happened to me. My problem is this: how to maintain a certain distance from that other man, keep him at arm's length, while at the same time practicing a sort of peaceful coexistence. He's a stranger to me but I see no way to repudiate him, maybe because he somehow represents the beginning of knowledge, the beginning of the mutation of someone called Souza.

Rejecting him would mean interrupting the process of revelation. Discovery. Any real change necessarily begins inside us, and only later affects the whole. External modification, the alteration of society, is a result of interior transformation.

Odd that I'm not being followed. Not even one Agent Suspicious By Nature popping up behind me, just my own footsteps, so loud they get on my nerves. I stop and look around. A neighborhood like this must be well protected. Hidden cameras? Men with binoculars on top of the buildings? Sharpshooters?

Drenched in sweat, limping from my goddamned arthrosis which is acting up again, I press on. I try to orient myself by the signs, but many of the symbols are unintelligible to me. They must be meant for some special category of people. My grandfather used to say: "When you're lost, the best thing to do is go straight ahead, so you don't risk walking in circles." If it worked in the forest, why not in the city?

A high wall stretches on to the end of the street, almost out of sight. Recently painted, which means at least there's some restoration work going on in this city. I drag myself along the wall, moving slowly, my leg is still bothering me. I lean up against the wall to rest, startled to discover that it's cold, icy, really, compared with everything else. Strange. I wonder if there's such a thing as a tactile mirage. What would you call it—a *tactirage?* I touch it again, definitely quite cool. Like the glass in a refrigerated case.

I sit down with my back to the wall, determined to spend the rest of my life right here. Too bad I don't have a good book, or a magazine. How long has it been since I've read anything? Sure would be nice to read some news, even the lies put out by the Intense Official Propaganda Agency. Or to talk to someone. How could Tadeu have killed himself without so much as an explanation?

Five minutes went by, or not even, and a man in a khaki uniform and old-fashioned leggings appeared. His nose was a bloody mess, unable to control his constant sniffling. He stopped directly in front of me and stared. Cautious, unsure what to expect. He paced back and forth, casual but suspicious. Finally, he asked in a loud voice?

—What are you doing here?

—Nothing. Resting.

—You'll have to be on your way.

—Why?

—This is a security zone.

—How come? What's on the other side of the wall?

—Residences. It's the Super-Climatized Project.

—Do people actually live there? I mean really?

—Of course, what are you talking about?

—Well, it's just that I heard they all died, all the people in the Super-Project.

—Not a chance, buddy. They're alive, all right. The Secret Functionaries live in there.

—Do you know any of them?

—No, they never come out.

—And you mean you never go in, either?

—No, our job is exterior security. We communicate with the inside by radio.

—Then you've never seen any of them at all? No one ever comes on foot, or by car? Or haven't you seen somebody open a window, maybe?

—How could I? Look how high the wall is. And as far as them coming out, they just don't. Why should they? They have everything they need inside, it's paradise.

This conversation intrigues me, but I'm having a real problem with the way this guy smells. Characteristic of people with ruined intestines—yes, I'm certain of it, he's one of the group that served as guinea pigs when they were first developing synthetic food. Before they got it quite right.

The System's labs performed experiments on human subjects to study the organism's reactions to various chemicals. The first synthetic food substances they tested apparently caused serious gastrointestinal damage. As a result, the subjects live surrounded by a virtual gas chamber of their own body's creation, the stench from which is hard even for them to bear. I understand what it all means, the tortured nose, constant sniffling, droopy head, and worst, this unsaintly halo that follows him everywhere. The sufferers of Portable Flatulence, as it's called, were barred from the downtown areas and instead restricted to semi-deserted zones like this one. So it's easy to see why he's not allowed in the Climatized Project.

—I still don't understand it. No one comes out at all? How can they stand it?

—Okay, I'll tell you something, but you have to promise not to tell anyone else, okay?

—Who's there to tell?

—Right. So there's no harm in telling you that once in a while they do come out.

—Really? Where do they go?

—Well, sometimes they spend an afternoon at the Alleviation Center.

—Rich people are something else. I'm the one who needs alleviation.

—Me too. Do you know what it's like doing rounds, back and forth, back and forth, along these walls, not seeing a living soul for days, sometimes weeks? It's like I was in jail.

—What about the people who live around here?

—Nice folks, but they're trapped. Scared to death of the street.

—Do they work?

—I don't know. I see some of them every once in a while, but they're not much for chitchat. Not like a small-town kid like me.

—Where are you from?

—Vera Cruz. In the interior of the state.

—What did you do there?

—The same as everybody else where there's a bit of land. Except, get this: they called it the Energy Harvest Division.

—You got tired of it?

—No, the ground got tired of it. The seedlings failed and the weeds took over.

309

—Look, I'm sorry to bring this up, but the trouble with talking to you is the smell . . .

—Would it help if we stood farther apart?

—Okay, but you'll have to talk louder. Tell me, what are these secret functionaries like?

—Same as anybody else—they have heads, hands, feet. There are bald ones, crippled ones, you know. But they're real pale, milk-colored almost, like a macaroon.

—Macaroons, ah, do you remember macaroons?

—Sure, I guess we all grew up on them.

—If you want, I can give you an address where they still make excellent macaroons. It's in the Forgotten Center of São Paulo. You have a CIRCA for that area?

—Sure, our passes are good for anywhere. But can they really taste like macaroons, I mean made with synthetic milk and coconut?

—The milk is natural. They buy mother's milk.

—Mother's milk? How could they?

Damn! I forgot this guy's in security. All I need to do is tell him about the pregnant girls and their illicit children and he'll sound the alarm, enter a complaint that Sterilization isn't doing its job. Even the most casual investigation might lead them to the Shelters of Children Who Squeaked By.

It would be a real disaster. All the Infant Systems destroyed in one fell swoop. Of course nothing would happen to the children, but the people who maintain the shelters would be sent to Isolation, and the mothers would be barred from any further social contact. Not to mention the end of the macaroons . . .

—Hey, I'm talking to you. What's this about mother's milk?

—Just a joke, do you think mothers have milk?

—Sure, when they have a baby.

—Right, but who has babies these days?

—Yeah, I get the point. That's what I was thinking.

—Well, I'd better be on my way . . .

This damn arthrosis. One of these days I'm going to

cut off the whole leg, I'd be better off. I could use a crutch even now, and I better get out of here fast, before he thinks any harder about this mother's milk business.

—Hey, wait a minute . . .

—What? Oh, I forgot to give you the address, didn't I?

—It's not that. The boss overheard our conversation on the walkie-talkie and he radioed for me to bring you in. He wants some more information.

—About the macaroons?

—About the mother's milk.

—But I told you, I was just kidding.

—What can I do? He's an ASBN, I have to follow orders.

—I'm getting out of here, there's no more to tell. It was a joke, that's all.

He drew his gun. I jumped. Guns scare me to death, they really do. I told him to keep calm. And then dove into the pestilential smell that surrounded him, catching him by surprise. We rolled on the ground, I spit in his eye. Once again surprised at my own strength.

My punch misses its mark, but I get him with my elbow, crack under the chin and he's gonzo. The walkie-talkie is squawking some kind of code mixed with continuous static. I turn it off. I go through the security man's pockets and appropriate his CIRCA, and two little black cookies. No money or ID. I also take the canteen.

Then I yank off his belt, tie his feet together, and sit down against the refrigerated wall again to catch my breath. Can't help thinking how nice it would be to stay here forever. But I pick myself up off the sidewalk and force the leg to work no matter how much it hurts. I have to get out of here, the guys on the other end of the walkie-talkie must be coming after me, they could appear at any moment.

It was stupid of me to bring up mother's milk. Though it is funny enough as a joke: a roomful of young women with their breasts hanging out, milking themselves for

311

the cooks in the next room busily whipping up batch after batch of macaroons. But I wasn't thinking. I endangered one of the most top-secret projects of all time.

Our maid had an illicit son once. Apparently somebody in the System's Sterilization crew slipped up somehow. Anyway, she got pregnant and decided she wanted the child. I had heard about the shelters because I had met a guy on the street who happened to know about the organization. I stepped on his foot, we talked, ended up good friends, and eventually he trusted me enough to tell me.

But it wasn't until our maid got pregnant that I became personally involved in the shelters. Then I became a contributor, donating money, water coupons, food. Not a lot, but it was something. I even learned something about taking care of children by putting in some hours at the nursery and preschool. I meant to bring Tadeu there one day, and Adelaide.

This wall goes on forever. Dull gray. If only they'd painted murals on it or something, slapped up some wallpaper with woodsy scenes. There's a purpose to this monotony, I'm convinced of it, I just can't figure out what it is. Boy, would I like to get a look inside, though. Maybe someday we'll invade!

Take the city by storm—like Troy, or the Bastille, or Jerusalem during the Crusades. Wait a minute, I'm all confused. Maybe these are the Acrylic Palaces! If so, then my nephew lives on the other side of this wall. And Adelaide must be inside there too.

I'm so absolutely sure she's at his house, the thought of it is a relief. Adelaide is safe. The only question is whether she's there by choice or against her will. It's possible that he's prevented her from communicating with me, quite possible. Though her absence really doesn't bother me anymore.

The street lights go on, but the heat hasn't let up yet. Maybe I'll find some corner of the world to sleep in before the cold hits. The security man's black cookies taste awful. One is enough.

Taken with water, it seems to swell up and completely fill the stomach. Like in the old days—Northeasterners used to eat flour and drink water, they said it made a cake in the stomach. Maybe if I lie down in a dark corner I'll blend into the wall. I curl up in a triangle of shadow and hope I'm camouflaged.

It's the smell that wakes me. the smell of rotten meat. The ground is cold now, I'll rest a little bit longer. I slept like a rock, no dreams. I better take advantage of the early morning to keep walking; besides, I don't feel half bad. But don't think I've forgotten how good it would feel to take a shower.

—You there! Identify yourself!

—Security.

—Security? You don't look the part.

—Look who's talking. Have you looked at yourself in a mirror lately?

—What do you mean?

—I mean that I should be the one asking for your ID.

—So, it's right here . . .

—So's mine. Can't you tell I'm undercover?

—Undercover? What for?

—Confidential mission. Even I don't know what it is.

—I know what you mean, pal—how can we do our job when they're so secretive about what's going on? All they do is complicate life for us. More bureaucracy every day. You heading up that way?

—I'm supposed to patrol the whole area.

—It's bad up ahead, I'll tell you. Complete chaos. They're calling for reinforcements. Things get more screwed up by the day. Crowds of people escaping from the Encampments.

—Is that the problem up there?

—No, it's the lines for the black silk umbrellas. You've heard about them, haven't you?

—Yeah, but I don't believe a word of it.

—But they do. Off the deep end because of the sun. They're grasping at straws, that's what it is. You know

313

the sun has killed more of them than hunger, disease, and the Guards all put together. It's dangerous, they're beginning to penetrate the inner circles. That damn Marquee, that's the other thing they're clamoring for. The System keeps promising, advertising, but the damn thing's not ready yet.

—If they heard you talking that way, bye-bye—send me a postcard from Isolation.

—People from Security don't get sent to Isolation!

—No?

—I think you just slipped up, buddy. Let me see some identification.

—I really don't think that's necessary . . .

—Well, at least give me a password.

—How about a cookie?

—Hey, fantastic! The black ones are the best, hand it over!

Everybody knows the way things work around here, shit for some, choice tidbits for the others. I'm glad I had one of those babies left. I walk away as fast as I can without arousing his suspicion more than I already have. Maybe since those cookies are special rations for Security on patrol it will last me a few days. So I gave one up— it got me out of a jam, didn't it? Besides, no use crying over spilt milk. Ha ha.

Straight ahead? Back where I came from? What difference does it make. Maybe I should just stay in one place. Zero equals zero. Or I'll walk until I collapse; that way I'll be able to sleep anywhere. If I survive until then. It's still pretty early and the pavement burns my feet, right through my shoes.

I bet if I spent one day at an Alleviation Center, I'd be able to shake off this anxiety, this oppressive feeling. I can barely stand to speak. But the Centers are restricted. Maybe my nephew could get me an authorization? Fat chance. I'm forgetting the ingrate wanted to kill me.

. . . street quivering like Jell-O, the houses are going to come tumbling down . . .

. . . a bus stop, a shelter, at least some shade, I'm

314

allowed to stand here, right? At least until the bus comes . . .

. . . a TV camera focused squarely on me, as I move back and forth it follows. Where are the controls? An unpleasant sensation—they transmit my image who knows where . . .

KEEP MOVING, CITIZEN. REPEAT: KEEP MOV-
ING. YOU ARE WASTING YOUR TIME.

The voice comes from somewhere in the shelter, one of those pipes over there maybe. There's no way I'm going to stand here talking to some iron pipe, even if it can hear me. I really should take a nap, the heat is suffocating. I can't go back into the sun yet. Better to pretend I didn't hear it.

After a little while, I feel better. Must be a drop in my blood pressure. I look up at more closed windows. The buildings here seem more working-class, they're plainer, there's laundry hanging out to dry, at least a sign that somebody actually lives here. Also, the smell seems closer: cadavers, excrement, garbage. The same old trio.

No fan or ventilating system could take care of a smell like this. I've heard, and repeated, that in some neigh-borhoods the residents wear gas masks at all times. And that the animals living at ground level are dying like flies. Has it gone that far already? At least the haze is higher today.

KEEP MOVING, CITIZEN. THIS IS NO LONGER
A BUS STOP. THE BUS LINES HAVE BEEN DI-
VERTED TO ANOTHER ROUTE.
PLEASE FOLLOW THE SIGNS & SYMBOLS, THE
ENDLESS MARQUEE IS READY.

Here I sit listening to the voice of no one. They expect me to obey a pipe? It's probably a tape. What do they think I am, stupid? Some tape playing over and over, and we're supposed to do what it tells us. Sorry, not me. I stare at the ground, the paving stones practically melting

315

away, turning to mush, thick, dark oatmeal.

Something glinting in one of the cracks between stones. A small metal box, square, not much bigger than a wristwatch. I tried to fish it out, but it seemed to be fixed in place. Someone had fit it into the space with great precision. Is that where the voice was coming from? A mini-radio transmsitter?

I tried to pry it out, using a little more force and the tip of the security man's belt buckle. A whirring noise coming from down there. That scared me a little, could be a bomb, some kind of explosive. It's been ages, though, since the days bombs were going off around the clock. Nothing to worry about, really. Anything unknown makes people apprehensive, what imaginations we have.

I examined and reexamined the silvery object. Until, irritated, I threw it on the ground. The whirring sound must mean there's some sort of gadget inside, but what? And why in a sealed box? I felt like a guilty child breaking his toy to figure out how it works.

Just as well I let the child in me take over. Eventually, the top came off and I could see it wasn't an electrical device, or at least it didn't look like one. There were hundreds of tiny wheels, not a millimeter in radius, all spinning with incredible speed, some of them turning others via interlocking teeth.

It didn't tick like a wound clock—just a sort of soft buzzing sound. What the devil is this thing? What's it do? What makes it run? I tried to make one of the tiny gear wheels stop turning by sticking the tip of the belt buckle into the works. Instead of stopping it, the wheel popped out of the case, flew through the air, still spinning.

That's the part I didn't understand—maybe it was due to the force I exerted with the buckle, maybe centrifugal force, but for a moment it looked like a miniature helicopter. Then it fell onto the sidewalk right next to me. When I went to pick it up, it shot off like a firecracker and landed in another crack between the paving stones.

Gradually it nestled into the hole, still spinning in

place. Like a little drill. Fine dust rose into the air. My attention turned, fascinated, from the tiny dislocated wheel to the mechanism itself, whose hundreds of wheels were still turning, independent of the one I had pried out.

I bent down close to the ground, my cheek against the stone, and watched. A minuscule perpetual-motion machine! But how can it work minus what seemed to be an integral part? The dislocated wheel itself was still spinning its way down into the dirt, practically out of sight by now. If I left it there, how far would it go? How did it work all on its own?

My relative Sebastião wanted so badly for his wheel to begin spinning, self-propelled. As if it could just automatically start moving, if it happened to be in the mood. But it didn't. It just stared back at him, motionless. And every one of us knew that was all it would ever do.

When I say "us," I mean me, my father, my grandmother, my aunts, and Sebastião's neighbors. But what did we know, outside of traditional, conventional knowledge? What did we know, aside from what had been handed down to us by our ancestors and what we had gathered from observing our surroundings?

Everything that made up our momentary, daily life. Ours = theirs. Of course, at seven-or-eight-years-old, I hadn't yet experienced much myself. I vacillated between admiration for Sebastião and silent respect for those relatives who nodded their heads gravely. Agreeing: Sebastião is crazy.

Sebastião is crazy, it's just a matter of time before . . . But some subjects were taboo. They whispered or fell silent when the children came into the room. As far as I can remember, no one, among all the people Sebastião loved, had encouraged him.

But there was one person who was sure the wheel would begin spinning someday: me. Though of course I was equally certain of many other things the adults didn't understand: my bamboo pole was a sword; the old washbasin, a ship; the highest point of the garden wall, an airplane; the chickens, monstrous hawks. Only me and

Sebastião had imagination.

One day, long after I realized I was no longer a child, I also realized that Sebastião Bandeira had died. I never managed to find out when or where. He had just disappeared from my life. Had he been hospitalized? Or had he died in the bosom of the family and I had wiped out the memory? There must have been a funeral, flowers, a burial with people crying, no family would dispense with that: the solemn procession through the streets, the necessity to exhibit tragedy, to look for pity and consolation.

It's irritating to think about that critical "initial impulse." It was all anyone talked about, without getting any closer to understanding or believing in it. Somehow, at a determined moment, some physical law, as yet unknown to man, would make the wheel start to spin. Something invisible: weather conditions, humidity, the wood expanding and contracting on its axle.

I spent hours and hours playing in that garden littered with rocks, leaves, bottles, cans, sticks, nails, wire— while I waited, along with Sebastião, for the initial impulse. Now I see the admirable patience of that man, sitting transfixed in front of his perfect mechanism.

Because he was absolutely sure it *was* perfect. That it could spin for years and years, until finally falling apart. There he sat under the mango tree in his straw hat from dawn to dark. What faith. He had worked for years— weekends, holidays, vacations, forty years of them— and then every day after he retired. He knew it hadn't been in vain. Perfection was around the corner, he could smell it—that simple, harmonious, delicate movement.

Bandeira had the face of a saint, thin, yellow-skinned, a sparse beard, his eyes bright, especially when he gazed at his wire and wood contraption. A saint at the altar, waiting.

I've come to the still somewhat mysterious conclusion that Sebastião himself was the initial impulse. His touch, energy passing from his body to the machine. After that, movement generated movement.

Just like the tiny wheels of this crazy thing. Each interlocking tooth feeds the next, all the way around, until the last feeds the first. Unfortunately I was too much a child and Sebastião too much a dreamer to understand that we, too, are no more than interlocking parts.

## IN CHORA MENINO: CONFUSION, LONG LINES, BAD DREAMS, AND A BIG SURPRISE REGARDING THE BLACK SILK UMBRELLAS

Attention! Your attention, please!
The vents will be opened in ten seconds.
Nine seconds to clear the area.
Attention! Your attention, please!

You now have only six seconds left
to clear the area. Five seconds,
four, three, two...
This is the last warning!

Clear the area! Clear the area! Clear the area!

It was like a broken record. Just as well. I hope the vents get stuck, too, probably been a long time since they were used. Sure, I bet they're clogged, someone stuck something down the pipe. You know how things like that happen, everybody in this country is up for a little petty sabotage.

But not this time. I get out at the last instant, the gas rises from the vents—built right into the sidewalk in this case. Which means some VIP's live in the neighborhood. They dreamed up these vents during the time of the Dangerous Fallacies, first in industrial sectors, later in the privileged neighborhoods.

Efficient little devices. They were hidden in a niche in the sidewalk, in mailboxes, trash cans, any apparently

319

abandoned object. A network of piping delivered their choice of gases that made you sneeze, cough, vomit, have diarrhea, go blind, you name it.

The type of gas used depended on the situation and the number of participants. Sometimes they used the whole battery at once, and all that was left afterward was a pile of bodies and a big stink. The Civil Guards themselves preferred other methods of crowd control—participation in the cleanup operation left a stench clinging to them for weeks.

The most important union committee was the Volunteers to Neutralize the Vents. Which was not an easy job considering the tight security, including very sensitive alarm systems which were tied into District Security Headquarters.

The era of the Dangerous Fallacies got its name because the System's policies in those days were based on various incoherent and paradoxical attitudes, to which, of course, they admitted no rebuttal. Save your money and consume faithfully, buy a car and economize on fuel, fight inflation and lift price controls, ask for the truth and tell lies.

As I walk along, I notice the buildings changing markedly. It's been quite awhile since I've been in an area that had air conditioning, though all that's left of that luxury around here are the holes for the units, most of them covered with tattered plastic. More ruins.

Admit it, it's a thrill to be finding out about events which are still to come. Not everyone has the privilege. But don't ask me: how can we prevent such a period from happening? If you so much as turn one screw in the order of things, what I am living through will not occur.

Think about it: not only would my age not exist, I wouldn't even be born. And if I weren't born, how would I be able to write down this account of my time? The problem at once concrete and impenetrable, is this: the account is written, already in circulation. If you manage to circumvent my generation, what does that make this record?

I could endure just about everything if it weren't for this soupy, sweltering heat. The things that come into my head. It's the sun. Ambitious Phaëthon, stealing his father Helios' Chariot of the Sun. Pulled by four gleaming horses, it streams across the sky, illuminating and heating up our days.

Standing over the gaping abyss, surrounded by such light and heat, unable to control the fiery animals, Phaëthon was afraid. In his fear he dropped the reins and the horses galloped off the road, hallucinating, no driver and no destination. Woodlands caught fire, rivers dried up, whole mountains burned.

The earth raised up its arms, begging for help. And Zeus, having no other recourse, struck Phaëthon with a thunderbolt, and his blazing corpse fell into the River Eridanus. I took a class in mythology at the university. That legend had always bothered me for some reason.

The pavement came to an end and the street became dusty, hard-packed dirt. Dilapidated buildings alternating with vacant lots. Piles of trash everywhere. Acrylic signboards, in ramshackle condition, hide the facades of what appears to be an old-time commercial district.

People swarm out of doors, alleys, narrow lanes, cellars. There are no grates on the windows here, nor do I see any armed doormen or closed-circuit TV systems. Piles of turds in the corners, a strong smell of urine.

The crowd get larger and more frenzied the farther I go. More tightly packed—and nervous—by the minute. Lots of flustered people, itching, sneezing, raw-skinned from all sorts of allergies, bodies colliding. Women shouting for husbands and children, men calling back, hurry up, everybody's busy, confused, pressing forward.

Banners announcing bargain prices. People climbing all over each other, pushing and shoving. Others weeping on street corners, or screaming for someone to do thus-and-so. The sun is hidden behind the blue haze, I have

321

no idea of the time.

Sweat running down people. Men in Bermuda shorts, no shirt. Women in miniskirts, shorts, panties. Everything in slow motion. Signs proclaim: THE SYSTEM PROUDLY PRESENTS—THE MARQUEE—THE ULTIMATE SOLUTION TO THE HEAT WAVE—THE SHELTER FOR EVERYONE—ANOTHER SPLENDID ACHIEVEMENT FROM THE MINISTRY OF SOCIAL WELL-BEING.

—Is this Chora Menino?

—I think so.

—Where are they selling the umbrellas?

—You have to get in line.

—But where's the line? All I see is a horde of people.

—I heard the line starts about two kilometers from here. That's what they say, anyhow. All rumors. But look at this, you can't even move.

—I wonder if there'll be enough umbrellas to go around...

—They say there will be.

—But do you think it's worth it? It looks like everybody's gone crazy.

Banners along the road, hung from telephone poles: 100% BLACK SILK, LOW, LOW PRICES! The haze hangs so low it almost obscures the banners. I mingle in the multitude. A spot opens up, I fill it. Somebody moves to the right, I take his place. Like a bus in heavy traffic.

I push through the crowd, feeling silly for believing the stories about black silk umbrellas. If the sun really starts beating down as in the Northeast, it will scorch everything, melting those umbrellas like plastic. I push on until I find myself in a park that is impossibly jammed with people.

Night begins to fall, I keep walking, still crushed, pushed, cursed, and ignored by everyone around me. I work myself to the edge of the park, which is surrounded by a green chain-link fence. From here I can see spotlights around the boundaries, Civil Guards and German shepherds. People curled up on the ground, trying to get

322

comfortable. Not enough room for everyone.

I realize that the fence is made to narrow like a funnel, the kind they have for cattle at the slaughterhouse, that's how they're turning this mass into a line, from the inside out. Way at the back of the park, in the distance (it's not really a park, more like a nation), I see a brick structure. The Guards won't allow me to climb the fence to get a better look.

The line of people between the two narrowing lengths of fencing appeared to be very organized. People were seated on folding chairs, inside tents, curled up in sleeping bags. Were they Privileged Ones? Or would we all reach that point eventually? They were strumming guitars, squeezing accordions, girls were singing, dancing, couples were making love.

In the chill of dawn the partying tapered off a little. Though I could still hear a rhythmic bop-bopping. A group of men arrived and carried hundreds of bicycles into the brick building. Nearby, two women were heating up lunch pails and offered me a mouthful. No, I don't want any, you won't have enough for yourselves.

—Where there's enough for two, there's enough for three.

—Not true. If two eat poorly, three eat worse.

—You sure you can afford to be hungry and proud, both?

—Well . . . I am pretty hungry, you're right about that.

—Then eat. Come on, just a little something, here's an egg, there's enough to go around. Besides, tomorrow afternoon my husband will bring another lunch pail. Only, it will be eggs again. Not much else to be had.

—Never mind, who's picky these days, eh! And that's a lot of eggs.

—He works at the Farm Laboratory.

—A chemist?

—Goodness, no! He never went to school a day in his life. The only thing he knows how to do well is paint, they say he's the best at painting on those little specks of chicken shit that used to come on natural eggs.

—Oh, so he's a painter.

—No, silly, we're farmers, what do you think? We had some land outside Parati. I studied to be a teacher but decided I'd rather stay down on the farm, as they say. But that was before everything went to hell.

—Oh, did you have to leave because of the nuclear reactor?

—No, it was the hot rocks. It was an inferno, I'll tell you.

—Hot rocks?

—You've never been out in the country around Parati, I can see.

—No, can't say that I have.

—It's all mountains of rock. Of course, in the old days there was vegetation growing all over, lots of green. But they sold off the land, cleared it, and built up the whole area, the slopes, the peaks, everything. Cut and cleared the forest, too. That's what started the erosion. Mountains scraped completely bare. It was even sort of pretty, all those gigantic black boulders. Except the sun beat down and superheated them something awful, they hardly even cooled overnight. Then absorbed more heat the next day, and the temperature just kept rising. People in the valleys were literally burning up. Like roasting a fish on a hot rock. We got out of there as fast as we could.

She passed me the lunch pail, it was some kind of soup. Hot water, salt, a few synthetic herbs, and boiled eggs. It felt good to eat, in spite of the fake eggs, calmed my stomach down. The bop-bop-be-bop, the rhythm from the other side of the fence, and another batch of men carrying bicycles.

—What could they possibly be doing with all those bicycles?

—They use the spokes to make the umbrellas.

—No kidding!

—Hordes of guys go off every day to steal more bikes. The Civil Guards own the umbrella factory.

—Unbelievable.

—I've heard it was the Guards who invented this whole big deal about the black silk umbrellas, that they protect you from the sun, especially in the heat pockets. Looks like everybody believes it.

All those stories about the Northeast came back to me, the tales told by the man-who-sat-at-the-head-of-the-table. People killing each other to open job vacancies in the factories, stuff like that. Could it be his stories were true? Weren't they too outrageous to believe?

I have to admit I fell for some of it at the time, but thinking about it now made me uneasy. He must have thought me a real jerk to believe him. He had to be an ASBN, or a Guard assigned to spread false propaganda, like this business of the umbrellas.

I was dumb to have believed a word he said, just plain stupid. But on the other hand, maybe it was understandable, since that's what the Intense Official Propaganda Campaign is all about. Didn't we all believe in the Economic Miracle, for example, or the copper bracelets that were supposed to cure all diseases?

The noise of a truck jolted me back to life. Gears changing, the feeling that it was going to run me down. But the truck was on the other side of the fence. Everyone was still sleeping, the spotlights glowed, day was just beginning to break. The blue haze hung low, obscuring everything, you could almost touch it.

An official was directing the maneuvers of the giant brown tractor-trailer as it backed up to a side door of the brick building. Paralysis again, this time before the blob even appeared. But at least now I know what it signifies: the overloaded logging truck pulling out of the forest.

I know now it was an old man's delusion to try to stop that monster truck, it was over before it began. No brake could have held it back, the truck slid out of control and right over him, he was standing there defiantly, arms in the air. My grandfather knew them all, the trucks, the loggers, the saws, the claws to hold the logs in place. He must have known it was the end.

No more ax vs. tree. Now it was the speedy, invincible

saw. I still can't figure out what the old man was really trying to do. An eighty-five-year-old man, white hands extended to the sky. For some reason he believed it would be possible to stop that truck, and that's why I still admire him today. He gave it all he had: his life. Not just an uneven match—a complete impossibility.

The area around the building is swarming with Civil Guards now, all armed to the teeth, walkie-talkies in hand. They're shouting, trying to rouse the people and channel us into lines.

I got separated from the two women with the lunch pails. Too bad, that one wasn't bad-looking, maybe we could have gotten to know each other better. One of these lonely nights. That's all I can think about lately, I guess I need it bad. Everyone in line, perplexed faces—*what's going on?*—reminds me of lines from the past.

The most liberal of the history books recorded them: Jews on the way to the crematoriums. It could be happening all over again, we're all so innocent. Another of my hallucinations. Sometimes I just can't control my sense of the dramatic. Tragedies are fascinating, engrossing, they captivate us.

Later:

—Do you own a house or an apartment?

—I did.

—What do you mean?

—I lost it.

—Look, you can lose money, CIRCAs, women, objects, but how do you lose a house?

—Well, I didn't exactly lose it. They took it over.

—Oh, you mean you didn't pay the mortgage. That happens to lots of people, I bet most of the people here lost their houses the same way. Got in over their heads.

—No, that's not what I meant, I never missed a payment! What happened was these guys invaded my house and threw me out. It's a long story, and confusing, there are parts of it I hardly believe myself. And I'm tired, you've been asking me questions for over two hours, who knows why.

—All the people from up north tell the same story, did you learn it from them? A bunch of liars, the whole seedy crew, liars and bums. You invaded the city limits, took over neighborhoods you're not supposed to be in, that's what happened. There are circulation laws, you know! It's not right, you're all escapees from the Encampments. And it's the System that has to cope with it, it's all dumped in their lap.

—Wait just a minute! What did *I* do? All I want is a black silk umbrella!

—What are you talking about? Nonsense, sheer nonsense.

—You mean this isn't where they're selling the umbrellas?

—Look, take a number, check your color and letter, and get in line. There'll be a slight delay, but we'll get everybody on a bus eventually.

—Who said anything about a bus?

—Go on, take your ticket, the buses will be along soon. In a couple days this will be another department entirely. See if you can take care of yourself and don't come to me with any more stories.

—But...

—Next, please.

—Look, I'd just like to know—

—Will the next person please step up!

—Please, mister—

—Next! I've already wasted enough time.


### HARD TO BELIEVE, BUT
### JUST LOOK WHERE I ENDED UP!
### THIS DEVELOPMENT'S NOTHING
### IF NOT EGREGIOUS—
### YIKES, I DREDGED THAT ONE UP
### FROM THE DEPTHS OF ANTIQUITY


We spent the first few hours getting settled. We had arrived in the dark, without the slightest idea of what the

Marquee actually was. Just that it was our only hope, our last chance for salvation, according to the propaganda. A minimal effort for minimal citizens, remarked an old man on the bus.

All we wanted was a little shade over our heads during the heat of the day. That's not too much to ask, really. Practically nothing. Yet in this nutty country, as I've said so many times before, somehow nothing turns into everything. So here we are—the Marquee—the final solution. The shade and the wait. It's odd to wait and wait without knowing what it is you're waiting for.

Somewhere inside me, though without a great deal of conviction, I know I'm waiting to find Adelaide again. I'm waiting to go home. Which is no little thing; I'm talking about my life, after all, everything that means anything to me. And shade during the day represents survival, at least for a little longer.

The promise of surviving for a little longer is enough for now. We'll see about later later. Actually, I never intended to come here. I was sure the Marquee was some kind of utopian idea invented by the System in order to keep us in the dark a little longer. To bolster our hope.

How could any sane person really believe in a gigantic marquee designed to shelter an entire population? Just a marquee? A cement roof on columns, a simple covering to keep us out of the sun? Doesn't seem to make sense, does it? Well, I have to say it does. Maybe not to you, on the outside, light years away from this solar age.

Now that I'm here, I understand my last official encounter, the interview before I was put on a bus. That gigantic concrete room, bigger than Grand Central Terminal, and just the two of us, me and the inquisitor, in all that vastness. A table and chair in the center of the room. A monotonous, authoritarian voice.

—So, Mr. Souza. You have no problem whatsoever.
—I never said I did.
—I'm just confirming it. You're perfectly fine.
—I know that, I don't need you to tell me.

—I'm telling you so you won't have doubts about yourself.

—But I don't.

—. . . and so that you won't argue with me.

—But I'm not.

—You're probably feeling like saying that what I do is unnecessary.

—I never thought about it.

—I'd like to congratulate you.

—That's not necessary. It's not my fault if I'm all right. Just luck, isn't it? I mean, I don't know *why* I'm okay, which in itself occasionally makes me a little suspicious.

—Uh-oh, now wait a minute! Don't start doubting yourself. You must blindly believe that you're perfectly fine. Because that's the only way you'll be able to function in society. As long as you know you're okay, you'll remain a peaceful man.

—Can I ask you something? What is this conversation all about?

—Why, it's about helping people. Our citizens need more self-confidence, more faith in themselves. And that's what we're here for.

—I don't get it.

—You don't need to. Just answer my questions sincerely and honestly.

—I am.

—Okay. Tell me frankly—no problems? None at all?

—Well, just the normal ones everybody has. The extreme heat, thirst, difficulty breathing, discomfort, permanent fatigue, hunger now and then, fear. And of course now I don't have anywhere to live.

—Fine. I can see we have a few problems here. But don't worry, we'll come up with a cure.

—A cure?

—First, let me tell you something: you're not hot. You couldn't possibly feel hot.

—But it's scorching!

329

—No, it's not, that's just your impression. It's spreading, I'm afraid, but nevertheless it's just an impression a lot of people happen to share. Do you know what the thermometers are registering? It's only sixty-three degrees Fahrenheit.

—What?! Then they're broken, every one of them.

—No, it's true. It's not hot. You think it is, so you feel hot. What you have to do is get "hot" out of your mind.

—Get it out of my mind, huh...

—That's the only way we can free you.

—You mean I've been arrested?

—No, of course not, this is a transitional phase, that's all. We're merely verifying your condition.

—Could you repeat that, please?

—It's a preparatory session, we need to find out if you're adjusting to community life.

—But I've lived in São Paulo all my life!

—Yes, of course you have, but life under the Marquee will be somewhat different. You see, we're studying all applicants for the Marquee so that we can put them in appropriate groups, and we also have a team of psychiatrists to help people adapt to their new life, so there won't be problems.

—Okay, okay. But who said I wanted to live under the Marquee?

—You got in line.

—I got in line to buy a black silk umbrella.

—That's what everyone's been saying, what kind of foolishness is that? We're checking into it. But in any case, now you're well on your way to a new life under the Marquee. I just have to keep you here under observation for a few more days. To evaluate your condition.

Three days. A week. I lost count. Adding up the days doesn't interest me anymore. I face them one by one, isolated moments. Innumerable conversations, special films, magazines, pamphlets to read, tests, more tests, interviews. I swallowed it all, until finally they decided I was ready. And here I am.

330

Could everyone in this whole crowd have gone through such lengthy psychiatric preparation? If so, they must have been at it for years. Oh, our neurotic necessity to *understand*. Some things just escape us, but unfortunately that doesn't make them go away. Given my capacity for hallucination, understanding what I'm saying here has probably become superfluous! But hallucination may be the only thing that can make people act nowadays, keep them alive, give them a reason to survive.

None of us had any idea what the Marquee would be like. I suppose we pictured the rationally conceived and organized shelters in Europe during the Second World War. Or something on the order of the bomb shelters that were so popular in the fifties and sixties. Or the famous Peking underground.

We expected space, a ventilation system, a reasonable amount of comfort, bathrooms, drinking fountains. I never planned on coming here, but that's the way I pictured it on the basis of the Intense Official Propaganda. As if we could expect something like that from the System! (If they knew about these pessimistic thoughts of mine, I'd be sent to Isolation.)

They let us off the bus (bus: a filthy, stifling rattletrap) at night. We were marched along a wide plain (what part of São Paulo is this?), still scalding hot from the day's sun. Unable to see a thing, we were cooperative, though we did think it odd that there were no lights. Total darkness, not even a moon.

"There's a problem with the electrical system, it will be fixed by tomorrow," promised our escorts. Exhausted, we accepted their excuses. In the morning when the sun came up, we hurried for shelter. There was the famous Marquee—not quite what we had expected. The construction of the century was nothing more than thousands upon thousands of columns supporting a cement roof.

The thing stretched into the distance as far as you could see. No sign of any ventilation system whatsoever. The people who ended up in the center sections were going to regret it. A few feeble light bulbs here and there.

The bathrooms must be hidden by the crowd. Drinking fountains? Even if they had them (which suddenly seemed highly doubtful), only the people in the immediate vicinity would be able to get close enough to get a drink.

"Security in a cool and eclectic environment." All sectors working full-bore for months to provide this state-of-the-art Marquee. No project had ever been as gradiose. Not the Rio-Niteroi bridge, not the canals of the northeast, not the Age of the Railroad, not the Hydroelectric project at Itaipu, not even the reclamation of the Trans-amazonian highway.

A Calamity Tax was instituted as a way for the population to finance this immense pharaonic construction, destined without a doubt to be the pride of Brazil. Speeches were made, papers delivered, architects extolled the "twentieth century wonder of the world," comparable to the Hanging Gardens of Babylon, the World Trade Center, the Eiffel Tower, the Colossus of Rhodes.

From space, photographed via satellite, the Marquee formed the word Brazil, visible even to the moon. Rhetoric flowed like wine in and around official circles, government ministeries, the Supreme Hierarchy of the Civil Guards, The Resistance Clubs, the District Access stations, the Society of Inebriated Aides, well—in every administrative or managerial department of the System.

Of course you have to understand that Brazil is a country where rhetoric had been flourishing for centuries—ever since the glowing report Cabral's scribe sent back to Europe announcing his wondrous discovery. Rhetoric was a national trait the System knew how to capitalize on, with the invaluable help of popular psychology. They turned rhetoric into a vast and eminently exploitable smoke screen.

The process of public rhetoric follows an invariable sequence. First comes the moment of so-called denunciation. Someone has to bring up the problem. Next, the delicate phase of indignant voices, in or out of government, rising to demand action.

The third phase requires some talent and not a little fast talking. The phase of promises: the government guarantees to appoint commissions of inquiry, promotes supervised demonstrations, permits editorials in the press, and grants "in-depth" interviews. This period is essential. It is of the utmost importance to maintain a continuous avalanche of exasperating rhetoric. Talk and more talk, until it becomes positively overwhelming.

Until it becomes impossible for anyone to remain rational. Cover the same ground over and over again to the point of saturation. And then, all of a sudden, no one wants to hear another word of denunciation, the subject has been exhausted. Anyone who goes on talking about it is automatically classified as Intolerably Boring.

Systems of government succeed each other, notions of politics are modified, but rhetoric remains, endures like a hereditary defect. Though of course it's constantly being perfected. History is full of examples of the process of rhetoric. During the famous Open Eighties, for instance, the dominant elite was suffering from a certain undefined preoccupation, almost dread. They tried to keep their eyes open, they wanted to know what was going on.

In those days, the people and the intellectuals, previously two separate and distinct classes, were fused into the Middle Class Automobile Owners. They joined forces with Those Who Hadn't Had Their Houses Repossessed. The only group that stood alone was the Privileged Class of Winners: those who had won the sports lottery, the Federal numbers game, the illegal numbers game, the Surreptitiously Approved Clandestine Roulette Games, or some other type of gambling venture. The Winners kept to themselves, jealously guarding their winnings and maintaining their privileges.

Everyone else was more than happy to denounce, comment, mouth off, criticize, take a stand, pick up a pen, shout, moan, agitate, testify, grumble, protest, make banners, sign petitions, pledge solidarity, demand public review boards, propose amnesty, lobby for *habeas corpus*, and generally raise hell in opposition to the government.

Absolute power, in the person of the System, hesitated for a while before reacting. The enthusiasm the people were bringing to their task was unexpected, a relatively new phenomenon in Brazil. The system had imagined the protest would develop slowly, in gradual stages. The country rising up against them was one they found totally unrecognizable; the only image they had of Brazil was the one they had tried to create.

After this short period (called the Days of Stupefied Hesitation), the System began to react. But its reactions were clumsy, almost crude—like those of someone who doesn't know how to act in the context of freedom, someone profoundly uncomfortable with the institutionalized freedom of the people.

First off, it was important to give a semblance of legality to governmental actions which might be (often were) violent and arbitrary. Existing laws were distorted, reinterpreted, stretched beyond recognition. Casuistic statutes were introduced; statutes, that is, which were easily adaptable to diverse necessities as they arose. Laws which were infinitely expandable. And so all kinds of organizations sprang up at the borders of the System. Paramilitary associations, clandestine para-official groups—given free rein. Bombs began to go off. Newspaper stands, churches, cars, blown to smithereens.

All of which may have been unnecessary if the System had allowed the process of rhetoric to take its course. Which they finally did, in the period called Voracious Craftiness. The flexing of rhetoric. I can remember how happy my father was in those days to be protesting, demonstrating, and most of all just plain talking about all that had gone wrong. Gradually, members of the System itself began to swell the ranks of the protestors. Until it seemed that everyone, absolutely everyone, was talking.

And while they talked, it was left to chance what

corrective measures would be taken. A perfect smoke screen, as I said. People wore themselves out talking. They got tired of the subject, so it died. People got tired of rhetoric itself. Which led to what the sociologists dubbed the Brief Period of Rest for Inflamed and Indignant Throats.

We had names for all the periods. Regardless of how long they lasted, they had to be labeled, characterized, personified. I wonder what this very moment in history will be called. That is, if anyone survives to baptize any more historic periods. The Body A-Politic Waiting for Death? The Age of Gullibility?

We're incorrigible, we believe anything they tell us. We even imagined that someday the foremen would go against tradition and build something that wasn't immediately obsolete. As if the construction companies would be stupid enough to spend any of their generous profits on insulation, ventilation, *creature comforts*.

Ah, Souza, you're too much. Utterly disconnected from the real world, lost in thoughts as useless as an impotent man between the legs of a woman. Starving, tongue burning, head exploding, feet on fire, eyes tearing, and still climbing up onto the soapbox.

Going over and over the obvious, a puerile moralism. None of it gets you anywhere. Besides, you don't even talk—you just think. Your whole life long you've been thinking, thinking. Inside your own head. You didn't even join in the rhetoric, and now you've finally discovered the truth about it.

So, what now? What can you do with this truth? Cover yourself? Fan yourself? Hop on it and ride far, far away from here? Find Adelaide? (And don't you think it's strange that when Adelaide disappeared you remained relatively indifferent?) How about trying to resuscitate Tadeu Pereira? Or running to look for Elisa? Will "truth" help you with that?

Say something! You win a prize if you come up with the right answer. Take it or leave it. Give up or play on. Double or pass. At least the game is obvious now, ob-

335

jective. Straightforward. Not like in the old days when it was multiple choice. A question and three little boxes. That's over now. And the time has run out. All you have to do is come up with an answer.

What's that? You'd like more time? Of course, take as long as you need. I know I said the time had run out, but I don't know what I'm talking about. It's just that I won't have you dying on me before you answer, okay? We'll make a deal. If you answer, you don't die. How about that? Well then, I'm waiting. Wait a minute, *who's* waiting? What answer do you want? Who are you, anyway? *Who are you?*

ATTENTION! YOUR ATTENTION, PLEASE! WE HAVE AN ANNOUNCEMENT. *Attention, please! All those who have been fortunate enough to make their way to the security and protection of the Endless Marquee, planned and constructed by the Ministry of Pharaonic Public Works:*

The question is this: which will last longer, us or the Marquee? Will this roof be able to take the strain of such extreme heat? And even if it does, will we be able to take the Marquee? The heat? We may well be long dead by the time it cracks and falls. Of course if we're alive, then we run the risk of having it fall on top of us.

I'd say this is what is called a no-win situation. If the animal gets you, he eats you. Simple as that. But these are just hypotheses for the future, anyway—and what good does it do to think about the future when you can't even solve the problems of the present? One of which is fatigue. The eternal quest for a position which is at least moderately tolerable, even slightly comfortable.

Though it's not really a question of comfort. We're simply trying to find a way to stay on our feet for hours on end. I remember a time when orientalism was all the rage, the body, the cult of the physical, the secrets of the masters, teachings that were thousands of years old.

How to fall asleep in five minutes. Exercises to eliminate fatigue in four seconds. How to go a week without sleeping and still be alert and at ease. Increase your body's potential. Stimulate your innate sexuality. Double your natural energy. Discover the power of touch at your fingertips. Make your skin tingle.

They offered everything, at completely unreasonable prices. Many of the thousand-year-old teachings had been dreamed up in incense-perfumed offices a week before they were divulged. I wonder if any of those miraculous formulas would be applicable here? Or does everyone have to discover their own solution?

Mine is simple. I let one leg go to sleep, and then the other. They return to normal. Then I let them go to sleep together. And wake up. And go back to sleep. Continuously. The tingling in my legs is constant, I can't imagine the damage this might be causing. Even if I could, what difference would it make? (The old refrain.) None at all.

ATTENTION! YOUR ATTENTION, PLEASE! WE HAVE AN ANNOUNCEMENT: *The security division of the Marquee has informed us that everyone must stay within the confines of the Marquee. Do not, we repeat, do not stray beyond the yellow lines which have been conveniently painted on the ground for just this purpose. Numerous heat pockets have been confirmed in the area, thus leaving the Marquee could mean immediate death. We repeat: immediate death.*

—Hey, you! Hey! That's right, Jack, I mean you.

—Me? I'm not Jack, and I'm not "Hey You" either.

—Doesn't matter, man, I got a deal for you. You aren't gonna want to miss this one, let me tell you.

—A deal? Here?

—You look like somebody, you know what I mean? Somebody. You shouldn't have to stand here in this crowd, nowhere to move. There are better spots, and I can tell you deserve one of them.

—Better spots? Where?

—What I got to offer is a nice little comfortable place, man, nobody around, plus it's near the bathrooms and the water fountain.

—Sure. A paradise like that would have to be in the Inner Sanctuary for Secret Functionaries. Or under the Clergymen's Geodesic Dome. And you propose to whisk me out of here, for a price, and get me in there, right.

—No, sir, we're talking about right here under the Marquee.

—In the middle of this crowd?

—You got it—in the middle. Far from the edges, safe and protected.

—What kind of a scam is this, anyway?

—It's no scam. It's an exceptional opportunity we're offering. For a short time only. Take advantage of it, man, there's only a few spots left.

—Okay, I'll consider it, why not? But you better explain the whole thing.

—I already did. You want me to repeat it all?

—I thought it was a joke, I wasn't paying attention.

—Okay, look. This is the deal: we've got well-located places, near the bathrooms, far from the edges, which you just heard are dangerous, and right next to the water fountain. And we're even going to arrange for some electric fans.

—Sounds terrific, but just a little hard to believe. I don't see an inch of space left.

—Yeah, and you don't have x-ray vision, either. We're talking about right in the middle of everything—you know the crosspiece between the two legs of the A? That's where the best spaces are.

—Even if I believed you, how do you get there?

—You leave that to us, we'll take care of it.

—How?

—At night, see, when it cools off a little, people leave the Marquee to lie down on the ground outside where there's more room, and it's cooler. Just for a little while, right between the last heat of the day and when it starts

338

heating up again before dawn. Right in there, that's when I give a signal and my buddies come get you.

—And how did you happen to come by these privileged spots?

—Are you buying?

—Not if you keep me in the dark.

—I see an awful lot of talk here, and no action.

—I never spend my money unless I'm well informed.

—Are you asking me how you get it or what you get?

—The "how" part is what interests me.

—Well, I guess there's no harm in telling. When the Marquee was first ready, the information leaked out prematurely. Some guys in the know told their friends about it, you understand how it is. So they rushed on down here and took possession. Divided up the prime spots. Fair and square.

—Will you accept an IOU?

—What? You kidding?

—Or a predated check, maybe?

—Of course not, what do you think this is?

—You don't have any sort of credit plan?

—You think we're nuts? You think anyone's going to last long enough to pay on time?

—What did you say?

—Nothing.

—No, come on, you know something, don't you?

—Me? I don't know nothing.

—You said, in effect, that we're all going to die.

—You dreamed it, man. End of conversation. You buying or not? I'm wasting a lot of time here.

—What you're doing is changing the subject.

—Look, pal, I got nothing to say to you. I don't owe you a thing.

ATTENTION! YOUR ATTENTION, PLEASE! WE HAVE AN ANNOUNCEMENT! *We repeat: it is extremely dangerous to remain near the edges of the Marquee where you risk slipping or being pushed over*

339

*the yellow line. We urge the utmost caution! Exposure to the sun means immediate death!*

Who could stand those blasted loudspeakers and their warnings. We knew it all. No one was foolish enough to want to get near the edges. But somebody had to. That's why there was continuous movement in the peripheral areas—people trying, at all costs, to improve their positions, usually without much success. Who lost ground most often? Who got pushed out?

The weakest, the oldest. Naturally. They were jostled toward the edge little by little; closest to the dangerous yellow line, you saw only skinny, anemic types, frightened old women. They clung to the people nearest them, and the people they clung to tried angrily to shake them off.

It doesn't do any good to rage at the loudspeakers, though. A waste of energy. Any movement, however small, saps the strength and could mean not being able to last as long. So we try to remain still: our last investment in the future. Meanwhile, it's almost impossible to breathe, it's like inhaling fire. The hairs inside my nostrils are singed.

We used to complain about bad smells a lot. To think that it was a thousand times better then. Somehow we endured and made it this far. We're alive. Thanks to some imponderable. That's what the last few years have been, really: a succession of imponderables. Now it's just a matter of wondering who will last longer, us or this silly roof.

The sun is so strong it seems to raise dust. Once in a while the dust settles and we get a glimpse of the tortured ground, houses in the distance, bones piled up in the sun. We derive an unusual degree of consolation from this, even though we know that in a little while we may be bones ourselves. Dust swirling in eddies outside the Marquee. Where there are eddies, there must be wind. But there is no wind. Let the physicists explain such phenomena. If they can.

340

The human sea, in its uncontrollable ebb and flow, sweeps me to the extreme edge of the Marquee. I've got to work my way back into the middle. What a laugh. No wonder I was considered pretentious at the university. Working my way back would be about as easy as scaling a wall a hundred meters high.

No sun, and yet it's clear. Shading my eyes from the glare, I look out at skeletons of viaducts, rotaries, cloverleafs, and seventy-lane freeways which circle the city, and which used to dispatch traffic in all directions. Now they look like phantasmagoric, abstract designs. Will time eventually wear away the concrete, or will these grand public works remain, testimony to an era?

In any case, they won't mean a thing to the people of the future, though they'll be contemplated with curiosity, no doubt. Featured in encyclopedias. Filmed and photographed by tourists from this planet or that. Mysterious relics. Dead objects.

Then I saw it. A tiny bush, low to the ground. Just two leaves, but they were green. Or something close to green. Maybe I made them green. I closed my eyes, opened them. The bush was still there. A cheerful little plant sprouting courageously from between the cracks in the sidewalk.

It's not really a matter of courage, I know. There's no acceptable explanation for the sudden appearance of any form of plant life on this sterile plain, no possible sustenance in this tired ground. Unless it's not real. Just a plastic branch someone stuck in the dirt. Maybe synthetic plastic, at that. (Is there any other kind?)

I've got to get closer. I push, curse, say excuse me. People gladly let me get by once they realize I'm trying to get nearer to the edge. Every centimeter farther away represents a victory for them, the probability of a few instants longer under the Marquee. They made room to let me squeeze by.

Finally, it's late enough, long enough after sundown, to cross the famous yellow line. Soon there will be lots of people out here for a quick stretch of the legs, a little room to move. No one stays out for long, though, for fear of not finding a place when they go back. The people in the middle stay there; nothing could get them to give up their choice spots.

I kneel down next to my find, the soil is cold by now. I stare at the plant. It's true, it's alive, it's growing, indifferent to the arid sand stretching to infinity. Alien to its own impossibility. Surrounded by negation, it asserts itself. How can it hold out, without a drop of water, against a sun powerful enough to consume flesh and bones?

Conversations with Tadeu Pereira drift back to me. (I still can't believe he's dead.) I remember his telling me that there were certain pine trees in Israel which sprang up, green, surrounded by nothing but rocks. It was a complete enigma: what nourished them, where did they get the moisture they surely needed, how did they survive? But they did, defying all odds.

Maybe this was a new species. Nature developing a process of reconstitution. Recreation. Why not? Finding new and indestructible forms. Organic resistance. Unbreakable, durable strength.

How strange. Suddenly it occurs to me that's what freedom is—the capacity to revive continually in new forms, reinvigorated. The process of renewal, of hitting the bottom and coming back up again, is a tactic, a way of tricking death. Death, which is a simple, surmountable stage.

It can only get us individually, not as a group. Man's permanence is proof of death's defeat. Bouncing back, restored, is this plant's victory. Surviving is its vengeance. Because in this game there are battles won and battles lost. Never total war, the end, extermination.

It's a bit shocking to contemplate. We're desperate enough to be pleased, grateful, for freedom born of sterility, nurtured on destruction. That's where our victory is found: in the permanent possibility of reconstruction. We'll have to revise our concept of living in order to adapt to an inferior stage, we've regressed to the pre-historic. Life as a battle to preserve non-life. Life reduced to not dying. Each sunset implying the time we lose, the time death gains.

There I go again, waxing dramatic. But wait, why not turn the idea inside out? Suggest that life as mere survival will lead us to a new sense of life, newly human. Our essence reconquered. Wipe out having in favor of being. Destroy "I have," and suddenly "I exist." Oh, my utopian dreams!

I nudge a sleepy-looking man sitting on the ground nearby. He starts: "What's wrong? Is it time to go back?" I shake my head no.

—Look. A plant!

I pointed. He looked perplexed. A mirage? Had I pointed at an empty space? He took another look.

ATTENTION! YOUR ATTENTION, PLEASE! YOUR ATTENTION, PLEASE! *Please take care to remain in your places under the Marquee. Reserving places is not allowed. We ask that you do not move around a lot, in order to facilitate our work.*

You want me to talk out loud, I'll talk out loud. There. Are you happy now. I SAID, ARE YOU HAPPY NOW? Another hallucination perhaps. Big news. I think I talked all night long. I woke up this morning with a sore throat, chapped lips. I've never talked in my sleep before, but I guess there's always a first time. The damn ground is heating up already, even before the sun comes up. We begin to move back under the Marquee.

I try to spot a place away from the edge. Impossible. People are pushing and shoving, climbing on top of each other, clawing wildly in utter panic. It's a good thing there aren't any children, they'd be trampled for sure. I continue talking out loud. The guy next to me gives me a look. So what.

Here we are crowded in under this idiotic Marquee to

343

escape being fried by the sun, and this guy's surprised to see somebody talking to himself. Only a jerk would be surprised at anything. Lucky him. To the physicists and chemists and biologists and meteorologists and geographers and historians and psychologists and sociologists and scholars and researchers I say: give up.

Give up on understanding. If there are eddies with no wind, it's because from now on anything is possible. Speaking of which, I'm even getting excited by this woman who's been leaning against me since yesterday. At first I didn't notice, the way we're packed in here. Like junked cars crushed into neat tin cubes.

Glass, metal, rubber, the whole works, all mixed together, interlaced, intertwined, wedded. Glued to each other intimately, trading bad breath, gasps for air, sweat, farts, it's sort of sickening. At first I didn't notice the way she was leaning against me; then I realized there was something different about the pressure between our two bodies.

A woman in her forties, full-figured, a face that shows some wear and tear. I sort of like thickset women. But this is the newest mystery: how can she manage to smell so good? Fresh out of the bath. A whiff of lavender. No, it's impossible, an olfactory mirage. Olfactory mirage?!

When I was a kid, I'd stand at the door to the movie theater, smelling the women as they walked past enveloped in that Sunday aroma of fancy soap and toilet water, talcum powder and cologne. I'll never be able to explain why it was so excruciating, standing there with my eyes closed, inhaling, aching all over.

I could tell who walked past by their smells. It was a small town. The same people always came to the Sunday matinee—it was as though we lived together! The woman next to me smells as if she came straight from her Sunday bath to the Marquee. Maybe she was on her way to a Supersubsistence Distribution Center when she was whisked away and brought here. Silly idea.

Around mid-morning the woman turned her head ever

so slightly in my direction. Even such a small gesture was difficult, but she managed to twist far enough to see me out of the corner of her eye. Then she gradually began to let herself go, relaxing into me even more, until her whole body fit close against mine. Hot, but a pleasant hotness (for a change). I began to relax, to get interested, and as she detected this she leaned even closer, adjusting to my every movement.

If she moves, leans away ever so slightly, my body looks for hers. We find each other again. Her flesh is soft, I could get lost in it. My left hand fumbles, pinches, gropes as best it can. The possibilities of movement are limited, my hand is wedged in place.

Finally I reach a vital spot. She guesses what I plan to do and pretends to pull away, but can't. Too tightly packed in to allow for a game of intentions. Should I try to lift her skirt with my right hand? Would the people near us be able to see? For a change, the sweat dripping from my brow is due to excitement.

How far will she let me go? I slide my hand from her waist up to her breasts. Erect nipples. Dust has begun to swirl in under the Marquee. Everyone starts coughing. In no time, there's a light covering of dust on everything. We're going to suffocate before the sun even gets to us.

There's nothing worse than being in a crowd of coughing people, unless it's being in a crowd of coughing people who have no way to put their hands over their mouths. Anyone lucky enough to have a free hand uses it to protect his eyes. Lucky our mouths are so dry, or we'd be spitting mud all over the place. I never could stand the hot, stale air that emanates from people's mouths. Or the smells. Unbearable. Must be because of the synthetic food.

General confusion, lots of nudging and shoving. Somebody screams—pushed out into the sun. The scream lasts only an instant. I can't see what's going on from where I'm standing. More screams, a general moan, followed by silence. Time passes. People calm down. We're suddenly very aware of death. It's right out there.

It happens. We were calm, confident of our impunity. Someone would come and save us. But who? No, that's not even it. The real question is much broader and clearly unanswerable: why should anyone come rescue us? Or, how about this one: why are we even here?

Of course death is there, it happens. It won't (to us), but it can. I stayed calm, considering this a momentary stage to get through. Thinking that I'd reached a point which I defined as peaceful uncertainty. Accepting it as normal, something I just had to learn to live with.

For years I was invulnerable, after all. Or at least I thought I was, blind to the effects of extremely high doses of tension—worse than any poison. My defenses were few, but solid, I thought. An optical illusion. They depreciated and disappeared faster than money.

And now I find I am vulnerable. There's nothing more debilitating than the knowledge that we're exposed, powerless to act, because all we know has been canceled, null and void. Suddenly I grasp the immediacy of death. It's there, in the sun, just beyond the edge of the Marquee. The game continues: I have to stay as far away from the yellow line as possible. That's all.

Somewhere in the middle of all the coughing, the dust, and the screaming, I slipped my hand down the dress of the woman next to me and squeezed her breasts. Her flesh in my hand. Soft, flabby. Different from Elisa's—just as sweaty, but not as firm. She laughed. Ticklish.

I wonder if I could convince her to turn toward me so I could kiss her full on the mouth. Feel her lips between mine. Dry, chapped, hot. I've got to work up a little saliva, moisten my tongue. And then explore her mouth, lick her teeth. Taste her taste.

Her warm skin. She trembles, as I do, with excitement. My fingers between her thighs. Damp. If I don't calm down, I swear I'm going to lift up her skirt and put it right in her. Here and now. But I know how to hold back. Ha! I've got a lot of experience in that department! Though right now I feel like erasing the past, all of it.

I pull her toward me. There's so much dust in the air almost everyone has his eyes shut. I struggle to keep mine half open. I press her closer, expecting some resistance, but she's giving in, giving herself to me.

—You're crazy.

—I wish I were, woman . . .

—I like it.

—What about all these people?

—Who's watching? Wait until a few days from now . . .

—What do you mean?

—By tomorrow, or the day after tomorrow, everyone will be doing it.

—You think so? Really?

—It's not a matter of thinking. It's written all over their faces. Or was, until this damn dust appeared out of nowhere.

—Can you turn a little more this way?

—UNCLE SOUZA!!

—Like this?

—Yeah, facing me, like that.

—UNCLE SOUZA! OVER HERE!!

—There's someone calling you. Look.

—HEY, UNCLE SOUZA!!

My nephew, pushing his way through the crowd, about fifteen meters away. Enterprising, as usual. Casually elbowing people aside. He doesn't even seem to realize he's in a crowd. But I don't get it. He can't be hiding out here, or running away. He must be working on something. Sure! He must be involved in that business of selling prime locations under the Marquee!

—Who's the madman?

—My nephew.

—Having a family reunion? You'd think you could arrange someplace else.

—It wasn't my idea.

—So what happens to me? I can't even feel you any

347

more, you've frozen up on me.

—Just give me a minute...

—Give me a minute—go to hell with your give me a minute, will you? You shouldn't start things you can't finish.

Terrific. My nephew has perfect timing. He waits until the most inconvenient moment and appears like an apparition. I should have shot him that morning. Rubbed him out. One less Mili-tech in this country. But I must admit that the fact he's here under the Marquee does intrigue me. What gives?

The woman is still fondling me. She has a light touch. Adelaide didn't have hands like that, even though she was a pianist. Maybe it's the way she holds it, trying to make me hard again. Adelaide had her little tricks too. Like that delicious way of looking at me. Decorous.

Decorous. I found that one in pre-history. Hot as hell, people dying right in front of us, damn dust everywhere, I'm all revved up and still coming out with words like *decorous*. Adelaide wouldn't even approve of my word choice, but I can't think of any other way to describe it.

Embarrassed, but not really. Shy, but that's not it either. There was always something of the well-brought-up little girl in her. And then she'd do a complete turn-around. It was the transformation that really did it. Turned me on. The possibility of change, constant surprise. Oh, my fantasies! My sweet daydreams.

—Yoo-hoo. Anybody home?

—Just give me a minute, I already told you. I'm working on it.

—Sorry, I don't think so. No more minutes left. Once I get started, I don't know how to stop, I'm just not the type that can put it off.

—UNCLE SOUZA!

—He's never going to shut up until you answer him. I know the type.

—How am I supposed to do everything at once?!

—UNCLE SOUZA, CAN YOU HEAR ME?

—Okay, okay, you don't have to yell.

He held up a silver canteen. Smiled. Not really a smile, a grimace. Ironic. Something else he must have learned at the Academy. A smile that smacks of distaste. You can't even see his upper teeth, and that irritates me. Such an air of superiority. Supercilious.

—I almost didn't recognize you, Uncle Souza. Some beard you've got there.

—Really. The barbershop in this place is closed, I tried to make an appointment three times.

—You disappeared.

—No kidding, you were trying to kill me.

—Me?!

—Tried to run over me with that truck.

—Don't be silly, it went out of control and you got scared and took off, that's all.

—You've always got a story, don't you?

—Am I the type that goes around killing people?

—Aren't you? What about the guys in the back room?

—That was different, we had to. Not a matter of choice.

—You admit it with such effrontery, you're a utterly shameless.

—Say that again—

—Shameless?

—No, the other one.

—Effrontery?

—Yeah, effrontery. I swear I'm going to try that out in the barracks, the guys will really be impressed.

—I wish I could understand how your mind works.

—Same here. It's beyond me, the way you think, what's in your head.

—I'd really like to know what you think you're doing.

—Living my life. Like everybody else.

—No, that's just it, you're not like everybody else.

—Course not. If I was like everybody else, who would be the else? Not bad, eh? See, I can play with words, too, Uncle Souza.

—You play with everything. Even people's lives.

—Say, what is this? Are you a judge now or what?

349

—I'm just following the logical thread.

—Sure, your idea of logic. Why don't you try to look at things from my point of view? You're somewhere in outer space, Uncle Souza, in another world completely. One that doesn't exist. Aunt Adelaide said so plenty of times, that's why it was so hard for her to understand what went on in your mind. First, you never talked to her. And second, you expected the rest of the world, including her, to be the way you wanted it.

—That's not true. I want a good world, a just world, what's wrong with that?

—Idle chatter, that's all. The world is what it is, can't you get that through your head? You're clinging to the train by the door handles—you've got to either come on in or jump the hell off!

People are staring at us. They turn toward him when he talks, toward me when I answer. Following the ball back and forth across the net, a game of tennis, for heaven's sake. Some faces are cynical, others smiling. I feel ridiculous caught in this conversation. It's going nowhere.

I'll never be able to change his mind about anything. He was brought up differently, that must be what it is. Who knows, maybe he's got a point. He does what he has to, the way he has to—the way he was taught. But where does that leave me? Where does that leave any of us who were brought up with different standards? Are we supposed to find refuge in Isolation? Kill ourselves?

—What are you doing here, anyway, Dominginho?

—Let's say I'm laying low. Just for a little while, until the dust settles.

—I thought you were going to go underground.

—I did.

—Here?! It's so open—not to mention the Civil Guards looking over our shoulders.

—Look around, Uncle Souza. There's not a Civil Guard in sight.

—Then the place must be full of ASBN's.

350

—Not a one.

—Then who's in charge of security?

—The System isn't the least bit worried about security here.

—What do you mean?

—This place is the end, Uncle Souza.

—You mean it's a trap? There's no way out?

—You can leave if you want. But all roads lead to the Pauper Encampments.

—If they could hear you now . . . You'd better be careful or you'll end up in Isolation.

—They're already looking for me, but they never figured we'd slip in under the Marquee. They consider us anything and everything, but not suicidal.

—Looks like you are, though, huh? Unless you have some grand plan for getting out of here.

—Oh, there's still time. We've got people negotiating the situation.

—What went wrong in the first place?

—Well, there was a falling-out, shall we say, so we split up. The group I belonged to didn't exactly come out on top. A slight crisis in influence. Better to stay out of it altogether for a while, people are still shifting around in the System. There's going to be a new president, how about that!

—Impossible. Without even telling us?

—Why should they bother?

—They're our government!

—Well, the people who really govern aren't going anywhere . . .

He took another swig from the canteen and laughed, as if he hadn't a care in the world. His friends will come get him, I'm convinced of it. He'll get out of here and continue on his merry way—if there's going to be any continuation at all, that is. I know I'm melodramatic, but I don't believe it will all end here. Not really. If I did, everything would be senseless.

Things are simpler than I used to think, you don't

351

need to look for hidden significance all the time. Facts are facts. True, naked, obvious. We spend our lives searching for answers, working out complex symbolic interpretations, trying to penetrate the profundities, when what's real is right on the surface, floating within view.

So obvious that we reject it. Because we're used to looking in the mirror of illusion. Because we no longer trust our own perceptions. Out of touch with that old, primordial wisdom: life is a series of rebirths. Each moment I'm a new person. The child in me, the experienced adult—continually trading places. Not a paradox: a sum. Simple arithmetic. Tadeu Pereira would be interested in all this, he'd take notes in his little notebook. I wonder if I'll ever get to see what's in that envelope he left me.

—You want some water, Uncle Souza?

—Sure, but how are you going to get it to me?

—I'll throw the canteen, you can take a drink and toss it back.

—If it gets this far.

He heaved it in my direction. I threw my arms into the air, desperate to intercept the pass. Nobody moved. The majority of the people around us had their heads down now. Drowsy, lethargic, suffocating from the heat. Maybe they weren't paying any attention, had no idea that water was flying through the air above their heads.

I take a small gulp, roll it around in my mouth. That's the ritual. So it's not too much of a shock to your system. I wet my lips. My head feels better already. After another swallow, I remember the woman in front of me. I nudge her, and she comes back to life. Takes one look at me and closed her eyes again.

—Hey!

—Leave me alone.

—Want some water?

—Water?!

—Ssssh, not so loud. Just tell me if you want any.

—Stupid question. Where is it?

—Easy now, easy There's only a little.

352

—Where'd you get it?

—From my nephew.

—Who are you, anyway? What do you want from me?

—Huh?

—I don't understand, I don't understand anything about you. No, I don't think I want any water. Who knows what I'd be getting myself into.

—The only thing I could possibly ask you for in exchange, you were about to give me before the water even appeared. Free. So what's the problem?

—I don't like tricks, games. You pawed me for a good long time, then left me hanging. I don't get it, and I don't want anything to do with you. You think I'm made of stone? You think I was kidding around?

—No. No, I don't. And I wasn't kidding around either. I wanted you. I still do.

—I don't know what to think . . . You must be here to spy on me.

—Whatever for?

—Who knows. This city is full of spies.

—Stop being silly and take a drink.

—Do me a favor, will you? Forget all about me. Pretend I don't exist. Pretend you're leaned up against a wall or something.

—I never met a wall with thighs as soft as yours . . .

—A dirty old man, that's what you are. Impotent, no less. Feel people up, that's all you do. Pervert. Go drool over your granddaughters, okay? But leave me alone.

—HEY, UNCLE SOUZA! SEND BACK THE CANTEEN!

One more swallow. A long one. My throat's a little less sore. I like the sound the water makes, glug-glug. Refreshing. Meanwhile, my clothes are filthy, I haven't changed in a week. I must stink like hell.

The water feels heavy in my stomach. If I tap my belly I can still hear a glug-glug. Feels awful. I drank too fast on an empty stomach and now it's giving me gas. The pain rises to my chest. What if it's a heart attack? That's how they start, a pain coming up from the stomach.

The water sloshes around inside me, splashing against the walls of my stomach. Like waves, pounding, pounding on the rocks. Fustigating. All right! Today's my day for bringing back retired words. Where do I dig up these old fossils? I burp loudly. A little explosion, like a hot light bulb hitting ice-cold water. A dead sound. Painful electric lights snuffed out in an icy sea. Strings of colored lights. Street decorations—in the park, for Christmas, for carnival, a church bazaar.

Hundreds of colored lights, thousands. It's a big party, I'm sure of it, I can hear the shouting. Odd, though, no music. Shouts punctuating complete silence, and the noise of the water. Turbulent. Turbulent, and yet calm. Dry explosions, one after the other.

All I can see is the immensity of the water, the heaving waves. The lamps have gone out now, I can't tell if the water is pounding rocks or... No! It's a dark hull, the dark hull of a sinking ship.

The image is so clear, but I don't understand it. I've never been to sea, never gone anywhere on a ship. A ship, darkness, lamps exploding as if they were heads. My God, it's Adelaide's dream. That's crazy, it can't be—I'm completely immersed in a dream that isn't even mine.

She told me the same dream every morning. It terrified me, though I wouldn't admit it. I just couldn't believe that the children's ship had sunk. I'm sure they made it to some port or other, and scrambled down the gangplank. They must be adults by now, living their own lives. There's just one thing that still bothers me.

Have they forgotten, or were they never told? As soon as they were old enough to understand, they were supposed to be told the reason for their exodus. That was our one condition: that one day they would hear the whole story and make their own decision. So they wouldn't see our giving them up as rejection. On the contrary, it was a profound act of love, the only solution.

That was why Adelaide waited for a letter every afternoon, hidden in the entryway corridor. The letter our son would write to say that everything was fine. My dear parents, I'm growing old, entering college, I landed my first job, I'm going to get married, you're going to be grandparents, we're broke but happy!

Every night before our good-night kiss, as I breathed in the exciting aroma of gooseberries, she would tell me the news. "Let me read it," I'd beg, her accomplice, her straight man. "No, let me tell you, I've memorized the whole thing word for word, just the way he wrote it." Long letters, short notes, cards with hugs and kisses.

We'd worry when he confided some problem, tension, heartache, loneliness. If he was happy, we were happy for him. Pleased when we could offer advice. That's how we brought up our son, from a distance. Day by day, we grew along with him, giving him all we could, all we knew.

Now I see that I loved that woman. Her illusions made me able to bear reality. Each night she made up a new letter, with a cleverness and imagination that novelists, whose job it is, after all, to create lives, don't come close to. It's true, you know—writers these days invent so little, the poor dears.

But we had our turbulent fantasies, Adelaide's chimerical letters. And they were a comfort to us. Our own little world. Because we wanted so badly to hear from him. I bet he's scared we'd make him come back. Which is something we'd *never* do, it doesn't make sense to live in this country.

All we'd ask, all we ever asked, is that he write us a few lines now and then. So we'd know we were right to do what we did, so we'd know that all the anxiety, the torture of his absence, had been worth it. We'd know that he had arrived somewhere—other parents got word, the ship arrived safely, the children were fine.

We had no other choice, I hope he understands that. We met with other parents to decide what to do. Hundreds of meetings. Thousands of mothers and fathers, ideas coming from all sides at first. We were lucid, conscious, determined to stick with it. Weeks and weeks debating, arguing, sweating it out, until we could accept the only solution.

Actually, the idea had come up at one of the first meetings. In a whisper—even the person who first suggested it was hesitant to call it his own. All our talking was aimed at keeping it at a distance. All we really needed was time, time to get used to the idea.

Time to live with the notion of separation. Time for our certainty that it was the right thing, our conviction, to ripen. Of course, there's nothing new under the sun, it's what the Jews did twice quite successfully. First on leaving Egypt, in antiquity, and then on their return to Israel, with the formation of the Jewish state in the forties.

Not that it was easy for us to reach the final consensus. We talked in circles for nights and days on end, we sweated and we agonized. Finally, the idea surfaced again, driven up from the depths of our uncertainty. Crystallized. I know, I'm being dramatic again, it's a vice. But it really was like that, I swear it.

I remember that as we got closer and closer to a definitive decision, our footsteps got heavier and heavier. But, in some strange way, on hearing the final vote, we felt confident. Daring, even. Serene. Because looking around us we saw no present, no present at all. Where, then, was the future?

Buried under the polluted sands of Angra dos Reis, radioactive. Evaporated in the dry riverbeds. Lost in the towering dunes of the Amazon desert. Smashed in pieces, littering the broken-down, closed-up gas stations. Lost forever in the landslides and fires which took whole neighborhoods, villages, cities, forests, countrysides.

Our bodies were decomposing as a result of the food

356

we ate, first over-fertilized, then over-insecticided, then synthesized. Little by little we were evacuating pieces of stomach, liver, intestine, coughing up whitish hunks of lung, fragments of pharynx. Which looked nothing like human fabric at all—more like rotten plastic.

Adelaide had been obsessed with the idea of having a child. Which, in itself, is nothing terribly surprising. For her, the main reason to get married was to have children. And so we had several. But each time our dream died prematurely in the clandestine clinics as Adelaide wept and bled and vowed to try again. And each time I was more worried that she wouldn't pull through.

She blamed herself—religious upbringing?—saying there must be something wrong with her, with her womb, which prevented her from carrying a baby. There wasn't a doctor (the bastards) who would risk explaining that women were becoming just plain too contaminated to bear children.

Little by little reports began to leak out. Surreptitiously. Whispers. Comments. Which of course started a great panic. Also surreptitious, because those were the days of the Watched Wombs, followed by the bitter period called the Great Cycle of Sterility.

Brought on, they whispered, by the catastrophe at the nuclear power plant. The immense failure which left us without electricity *and* without children, a country on the edge of the abyss, so many dark nights. Then came the Age of Great Insecurity. How would we keep alive the children who *did* exist?

Protest groups that had been crushed earlier resurfaced timidly—people who had railed against the foolish, even irrational, application of technology to every facet of life; who had urged a return to the earth, declaring their allegiance to everything green; who had fought for natural, healthy food, instead of the products crammed down our throats by multinational chemical companies and government laboratories.

Small in membership, but determined, these groups

357

banded together and pressed ahead with the Grand Plan to Save the Children. Funny, everything was "great" or "grand." Were we suffering from delusions of grandeur or something? The Great Era, the Grand Plan, almost as if we were mimicking the System and its Pharaonic projects.

It was hard to get people involved in reform activity, in underground movements. To pull them out of their houses, wake them up, provoke them. To get them to attend meetings and rallies. It took time to whip up their enthusiasm. But the day came when the movement began to resemble the workers' assemblies of the Open Eighties, with thousands of people participating, demonstrations, slogans, rhetoric without end.

It took time, but those romantics were patient. More than that, obstinate. Even a little elephantine. Yes, elephantine. There I go, dipping into the well of archaisms once more. Heat makes your head go soft, that's what Tadeu Pereira used to say. Now what did Tadeu go and kill himself for? Could it really be true? I refuse to believe it.

Anyway, the government was organized, interconnected. Once the decision was made, things began to happen. Task forces spread throughout the country, cities, villages, rural areas, everywhere. Working underground like ants. More and more people joined, donated money, food, water coupons, clothing, weapons. The parents stayed out of it. Their job was to wait.

We were registered, catalogued, each given a number. Six or seven months passed. Finally, we were summoned. We descended on the port of Santos one summer night, each child's documents safe in his or her suitcase. If they had been older, they would have been thrilled. There at anchor was the ship: majestic. Deteriorating but monumental.

We were fascinated by the idea that the people on board had crossed an ocean as a floating party with fancy dinners, gambling, theater, elegant clothes, swimming pools, grand debauches, wild drinking parties. The rest of the world sure knew how to have fun. I remember I was worried about whether that barge would last for one more crossing. It looked awfully rusty to me.

It was called the *France,* and dated to the age of the transatlantic liner. The last one before the Jet Age was upon us. We begun putting the children on board just after ten. Two thousand of them. And all of us, parents and relatives. The most silent mass of people I've ever seen. The holiday passengers on the *France* must have thought it odd, such a funereal aura.

The children themselves varied in age from two (like our son) to eight. Very few of them stayed at the rail to wave good-bye. The older ones understood the necessity of the separation. I'm sure of it. And unconsciously withdrew, to avoid suffering.

We didn't talk much. No one wanted to air the fears we all were feeling. We didn't even know what their chances were. We were risking everything, gambling with high stakes, the highest of all. In some corner of the world those children would find a home, a soil, new parents. They would have a normal childhood.

Instead of just growing up, they would live, really live. As that ancient transatlantic liner left Santos at a list, we heaved a sigh of relief. It set sail for the unknown, like the Portuguese caravels in the seventeenth century.

There was no clamor of despair, no mass hysteria or gnashing of teeth. Just stifled sobs, silent tears. The ship was strung with hundreds of colored lights, giving it a festive look—such a contrast to our somber mood that it was almost comforting. It headed slowly out to sea and disappeared into the dark.

That ship took with it the probable certainty of continuity. We watched immobile until the lights were gone, swallowed in the mist. We were slow to shake off our torpor, eyes dreaming in the dark. As usual, I intellectualized. My response to Adelaide's grabbing my hand was to make a pronouncement.

"Life is born of darkness—it was out of the depths of primitive chaos that the world emerged. The seed will come back one day to this unknown place." Something like that. Adelaide rubbed her eyes and looked at me in that irritated way with which she put me in my place: "This is no time for a lecture. Our baby just disappeared."

—I changed my mind, I'd like some water.

—

—Hey, I said I'll take you up on the water.

The dream became a constant in our lives from that day on. At first Adelaide would wake up screaming, sweating, exhausted. She'd tell me how she had seen the ship sinking, then the calm sea. She never actually saw the children dying, it's true. So I consoled her: they were saved, they were surely picked up by lifeboats, another ship came along.

Little by little the dream became real. A part of our life. Like the letters. We got used to it. When she went without dreaming it for a while it seemed strange, almost frightened us. That ship made ninety trips before finally being relegated to an oceanographic museum somewhere in the world.

—Hey, what is it with you? Now you're pretending you're deaf? I thought you offered me some water.

My neighbor nudged me and leaned closer. Foul-smelling breath in my face. How could I have thought about kissing this woman? Then again, not much chance my own mouth smells substantially better, is there? I was always such a maniac about brushing my teeth, gargling, keeping my mouth fresh-smelling.

My clothes feel as if they're stuck to my body permanently, the synthetic fabric has become part of my skin. Sweat drips down my face and I catch a drop with my tongue, it's salty, distasteful. I don't know how much longer I can take this, my headache is starting up again.

—Are you going to give me some of that water or not?!

I rouse myself, must have been dozing, the heat feels so thick it's no wonder we can't move. Everyone is motionless, tense. A murmur of voices. The sluggishness is general, as if we were indulging in a collective nap. The woman has turned to face me now, glued against my body. I feel indifferent, distant.

—Huh?

—Give me a little water?

—Just a swallow. It's my nephew's.

—Just let me have some fast, okay, or I'm going to scream.

—So scream.

—You really want everyone in the crowd to know you've got water?

—Okay, so take a drink, but hurry up, I'm losing my patience.

She grabbed the canteen and gulped greedily, glug-glug-glug-glug-glug, the harpy is going to drain the thing! I yank it out of her hand, she grabs it back, water spurts into the air, dripping all over the guy next to her, who wakes with a start without knowing why. Before he has a chance to figure it out, I snatch the canteen away from the woman and hide it under my arm.

—What's going on, is it raining?

—What are you, out of your mind?

—Look, I'm all wet.

—So is everybody else, must be sweat.

—Sweat doesn't feel cool like this. Wow, it's nice!

—You must have dreamt it, pal.

—Yeah, maybe. I've been dreaming all morning, I'm dying of hunger. They promised there'd be food, but I'm beginning to wonder.

—The trucks must come at night. How else could they get through the heat pockets?

—I don't know ... But they said the Marquee would be cool and comfortable, plenty of room for everyone. Bunk beds, footlockers. They talked it up so much I left my apartment, it sounded like I'd be better off here.

—Yeah, I left my apartment too. But not really by choice.

—Well, it wasn't really mine, it was a sublet. We

361

bribed some guards to get into the city and then some
guy from the New Army came along and told us he could
get us a place to live. We talked, gave him some money,
water coupons, everything we had. He found us an apartment all right—filthy and ridiculously overcrowded. And
that's not all—you know where it was? Get this: in the
middle of the Housing Project for the Lice-Infested. I
kid you not. Some deal, I'm telling you. By the time we
realized what was going on, it was too late, there was
nothing we could do. In less than three days we were
crawling with lice. We shaved our heads, nothing helped.
We scratched so much our skin was like one big wound,
and of course we kept reinfesting each other. Finally the
Civil Guards came with insecticides. They thought they
were firemen, I swear to God, hosed us down good. And
it just made things worse, the insecticide stuck to your
skin. Killed people left and right. I thought I'd go out
of my mind.

—Why didn't you get out of there sooner?

—You mean you didn't hear what happened down
there?

—I never even heard of any such housing project.

—Well, three days after we got there, the government
isolated the area. Surrounded it with a circle of fire. Every
now and then they'd cross through in armored cars, they
kept telling us it was only temporary, just as long as it
took to get rid of the lice. But it was too much, I tried
to jump out the window, my friends wouldn't let me. So
what could we do? We decided to burn all the furniture
and household articles, take on the lice ourselves. It
helped a little. But when I heard about the Marquee—
well, anything sounded better than that hellhole, at least
I'd be in the open air. As soon as they started talking
about the fabulous Marquee, there were Civil Guards all
over the place trying to sell us places here. I scraped
together everything I could get my hands on, don't ask
any questions, and bought a spot. What I was really
buying, of course, was the right to leave the Circle of

362

Fire and get away from those damned lice. So here I am, and I'm still not sure if it's better or worse.

—It wouldn't help if you knew. There's no getting out of here.

Every once in a while a ripple of movement goes through the crowd. The humidity, human and meteorological, is actually visible, it seems to hover somewhere overhead. No one can remain motionless forever, and when one moves we're all affected. More screams. Someone else has fallen outside. No one dares to try pulling him back for fear of being dragged along. Solidarity is dead, that's plain to see.

—HEY! UNCLE SOUZA! TOSS IT BACK!

I realize I'm getting dangerously close to the edge myself, but there's not much I can do about it, I'm swept along by the sporadic movement of the crowd, like riding the waves against your will. I can feel the pull even before the movement starts: the tide. Before giving back the canteen, I should offer a little bit to my friend here. But I don't even make a gesture.

—Okay, I'm sending it back. Will you be able to get more?

—If one of our men comes tonight.

—Do you think he will?

—Maybe.

—And what about your eradicators?

—Eradicators? What does that mean?

—The goons.

—What?

—The guys in your group, my good friends.

—You use so many words I never heard of.

—Thugs. Hoodlums. You know what that means, don't you?

—You think I'm a hoodlum, don't you? You really do. How come?

—What would you call yourselves?

—We're a commercial and financial organization, a partnership, like all the others.

—You know, I can't understand it. You had a good, solid upbringing.

—Sure, I did. And it got in the way something awful. What you taught me had nothing to do with reality, Uncle Souza. It really messed up my head.

—I doubt that's how your head got messed up.

—I was brought up on ideas from the past, things the world had already left behind. Useless customs. I ended up with nothing, I didn't know how to act in the real world, I mean really act, to take a step on my own.

—Why? I don't get it. Come on, tell me why.

—Why. That's what your life consists of, Uncle Souza. You hide behind the why, the how. I don't know why you make things so complicated, it's really very simple. I do what I do for money, that's all.

—For money?

—Why are you so surprised? Money. Sure. I need money. I want a house in the Super-Climatized Block someday. Do you think I like living in a stifling hot apartment building, filthy, no ventilation, counting pennies to get from day to day? I want to eat, drink, and be merry, I want a pool, I want to be able to visit the Alleviation Centers a couple of times a week. You need money to live like that. It's that simple.

—Now I wouldn't mind a membership in an Alleviation Center . . .

—Are you still mad at me, Uncle Souza?

—You know, I'm not even sure.

—You better behave yourself, or I won't take you out of here with me.

—You expect me to believe you're intending to?

—Well, even if I did get you out, you wouldn't have anywhere to go. They confiscated your apartment. We lost our base of operations and everything.

—Say you could get me out, how much would it cost?

—Leave that for later.

He laughed. For some reason, this time his laugh cheers me up. He's so sure of himself a little hope rubs off on me. I can't shake the idea that maybe we're really getting out of here, together. Unless of course he's completely unconscious, a real maniac. Well, okay, he *is*, but that doesn't mean we're not getting out of here.

Someone's staring at me. You know how you can feel it when somebody's looking at you? You don't need a sixth sense. I crane my neck until I can see him—a tall, dark guy, looks like a basketball player. He nods his head slightly, an affirmative gesture. Then he holds up his hand. Unbelievable!

He's got a hole exactly like mine. It must be some kind of sign of recognition, a signal. I raise my hand and motion to him. Nod my head as he did. As I lower my hand, I pause to admire our common trait. But I can't believe this—I must have finally gone crazy for real! Was it all a dream? Or is *this* the dream?

The hole in my hand has disappeared. It's true—the hole is gone. Poof. Where did it go? Could I have dropped it? I try to push people aside, but they don't move. Madness—a hole falling to the ground! Some imagination. I've got to concentrate. When did I last see it?

I can't remember, I got so used to it, I never even noticed it anymore. Maybe it closed up days ago. Do you think I ... no, no, that's impossible. It was there, I saw it, it was part of me for months. Has it been months? How long have I had this hole? Past tense. But what if—

No, impossible, God help me, that's a crazy idea. One more proof that I've gone off the deep end. You saw it, after all. I showed it to you. I had a hole in my palm, right? Tell me I did, or I'm getting out of here, I'll shoot myself. Never mind. There's no way out, plus where would I get a gun.

The hole never existed. Could it be? Could it be that there was never anything wrong with my hand? No hole, just as there were no letters from my son? Look at that palm. Intact. Not a mark on it. If there had been a hole in my hand, wouldn't it at least leave a mark? I swear it's medically impossible.

Unless of course I had plastic surgery. But still, there's always a telltale scar. Besides, plastic surgery? That's preposterous! The hole was a product of my imagination, and I came to believe in it as if it were real. That's the only explanation. Of course, you could say it had to be real—it's the reason Adelaide left me, after all. And I'd have to agree with you, though don't think I don't know you're on her side. Not that I blame you, I would be too if I were you. How many times I've said to myself these many months that it must not have been easy to live with a person like me. I know I wouldn't have been able to stand myself. And now that I can stand myself, it's life that's become intolerable.

Pretty complicated, wouldn't you say? If we can't tolerate ourselves, how can we expect anyone else to put up with us? So there's no reason for me to expect you to be on my side, no matter how much you love me. Because even the largest love dies, falls from on high like the gigantic trees I watched cut off at the feet by those maniacal saws.

My headache is back with a violent pounding, I feel paralyzed, but no blob appears in my head. No, now I know that my grandfather is dead, crushed under the truck he was trying to stop. Poor old man. But what does that have to do with me and Adelaide? Nothing. Just my raving mind, off on a tangent again.

What I've been half admitting to myself, without the courage to face it, is that Adelaide left because it was time to go. Her decision wasn't sudden at all. The idea had been forming in her head for a long, long time, gradually taking shape. She even tried to talk to me a couple of times, but I didn't listen, I didn't want to know.

If only I'd read the note she left me. I didn't need to. I knew what it said, because she was gone. But if I'd just opened it, I would have read it. I'm ashamed of how I let my wife get away, how I let everything go to hell like one fine son-of-a-bitch.

I made it sound like Adelaide was neurotic, ordinary. Selfish, the way she abandoned me, overnight, when I needed her most. When an inexplicable hole appeared in my hand. It's just that I had to keep up my self-image.

366

You understand, we all do things like that now and then.

Adelaide didn't, in fact, abandon me. She simply went away, with the same directness and artlessness she did everything else. She was straight and strong, a fine woman, a shame you didn't have a chance to get to know her. I admit I haven't done her justice. Everything I've said up until now has been distorted. But I'm sure you understand I was in great distress.

The loneliness of no Adelaide, after thirty-two years. I loved that woman, I swear that gesture of putting my hand on her shoulder every morning was never automatic. It was real affection, tenderness. There were days when I missed the bus because that simple touch sent us running back to bed.

It's true, whether you believe it or not. I don't have any more reason to lie, to pretend, make up fantasies. And I'm not hallucinating, either. You're already used to my hallucinations, this is different, this time I'm unburdening my heart to you. It's the truth. And it's a great relief.

I even feel hopeful that some day Adelaide will hear all this, though I don't know how, unless one of you runs into her one of these days and happens to recognize her. But I haven't really described her physically, which would make things difficult. Have any of you ever described someone you love? Think about it.

Sounds easy, right? A real snap. But it's actually impossible. You can never get it right. Because we're afraid of facing, analyzing, who it is we love. It's not that we intentionally distort things, it's just that it comes out all wrong. It's not the real we've described, but the filtered real.

Changed by what we've added. Since the other person is really precisely that: whatever she is, plus what I add, what I make of her. Which comes from what I see, what I feel, what I receive, what she gives me each moment we're together. So she is the sum of both of us, intermingled, a hybrid.

Someone on the outside, not feeling what I feel, perceives two images that don't match. Like watching a 3-D movie without the special glasses. And meanwhile, for me it's not 3-D, I'm entering the fourth dimension. Sure, that's it! With this heat and my head throbbing, it's that fuzzy.

In any case, I'm suggesting that Adelaide didn't leave because of the hole, because the hole never existed. I created it, by sheer force of will, to give myself a motive, a way to change, to confront the world. What's that you say? A crutch? Why not? I'd rather hobble along on crutches than be stuck standing on the corner like a stupid fool.

Adelaide left because she decided to. Christ, if a simple hole in the hand was reason enough for people to abandon each other, the great majority would be separated by now. Just look at all the people missing a finger, a leg, an arm, an eye, a nose, teeth, feet, knees, ass. (And that's not even counting the ones with no head to begin with.)

—Strength, energy, vigor, vitality.

—What?

—Strength, energy, vigor, vitality.

The tall, dark guy had moved closer. I was eye level with his neck. Hanging from a thin chain I saw a tiny stainless-steel mechanism. Spinning around. Identical to the one I found between paving stones. There's got to be a reason, it must *mean* something. We look at each other. Some force bringing us together.

—Strength, vigor, energy, vitality.

Okay, okay, one more crazy person, talking in code. People like that can be really esoteric, they express themselves in signs and symbols. And hope everyone will understand their private symbology. Well, here I am, living in the open air. At this point I'm not really interested in racking my brain to try and understand. I just want to live.

More than that, I'd like to enjoy a little bit. I've already just lived. That wasn't enough. I'd like something better this time around. I'd like to see it to the end. To be the very last person, if possible, when it all comes tumbling down. The last—what pessimism!

The man with the hole in his hand leans forward, straining, but remains rooted to the same place. Patience, my friend. Every once in a while you get a brief chance, the multitude flows backward, panic-stricken, when someone falls out from under the shelter. Little gaps open between bodies. The thing to do is squeeze in, and wait.

And die on your feet. No one would fall down dead here. Maybe to some that's a consolation. The ones who are always proud of landing on their feet. Imagine if there were children here—they'd be crushed. How old must Daniel be by now? (Adelaide's the one who picked the name, I wanted to name him André.)

I dozed off. I think I dozed off. I can't be sure of anything anymore, ever since that hole disappeared. I must have been asleep for a while, because now the tall, dark guy is standing directly in front of me. His stainless-steel gadget is spinning at an amazing speed. I'm hypnotized. One question nags at me: who gave it the initial push?

—Have you had that hole for a long time?

—Yes, quite awhile.

—I used to have one.

—Really?

—But it disappeared. I know, you don't believe me.

—Sure I do. Anyway, does it make a difference?

—I thought it might. I thought it was some kind of sign.

—A sign of what?

—That's what I was going to ask you.

—Do I look like someone who knows?

—Well, I figured you might know something about it.

—Not even my doctor knew what to make of it.

—Okay, but how about explaining that little contraption you've got around your neck?

—You're an odd duck. Looking for a lot of explanations.

—I saw one of those things once...

—Yeah?

—It's extraordinary!

—Then why didn't you buy one?

—You can buy them?

—Sure, all over the place.

—I don't go to stores much anymore. What's it for, anyway?

—Nothing, decoration. One of those hi-tech toys they're coming out with every day.

—What do you mean, nothing?

—You know, it's just something to wear, a piece of jewelry.

—How does it work?

—The guy told me something about solar energy, I don't remember. But it doesn't work in the dark. Except if you light a candle.

—Still, it must have some use, some purpose.

—Yeah. And those little bracelets people used to wear alongside their watches, do they have a purpose? Or the pendants women wear around their necks? They're just pretty things, nothing more.

—Sure...

I go limp, the bodies around me hold me up. I'm so exhausted, my feet ache. Legs went to sleep again. I worry about my circulation. I close my eyes. It's late afternoon, heat still at full blast. It's not until late at night that it gets cooler. Hot/cold, cold/hot.

By morning many of us will be dead. The changes in temperature are so rapid, so extreme. Tomorrow at first light we'll start throwing the bodies out to be incinerated in the sun. Just part of our day-to-day. Horror is no longer horrible when it becomes the daily.

—Do you have any idea where we are?

—Not really, the windows on the bus were painted black, you couldn't see a thing. I'm not even sure whether we came straight here or drove in circles.

370

—I bet we never even left São Paulo. I think I recognize that freeway, what's left of it.

—Could be any one of them, they're all the same.

—I wish I knew what we're doing here, that's the
main thing.

—I know what you mean. I feel ridiculous, huddling
here under this Marquee, whatever it is, completely ridiculous. Like someone's making a fool out of me but I
don't know who. The whole situation is grotesque. It
would be comic if it weren't teratoid. Humiliating. Like
standing bare-assed in the middle of the street, everyone
looking at you.

It's been a good day for archaic words, maybe I can
come up with another one. I liked this guy. I was glad
I'd met him. He took a weight off my shoulders somehow, he defined perfectly what I had been refusing to
accept. This is truly an egregious turn of events. All
right! I told you I'd revive yet another dead word.

Tell me: have you ever seen anything more ludicrous
than what I'm describing here? Burlesque! All these people under an immense Marquee, some pharaonic public
works project, the pride of the government, marvel of
marvels! And we buffoons, we don't so much as have
an audience for our foolishness. The public around here
doesn't know how to clap.

—You think we'll ever get out of here?

—If we put our heads together, maybe there's a chance.

—But how?

—I've got a nephew, a captain in the New Army. He's
a slippery character, but well connected.

—And he could get us out of here?

—He said he could. He's so sure of himself, confident
that his friends will come get him.

—If only we knew where we were, we could chance
it and just take off some night.

—Right. And what about when the sun comes up?

—We could get organized, send a group on ahead to
scout things out.

—You think if anyone made it they'd come back and

tell us all about their trip? Nobody's that stupid.

—We've got nothing to lose ...

—Okay, Mr. Optimist, would you go in the first group? Without knowing whether you'd find shelter before sunrise?

—Maybe.

—Easy for you to say. What you're really suggesting is leaving somebody else's ass hanging in the breeze.

—Well, it definitely looks like we're going to be here a little longer, so we ought to get organized at least.

—Huh?

—I said we need to get organized.

—Organized?

—WHAT'S THE MATTER, HAVE YOU GONE DEAF OR SOMETHING?!

People turned, as much as they could, in surprise. Silence. This man had some kind of power. Charisma. There must be other people around who understand what's going on, it can't just be the two of us. I feel like I'm being called to action. Me, the theoretician, moving to put my ideas into practice! But how?

—I'm not sure yet how it will work. Meanwhile, let's get to know each other better and work on the plans. What do you say?

—But we can't even move.

—By tomorrow there will be more room. We'll take over the places of the people who fall down.

—Or keep them from falling.

—There's no way. We might as well cut our losses, count on a certain number of vacancies each day. We can split up and go around talking to people.

The night drags on. A few more hours of weak, artificial light. A penetrating yellow brightness. "The painful light of the electric bulbs."

It's agony to look at them, they hurt so. People are snoring, snorting in their sleep. I hear irregular breathing, cries, murmurs. I wake up to the noise of the wind.

The noise of the wind whistling. I say it over and over

to myself. The noise of the wind. A dream, a light sleep. The light bulbs are motionless.

Painfully so. No play in the wires. Dust swirls in my face. The wind is very hot, and still. That's right, still wind. No kidding.

It's enough, for me, that it exists at all. Doubt it, if you like. This is not one final hallucination. But just to be sure, I elbow my friend, who's dozing, and who wakes up with a start, rubs his eyes.

—Do you feel it?

A studied pause, then he shouts out loud.

—YES, oh my God, yes, WIND! SON-OF-A-BITCH, I FEEL WIND!!

—That means it's real, two people couldn't dream the same thing!

—And I smell rain, don't you?

—I think that's going a little too far . . .

—No, I mean it, rain. Concentrate.

—I don't even remember what rain smells like any-more.

—Don't be silly, it's one of those things you never forget. Like swimming, riding a bicycle, making love.

—I hope it's not acid rain.

—No, acid rain smells bad, Christ, how it stinks! Remember? Nobody could stand it, people sealed their doors and windows, it was lethal. This smells good. Like wet earth.

Even though I couldn't smell it, I let the sensation surround me. Penetrate me. I want to feel the cool wind in my face, after so very long. Longed for. Like the smell of dirt, you recognize that wind. It brings rain. Prophetic wind.

—Are you sure we're not imagining this?

—Even if we are, what harm can it possibly do? For a long time now I've preferred living in my imagination.

I didn't fall back to sleep, I was alert, electric, waiting for that promised rain. It was on its way, I was sure of it. It would arrive sooner or later. Even if it was still a long way off, it was moving in our direction. In this rarefied atmosphere sounds and smells travel amazingly fast.

Like light from the stars. By the time it reaches us, it's been shining for thousands of years. Maybe the moist smell we were smelling came from somewhere so remote it would take a long time to arrive. But I'll bet you anything it's rain. Hey! Is it raining somewhere out there?

*E pur si muove*
And yet it moves
Galileo

IGNÁCIO DE LOYOLA BRANDÃO began his career writing film reviews and went on to work for one of the principal newspapers in São Paulo. Initially banned in Brazil, his novel *Zero* went on to win the prestigious Brasilia Prize and become a controversial bestseller. Brandão is the author of more than a half-dozen works of fiction, including *Zero*, *Teeth Under the Sun*, *Anonymous Celebrity*, and *The Good-Bye Angel*.

ELLEN WATSON, a poet and translator of Brazilian literature, is the director of the Poetry Center at Smith College in Northampton, Massachusetts. Her poems have appeared in *American Poetry Review*, *Field*, *Boulevard*, *Ploughshares*, and *The New Yorker*.

MICHAL AJVAZ, *The Golden Age.*
*The Other City.*
PIERRE ALBERT-BIROT, *Grabinoulor.*
YUZ ALESHKOVSKY, *Kangaroo.*
FELIPE ALFAU, *Chromos.*
*Locos.*
IVAN ÂNGELO, *The Celebration.*
*The Tower of Glass.*
ANTÓNIO LOBO ANTUNES, *Knowledge of Hell.*
*The Splendor of Portugal.*
ALAIN ARIAS-MISSON, *Theatre of Incest.*
JOHN ASHBERY AND JAMES SCHUYLER,
*A Nest of Ninnies.*
ROBERT ASHLEY, *Perfect Lives.*
GABRIELA AVIGUR-ROTEM, *Heatwave*
*and Crazy Birds.*
DJUNA BARNES, *Ladies Almanack.*
*Ryder.*
JOHN BARTH, *LETTERS.*
*Sabbatical.*
DONALD BARTHELME, *The King.*
*Paradise.*
SVETISLAV BASARA, *Chinese Letter.*
MIQUEL BAUÇÀ, *The Siege in the Room.*
RENÉ BELLETTO, *Dying.*
MAREK BIEŃCZYK, *Transparency.*
ANDREI BITOV, *Pushkin House.*
ANDREJ BLATNIK, *You Do Understand.*
LOUIS PAUL BOON, *Chapel Road.*
*My Little War.*
*Summer in Termuren.*
ROGER BOYLAN, *Killoyle.*
IGNÁCIO DE LOYOLA BRANDÃO,
*Anonymous Celebrity.*
*Zero.*
BONNIE BREMSER, *Troia: Mexican Memoirs.*
CHRISTINE BROOKE-ROSE, *Amalgamemnon.*
BRIGID BROPHY, *In Transit.*
GERALD L. BRUNS, *Modern Poetry and*
*the Idea of Language.*
GABRIELLE BURTON, *Heartbreak Hotel.*
MICHEL BUTOR, *Degrees.*
*Mobile.*
G. CABRERA INFANTE, *Infante's Inferno.*
*Three Trapped Tigers.*
JULIETA CAMPOS,
*The Fear of Losing Eurydice.*
ANNE CARSON, *Eros the Bittersweet.*
ORLY CASTEL-BLOOM, *Dolly City.*
LOUIS-FERDINAND CÉLINE, *Castle to Castle.*
*Conversations with Professor Y.*
*London Bridge.*
*Normance.*
*North.*
*Rigadoon.*
MARIE CHAIX, *The Laurels of Lake Constance.*
HUGO CHARTERIS, *The Tide Is Right.*
ERIC CHEVILLARD, *Demolishing Nisard.*
MARC CHOLODENKO, *Mordechai Schamz.*
JOSHUA COHEN, *Witz.*
EMILY HOLMES COLEMAN, *The Shutter*
*of Snow.*
ROBERT COOVER, *A Night at the Movies.*
STANLEY CRAWFORD, *Log of the S.S. The*
*Mrs Unguentine.*
*Some Instructions to My Wife.*
RENÉ CREVEL, *Putting My Foot in It.*
RALPH CUSACK, *Cadenza.*
NICHOLAS DELBANCO, *The Count of Concord.*
*Sherbrookes.*
NIGEL DENNIS, *Cards of Identity.*

PETER DIMOCK, *A Short Rhetoric for*
*Leaving the Family.*
ARIEL DORFMAN, *Konfidenz.*
COLEMAN DOWELL,
*Island People.*
*Too Much Flesh and Jabez.*
ARKADII DRAGOMOSHCHENKO, *Dust.*
RIKKI DUCORNET, *The Complete*
*Butcher's Tales.*
*The Fountains of Neptune.*
*The Jade Cabinet.*
*Phosphor in Dreamland.*
WILLIAM EASTLAKE, *The Bamboo Bed.*
*Castle Keep.*
*Lyric of the Circle Heart.*
JEAN ECHENOZ, *Chopin's Move.*
STANLEY ELKIN, *A Bad Man.*
*Criers and Kibitzers, Kibitzers*
*and Criers.*
*The Dick Gibson Show.*
*The Franchiser.*
*The Living End.*
*Mrs. Ted Bliss.*
FRANÇOIS EMMANUEL, *Invitation to a*
*Voyage.*
SALVADOR ESPRIU, *Ariadne in the*
*Grotesque Labyrinth.*
LESLIE A. FIEDLER, *Love and Death in*
*the American Novel.*
JUAN FILLOY, *Op Oloop.*
ANDY FITCH, *Pop Poetics.*
GUSTAVE FLAUBERT, *Bouvard and Pécuchet.*
KASS FLEISHER, *Talking out of School.*
FORD MADOX FORD,
*The March of Literature.*
JON FOSSE, *Aliss at the Fire.*
*Melancholy.*
MAX FRISCH, *I'm Not Stiller.*
*Man in the Holocene.*
CARLOS FUENTES, *Christopher Unborn.*
*Distant Relations.*
*Terra Nostra.*
*Where the Air Is Clear.*
TAKEHIKO FUKUNAGA, *Flowers of Grass.*
WILLIAM GADDIS, *J R.*
*The Recognitions.*
JANICE GALLOWAY, *Foreign Parts.*
*The Trick Is to Keep Breathing.*
WILLIAM H. GASS, *Cartesian Sonata*
*and Other Novellas.*
*Finding a Form.*
*A Temple of Texts.*
*The Tunnel.*
*Willie Masters' Lonesome Wife.*
GÉRARD GAVARRY, *Hoppla! 1 2 3.*
ETIENNE GILSON,
*The Arts of the Beautiful.*
*Forms and Substances in the Arts.*
C. S. GISCOMBE, *Giscome Road.*
*Here.*
DOUGLAS GLOVER, *Bad News of the Heart.*
WITOLD GOMBROWICZ,
*A Kind of Testament.*
PAULO EMÍLIO SALES GOMES, *P's Three*
*Women.*
GEORGI GOSPODINOV, *Natural Novel.*
JUAN GOYTISOLO, *Count Julian.*
*Juan the Landless.*
*Makbara.*
*Marks of Identity.*

# SELECTED DALKEY ARCHIVE TITLES

HENRY GREEN, *Back.*
*Blindness.*
*Concluding.*
*Doting.*
*Nothing.*
JACK GREEN, *Fire the Bastards!*
JIŘÍ GRUŠA, *The Questionnaire.*
MELA HARTWIG, *Am I a Redundant Human Being?*
JOHN HAWKES, *The Passion Artist.*
*Whistlejacket.*
ELIZABETH HEIGHWAY, ED., *Contemporary Georgian Fiction.*
ALEKSANDAR HEMON, ED., *Best European Fiction.*
AIDAN HIGGINS, *Balcony of Europe.*
*Blind Man's Bluff*
*Bornholm Night-Ferry.*
*Flotsam and Jetsam.*
*Langrishe, Go Down.*
*Scenes from a Receding Past.*
KEIZO HINO, *Isle of Dreams.*
KAZUSHI HOSAKA, *Plainsong.*
ALDOUS HUXLEY, *Antic Hay.*
*Crome Yellow.*
*Point Counter Point.*
*Those Barren Leaves.*
*Time Must Have a Stop.*
NAOYUKI II, *The Shadow of a Blue Cat.*
GERT JONKE, *The Distant Sound.*
*Geometric Regional Novel.*
*Homage to Czerny.*
*The System of Vienna.*
JACQUES JOUET, *Mountain R.*
*Savage.*
*Upstaged.*
MIEKO KANAI, *The Word Book.*
YORAM KANIUK, *Life on Sandpaper.*
HUGH KENNER, *Flaubert.*
*Joyce and Beckett: The Stoic Comedians.*
*Joyce's Voices.*
DANILO KIŠ, *The Attic.*
*Garden, Ashes.*
*The Lute and the Scars*
*Psalm 44.*
*A Tomb for Boris Davidovich.*
ANITA KONKKA, *A Fool's Paradise.*
GEORGE KONRÁD, *The City Builder.*
TADEUSZ KONWICKI, *A Minor Apocalypse.*
*The Polish Complex.*
MENIS KOUMANDAREAS, *Koula.*
ELAINE KRAF, *The Princess of 72nd Street.*
JIM KRUSOE, *Iceland.*
AYŞE KULIN, *Farewell: A Mansion in Occupied Istanbul.*
EMILIO LASCANO TEGUI, *On Elegance While Sleeping.*
ERIC LAURRENT, *Do Not Touch.*
VIOLETTE LEDUC, *La Bâtarde.*
EDOUARD LEVÉ, *Autoportrait.*
*Suicide.*
MARIO LEVI, *Istanbul Was a Fairy Tale.*
DEBORAH LEVY, *Billy and Girl.*
JOSÉ LEZAMA LIMA, *Paradiso.*
ROSA LIKSOM, *Dark Paradise.*
OSMAN LINS, *Avalovara.*
*The Queen of the Prisons of Greece.*
ALF MAC LOCHLAINN, *The Corpus in the Library.*
*Out of Focus.*
RON LOEWINSOHN, *Magnetic Field(s).*
MINA LOY, *Stories and Essays of Mina Loy.*

D. KEITH MANO, *Take Five.*
MICHELINE AHARONIAN MARCOM, *The Mirror in the Well.*
BEN MARCUS, *The Age of Wire and String.*
WALLACE MARKFIELD, *Teitlebaum's Window.*
*To an Early Grave.*
DAVID MARKSON, *Reader's Block.*
*Wittgenstein's Mistress.*
CAROLE MASO, *AVA.*
LADISLAV MATEJKA AND KRYSTYNA POMORSKA, EDS., *Readings in Russian Poetics: Formalist and Structuralist Views.*
HARRY MATHEWS, *Cigarettes.*
*The Conversions.*
*The Human Country: New and Collected Stories.*
*The Journalist.*
*My Life in CIA.*
*Singular Pleasures.*
*The Sinking of the Odradek Stadium.*
*Tlooth.*
JOSEPH MCELROY, *Night Soul and Other Stories.*
ABDELWAHAB MEDDEB, *Talismano.*
GERHARD MEIER, *Isle of the Dead.*
HERMAN MELVILLE, *The Confidence-Man.*
AMANDA MICHALOPOULOU, *I'd Like.*
STEVEN MILLHAUSER, *The Barnum Museum.*
*In the Penny Arcade.*
RALPH J. MILLS, JR., *Essays on Poetry.*
MOMUS, *The Book of Jokes.*
CHRISTINE MONTALBETTI, *The Origin of Man.*
*Western.*
OLIVE MOORE, *Spleen.*
NICHOLAS MOSLEY, *Accident.*
*Assassins.*
*Catastrophe Practice.*
*Experience and Religion.*
*A Garden of Trees.*
*Hopeful Monsters.*
*Imago Bird.*
*Impossible Object.*
*Inventing God.*
*Judith.*
*Look at the Dark.*
*Natalie Natalia.*
*Serpent.*
*Time at War.*
WARREN MOTTE, *Fables of the Novel: French Fiction since 1990.*
*Fiction Now: The French Novel in the 21st Century.*
*Oulipo: A Primer of Potential Literature.*
GERALD MURNANE, *Barley Patch.*
*Inland.*
YVES NAVARRE, *Our Share of Time.*
*Sweet Tooth.*
DOROTHY NELSON, *In Night's City.*
*Tar and Feathers.*
ESHKOL NEVO, *Homesick.*
WILFRIDO D. NOLLEDO, *But for the Lovers.*
FLANN O'BRIEN, *At Swim-Two-Birds.*
*The Best of Myles.*
*The Dalkey Archive.*
*The Hard Life.*
*The Poor Mouth.*

FOR A FULL LIST OF PUBLICATIONS, VISIT:
**www.dalkeyarchive.com**

## SELECTED DALKEY ARCHIVE TITLES

*The Third Policeman.*
CLAUDE OLLIER, *The Mise-en-Scène.*
*Wert and the Life Without End.*
GIOVANNI ORELLI, *Walaschek's Dream.*
PATRIK OUŘEDNÍK, *Europeana.*
*The Opportune Moment, 1855.*
BORIS PAHOR, *Necropolis.*
FERNANDO DEL PASO, *News from the Empire.*
*Palinuro of Mexico.*
ROBERT PINGET, *The Inquisitory.*
*Mahu or The Material.*
*Trio.*
MANUEL PUIG, *Betrayed by Rita Hayworth.*
*The Buenos Aires Affair.*
*Heartbreak Tango.*
RAYMOND QUENEAU, *The Last Days.*
*Odile.*
*Pierrot Mon Ami.*
*Saint Glinglin.*
ANN QUIN, *Berg.*
*Passages.*
*Three.*
*Tripticks.*
ISHMAEL REED, *The Free-Lance Pallbearers.*
*The Last Days of Louisiana Red.*
*Ishmael Reed: The Plays.*
*Juice!*
*Reckless Eyeballing.*
*The Terrible Threes.*
*The Terrible Twos.*
*Yellow Back Radio Broke-Down.*
JASIA REICHARDT, *15 Journeys Warsaw*
*to London.*
NOËLLE REVAZ, *With the Animals.*
JOÃO UBALDO RIBEIRO, *House of the*
*Fortunate Buddhas.*
JEAN RICARDOU, *Place Names.*
RAINER MARIA RILKE, *The Notebooks of*
*Malte Laurids Brigge.*
JULIÁN RÍOS, *The House of Ulysses.*
*Larva: A Midsummer Night's Babel.*
*Poundemonium.*
*Procession of Shadows.*
AUGUSTO ROA BASTOS, *I the Supreme.*
DANIËL ROBBERECHTS, *Arriving in Avignon.*
JEAN ROLIN, *The Explosion of the*
*Radiator Hose.*
OLIVIER ROLIN, *Hotel Crystal.*
ALIX CLEO ROUBAUD, *Alix's Journal.*
JACQUES ROUBAUD, *The Form of a*
*City Changes Faster, Alas, Than*
*the Human Heart.*
*The Great Fire of London.*
*Hortense in Exile.*
*Hortense Is Abducted.*
*The Loop.*
*Mathematics:*
*The Plurality of Worlds of Lewis.*
*The Princess Hoppy.*
*Some Thing Black.*
RAYMOND ROUSSEL, *Impressions of Africa.*
VEDRANA RUDAN, *Night.*
STIG SÆTERBAKKEN, *Siamese.*
*Self Control.*
LYDIE SALVAYRE, *The Company of Ghosts.*
*The Lecture.*
*The Power of Flies.*
LUIS RAFAEL SÁNCHEZ,
*Macho Camacho's Beat.*
SEVERO SARDUY, *Cobra & Maitreya.*

NATHALIE SARRAUTE,
*Do You Hear Them?*
*Martereau.*
*The Planetarium.*
ARNO SCHMIDT, *Collected Novellas.*
*Collected Stories.*
*Nobodaddy's Children.*
*Two Novels.*
ASAF SCHURR, *Motti.*
GAIL SCOTT, *My Paris.*
DAMION SEARLS, *What We Were Doing*
*and Where We Were Going.*
JUNE AKERS SEESE,
*Is This What Other Women Feel Too?*
*What Waiting Really Means.*
BERNARD SHARE, *Inish.*
*Transit.*
VIKTOR SHKLOVSKY, *Bowstring.*
*Knight's Move.*
*A Sentimental Journey:*
*Memoirs 1917–1922.*
*Energy of Delusion: A Book on Plot.*
*Literature and Cinematography.*
*Theory of Prose.*
*Third Factory.*
*Zoo, or Letters Not about Love.*
PIERRE SINIAC, *The Collaborators.*
KJERSTI A. SKOMSVOLD, *The Faster I Walk,*
*the Smaller I Am.*
JOSEF ŠKVORECKÝ, *The Engineer of*
*Human Souls.*
GILBERT SORRENTINO,
*Aberration of Starlight.*
*Blue Pastoral.*
*Crystal Vision.*
*Imaginative Qualities of Actual*
*Things.*
*Mulligan Stew.*
*Pack of Lies.*
*Red the Fiend.*
*The Sky Changes.*
*Something Said.*
*Splendide-Hôtel.*
*Steelwork.*
*Under the Shadow.*
W. M. SPACKMAN, *The Complete Fiction.*
ANDRZEJ STASIUK, *Dukla.*
*Fado.*
GERTRUDE STEIN, *The Making of Americans.*
*A Novel of Thank You.*
LARS SVENDSEN, *A Philosophy of Evil.*
PIOTR SZEWC, *Annihilation.*
GONÇALO M. TAVARES, *Jerusalem.*
*Joseph Walser's Machine.*
*Learning to Pray in the Age of*
*Technique.*
LUCIAN DAN TEODOROVICI,
*Our Circus Presents . . .*
NIKANOR TERATOLOGEN, *Assisted Living.*
STEFAN THEMERSON, *Hobson's Island.*
*The Mystery of the Sardine.*
*Tom Harris.*
TAEKO TOMIOKA, *Building Waves.*
JOHN TOOMEY, *Sleepwalker.*
JEAN-PHILIPPE TOUSSAINT, *The Bathroom.*
*Camera.*
*Monsieur.*
*Reticence.*
*Running Away.*
*Self-Portrait Abroad.*
*Television.*
*The Truth about Marie.*

DUMITRU TSEPENEAG, *Hotel Europa.*
  *The Necessary Marriage.*
  *Pigeon Post.*
  *Vain Art of the Fugue.*
ESTHER TUSQUETS, *Stranded.*
DUBRAVKA UGRESIC, *Lend Me Your Character.*
  *Thank You for Not Reading.*
TOR ULVEN, *Replacement.*
MATI UNT, *Brecht at Night.*
  *Diary of a Blood Donor.*
  *Things in the Night.*
ÁLVARO URIBE AND OLIVIA SEARS, EDS.,
  *Best of Contemporary Mexican Fiction.*
ELOY URROZ, *Friction.*
  *The Obstacles.*
LUISA VALENZUELA, *Dark Desires and
  the Others.*
  *He Who Searches.*
PAUL VERHAEGHEN, *Omega Minor.*
AGLAJA VETERANYI, *Why the Child Is
  Cooking in the Polenta.*
BORIS VIAN, *Heartsnatcher.*
LLORENÇ VILLALONGA, *The Dolls' Room.*
TOOMAS VINT, *An Unending Landscape.*
ORNELA VORPSI, *The Country Where No
  One Ever Dies.*
AUSTRYN WAINHOUSE, *Hedyphagetica.*
CURTIS WHITE, *America's Magic Mountain.*
  *The Idea of Home.*
  *Memories of My Father Watching TV.*
  *Requiem.*

DIANE WILLIAMS, *Excitability:
  Selected Stories.*
  *Romancer Erector.*
DOUGLAS WOOLF, *Wall to Wall.*
  *Ya!* & *John-Juan.*
JAY WRIGHT, *Polynomials and Pollen.*
  *The Presentable Art of Reading
  Absence.*
PHILIP WYLIE, *Generation of Vipers.*
MARGUERITE YOUNG, *Angel in the Forest.*
  *Miss MacIntosh, My Darling.*
REYOUNG, *Unbabbling.*
VLADO ŽABOT, *The Succubus.*
ZORAN ŽIVKOVIĆ, *Hidden Camera.*
LOUIS ZUKOFSKY, *Collected Fiction.*
VITOMIL ZUPAN, *Minuet for Guitar.*
SCOTT ZWIREN, *God Head.*